REALMS

REALM OF FLAMES & STEEL

ALLISON SIPE

LIKE MAGIC
STUDIO

To my brother, Matt. Thank you for all the late night chats about made up worlds, magic, and book covers. And for helping me fix the plot holes, not just in fiction, but in everyday life with your talent, precision, and skill.

BOOK PLAYLIST

If you like to listen to music while you read, then you're in luck! I've created a playlist just for Realm of Flames & Steel. Enjoy the music that inspired the story.

HEED OUR WORDS,
ALL CLASSES OF CREATURES,
YOU GREATER AND LESSER
CHILDREN OF YGGDRASIL.
YOU SUMMONED US,
TO TELL WHAT WE RECALL
OF LOVE AND DEATH
AND THE LEGENDS OF,
FLAMES AND STEEL.

PROLOGUE

SIGURD

My sword ripped through the tender flesh of an enemy soldier, and he crumpled to the blood-soaked earth with a thud. Turning away from his body, I wiped my blade free of blood on my leather trousers and took in the scene around me. Flames licked up the homes of our village as the sound of steel clashing against steel died down. Only a handful still fought, but it was a lost cause. The battle was all but won. Our home defended, if not a little worse for the wear.

I searched for Kara among the few still fighting, but she wasn't among them. Once I would've worried about her, but I'd learned she was far more capable than most of the men I fought beside.

I moved through the village, looking to aid anyone who might need help. To my left, Leif threw a bucket of water on the flames, trying to lick up the healer's front door. And a few feet ahead of me, Astrid knelt over someone, wrapping a bandage around their leg as three men rounded the corner, locked in battle.

Someone gripped my shoulder, and I turned to find Kara, a secret smile curling the corner of her lips. A spray of blood stained her chain mail, and with the sun behind her silhouetting her wings, she looked like a Valkyrie right out of the legends.

"Hello beautiful." I pulled her against me and her wings

1

vanished in a wisp of Magik, waiting to be called upon once more. She wrapped one arm around my neck, and I pressed my forehead against hers. There's nothing I loved more than the rush of battle, but this woman, my Valkyrie, could make me walk away from everything with one word.

I brushed my lips against hers, and she melted into my arms, deepening the kiss. She tasted of dust, sweat, and the honey mead we had with breakfast. Her hand found its way into my hair, and her lips parted as she deepened the kiss.

My fingers slid down the middle of her back, following the same path as last night. The memory of her supple skin was still fresh in my mind despite the armor separating us.

The air was ripped from my lungs and agony tore through my chest as if someone had lit my blood on fire.

I pulled away from her and tried to suck in a breath. A warm trickle of blood oozed down the inside of my shirt. I stared down at the dagger shoved through my leather chest plate and into my heart. My vision fractured at the sight of Kara's hand holding the hilt in place. I looked back up, only to be met with a smirk on the lips I'd just kissed.

My sword slipped from my hand and clattered to the dirt. I met her eyes, but the vibrant, lively green I'd fallen in love with was replaced with a stone cold grey-green that left me hollow.

"Why?" I coughed. I didn't know what hurt more, the weapon piercing my heart or the knowledge that the woman I loved and trusted above anyone else had just shoved a dagger into my chest.

She pulled the blade free, and I took a woozy step backward, trying to maintain my balance. The heaviness of her blade was replaced with a scorching fire that ripped through me. Tears stung my eyes as my ears rang. *How was this happening?* Even with her hand wrapped around the hilt, my heart refused to believe what I was seeing. She wouldn't do this.

Her gaze didn't break from mine, but it wasn't the look of a lover, nor an assassin. It was predatory. Unnatural.

"Kara." I wheezed as I tried to fill my lungs with fresh air. My vision doubled as pain thundered through me. My heart beat wild and irregular, pumping more and more blood down my chest. I gripped the wound, a feeble attempt to stay the bleeding.

Not that it would do any good. Her aim was true, and I had only moments of my mortal life left.

A chill akin to a frozen lake expanded in my core. I... was... dying. My life forfeit too soon. I'd yet to make a name for myself, or leave my mark on the world. No one will remember my name. No one will sing songs about my heroics. Everything I'd worked toward, fought for my whole life, gone in an instant. She'd taken everything from me in the space of one breath. The future we planned, the home we'd build together, the love we shared. All of it gone.

I searched her face as a wave of torment crashed on the shores of my heart. Every word out of her mouth, every memory we shared, stared back at me, taunting me. Was it all a lie?

She moved toward me, her eyes raking over my face and down my body. Something deep and eternal broke free inside me, and reached for her in a way that left me empty.

My legs gave out, and I fell to my knees, joining the bodies of the fallen. The world tilted and spun around me in a cacophony of colors and sounds. The distant shouts of celebration, the glint of sunlight off a blade, the red paint of a shield, the crackle of wood burning. I couldn't grab onto any one thing as I swayed and fell onto my side.

A shadow moved over me, followed by a ripple of auburn warmth I knew all too well. Kara. She rolled me onto my back, sending a bolt of agonizing pain through my chest. A tear rolled down my temple as she leaned over me.

"I don't... understand." Each word sent a lightning bolt of

agony through me, as if Thor himself was abusing me for each word I spoke.

She placed a hand on my face, a familiar caress that once warmed me to her advances. I shivered at the touch, unable to reconcile the affection in my memories with the coldness of the woman above me.

Something in me stirred as her eyes bore into mine. It was like I was being called to her. I tried to resist the urge, tried to ignore the siren call singing from under my skin, but the more I wrestled against the tide, the stronger it pulled on me.

A cough rattled through my body. "You... wouldn't... do this." My words tasted like blood, like death. I struggled to breathe, each breath short and clipped.

She leaned closer, her cheek brushing mine, and the warm, floral aroma of her hair filled my nose. "Why? Because I love you?" A deep, humorless chuckle rumbled through her.

A fissure opened up inside me and my heart shattered into more pieces than all the stars in the nine realms.

She repositioned herself, and for the first time, I saw her for what she was.

A harbinger of death.

As she stared at me, a look of hungry lust flitted across her face. She was no longer my Kara, no longer the woman I loved and trusted. She was a stranger to me, cold and unfamiliar. Her hand slid up my chest in an act that would seem intimate to anyone on the outside.

"Was it"—pain radiated through me, stealing my breath—"all a lie?" I searched her eyes, desperate to find even a sliver of the woman I'd welcomed into my heart.

She leaned closer, her face an inch from mine, and my soul cried for release. My mind shattered, and the world spun as if I'd finished an entire cask of ale. A lightness settled over me and the pain from my wound fizzled into a fuzzy warmth as I lost all sensation in my arms and legs.

I never considered that my heart would be my undoing and not my blade.

She brushed her lips against mine, and the nine realms shifted above me. A low hum buzzed under my skin, and the hairs on my arms rose. Her Magik galloped over my bones as if her power were my own. A deep ache settled in the pit of my stomach, and I wanted nothing more than to become one with her. The fight left me, the pain, the heartache. The betrayal.

"Kara!" someone yelled from the other side of Yggdrasil and pulled her off me.

The siren song of Kara's Magik vanished, leaving me empty and cold as the pain in my chest returned. I lay among the dead and dying. Alone as my mortal life slipped through my fingers. No more plans to be made. No more wondering what the future might hold. No more battles or glory.

Soft brown eyes and iridescent wings so bright they were like the sun reflecting off a lake, filled my view. "It's time." The Valkyrie's voice was a balm to my frayed nerves and battered soul. "Are you ready?"

I nodded. There was nothing left for me here.

She placed a hand on my chest and her wings folded around me. Midgard shook, each piece falling away as we rose into the sky. The echo of Kara screaming hit me like a blast of cold air as the last remnants of Midgard fizzled into nothing.

We moved through the dark, and it was as if I could reach out and touch the beginning of the universe. Wind whipped around me once more, and we were soaring over fields of green. My life in Midgard had come to an end, but my life among the Gods had just begun.

KARA

"Kara." Rough hands grasped me by the shoulders. "What in the name of Yggdrasil is the matter with you?"

I felt like I was waking from a dream before I was ready to.

"Kara, this isn't you." Her words were muffled and slowed down as her fingers dug into my flesh. "Look at me," she demanded as she shook me. "Kara!" she screamed, and smacked my cheek. The sting of her assault barely registered.

I could hear her, feel the grip of her fingers on my skin, but it was as if I was trapped in my body behind a wall.

"Kara, for sorðinn's sake." She slapped me and pain sliced across my face, blood filling my mouth as the heaviness in my rib cage softened.

A sharp ringing pierced my ears and cleared my head. Chills ran down my arms as dread replaced the intoxicating, primal hum of Magik that had been coursing through me a moment ago.

I let out a shaky breath as the world around me rushed into focus. Everything was too bright, too loud. I blinked against the sun, and my ears adjusted to the cheers of celebration, the groans of men yet to pass into the afterlife, the screech of a bird, and the crackle of flames around me.

Talon's grip on me loosened. "There you are." Russet eyes stared back at me.

As my mind cleared, I noticed she was dressed head to toe in battle armor. Her box braids were pulled up into a crown atop her head, and the gold filaments she weaved into her hair caught the sun and shimmered like drops of dew at first light.

"What happened?" I wiped a hand over my face. "And why are you dressed for a fight?"

"You're joking, right?" Her brow knit together as she studied me.

"And why do I feel like I've been drinking for days on end?" I rubbed my temple.

"I don't know how to tell you this..." Her eyes darted over my shoulder, and I turned to follow her gaze.

Si lay motionless in the dirt. *No, no, Gods, no.*

The nine realms turned upside down and my heart clambered into my throat. I ran to his side and fell to my knees next to him. Panic burned through me like a cornered animal.

"For the love of Yggdrasil, please." My hands hovered over him, unsure of where he was hurt or how badly. Blood covered most of his torso and pooled under him. "Si?" Tears blurred my eyes as I shook his shoulder and begged him to wake up.

Tearing my gaze from the blood, I searched his face for something, anything, that would tell me he'd be okay. But his body was too still, and all the life had drained from his eyes.

He was already gone.

I could feel it now, the emptiness, the absence of his soul, as I placed my forehead against his. The Magik that connected us, Valkyrie and her charge, was an empty void. He was gone, his soul taken to the afterlife without my guidance. My love, my charge, stolen from me.

A sob broke from my throat and I screamed. Unyielding grief poured into me, drowning out everything and everyone until every heartbeat ached, every breath burned, and every tear felt like acid on my skin.

He was gone.

I reached out to the nine realms once more, searching for the familiar song of his soul, but there was nothing. Not him, not the smell of Folkvang, not the chaos of Asguard, nor the chill of Niflheim.

There was only Midgard, this mortal realm, that answered my call.

My mind raced, searching for an explanation. I opened up my senses, tapping into the Magik inside me, looking for a glimmer of another realm. Why couldn't I feel anything?

Why couldn't I feel him?

"Kara." Talon touched my shoulder and I flinched.

"Why can't I feel him?" My voice broke on the last word.

"You don't remember, do you?" She held her hand up like she was approaching a coiled snake.

"Remember what?" I shook my head. "I have no idea how I got here." Tears burned my eyes, and the lump in my throat made it hard to breathe. "The last thing I remember is falling asleep last night."

"Oh, Kara." Worry creased her brow.

"What aren't you telling me?" My chest tightened as I recognized the pity in her eyes. "Who did this to him?" I pushed to my feet, my soul screaming for revenge. "Tell me," I shrieked like a wild animal. My vision blurred through my tears as fury tore through me.

I'd rip whoever did this, limb from limb.

Talon held my gaze as she lifted my hands between us. "I'm so sorry." She glanced down and back up at me. "But it was your blade that was his undoing."

Shaking, I looked down at my hands covered in blood. "No." I stumbled backward and struggled for every breath. The amount of blood coating my fingers, and beneath my nails, couldn't be from trying to wake him. "I don't understand." My stomach rolled as Talon stepped aside. My dagger lay in the dirt next to Si, covered in blood.

His blood.

Tears burned my eyes, and the lump in my throat made it hard to breathe. "I... I wouldn't... I..." I fell to my knees, the jolt of hitting the ground barely registering.

"I'm so sorry, Kara." Talon knelt in front of me.

Bile rose to the back of my throat, and I turned just in time to vomit into the dirt.

Si's mortal body lay before me, ready for his send off into the afterlife. I placed a hand on his, and brushed a strand of his dark hair off his face. I was still in disbelief that this wasn't some horrible dream. The fact that he was gone hurt more than words, but the knowledge that his death was by my hand made me sick to my stomach.

It didn't matter that he was with the gods now. That he'd be happy and cared for until the last star blinked out of existence. He would never walk this realm again. Never see his mother, never achieve his dreams, or build the life he wanted. He would live on in the afterlife, but for a man like Sigurd, it would never be enough.

He'd given me his love and trust, but I didn't deserve it. Nor did I deserve the freedom Freya's Magik granted me. I understood why Folkvang, Freya's domain over fallen warriors, was taken from me. And Valhalla, Odin's own army of worthy men and women. And the nine realms. I deserved to be stranded in Midgard for breaking the one law placed upon Valkyrie.

Never kill your charge.

Soft footsteps sounded behind me, but I didn't care to see who had come to say their goodbyes.

I adjusted the hood of my cloak to hide my face. I'd become the most hated woman in the village in a matter of hours. True, I deserved their ire, the insults they threw at me, but for just a moment, I wanted to be alone with him and my pain.

"He was something else." A male figure came to a stop next to me. His gruff voice grated on my nerves. "A true warrior through and through."

I didn't acknowledge him. I'd learned long ago, some people grieved out loud while others, like myself, preferred to suffer in silence.

"Do you have any remorse for killing him?" His words struck me like a knife to the gut.

I snuck a glance in his direction. He too, wore a cloak, his face hidden in the hood. I could just make out the smirk on his face and it took everything in my power not to knock him into next week.

"You think I wanted to kill him?" Tears stung my eyes. The image of his blood on my hands flashed in my mind, and I flinched at the memory. I pulled my cloak tighter, as if it could protect me from what I'd done.

"Then why?" He stepped up to Si and placed a hand on his chest.

The words sprung from my mouth as if Magik had compelled me to speak. "I don't know. I have no memory of the act."

He shook his head. "I warned her this might happen."

The familiar cadence of his voice scratched the back of my brain. "Warned who?" I asked as I studied him a little closer.

He continued to look down at Si as if the two of them were having this conversation. "Freya wouldn't listen to reason. She never does."

"Freya?" I furrowed my brow in confusion. *Who was this*

man? Very few mortals had the privilege of speaking with the Gods.

I tried to get a glimpse of his face, but he was careful to keep himself hidden from my view.

"She's a stubborn woman." His voice was laced with vitriol.

Alarm bells went off in my head, and I took a step back. I swallowed the lump in my throat. "You shouldn't speak ill of the Gods."

He turned to me, his bright sapphire eye meeting mine. Not for the first time today, I wished I was the one who was dead. "It's good to hear you still have some sense left in that head of yours."

"Alfather." His name escaped my lips, and I inclined my head.

"Kara." His smirk faded as he removed his hood. The bitter taste of his Magik filled the small space, making it hard to breathe.

I closed my eyes, bracing for the end. *I deserve to pay for what I did.*

His deep chuckle startled me, and I opened my eyes.

"Death would be too sweet a release for what you've done. You deserve to suffer." He took a step toward me. "And so does Freya." His eye brightened as he said her name. "She took one of mine, so I shall repay the favor."

"I don't understand? One of yours?" I choked on the last word as my eyes slid back to Si.

"Sigurd was meant for Valhalla. He was mine." Odin seethed as he stalked toward me, forcing me to take another step backward. I wasn't scared to die, but Odin could do far worse than kill me. "You and Freya have conspired against me, and I won't allow it."

"I didn't—"

"I don't give a dwarf's ass what you have to say." He rushed me, forcing me against the wall. "You're a disgrace to your kind, killing your charge." His face scrunched up in disgust. "You're an abomination that should've been put down the moment you were born."

The endless cavern of pain inside me swallowed his words, their meaning registering before disappearing into the screaming agony of my heart.

"I don't know what game Freya is playing, but let's see how she does without you to help her." A short, clipped laugh escaped his throat.

"I—"

He raised a hand, and the words died on my tongue. "You don't deserve the wings Freya gifted you to serve the mortal world."

Terror gripped me. I'd rather die than give up my wings.

"Freya's Magik may have barred you from traveling the realms temporarily, but it's not enough. You don't deserve to be a part of the nine realms." His eye glowed and his Magik crackled in the air. He turned me around and ripped through my cloak and clothes, exposing my back. He placed his hand on my spine, in the middle of my wing tattoo, and recited a spell in the Aesir tongue.

Blinding pain seared through me like a hot knife, and I bit back the scream that threatened to escape my throat.

I deserve this.

He continued the spell, his Magik battling for control inside me. Light exploded behind my eyes and I screamed.

I screamed for the man I loved. I screamed for the loss of the nine realms.

"A mortal life, with an immortal soul." His voice echoed around me, through me. "You'll spend the next hundred years without the nine realms, without Magik, without your home."

My heart faltered, and a sob stuck in my throat.

"It will be as if you died with him." Rage roiled off him, thick and heavy, making it hard to breathe.

Each word felt like it would be my undoing.

He shoved me harder against the wall, his Magik burning away any last shred of a connection I had to the nine realms.

I could feel him in my mind, flicking through memories, feel him in my blood, my heart. A scream tore through me again as he battled for control of the Magik inside me. My soul felt like it was being shredded into a million pieces. Every bone in my body was at the point of breaking.

Thunder rolled overhead, and the hairs on my arms rose as Magik crackled through the air.

"You will be nothing," he growled.

He continued the spell, and my wings erupted from my back. He took hold of Freya's Magik in my soul, the Magik that gave me my wings, and twisted.

I heard the snap before I felt the mind numbing pain radiate across my back. With my face pressed to the wall, I watched as my wings, the one thing that had always given me purpose, catch fire and disintegrated to nothing. Their presence within me vanished, leaving behind a shell of who I once was.

I fell to my knees, his hand still on my back as he dug through the tattered remains of who I was.

The pain gave way to a cold numbness, and I no longer cared what he did to me. He could steal every memory, destroy every part of my heart and soul. I had nothing left to live for, nothing to hold on to. He pulled at the last shred of my tattered soul and a door slammed closed inside me.

He let go, as if he'd been forced to, and I collapsed to the ground. I gasped for air, but each breath burned down my throat and scorched my lungs as if I was inhaling the flames of Muspelheim.

Odin's shadow fell over me, and his eye held mine. Something passed over his face, and the calm mask I was used to fell over his features. Some decision had been made within himself, and I tried not to think of what that meant for my fate.

He leaned down and brushed the hair off my face. "You're

13

lucky Freya's Magik binds me from making a true example of you." He pushed to his feet and within a blink, he was gone.

I looked up at Si, still lying a few feet away from me as a new brand of sorrow cradled me.

It is done. A voice said from the shadows as my mind snapped and everything went dark.

100 YEARS LATER

CHAPTER ONE

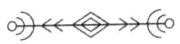

KARA

A HUNDRED YEARS is a long time without Magik, without the freedom of the nine realms. Tapping my foot, I leaned back to get a view of the open double doors to check the position of the sun for the millionth time.

Any minute now.

The last twenty-four hours had moved slower than the last hundred years. I downed the last sip of my ale and sat the empty glass on the table. My gaze drifted to the wood carvings in the pillar in front of me, and I followed the twists and swirls upward toward the pitched roof of the mead hall. Firelight cast shadows onto the wood, giving the design a living and breathing quality. A memory too far in the past pulled at the corner of my mind, and a swell of nostalgia filled my chest.

"Another one?" Davlin asked, bringing my attention back to the present. Without waiting for an answer, he grabbed the bottle closest to us and he filled my cup.

"You're a lifesaver." I tapped my fingers on the tables smooth wood surface. Music and laughter floated through the air, but I was wound too tightly to enjoy any of it.

"So this is it. You're finally free of Odin's curse." His grey eyes met mine as he pushed my cup across the table toward me.

"Let's hope," I huffed, and tried not to check the sun again.

"I still think a hundred years trapped in Midgard is cruel and

17

unusual punishment." He poured his own cup of ale to the very brim.

A half snort, half laugh escaped my throat. "Have you met the Gods?" I took a sip of my ale, letting the drink warm my chest and numb my nerves.

"Rub it in, why don't you?"

"Trust me, you're not missing anything."

"Says the woman who rubs shoulders with the Aesir and Vanir like it's nothing." He leaned over, sipping from the rim of his cup to keep the ale from spilling over.

"Used to rub shoulders," I corrected him.

"And you will again." He smiled, bringing out the wrinkles around his eyes.

"Maybe, maybe not." I bit the inside of my cheek. "What if whatever Odin did to me is permanent?"

"Huh," he paused with the cup halfway to his mouth. "I wouldn't have thought..." Davlin looked me up and down.

"What?" I tried not to squirm under his scrutiny.

"Nothing, nothing." He raised his hand in surrender.

"Out with it." I took a sip of my drink.

He looked me over, and his eyes landed on my tapping fingers. "You're nervous." He leaned forward and placed his forearms on the table.

"Am not." I shot him a glare over the rim of my cup.

He cocked an eyebrow. "Oh, we're playing dumb now, are we?" He placed his hand over mine and lowered the glass from my lips. "When are you going to learn? You can't bullshit me?"

From the moment I met Davlin, he'd seen right through my walls and never let me hide behind them.

I shook my head. "For the love of Yggdrasil, I don't know why I keep drinking with you."

"That's easy." He pulled back and shrugged one shoulder. "You're in love with me."

"Ha. Ha." I rolled my eyes. "In your dreams."

"Every night darlin.'" He winked, and I couldn't help but smile.

"Does that line ever work for you?" I took another drink, the sharp edges of my nerves falling away.

"A gentleman never tells." A secret grin pulled at the corner of his lips.

I leveled my eyes on him. "I thought we weren't bullshitting each other." I fought to keep the grin from my lips.

"You first."

Unable to help myself, I looked to see if the sun had dipped below the horizon and then back at Davlin.

I met his eyes, and the tiny sliver of peace inside me vanished.

"Kara." Davlin reached for my hand and I let him take it.

"I don't know who I am anymore," I said in one breath. "I haven't felt like a Valkyrie in decades. I've never quite felt like a citizen of Midgard. And now that I'm about to be free of Odin's Magik, I'm not sure where that leaves me."

"Don't be ridiculous." He squeezed my fingers. "You're Kara. Valkyrie of the nine realms. Purveyor of the best horseradish in Midgard."

I snorted at the last part. It was true, but not the point. "A Valkyrie's who I used to be." I pointed out. "A long time ago."

"You may have lost your wings, but they never made you who you are." He kept his voice low even though music and enthusiastic conversations filled the mead hall, making it unlikely anyone would overhear us.

"People change."

"Maybe you've changed a bit." He ran a hand through his short-cropped blond hair. "But that doesn't change what you are."

"And what am I, exactly?" I rolled my eyes.

"Powerful. Cunning. Kind." He offered me a warm smile and squeezed my hand. "Loyal."

19

It wasn't the first time he was saying these words to me. And in practice, I knew he was right. But the voice in my head–Odin's voice–the voice that haunted my dreams and took advantage of my darkest nights, told me I didn't deserve to be a Valkyrie. That I didn't deserve to be alive. No matter how kind Davlin was, or how much time passed, those words lived in the deepest parts of me and were impossible to root out entirely.

"Do you want your old life back or are you content with this?" He motioned around the hall, but he clearly meant this realm, this ordinary life.

"I—" The words lodged in my throat as I thought about everything I'd lost. No matter what happened tonight, I could never go back to the moment before I plunged my blade into his chest and ended his mortal life. Having my wings back wouldn't change the past, and it wouldn't give Sigurd his life back.

"You're spiraling."

I leveled my eyes on him. "I'm thinking, there's a difference."

"Share with the class."

I studied the contents of my cup and bit the inside of my cheek.

"Ahh, him again." He shook his head and sighed.

"Jealous?" I jabbed, trying to get the attention off of me.

"Of a dead man, never."

I leveled my eyes on him and bit back the retort on my tongue. He didn't mean anything by it, and I knew that.

"Too soon?" He grimaced.

I shook my head and ignored him. "I just don't understand what would have driven me to—"

"I thought we were past blaming ourselves?" He raised one eyebrow.

"Old wounds die hard." I let out a huff, trying to shake the nerves bouncing around in my chest.

"I think you mean habits."

"You know what I—"

Thunder rolled overhead, setting my teeth on edge. Of course, thunder didn't mean Odin was among us, but I'd never forget the day that it did. The day I lost my entire world.

"Is this it?" Davlin's brow furrowed as his gaze darted around the room.

Lightning flashed, reflecting off of every piece of metal in the hall, and thunder roared overhead, rattling my bones.

"Your guess is as good as mine." I met his eyes and for the first time in a century, the gentle brush of Magik touched my awareness. Excitement bubbled through me, quickly followed by the cold zing of fear.

This was it.

I'd watched the world change and change again as I waited to shed Odin's curse. For so long I waited to be free, to feel the nine realms again. But with each decade that passed, my longing for the familiar turned to apprehension. The nine realms might not want me back.

"Come on." I jumped up and stepped over the bench before rushing out of the hall. I'd spent the last century both hoping for and dreading this day. I didn't want or need an audience as the universe shifted around me.

Cool air washed across my face as I pushed through the double doors. The smell of petrichor filled my nose, and I breathed deeply. Another bolt of lightning zig-zagged and splintered across the sky, making me flinch.

Whispers whisked past my ear. The voices of Jotunheim, the sensations of Niflheim caressing my skin, the thread of Asgard bloomed in my chest. I could hear them, almost taste them all again. I felt like a child, experiencing the nine realms all at once for the first time again.

Another streak of lightning, and a shiver moved down my spine as a warm hand landed on my shoulder, bringing me back to the present.

"So this is goodbye, then?" He smiled, but his eyes didn't crinkle. "Promise you'll visit?"

"You might be waiting a while." Lightning struck a few feet in front of us. The thick, sharp scent of the sky being split in two filled my nose, and the current set my hair on end.

"I've got all the time in the world." And he did. I didn't know what his connection to the nine realms was. He was never keen on talking about his past, but he'd been with me the last fifty years and hadn't aged a day.

As if on queue the swollen clouds unleashed a torrential downpour. Anyone and everyone outside scattered, running for cover except for us. Rain streamed down our faces and soaked through our clothes as another bolt of lightning struck a few feet away, and the sharp crack of thunder rattled my bones.

For the first time in a long time, I turned my face up to the rain and smiled.

"Promise me something?" Davlin shouted over the roar of the storm.

"What?" Freya's Magik unfurled inside me as the threads that tied this world to the others made themselves known to me once more.

"If you get a second chance with him, don't fuck it up." He smiled, and I pulled him into a tight embrace.

"I wouldn't have survived without you," I said against his cheek.

He held me at arm's length. "That's too close to a goodbye for my comfort."

Lightning streaked across my field of vision. "I mean it. You saved me when I didn't want to be saved."

"We saved each other." He cupped my face in his hands, and tears stung my eyes.

Once I had my wings back, I knew I could visit Davlin whenever I wanted. But deep down, I knew it would never be the same again.

Magik exploded inside me, sharp and urgent. I threw my arms around my torso. I sucked in a breath as the force of a thousand lashings ripped across my back.

"Kara, what is it?" Davlin's eyes searched mine as I fought for control of the Magik inside me.

My vision blurred and my knees gave out as raw, untethered power exploded in my marrow. Wildfire burned down my spine and over my ribs, making it hard to breathe. "My back," I choked out.

Fire burned through my lungs as I shook with the effort to rein in the Magik inside me.

"What is it? Are you okay?" Concern laced his voice as he turned me around.

I concentrated on the hum vibrating in my chest; the core of my Magik, and sucked in a ragged breath. "Do you see anything?" Every fiber of my being hoped he was looking at the intricate tattoo that spanned from shoulder to shoulder and down the middle of my back.

"No, nothing."

I let out a ragged breath. "Bastard." Tears pricked the corners of my eyes, and I hated myself for it. I hated myself for hoping even a little. "I still don't have my wings." I forced the words from my lips as Magik rippled through me once more. I gasped again, trying to gain the upper hand on the power burning through me.

"But I thought you said the curse was only for a hundred years." He reached out tentatively, his hands a feather light touch on my sensitive skin.

You can do this.

I breathed through my nose and exhaled, quieting my mind. Magik swirled in my marrow, wild and free, as I took another breath. I reached out with my mind, caressing the power inside me. Focusing on my heartbeat, I invited my Magik to match the tempo of my soul.

On shaky legs, I turned to Davlin as the pain shifted to a warmth I remembered well.

"I'm free of the curse." I took a steady breath. "I can feel Freya's Magik inside me. I can hear the distant call of the nine realms." I closed my eyes, the familiar sensation of each realm caressing my soul like a long lost lover. "But when he took my wings..." I winced and let out a heavy breath as the memory flashed through me. "I guess that was permanent."

The walls I built around my heart crumbled. This was a far worse punishment. To feel the realms, to hear them calling to me, and know I could never touch them, never see them again. Maybe the curse was only the start of Odin's torment. To take everything away, tear me down to nothing, and then only give back the piece of my soul that would break me over and over again. The Magik inside me burned like poison. I didn't want it. Not like this.

"Hey, look at me." Davlin placed a hand on my shoulder. "We'll figure this out. I promise."

Lightning cracked again, and the ground trembled under our feet.

"We're going to be struck down by the Gods if we stay out here any longer." He grabbed me by the arm and started to pull me inside.

Lightning struck the tree closest to us, splitting it in half as flames licked up the twisted branches.

I doubled over and cradled my stomach. Something tugged on my Magik, and I had to fight a wave of nausea.

"What is it? What's wrong?" Davlin's brow furrowed as he reached out to me.

Darkness fell over my eyes, and my boots no longer touched the ground. My Magik pulsed, and a heaviness settled into my bones. Every fiber of my being felt like I was being sucked between space and time.

"Kara!" Davlin's voice barely reached me as I was propelled into the place between realms.

I tumbled end over end. No longer sure which way was up or down. It was impossible to get my bearings in the darkness. I was nothing more than a wingless bird being tossed around in a storm with no true north to guide me.

Welcome back to the nine realms, Kara.

CHAPTER TWO

SIGURD

LATE AFTERNOON SUNLIGHT glinted off my blade as I caught his sword with my own. "Always the same move." I resisted the smile threatening to pull at my lips as I scraped my blade against Daiman's and pushed him back into a defensive position.

He dug his heels into the grass and smirked. "Why mess with perfection?" Shrugging, he flipped the hilt in his hand.

"It's hardly perfect." I fought the urge to roll my eyes. "Even the sheep can see it coming from a mile away."

"This isn't a tea party," Ragnar yelled from outside the training ring. "Fight as if you mean it! Or do you need someone to show you how it's done?"

I pointed my sword at Ragnar as he mounted the short wood fence. "Wait your turn." I turned toward him, and he took a seat on the top of the barrier in a huff.

Out of the corner of my eye, I saw Daiman take the opening and shoot forward.

Always the aggressor. I turned my attention back to him and met his blow, dodging out of his path.

I swung my sword in an arch from my hip up to his face. Daiman leaned out of the way and spun to the left. I turned just in time to catch a glimpse of his blade slicing through the air. The sharp edge of his weapon skated across my cheek. The sting of my exposed flesh bit across my face, and a trickle of blood dripped down my cheek. I wiped it away with the back of my hand and stared daggers at him.

He cocked his head to the side and raised an eyebrow. "I guess you didn't see that coming." He paced in front of me, arms held out as an invitation.

"Cocky doesn't suit you." If he wanted a proper fight, I'd give it to him. I wouldn't let him draw blood and walk away unscathed.

I shot forward, my sword slicing through the air as if it was an extension of my body. Blow after blow, I pushed him around the ring, keeping him on the defense. With his back against the fence, I knocked his sword out of his grip, grabbed him by the front of his shirt, and slammed my forehead into his nose. The crunch of bones breaking sounded around us.

"For sordinn sake," Daiman cupped his nose. "I was just starting to breathe through both nostrils again." He let out a string of curses.

"You know the rules." I pulled a cloth from my pocket and handed it to him. "Blood for blood."

He grabbed the makeshift bandage and held it to his face. "Asheria's going to charge me twice as much to fix this again."

"Not my fault you left yourself wide open." I shrugged and started across the field toward Magnus and Ragnar.

"That was too easy." Ragnar jumped into the ring, a shit eating grin plastered on his face. "Care to make it more interesting?"

"What'd you have in mind?" I motioned him forward with my sword. Daiman was always a good fight, but never quite the confrontation I craved. He was too predictable and pulled his punches. It was never enough to get my heart pumping.

"How about something a little more challenging?" Ragnar held his arms out, insinuating that he was a better fighter than

Daiman. To be fair, he was, but only because he was ruthless and wild. You could never predict what he'd do next.

"Should I have one arm tied behind my back to make it a fair fight?" I cocked an eyebrow as we circled each other at a distance.

"You know you're not the only one chosen by the Gods." Ragnar rolled his eyes and pointed the tip of his blade in my direction.

"True, but when was the last time Freya asked for an audience with any of you?" I raised an eyebrow. It had always irritated him that Freya had chosen to favor me instead of him.

"That just proves her taste is questionable." He stalked forward, swinging his blade from side to side.

"The words of a jealous man." I relished in the annoyance that flickered across his face.

"Jealous." He threw his head back and laughed, but there was no humor in it. "Of what? Being a pet?"

"Would you call a dragon a pet?"

Daiman groaned from the sidelines. "You think too highly of yourself."

Magnus chuckled and jumped the fence. "He's a cocky dick and deserves to get his ass handed to him." He pulled his sword, turned it over in his hand, and nodded in Ragnar's direction.

I sighed. "Two against one is hardly a challenge."

"Then make it three," Daiman said behind me.

I turned to him just in time to block his blow. He cocked an eyebrow and laughed.

"Don't make me break another bone." I pushed him backward and turned to face Ragnar and Magnus.

"So smug for a man about to surrender." Ragnar shot forward, turning his blade over his wrist and swinging upward. I shifted my weight as he swung past me and his sword *whooshed* through the air.

Magnus lunged forward, and my sword connected with his.

I kicked out my leg and shoved Magnus back in time to turn and see a flash of steel as Daiman's sword swung toward me. I ducked under his sword and shifted to the right before shooting upright into a defensive position.

The three of them moved on me at once, and I planted my feet. Ragnar reached me first. His sword connected with mine, sending a jolt through my arm. He was out for blood and nothing less. We disengaged, and he spun around me.

Magnus was next, his blade swinging over his head and twisting sharply toward me. Raising my sword, I caught the brunt of Magnus's blow as I turned and kicked toward Ragnar, my foot connecting with his chest, and he let out a grunt as he stumbled backward.

Daiman sauntered forward, the tip of his blade trailing in the grass behind him. Twisting from side to side, I blocked each of Ragnar and Magnus's attacks effortlessly.

Daiman shot forward like a cat, his sword in both hands as he swung. I ducked out of the way of the other two to meet Daiman halfway. Our swords connected, the ring of steel echoing across the training field. He spun around me and kicked the back of my knee. A jolt of pain flashed through my leg as I hit the damp grass.

"Yield?" Daiman pressed the tip of his blade between my shoulder blades.

"Never."

I whirled toward him and grabbed his wrist. Twisting to the side, I forced the weapon from his hand. I stood and spun him around the front of me. I held Daiman like a shield, and pointed my sword toward Ragnar and Magnus.

"Call it," I growled at Daiman.

The tension in his body relax in my grip and knew victory was mine. He fell to his knees, and before I could register the smirk on Ragnar's face in front of me, Daiman's elbow shot back into my groin.

The air was ripped from my lungs and I buckled over. Stars flashed across my vision as I gasped for air. The three of them stood over me, the tip of each of their swords an inch from my throat.

"You have no dignity," I said through gritted teeth.

"None, whatsoever." Daiman grinned and held out a hand for me.

I swatted his hand away and got to my feet.

"So much for being a dragon." Ragnar slapped the flat side of his blade against my chest. "More like a mouse." He chuckled. "Looks like—"

Two Valkyrie flew toward us, cutting off whatever Ragnar was about to say. I recognized Bryn immediately with her gold tipped wings and bright white hair flowing behind her.

"This can't be good." I started across the field with Magnus, Ragnar, and Daiman in tow.

Their wings created an unnatural breeze, sending ripples through the tall grass as they came in for a landing on the other side of the training field. As their wings vanished into their backs, I recognized Hildr and cringed. She'd been cross with anyone who associated with Ragnar for weeks now. Whatever transpired between them, it must have been bad, because Ragnar still wouldn't come clean.

Bryn hurried toward the weapons room and disappeared inside, while Hildr called to a group of men who were lounging in the shade, having already finished their training for the day.

Several men rushed past us, shields and swords drawn as we reached the weapons room.

Adrenaline pumped through me. Finally, a real fight. It had been an age since the last time we were called to arms.

"Hildr, what's happened?" I called to her.

She turned in my direction, the green in her iridescent wings catching the light and shifting with her movements. "Just a minor disturbance on the southern border."

"Need some extra muscle?" Ragnar offered as the others pushed around me.

"If we did, I wouldn't be asking you," she fired back.

I looked between Ragnar and Hildr, and he rolled his eyes.

"Ah come on, you can't still be mad." Ragnar took a step toward Hildr and she shot him a look that would have had most men shaking in their boots.

"How do you manage to piss everyone off?" Magnus shoved Ragnar in the back.

"Whatever Ragnar did, I apologize. He was raised by a wild boar." I attempted to salvage the conversation in the hopes she'd ask us, or even just me, to join her.

"Don't apologize for me," Ragnar scoffed. "She doesn't—"

Hildr moved at lightning speed, creating a wind that brushed over all of us as she got in Ragnar's face. "She doesn't what?" she said through gritted teeth.

"Nothing, never mind." Ragnar shrank under her gaze and took a step back.

I smirked as Ragnar slunk away from Hildr. *Now, who's the mouse?*

"What kind of disturbance has called you to arms?" I attempted to call her attention back to the reason she was here. If we weren't going to get to be a part of the fight, she could at least tell us what was going on.

"Let us help," Daiman added.

Hildr looked him up and down. "You need to help yourself first." She turned and started toward the weapons room.

I turned to Daiman. A trickle of blood dripped from his nose. He was not the image I wanted to leave her with. Hopping the fence, I followed after her. "How bad is it?"

"It's minor and the kind that doesn't involve you," she sighed.

I opened my mouth to speak, but she raised her hand to silence me. "Sigurd, you're not missing out on anything."

"It looks like we're missing out." Magnus pointed to the

31

weapons room, and a few more men and shield maiden ran down the ramp and away from us.

"Freya ordered us to gather a small group, nothing more." Her voice held an edge of finality to it.

The hope in my chest deflated, and a sinking feeling settled in the pit of my stomach. Too often now, Freya was leaving me out of the fray. Maybe being her *pet* was doing more harm than good if she wasn't allowing me to do what I was born to.

"I'm sure Freya wouldn't mind a few—"

"It's nothing to get excited about." Her eyes met mine, and her head fell to one side. "I promise it's not worth your time."

I nodded once as the sharp sting of disappointment radiated through me. I was itching for a real fight. It had been too long since we were called to arms. Too long since I'd felt useful in a meaningful way. While I was grateful to be chosen by the Gods, and spend my second life in Folkvang, there had to be more than just drills and training until Ragnarok. I needed more.

"Hildr," Bryn called to her. "We've got all we need." She beat her wings and took off without another word.

Hildr glanced back in our direction once more, her eyes landing on Ragnar before her wings sprung out from her sides and she shot into the sky without another word.

I stared at the horizon until they disappeared into the glow of the setting sun.

Unease settled in my chest, like a shadow over a grave. In all my time here, there'd never been a disturbance that didn't turn into something more sinister. Whether it was another pissing match with the Gods, or Loki playing with things that ought to be left alone.

It was never just a small disturbance.

"You alright, Si?" Magnus asked, pulling my attention away from the western border.

"Yeah, all good," I said, catching up to him.

As we made our way back to the ring, I glanced toward the

setting sun once more and tried to push my disappointment aside. It would do no good to dwell on things out of my control. And we'd know soon enough from the rumor mill or from Freya herself what was going on.

I hopped the fence into the training ring and pulled my sword. "Who's ready for another round?"

CHAPTER THREE

KARA

THE SMELL of damp earth filled my nose, and the rhythmic sound of water reached my ears as I came to. It wasn't the constant roar of rain falling against the roof, nor was it the thunderous sound of the ocean.

I opened my eyes and a few feet in front of me, a delicate stream of water was alive with movement, bubbling and tinkling as it flowed through the forest surrounding me.

Forest?

I lifted my head from the dirt and a sharp pain shot across my eyes. My heartbeat took up residence in my temples and my stomach heaved. Pushing to a sitting position, I took stock of myself. Soft, wet earth soaked through the front of my clothes, and my body ached as if I'd been trampled by horses.

Where in the name of Yggdrasil was I?

Flashes of lightning and the chaotic feel of tumbling between realms hit me like a tornado. *The curse.* Adrenaline shot through me, and I turned to see my reflection in the stream. My fingers brushed along the nape of my neck, but the tattoo of delicate swirls was nowhere in sight.

Right. No wings. My stomach lurched. How did I get here? And where the Hel was I?

Pushing to my feet, I followed the edge of the stream toward a brighter, less dense part of the forest. If only I could place the forest I was in, but there were many locations in the nine realms similar to this one. Hel, for all I knew, I was still in Midgard.

As I trekked through the underbrush and stepped over fallen trees, the light shifted to a soft orange glow. If I didn't find civilization soon, I'd have to seek shelter before Mani chased the sun below the horizon, and graced us with the light of the moon. There were monsters in more than a few realms that even *I* didn't dare cross paths with in the dead of night.

I ducked under a low branch, and the trees gave way to a lush valley. Lime green grass stretched as far as the eye could see. Greenish grey mountains rose on either side of the valley, their peaks painted with a dusting of snow. And deep velvet green trees ran the length of the eastern border.

Warmth spread through me as my gaze followed the serpentine river that carved its way through the valley floor, and led to a waterfall off in the distance. If I squinted, I could make out the buildings that rose up through the trees, and stood out against the granite rock to my left.

"Folkvang." The word trembled on my lips. I'd dreamed of this day for so long it was hard to believe it was real. I was home. "I'm free." A chuckle bubbled up in my throat. "I'm free!" I yelled at the sky and laughed like a madwoman. "I'm free," I breathed, and let my head fall back. Closing my eyes, I inhaled the air of another realm for the first time in a hundred years. *I'm free.*

My debt had well and truly been paid. Now I was here, I could admit to myself that I never thought I'd be able to return. That my banishment would continue until the last star blinked out. And honestly, I wouldn't have argued for my freedom. The heartache of what I did would stay with me for the rest of my existence. It didn't matter that a century has passed. Even a thousand years wouldn't dull the ache I felt every time I thought of Sigurd. I may have made peace knowing that he'd never be mine like he once was, but he'd always be a part of me and my story.

Two figures cut through the skyline like giant birds. One with obsidian and gold tipped wings, and the other with iridescent wings that caught the sun and sparkled like a prism. My heart lept into my throat and my excitement turned to ash in my mouth. What if I wasn't welcome here? What if my actions were too heinous to forgive?

Their wings beat against the grass, flattening the terrain as they came in for a landing a few feet ahead of me. They started toward me and drew their swords in unison. The trees rustled to my left, and every hope I'd felt upon seeing Folkvang again vanished. Warning bells went off in my head as I scanned the trees. The shimmer of steel caught my eye, and half a dozen shields stepped out of the treeline.

I wasn't welcome.

I held my hands up as the Valkyrie stalked toward me. Hopefully, they were in the mood to ask questions first.

"Who are you? And what business do you have here?" The one with the iridescent wings pointed their sword at me.

I opened my mouth to speak and clamped it shut. They didn't know who I was. They only saw me as a threat to the realm for dropping out of the sky unannounced. A tiny spark of hope sizzled under my breast bone. Maybe my return would be welcomed.

"I'm a Valkyrie, just like you." I looked down at my dirty trousers and muddy linen top, then back up at them. Maybe they wouldn't judge a book by its cover, because at the moment it looked as if I had made my bed in a pig pen.

"Do you take me for a three-eye toad?" She chuckled, and her sword dipped ever so slightly. She'd already assessed me and deemed me not to be a threat.

Not going to lie. That stung a bit.

"Look, I know how this looks." I kept my hands raised in

surrender. Just because she didn't see me as the weapon I was, didn't mean she wouldn't rip my head off and present it to Freya. "But I swear I'm not your enemy." To them, I was just a trespasser, someone they'd never seen before. So I'd have to prove I belonged here.

"Go on then," the gold tipped wing Valkyrie said. "Show us your wings."

Her words were a blunt dagger to the stomach, and my chest tightened. Of course, they'd want a display of the one thing I couldn't give them. "I can't." I let out a heavy breath. "They were taken from me." Freya's Magik pulsed through my core, over my chest, and across my back. But there was no tattoo, no remnant of wings to call to the surface.

"By the runes. How?" The white haired Valkyrie exhaled and took a step forward.

The dark haired Valkyrie with sharp eyes held out a hand to stop her companion. "How convenient. The one thing that would prove you're telling the truth and they just so happen to be missing."

"Yeah, it's not a great look for me. But it's the truth." I took a step forward, and the warriors in the trees stepped with me. I glanced at the men and women to my left and then to my right. "For the love of Yggdrasil, put your swords down. There'll be no fighting today."

"You have no right to command them." The dark haired Valkyrie shot across the space between us in half a breath and pressed her blade against the delicate skin at my neck.

"Then why have they laid their swords at their feet?" I was careful to take shallow breaths so the blade wouldn't cut me.

The Valkyrie looked at the warriors surrounding us, and sure enough, they'd dropped their weapons in the grass.

She pushed me backward and stepped away as if she feared I might take her blade from her, too.

My hand went to my throat, and I breathed a sigh of relief. "These warriors are bound to Freya, same as you and me."

"How is this possible?" The white haired one frowned at me.

"I used to command legions of Freya's warriors. It would seem I still have that ability." *Thank the Gods.* I wasn't sure if that would work, and I wasn't in the mood to fight my way out of this without a single weapon to my name.

"Now that you're not trying to kill me." I placed a hand on my chest. "I'm Kara." I held my hand out, but when neither of them moved to take it I let it drop to my side.

"Bryn," the one with the Black and gold wings said. "And Hildr." She motioned to her dark haired companion.

"Why have we never met you before?" Bryn studied me as if she was trying to pluck the memory of me from some lost corner of her mind.

"I was banished to Midgard for quite some time. I've only just become free." They didn't need the whole story, at least not until I knew they'd let me live to tell it.

"Banished?" Bryn frowned. "What God did you piss off?"

I shrugged. "Better question is, which of the Gods haven't I pissed off?"

The heavy beating of wings sounded as another Valkyrie landed behind me. I groaned internally. How many people was I going to have to plead my case to before I could change into dry clothes, and grab a stiff drink?

"You were supposed to dispose of the intruder, not chat them up like they're your long lost mother." I'd know that voice anywhere. Excitement jumped through me, quickly followed by a stab of nerves. It took all of my control not to tackle her to the ground in a bear hug.

What if she wasn't happy to see me? What if time had allowed her to rethink her feelings toward me? What if she looked at me like I was a monster? I wasn't sure I could handle that.

I turned, forcing myself to face her. Black and midnight blue wings spread out on either side of her, and warm sunlight kissed her golden brown skin.

"Talon?" My eyes met hers.

"Kara?" Her eyes widened and her mouth fell open as she closed the gap between us. "You're alive?" She grabbed my shoulders and her wings shimmered into her back. "How is this possible?" Her hand touched my cheek and tears sprung to my eyes as I nodded. "We thought you were dead. That day with Si. You vanished. Even Freya couldn't feel you anymore."

"You can thank Odin for that." I wrapped my arms around her and she pulled me in to her embrace. One of the many cracks in my heart swelled as she held me.

She didn't hate me.

Talon had been my best friend, my right hand, my other half for longer than I could remember. It felt like a dream that she was in my arms right now.

She pulled back and held me at arm's length. "Odin?"

"It's a long story."

"It would have to be. You've been dead for...how long has it been?" She took a step back and examined me. The initial excitement seemed to wear off, and she eyed me with an edge of suspicion.

"A century and not dead, just cursed to a lifetime in Midgard." I sighed. "Without Magik, without the nine realms, without my family and friends."

"You've been in Midgard all this time?" Her eyebrows knitted together.

"Before you get all cozy, she should speak with Freya," Hildr interrupted our reunion.

"Of course." Talon's wings spread from her back. "Shall we?"

I opened my mouth to tell her I couldn't fly, but my throat went dry and I couldn't speak. It was one thing to tell strangers I didn't have wings, but my friend? She'd known me in all my glory and now I was just this broken thing, barely pieced back together again.

"She can't fly." Bryn leveled her eyes on me. "She doesn't have any wings."

Talon took a step back, and her gaze skated over me. "Then I'll walk with her." She draped an arm over my shoulders. "Hildr, let Freya know one of our own has returned to Folkvang." She still wore that look of skepticism, but until proven otherwise, she was willing to trust that I was Kara, her long lost friend.

We started toward the city on foot while Hildr and Bryn dismissed their makeshift army and took to the sky.

Talon turned, so she was walking backward. A mischievous smile pulled at her lips. "Alright, tell me everything."

CHAPTER FOUR

KARA

AFTER A BRISK HOUR OF WALKING, Talon and I reach the Vanir atrium, named for Freya's family. It was only ever used for official business with outsiders since it was tucked in the hills away from the city center. It wasn't lost on me that I was brought here and not somewhere more casual. To them, I was an outsider until proven otherwise. Freya would never risk the people of Folkvang if it turned out I was here for more nefarious reasons.

Double doors large enough to allow clearance for the giants of Jotunheim towered above us. Scenes of epic battles, births, and deaths were carved into the heavy wood doors. An homage to the Vanir family and their influence over the realms. In the middle was a likeness of Freya, Goddess of fertility, love, war, and Magik. Her wooden eyes stared down at me and my mouth went dry. Talon might be happy to see me, but I doubted a reception with Freya would be an easy reunion.

"Ready?" Talon asked as she reached the entrance.

Butterflies flapped in my stomach, over my heart, and formed a lump in my throat. "As ready as I can be, considering I look like a drowned rat." I tried to make light of the situation so she wouldn't know how nervous I was.

"You look..." she inspected me. "Like you've had a long journey home." Even if she was unsure of me, she remained friendly, which eased some of the tension in my shoulders. At least I wasn't alone.

She pushed the door open, and my eyes widened as the soft glow of the setting sun brushed over my face. Though this wasn't my first time visiting the atrium, my memory didn't do it justice. The open arches to my right framed the beautiful valley below like a painting. Trees sprung up from the marble floor unnaturally and reached for the sky. A cool breeze rustled the leaves, and white flowers blossomed on the branches above us. The sweet smell of jasmine mixed with the earthy scent of a hearth, and goosebumps shivered across my skin.

The stone wall to my left was painted to depict each member of the Vanir family. Swirls of decorative gold so bright I had to squint, tied each portrait together while showcasing the unique attributes of each God. It was a masterpiece, but a bit over-whelming after the subdued tones of Midgard.

A dozen pairs of eyes swiveled in my direction, and my heart skipped a beat. Bryn & Hildr, were among the onlookers, and had obviously shared who I claimed to be with the others. Some studied me with curiosity, their eyes tracing my form. While others stared daggers into my skull and sneered as I passed them.

I wasn't expecting an audience, and I certainly wasn't prepared for this level of scrutiny. Having so many pairs of eyes on me, when I was very clearly missing my wings, left me feeling exposed and vulnerable.

The crowd split as we drew closer to the head of the atrium. Freya stood about a dozen feet away, her long golden hair flowing down her back as if the most skilled painter in the nine realms had stroked each strand into perfection. My heart slammed against my ribcage, and my mouth went dry. *This was it.*

She turned to me and froze mid-sentence. "By the Runes," she exhaled and took a step in my direction. A smile pulled at her lips, but she quickly wiped it from her face. "So you're the one who claims to be Kara, The Wild Storm." She used the title that was given to me at my wing ceremony, and my spine went rigid. It was a deeply personal name I thought I'd never hear again.

"Let me have a look at you." She scanned me from head to toe as if she could see right to the core of my soul. Motioning me forward, she schooled her expression into an unreadable mask.

I felt rather than saw Talon leave my side, and I took a breath as I stepped forward. Even though I knew I was telling the truth, I also knew the truth rarely set you free. And I had no proof of who I was or that I once carried the mark of Valkyrie.

I took another step forward, determined to meet my fate head on even if my heart was in my throat.

Each step felt like a step through time. A month without Sigurd. *Step.* A decade of loneliness. *Step.* A century without my wings. *Step.* A lifetime of guilt. *Step.*

Freya moved toward me and held out her hand as I approached her. Her personal guards shifted with her, but she motioned for them to fall back.

"You resemble the one we lost, but a face does not determine the truth of one's soul." She ran a finger along my cheekbone and tipped my chin up.

"I don't sense another's Magik about you." Her eyes flicked between mine. "But I felt the light blink out inside you all those years ago. How is it possible you stand here today with my Magik in your veins?"

I let my gaze drop to the floor and swallowed. "Odin."

"I'd have guessed he might have something to do with this." The malice in her voice was unmistakable. "But why? To what end?" Her brow furrowed as she pinched my chin and moved my face from side to side.

"It's a long story." I let out a breath.

"It usually is." She let go of my face and circled me. My shoulders stiffened. I knew she'd look for the tattoo of my wings, but there was no trace of the Valkyrie I once was. Her finger trailed across my shoulders and it was as if someone had walked over my grave. "Interesting."

"They were taken—"

"I didn't ask for an explanation." The coolness in her voice sent a shiver down my spine.

She circled back in front of me and took a step back, steepling her fingers and pressing them to her lips.

I opened my mouth to speak, and she raised her hand to silence me. "I'd hate for you to waste your breath and my time." One corner of her lips curled as she narrowed her eyes at me. Gold swirls of Magik sparked to her fingertips. Her eyes wrinkled at the corners and, for the first time since I returned, a yawning pit of dread opened up inside me.

Please, for the love of the nine realms, don't let there be any lingering effects of Odin's Magik. I just want to be free. I swallowed the lump in my throat and nodded for her to confirm my identity. After all, I had nothing to hide.

So why did it feel like I might hyperventilate at any moment?

She held her hands out in front of her face, palm up. Pursing her lips, she blew a gust of air over her palms. Gold starlight Magik left her fingertips and floated toward me like dandelion seeds.

I raised my head and took a breath as the first touch of Freya's Magik landed on my skin.

The Magik, already a part of my soul, bloomed in my chest and filled every corner of my body as it called to its likeness. Freya's power clawed at my skin, digging its talons into the core of who I was, and took hold. Memories flashed through my mind like cards being shuffled. Before I could grab onto one, the next was falling into place.

Me as a child. Reading a book outside. My first fight. Folkvang. A flash of my wings. Sigurd laying in bed. Midgard. Odin. Flames. Steel. Shadows and a sapphire eye.

I held my breath as memory after memory assaulted me. My heart raced and sweat gathering on my brow. I locked my knees in place, forcing myself to stay upright when all I wanted to do was crumble to the floor and succumb to the onslaught of Freya's Magik.

Whispers filled the room. As much as I wanted to look for a friendly face, I kept my eyes on Freya. She was the only one who mattered right now.

My life, my future, was in her hands.

She cocked her head like a raven inspecting a worthy trinket and hummed as she released me.

I let out a ragged breath as my vision blurred and a wave of nausea rolled through me. If this was what honesty felt like, I didn't want to know what it would feel like if her Magik found me to be a liar.

She closed the distance between us and cupped my face with both her hands. "I thought you were dead." Her voice was barely a whisper. She smiled and kissed my forehead. "I've never been happier to be wrong." She wrapped her arm around my shoulder and guided me toward the front of the room.

"You and me both." A nervous chuckle bubbled out of my throat. "Though without the nine realms, without my wings..." I hesitated. "I fear a part of me did die."

"I can only imagine." She squeezed my arm, and her lips formed a hard line. "But now you've returned to the nine realms, we only need to remedy your wings to make you whole again.

"Can you?" My heart raced as the words left my mouth. I was dangerously close to getting my hopes up, and if I did, there'd be no going back to Midgard to live a simple life.

She studied my face and frowned. "The choice is yours, same

as before. And if you decide to forgo the ritual, you can always–"

"I'll do it," I said without a second thought. Davlin may be right, that my wings don't define me, but if she was offering to make me whole again, I wasn't going to pass up the opportunity.

She beamed at me the way a mother might look upon her child. "Very well. Until then, it would seem you have quite the tale to share with us." She motioned for me to take a seat.

I nodded as my heart threatened to beat out of my chest. I hadn't told this story in a very long time. In fact, I spent the majority of my time in Midgard trying to avoid thinking about what happened the day I ended Sigurd's mortal life, and Odin cursed me.

Talon took a seat on the pillow next to me and squeezed my shoulder. "For half a second, I was worried." Her eyebrows nearly met her hairline.

"And here I thought you believed me."

"I did. I do," she amended. "But you looked like your head was about to explode," she chuckled.

Freya took a seat on a raised section of cushions and turned toward me. "So tell me, my Wild Storm, how does one disappear from the nine realms?"

CHAPTER FIVE

SIGURD

As THE NIGHT WENT ON, more and more people filed into the Great Hall. Music carried through the room, mixing with laughter and chatter as we waited for Freya's big announcement. The atmosphere was charged with anticipation. Glancing around, I realized I hadn't seen this many people gather under one roof in an age. I couldn't help but wonder if it had anything to do with the disturbance. Irritation prickled over my skin. I should have been there.

Ragnar slammed his cup on the table, calling my attention back to our group. I took a sip of my crisp honey ale and wiped a few droplets from my beard with the back of my hand.

"Don't know who you think you're fooling." I cocked an eyebrow at the tale Ragnar was attempting to spin. "Magnus had you cornered." I gripped Magnus by the shoulder in a congratulatory spirit.

"It was a cheap shot, and you know it." Ragnar pointed at Magnus and scowled. It wasn't often someone got the better of him, but when they did, he'd pitch a fit for hours, even days, depending on who bested him.

"You're just sore you'll be keeping the sheep company tonight." Magnus taunted Ragnar.

"I should warn you, the ram is a right bastard." Daiman rubbed his ribs. "I'm still not breathing right."

"That was a week ago." I choked down my laughter. "How are you still such a mess?"

"Maybe if I wasn't always patching up a broken nose, I'd be able to afford some real healing." He leveled his eyes at me over his swollen nose, and I stifled a chuckle.

"Maybe if you learned some better defensive skills, you wouldn't need mending so often."

A door slammed open with a bang, the echo reverberating through the hall. The music halted, and the chatter swiftly turned to whispers as Freya barged across the dais at the head of the hall. Her blue and gold dress clung to her curves, and her black feather cloak trailed behind her.

"She knows how to make an entrance, doesn't she?" Ragnar said under his breath.

She turned to face us, her golden braid falling down her shoulder as she came to a stop at the top of the dais. "As some of you may know," she started and all the whispers ceased, "there was an incident earlier today." Her voice carried over all of us with ease. "One of our own has found their way back to us."

Freya's eyes met mine across the room, a small smile pulling at the corner of her mouth. "I ask that you welcome her with open arms and celebrate her homecoming." She motioned toward the entrance of the great hall, and everyone in the room swiveled as one. As the carved doors swung open, a steady beat of drums filled the hall.

Torches lined the path leading to the main entrance. Their flames flickered as if the tempo of the music intoxicated them. A figure stepped out of the shadows, and someone in the room whistled in celebration.

My grip tightened on the cup in my hand as every nerve in my body flared to life.

My vision focused on the woman standing at the threshold of the Great Hall. Firelight cast a glow upon her as if Sol himself was lighting up her presence with the sun. The music fell away, the cheers and shouts no longer reached my ears as everything and everyone disappeared from my vision. Leaving only her.

It had been a hundred years since I last laid eyes on her, and still, I felt something primal rumble deep in my chest, quickly followed by the cold stab of betrayal.

"I wonder what her story is," someone behind me grunted as she took a step.

"Why haven't we ever seen her before?"

The words floated in and out of my ears, barely taking on meaning, and the steady beat of drums thundered through me once more.

The back of my neck tingled, and a shiver passed over my chest. She was here. After all this time. Why?

Talon and Bryn led her through the throng of onlookers, dancing and swaying to the beat of the drums as they ushered her into the hall. Each Valkyrie they passed reached out and touched her hand, her arm, her shoulder. Each warrior and shield maiden they passed inclined their head or raised their cup to her.

She moved through the crowd with ease and grace. Her body swaying with the music as if the tempo was branded on her soul. The Valkyrie had outdone themselves for her home-coming. The sleek gold dress complimented her burnt auburn hair that was swept off her face into intricate twists and braids. Inky black runes covered her arms, and resting on her chest was an assortment of beads and silver pendants that displayed her loyalty to Freya.

"She's a sight to be sure," Ragnar said, and I had to agree. The last century had done nothing to dull her beauty.

My gaze swept over the curve of her hips, the swell of her chest. The memory of what she felt like burned thorough me, letting loose the embers of a long lost love.

"You alright Si?" Magnus asked from what seemed like the other side of Yggdrasil.

49

"Kara." Her name was barely a whisper on my lips, but I might as well have shouted her moniker at the top of my lungs.

As she danced in another circle, her eyes caught mine. She froze, her bottom lip falling open as her hand moved to her chest and she took a breath.

I forced myself to look down at the cup in my hands.

So much time had passed and still, the sight of her made my blood sing and made my heart beat as if I was fighting for my life once more. She was here, really here, after all this time.

I'd waited decades, hoping we'd be reunited, hoping I'd finally get some answers. But when I died, it was as if she'd vanished from the nine realms.

"Si?" Someone called my name, but I ignored them and poured myself another cup of mead.

"What in the name of Hela's gotten into him?" Daiman said as I downed my cup and stared at the half eaten plate of food in front of me.

The beat of the drums echoed in my blood, amplifying the beat of my heart and making my head spin.

"Svava said she was cursed for betraying the one restriction the Alfather placed on the Valkyrie." Ragnar leaned into the middle of the table, eyeing each of us as if he was privy to some secret information.

"Svava, really?" I spat without looking at him. "You know she'll spin a tale just for the attention." I filled another cup to the brim, eager for him to continue, but trying not to show it.

"What other reason would she have for staying away from Folkvang so long that none of us have ever seen her?" Ragnar shrugged.

"Good question," I said into my cup.

"She heard you were here and didn't want to be annoyed for all eternity." Magnus laughed at his own joke, slapping his hand on the table.

"Odin doesn't have any say over the Valkyrie," Daiman challenged Ragnar's story.

"Well then, it's a good thing Talon confirmed Svava was telling the truth."

"Talon? Really?" I hated how hungry I sounded for any scrap of information. If Talon had confirmed anything Svava had said, then maybe it was true. She'd always been kind to me and a loyal friend. She didn't have the penchant to lie like Svava.

"Yes, Talon. I'm not the daft cow you all take me for. I'm well aware of Svava's reputation for bending the truth."

"I bet you are." Magnus raised his cup in salute as the tempo of the drums and shouts of celebration took on a life of their own.

"Are you ever going to get to the point?" I tried to sound bored, but every nerve in my body was strung tighter than a quiver as I tracked the loudest of the shouts through the room. She was getting closer. Every beat of the drums, every heartbeat was bringing her closer.

The corner of Ragnar's mouth lifted with a wry grin. He loved the attention just as much as Svava. They were two peas in a questionable pod.

I raised my cup to my lips as a shadow moved over me.

"Sigurd." Her voice rang through me like honey and knives.

Every muscle in my body went rigid. I pushed every trifling emotion back into the shadows where they'd been for the last hundred years and turned toward her.

"Kara." I looked up the length of her, taking a few extra seconds before meeting her eyes.

They were the same brilliant green I looked into as my life was stolen from me.

Her gaze danced all over me before settling on my face. "You look well." Her lips pulled at the corner ever so slightly, but it didn't take a God to see the unease in her expression.

"As do you." I was surprised by how even my voice sounded when really I wanted to drag her out of the hall and—

And what? Love, confusion, hatred, lust and betrayal warred for control within me. Even if I did get her alone, I was just as likely to bed her as I was to strip her of her own life.

"You two know each other?" Magnus grabbed my shoulder, but my eyes stayed glued to Kara.

"Were you raised by trolls?" Ragnar grunted. "Obviously they know each other."

She stared down at me as I took a sip of mead and refused to say anything more.

"I'm sure you're happy to be back," Daiman interjected when it was clear neither of us was going to say anything more on the topic.

Her eyes shot to Daiman, and I turned away, thankful to be free of her roaming gaze. Now was not the time for a very public reunion. Nor was it the time for answers I deserved.

"You have no idea." I could hear the smile in her voice.

Decades of hope, disappointment, and loss bloomed in my chest.

"You'll have to regale us with your adventures once you're settled in," Magnus said.

"Not much to tell. Midgard's been dull since it lost some of its best." The warmth in her voice sent a chill down my spine.

From the smile on Daiman's face, I could tell her flattery had already won him over.

I stifled a dry laugh and shook my head.

"From the looks of you"—Ragnar's eyes raked up and down the full length of her—"I find that hard to believe."

"Now, now," Talon tisked behind me. "You boys can't hog Kara all to yourselves." Leave it to Talon to politely move her along. I'd have to thank her later.

"I'll see you all around, I'm sure."

"You can count on it," Daiman called after her with a shit-eating grin on his face.

A knot formed in my stomach.

"Well, well." Ragnar folded his arms over his chest and three pairs of eyes turned to me.

"I don't want to talk about it," I said without meeting any of their gaze.

"Like Hel you're not going to talk about it." Ragnar leaned forward. "A Valkyrie no one knows shows up out of the blue and we find out you two are acquainted?" He shook his head, a grin spreading across his face. "We're hearing this story one way or another."

"Leave it, Ragnar," I said through gritted teeth.

"Or what? You'll make me?"

"Don't tempt me." I tightened my grip on the cup in my hand and fought the urge to hit something.

"She must really be something to have you so rattled." Daiman cocked his head.

"A beauty like that." Ragnar whistled.

I followed Ragnar's gaze and as much as I didn't want to admit it, she was a sight for sore eyes. I took another gulp of my drink, trying to erase the sound of my name on her lips.

"Looks like you struck a nerve." Magnus punched Ragnar's arm.

"How about I just ask her?" Daiman got to his feet. "I wouldn't mind getting to know her a little better."

I grabbed Daiman by the arm and pulled him back down to the bench.

"The way you lot feed off gossip isn't healthy," I grumbled.

"Come on, it can't be that bad." Magnus clapped a hand on my back.

Actually, it can. I took a sip of mead, barely tasting it, and sighed. "She was the love of my life."

"So she broke your heart?" Ragnar scoffed and rolled his eyes. "We've all been there."

"In more ways than one." I drained the rest of my mead. "She shoved a dagger into my chest and ended my mortal life."

Three pairs of eyes settled on me, and for the first time in recent memory, they were at a loss for words.

CHAPTER SIX

KARA

"And you thought it'd be awkward," Talon snorted as she pulled me away from Sigurd and his companions.

Heart still pounding, I gave her a sidelong glance as we moved through the throng of people toward Freya.

"Okay, it wasn't the greatest reunion of all time." She shrugged. "But at least he didn't kill you on sight."

A flash of his penetrative gaze burned through me. "I think he might have if he wasn't so taken off guard." I shook my head as Talon guided me forward, turning me in a circle to the beat of the drums once more.

"It's a problem for tomorrow." She smirked. "Tonight is for celebrating."

She pushed me in front of her, and as much as I wanted to squash the history between us, she was right. There would be no quick reconciliation now or in the days to come. It would take time, time we now had. So tonight I'd celebrate me and my freedom, and tomorrow I'd start making things right with him.

I grabbed one of the raised cups offered to me and drained the contents. The music called to my soul, the beat filling my body while the melody of the strings caressed me like a lover. I gave myself over to it, allowing the music to banish the shadows of the past as I made my way toward Freya at the front of the hall.

My vision blurred as I moved through the throng of people. My head felt like it was in the clouds, and my feet skated along the ground of their own accord. It had been far too long since I'd been part of a celebration with my people.

In Midgard, the old ways were waning, giving way to a new, more rigid practice. With each day that passed, the heart and soul of an entire people was fading to history. And yet, here I was in the midst of that soul, that life I'd missed more than I ever realized.

As I reached the head table, Freya motioned me forward and pulled out a chair for me. I took a seat and without trying to, my eyes landed on Sigurd. He was the only one of his group that kept his gaze on the table in front of him, and my heart sank. I spent every day of the last hundred years thinking about what it would be like to see him again. But my imagination was frightfully dull compared to the real thing.

A swell of sadness filled my chest as I pulled my attention from him, and looked out over the assembled crowd.

Every square inch was filled to the brim with people in varying degrees of dress. Some still wore armor, others had dressed down for the occasion.

But the Valkyrie were shining beacons around the room. They wore flowing gowns of varying colors and fabrics, accentuating their ethereal beauty. A slit up each of their legs showcased the weapons strapped to their thighs. It was no wonder people thought of us as angels of death.

Freya raised a hand, and the hall fell silent save for a lone drum that continued the tempo that had swept me through the hall.

"Tonight we celebrate Kara's return to the nine realms." Freya's eyes met mine. "It's been an age without you," she cooed.

Several people cried out in excitement and threw their hands in the air. Someone else let out a high pitched whistle in celebration. Another person let a war cry that belted through the great hall as the drums got louder once more.

"Many of you will not know her." She turned back to her subjects, and I glanced at Sigurd again. His eye caught mine for a split second before he turned away. "But she's family, no matter the time spent away. I beseech each of you to treat her as such while she gets her footing again."

Another round of cheers as Freya nodded to the musicians to her right. One woman pulled a bow across the tagelharpa strings, and a warm, resonant tone echoed through the hall. A guttural hum moved through the crowd, and the string instrument and drums wove a soft melody that I recognized from Asgard.

A welcome back to warriors after their return from battle.

My heart swelled as I looked over the crowd. Their reverent and curious faces stared up at me, and tears prick the corner of my eyes. I didn't deserve this kind of homecoming, I thought as Freya sang a high pitched note.

Her voice pierced the fog in my mind, as the deep thrum of the strings and even tempo of the drums grounded me to the here and now. She belted another note, her voice pitching up another octave, calling to the Magik inside me. The whimsical, almost calming quality of her voice pitched into a battle scream, sending the congregation into a frenzy of whooping and hollering.

The drums grew louder, each hit reverberating through my bones and filling the great hall. Freya's song carried on as the chanting of the others grew stronger and louder.

I gave myself over to the music, becoming a part of the collective energy moving through us all.

We were one at this moment. Everyone chanting together, everyone moving to the beat of the drums. My head spun again and this time I didn't fight it. Everyone shifted in and out of focus, and the world turned upside down. I may've been afraid to step back into this life, but now I was here, I couldn't imagine returning to my mundane life in Midgard.

Davlin was right. I was made for the nine realms.

I closed my eyes, letting myself free fall into the celebration. I was one with Freya again, one with my sisters.

Freya's voice faded into a soft hum. The chanting grew quieter, and the drums banged once more as the hall fell silent.

Torches flickered along the walls as a moment of silence opened up around us.

"Skal." Freya raised her cup.

"Skal." Everyone raised a stein, drank deeply, and erupted in shouts of celebration.

The music flared back to life, taking on a life of its own as Freya took her seat.

Before I had the chance to even take a bite of food, Talon and Bryn dragged me toward the right side of the room. Which was in the opposite direction from Sigurd and his companions. I couldn't help but wonder if she was deliberately putting space between us or if it just worked out that way.

We stopped at a table, and I recognized a few friendly faces from my meeting with Freya earlier today.

"I don't want to see you empty handed tonight," Bryn said, passing a stein to me and tapping her own against mine.

"You don't have to tell me twice." I took a sip of the decadent mead. Nothing in all of Midgard came close to the sweetly spiced flavor of Folkvang's mead.

"I guess congratulations are in order." Svava sauntered up to our table and smirked down at me.

My spine went stiff at the shrill sound of her voice.

"This time, try not to forfeit your freedom so carelessly." She smirked and batted her lashes.

My grip tightened on my stein as I fought the urge to shut her up.

"That's enough, Svava." Asheria slammed her drink down harder than was necessary.

"I'm just saying." She raised her hands in defense.

"Ignore her." Bryn rolled her eyes. "I do."

I turned to Svava, a sickly sweet smile plastered on my face. "Glad to see you're still lovely as ever."

"You may not have taken your banishment seriously." She held my gaze, a fire burning in her eyes. "But those of us who know the truth will never forget what a disgrace you are." She pulled back with a devilish smirk on her lips and stalked away.

Talon cursed under her breath and stared daggers at Svava's back.

"Don't listen to her." Asheria touched my arm. "She's a nightmare. Always has been."

I huffed as I sat back down. "She's not wrong, though. There are plenty of people, I'm sure, who feel the same way."

"Don't do that." Talon held up her hand to keep me from speaking. "She just wants to get under your skin. She always has."

"You'd think she would've found another hobby in the last hundred years." I shrugged and took a sip of my drink. The tart berry flavor coated my tongue as a small smile pulled at the corner of my mouth.

"Oh, believe me, we've all taken our turn in your absence." Talon smirked. "Thanks for that." She raised her stein to me and drained the contents.

I let the conversation drop. I was in no mood to let Svava ruin my night, even if her words did strike a nerve.

It seemed as if everyone in Folkvang came up to our table, sharing a drink with me and telling me harrowing tales of their life in Midgard. With every cup of mead I downed, I slipped further and further away from reality.

The chatter and laughter became an indistinct murmur as I watched the other Valkyrie move through the hall like birds cutting across a graceful wind. The steady cadence moving through the hall was no longer just music, but a call to a wild instinct inside me that was heavy and electric. It was as if I was the lightning to the storm that was building, and the drums were my thunder.

My heart lurched at the thought of waking from this perfect dream, and I was on my feet in an instant. If I was cursed to wake tomorrow in Midgard, I would not waste my one night of freedom watching everyone live. I would join them.

I started toward the throng of people in the middle of the room, who were already swaying to the drums. Their bodies tangling together so I couldn't tell where one person started, and the other ended. As I drew closer, my head swam from the warmth of their bodies and the copious amount of mead I'd consumed.

I scanned the hall again, but there was no sign of Sigurd or the men he'd been sitting with earlier. I'd hoped I'd be able to steal a few moments with him this evening, but he'd cleared out just as soon as I turned my back. A part of me was relieved that he was gone, which immediately made me feel guilty.

I'd spent the better part of the last few decades imagining what it would be like to see him again, but never thought it would hurt so much. When his eyes reached mine, it was like the nine realms blinked out of existence, leaving me in the dark once again. One would think the time apart would've dulled the pain, but seeing his face again brought on a flood of memories and emotions I wasn't prepared for.

I didn't want to think about our heartbreak or the pain I've caused. For once, I didn't want my past to dictate the present. I let the music take me and joined the rhythmic dancing of those around me. Arms tangled with mine as I raised them over my head. A hand landed on my hip and slid along my back. The warmth of someone's breath brushed over my shoulder as I turned and moved further into the crowd.

The song came to a close and a new tempo took its place. I glanced around for a familiar face. My head spun from the heat of the bodies around me and the sheer quantity of alcohol I'd consumed over the last few hours. Sweat glistened over my skin and not for the first time tonight, I was grateful for the thin fabric they dressed me in.

Moving to the heady, rhythmic beat of drums, soft blue eyes met mine from across the room. He pushed off the wall, downed his cup, and moved through the crowd toward me.

My gaze traveled over him as I swayed to the beat. He towered over half the people in the room, and his dirty blonde hair was tied half up. His shirt hung loose at the neck, showing off his well muscled chest and sun-kissed skin. My eyes met his again, and his lips pulled into a smile.

He's the perfect distraction. I thought as the music coursed through my body, making my heart pulse through every inch of me.

He held out his hand, and I took it. Spinning me around so I was facing away from him, his hand moved down my arm, over the curve of my body, and settled on my hip. He matched my movements, swaying and dipping to the music as he pulled me against him.

"You look like you've been enjoying yourself tonight." His voice was husky against my ear and his beard tickled my neck, sending a shiver across my skin.

I looked over my shoulder, his face only inches from mine. "I have a lot to celebrate."

"So I heard." His hand moved from my hip and over my

stomach. The thin fabric did little to separate the warmth of his splayed fingers from my overheating skin.

His gaze drifted to my mouth. "Care to let me celebrate with you?" Flames flickered in his eyes and a bit my lip as I turned toward him, draping my arms over his shoulders.

I smirked up at him, already enjoying the feel of his hands on me. "Only if you can keep up."

His fingers dug into my hips as he leaned in. "I think I can manage." His words were a caress against my lips, heating my blood. "Maybe somewhere a little more private?" He raised his eyebrows, and I nodded.

He pulled me outside, the night air hitting my sticky skin and making me shiver. The beat of the drums followed us as he guided me around the back of the Great Hall.

Every few feet, stone benches sat in between decorative pillars that rose high above our heads to the ceiling. A stunning view of Folkvang spread out below us. Lanterns twinkled in the city like stars, and the night sky reflecting in the river took my breath away.

He turned toward me, reaching out with his other hand he guided me into the shadows. My back pressed against one of the pillars, the cool stone a welcome reprieve from the heat of the hall. His hand coasted along my waist, resting on my hip as my hands trailed up his arms, taking in the solid strength of him.

His lips met mine, soft and commanding, and I pressed against his chest. His other hand trailed up my side, over the curve of my breast, up my neck, and into my hair. The image of Sigurd looking up at me in the great hall flashed in my mind.

He'd haunted me for a hundred years. Every touch of another, every kiss, felt like a betrayal to his memory. But I had a chance to start over, live for myself again without the weight of him on my heart. Pushing him from my mind, I gave myself over to the present and the man pressed against me.

Letting my head fall back, his mouth burned a trail down the side of my neck and over my collar bone, making my heart race. I let out a shaky breath as his teeth grazed my skin.

"You are a rare beauty." His mouth found mine again. "Divine." He bit my bottom lip, and I tangled my fingers in his hair. Deepening the kiss, I gave myself over to the intoxicating heat of his lips, his hands, his body pressed against mine.

His mouth moved down the middle of my chest and over my breast as his hand cupped my ass. The warmth of his breath sank into the fabric, and his teeth grazed my nipple, eliciting a soft moan from me.

A chuckled rumbled through his chest. "Is that so?" His grip tightened on my back side, and he pulled my hips toward him. The length of his sex pressed against me and heat pooled between my legs as his mouth coasted over my other nipple.

My mouth fell open, and I sucked in a breath. He looked up at me, his eyes piercing through me as his lips pulled into a wicked grin. Screw drinking and dancing. This is how one should celebrate.

He continued down my torso, his hands trailing down my body as if he wanted to feel every curve, every line, every scar. He gripped my thighs, the pinch of his fingers in my flesh sending a jolt through me as he dropped to his knees in front of me.

There was nothing I loved more than a man willing to worship a woman.

Gathering my dress in his hands, he lifted the delicate fabric, exposing my thighs and sending a chill over my feverish skin. Running a hand up my leg, he gripped the back of my knee and lifted my leg over his shoulder. I gripped his shoulder to steady myself as his mouth moved up the inside of my thigh. Goosebumps rose on my skin and a flutter ran through my abdomen. Every brush of his lips, lap of his tongue, and graze of his teeth sent a wave of pleasure through me.

His other hand found its way through the fabric of my dress

and his fingers skated over the swollen part of me, tentative and teasing, and I let out a shaky breath.

I've had plenty of lovers in the last hundred years, but it's always been transactional; an itch that needed scratched. It's what I was looking for tonight, a distraction from everything that would come tomorrow. A distraction from the way Sigurd looked at me tonight. But the way he was taking his time with every caress, every brush of his lips, was so unlike the others who rushed to get to their own pleasure. I hadn't realized how much I missed being desired until now.

The heat of his breath against the inside of my thigh made the ache inside me grow tenfold. He looked up at me like a man starved as he bit the sensitive skin on my inner thigh.

Gods.

His fingers made another sweeping pass up my center, and I closed my eyes. My skin flushed, the cool night air unable to fan the flames of the fire building inside me. His tongue replaced his fingers. My heart beat in my ears, my chest and between my legs, making my head spin. A breathy gasp escaped my throat.

He hummed against me as he slipped one finger inside me and pressed his thumb on the bundle of nerves crying out for attention. My head fell back against the solid pillar and I tried to catch my breath. My hips rocked against his hand as his finger coaxed another moan from me.

A delicious warmth spread through me. Had I known I'd be welcomed home like this, I wouldn't have been so nervous about my return.

He slipped another finger inside me, and his mouth replaced his thumb, sending a jolt of raw, feral pleasure zipping through my core. My head emptied and there was only the solid feel of him between my legs, the rise of my chest and the pressure building between my legs.

I dug my fingers into his shoulder as his fingers curled inside me, and his tongue swirled and sucked.

I lost all sense of where I was, who I was, as he devoured me.

The sound of voices and laughter pulled me out of the fog and back to the present. A group of people stumbled out of the hall, hanging on each other as they moved toward us.

His mouth left me, leaving me teetering on the edge. "Unless you want an audience, we should take this elsewhere."

I forced myself to take a breath and look down at him through heavy lids. "And here I was, starting to think you could keep up."

He rolled his shoulder so my leg dropped back to the ground as he rose to his feet with a grin that promised trouble.

Gripping my chin between his thumb and finger, he said, "I'm far from done with you."

Heat coursed through my veins, sending a spark of anticipation through my core.

He took a step back and held out his hand. "Unless I've already satiated your appetite." He cocked an eyebrow at me and his gaze dipped between my legs.

I reached for his hand. "You think very highly of yourself."

"I intend for you too, as well." He folded his hand over mine and stole me into the night.

CHAPTER SEVEN

SIGURD

SWEAT DRIPPED down my forehead as Magnus blocked my punch yet again. My every move was sluggish and predictable, with my mind split in ten different directions. Seeing Kara again left me more unsettled than I wanted to admit. Foolishly, I'd spend the last dozen years believing I'd let go of my love for her, my hatred at what she'd done. But the embers of love smoldered in the shadows of my heart and warred with the scars on my soul once more.

I dodged and ducked as Magnus swung. His eyes narrowed as he bounced from one foot to the other, graceful and light. His fist shot forward again, and this time he connected with my jaw, sending a jolt through my face and rattling my skull. I stumbled backward and rubbed the ache throbbing across my face.

"Someone's head is in the clouds today." He took a step back and studied me. "Even the sheep would have seen that punch coming," he said, letting me catch my breath. "What's going on with you?"

I chuckled. "Just tired."

"Something or someone keep you up all night?" I could tell he was trying to keep the conversation light, but I didn't miss the way he studied me.

He moved into a defensive position, ready for me to strike as the image of Kara dancing through the Great Hall, like a leaf on the wind, flitted through my mind. "It's nothing I want to bore you with." I advanced.

He blocked my punch and returned his own. I caught his blow with my forearm as he swung with the other arm and I ducked. Air whistled over my head. *Too close, Si. Focus.*

"I'd hardly call something that's got your focus all over the place boring." He danced back and forth, keeping his arms up to defend himself. "It wouldn't have anything to do with the murderess redhead we met last night, would it?" He cocked an eyebrow.

My stomach churned. "I don't want to talk about it." I swung out of frustration and he leaned back, just out of reach.

"I'll take that as a yes." He bounced back, his right hand swinging toward my face. I avoided the blow only for his left fist to connect with my chest, right over the scar Kara had left me with. Pain rippled through my lungs as I sucked in a breath.

My heart squeezed as the violent memory of her plunging a dagger into my heart assaulted me. I flinched as pain shot through me like an arrow. It had been years since I'd thought of that day, but it was all coming back to me, violent and in focus, like it was yesterday.

Anger rose like a tidal wave. Adrenaline pumped through my veins, making my heart thrash like a trapped animal. Time was supposed to heal all wounds, but some things left a mark on one's soul that no amount of time could fade.

Magnus furrowed his brow. "Are you just a glutton for punishment this morning?" He dropped his arms and rolled his eyes. "A sack of potatoes puts up a better fight. Either fight like you mean it or talk." There was an edge of annoyance in his voice that I understood well. He deserved a worthy opponent, and I was anything but at the moment.

I met his eyes and raised my hands to fight.

His shoulders slumped, and his hands fell to his sides. "Si, I didn't—"

"No, you're right." I motioned him forward.

He looked me up and down, not convinced, but raised his hands nonetheless.

My fist shot through the air, every emotion bubbling to the surface and begging for release. Magnus blocked the punch, and I swung again, and again, and again. He blocked every blow I threw at him without retaliation as I pushed harder.

"Stop holding back," I snarled, as he blocked another punch. "Fight me."

His eyes met mine, and he pursed his lips and nodded. That was the only invitation I needed. I swung, but instead of blocking, he caught my fist and twisted my arm to the side. Fire shot down my wrist as I pulled free.

Blood boiling, I attacked again.

He dodged and circled around me. I turned to face him and this time, his fist launched at me. I blocked every punch, savoring the pain shooting through my body until the sharper edges of my torment faded to a manageable ache.

I swung, but the fire had left my veins, and he caught my fist again. His other hand landed a blow to my gut, knocking the air from my lungs. I doubled over and fell to one knee. Lightning shot up my leg as I hit the floor. I was thankful I hadn't eaten yet as I coughed and dry heaved.

"Feel better?" He cocked an eyebrow at me.

"A little." I smirked up at him.

"You still want to pretend like you aren't tied in knots?" He paced in front of me.

"It's nothing, really." I pushed a few loose strands of hair off my face.

He scoffed. "Is nothing the reason you're fighting like a child barely weaned from his mother's milk?"

I let out a shaky breath and shook my head. "Sorðinn off."

He chuckled. "Look, if you don't want to talk about it, fine." He held his hand out. "But you should talk to her, resolve things, even if only to clear your head." I grabbed his hand and pulled myself upright.

"I don't know if I can face her again." Saying the words made me feel about two inches tall.

"You still love her?" It was phrased as a question but came out more like a statement.

"No."

He cocked an eyebrow at me.

I ran a hand over my face. "Maybe. I don't know." I walked over to the wall of windows and poured myself a cup of water. "I don't think what I feel is love, not in the way you mean."

He leaned against one of the wood posts that stood between each pane of glass. "Then what?"

I downed the cup of water and looked up at the beams criss-crossing high above. "I remember what I used to feel for her." I tracked a fleck of dust floating in the early morning light. "The man I used to be." I bit the inside of my cheek. "But I thought that man died." The memory of her lips against mine as she shoved the dagger into my chest screamed through me, and I clenched my fists.

He eyed me and I could tell he was holding back whatever he wanted to say, allowing me the space to sort through what I was feeling.

"I thought I was past all of this, but seeing her again..." The image of her standing over me last night, her gaze holding mine, pulsed down my torso, and I let out a breath. "Everything between us is unresolved. What she did—"

He pushed off the post and clapped a hand over my shoulder.

"I always wanted to know why." I met his eyes, and there was nothing but compassion on his face.

"Knowing why won't change what happened."

"No," I shrugged. "But it might make it easier to coexist now that she's returned."

"Is that what you want? To coexist?" He folded his arms over his chest.

"Do I have any other choice?" I looked up at the ceiling. "She's a Valkyrie. This is her home just as much as it's become mine."

"True, but you have Freya's ear. You'd be well within your rights to ask her to send Kara away. Folkvang's meant to be your reward, not your torment."

"Would I even be worthy of Folkvang anymore if I asked Freya to fight my battles for me?"

"You will always be worthy." He gave me a tight lipped smile. "Whatever you decide, do it quick. Because this." He waved his hand at me. "It's pathetic, and it isn't doing anyone any good." He grinned and shoved my shoulder. "Not that I don't enjoy kicking your ass for a change."

A chuckle rumbled in my chest. "Thanks for the pep talk."

"Hey, what are friends for?" He shrugged as he poured himself a cup of water. "Look, no one's saying you have to forgive Kara. Hel, you'd be a bigger man than most if you did. But you need closure."

"Yes, oh wise one." I gave him a mocking bow.

"You're such an ass." We both laughed and the tension in my chest eased a fraction.

The door to the training room swung open, letting in a breeze of fresh air as Bryn and Talon sauntered in. The corner of Magnus's mouth twitched as he tried and failed to look at Bryn discreetly.

I raised my eyebrow. "Closure, huh?" I looked between him and Bryn as Talon headed toward us.

He grinned and shrugged. "Sometimes closure leads to new beginnings," he said under his breath and backed away.

"I don't think that's how it's supposed to work," I called after him, but his attention was already elsewhere.

Talon approached me as I took a seat on the floor. "I was hoping to find you here."

"Oh, trying to rope me into another beating?" I wiped the sweat off my brow with the back of my arm. "Unfortunately for you, Magnus beat you to the punch today."

"Magnus got the better of you?" She looked over her shoulder. "Not that he can't hold his own, but I expect better from you."

"I had a long night." I shrugged.

"Oh, do tell." Her eyes widened, and a grin pulled at the corner of her mouth.

I shook my head. I was in no mood to share with anyone else today. "You wanted me for something?" I reminded her.

"Well, you're no fun." She frowned and leaned against the floor to ceiling windows.

"Are you planning to talk to Kara?" She folded her arms.

"Not you too," I grumbled as I extended my left leg in front of me and stretched.

"I know you want to avoid her, because that's what you do."

"What's that supposed to mean?" I looked up at her as I tucked my left leg in and extended my right.

"Once you make up your mind about someone, it's damn near impossible to get you to see them any other way."

"That's not true." I folded over my leg, the tightness in my hamstring screamed at me.

She leveled her eyes on me, and a pang of irritation flared in my chest. She knew me too well, and I hated when she used her knowledge against me.

"What's your point?"

"I think you should give her a chance," she said in a huff.

I lay back, pulling my left knee to my chest. "You realize you're asking me to give the woman who ended my mortal life a chance to explain herself?"

"You're not the only one who lost something that day." Her tone shifted from playful banter to all business.

"What do you mean?" I let go of my knee and sat up.

"It's not for me to say." She looked away, but the furrow of her brow made me wonder what Kara could have lost that would have Talon in knots.

I lay back down and pulled my other leg to my chest. "Magnus thinks I should try to get closure, too."

"I've always liked Magnus." The warmth was back in her voice.

"You and I both know that's not true."

"Yeah, well, he was a little too arrogant when he first arrived." She leaned over me. "Just promise me you'll think about talking to her?"

"Why do you care?" The words came out harsher than I meant them to.

"I have my reasons." She folded her arms over her chest.

"Which are?" I folded my knee over my other leg and stretched to the side.

"You forget I was there that day." Her voice was cold steel. "I was the one who had to tell her she killed you."

I let go of my leg and sat up. "I don't want to hear how hard it was for her, Talon. She took my life, not the other way around. Whatever she lost is of her own doing." My chest heaved with each breath and my heart slammed against my ribcage. All the anger I'd worked off with Magnus was back with a vengeance.

"You of all people should know things aren't always black and white."

"If that were true, then why did Odin punish her?"

Her lips pursed into a hard line and anger flashed across her eyes. "It's a fool who thinks he knows the motivations of the Alfather. And you are anything but."

I rubbed the ache in my eyes and let out a sigh. "I don't have the energy to fight with you today."

She knelt in front of me so we were eye to eye. "Then don't." A soft smile touched her lips.

"You're relentless."

"And you love me for it." She crinkled her nose and despite myself, I softened a bit.

"Debatable." I laid back down. "If I say I'll think about it, will you leave me in peace?"

"Absolutely." She rose and the corner of her lips curled into a smile.

"Fine." I felt like I was making a deal with Mimir that I'd regret. "I'll consider hearing her out."

"Was that so hard?" She said, looking down at me.

"Excruciating, actually."

CHAPTER EIGHT

KARA

I MADE *my way through the city streets of Jotunheim. Gas lanterns flickered, lighting up the path in front of me with a warm glow. Snow crunched under my boots and a chill bit into my skin. I pulled my cloak tighter to keep out the frigid air as I shivered.*

Ahead, a door opened, the sound of music and laughter spilling out into the night as a patron stumbled into the street in front of me. A soft glow sat above the crown of his head, marking him for death.

Right on time.

My heart thundered in my chest and Magik thrummed under my skin like the steady current of the ocean. I pulled the dagger from its sheath on my hip and followed my mark. He stumbled, and I smirked. This one would be easy.

I closed the distance between us, not even bothering to quiet my footsteps. As he reached the alley, I pounced, shoving him into the shadows.

He slipped on the tight packed snow, but I caught him before he could hit the ground. I shoved him against the wall, and he grunted as he stared down at me. His gaze flicked over my face as he tried to puzzle out what was happening. By the time his addled mind registered the blade in my hand, it was too late. I shoved my dagger into his heart.

His eyes widened and his knees gave out. I pulled the blade free as he collapsed into the snow. Grabbing a vial from my pocket, I dragged the edge of the dagger across the top, letting his blood drip into the glass container as I watched the light go out in his eyes.

Kneeling, I pressed my fingers to his neck to make sure he was dead. I stood, turned my back on him, and transformed into a hawk, flying off into the night sky.

My eyes fluttered open as a chill ran over my skin. What was wrong with me lately? My dreams had never been filled with bloodshed like this before, even when I was in the midst of war. I couldn't shake the feeling that all these dreams were a warning or a bad omen. As if the powers that be in the universe were trying to tell me something.

But what? I thought as I stared at the ceiling.

Ezra was gone and the blanket of night had been banished by the sun already high in the sky. I was alone, but I could still feel the anger from my dream just under my breastbone.

"It was just a dream." I took a deep breath and ran a hand through my hair. "Just a dream." As my heart rate returned to normal, I leaned back against the bed.

I'd barely looked around last night when Ezra and I came barreling into the room. Freya had given me one of the distinguished guest bedrooms until I found a place of my own down in the city. In days gone by, I'd escorted a few lesser Gods to these rooms, but I'd never been inside any of them and I was stunned by its beauty.

Vines were carved into the domed ceiling, echoing the lush greenery outside. Floor to ceiling arches looked out over Freya's domain. Waterfalls cascaded down the hillsides, flowing around the buildings that were carved into the side of the mountain. Just off to the left, I could make out the stone bridge that led to the Great Hall.

It was a version of heaven mortals dreamed about.

With my heart rate back to a normal tempo, I slipped out of bed and padded across the room. The gold dress I'd worn last night sat in a pool of fabric on the floor. The memory of Ezra pulling it over my head and groaning at my naked body sent a jolt of pleasure through me. He'd been much better company than I'd expected, and I found myself keen to see him again, which was rare.

My reflection caught my eye as I passed a mirror and I froze mid-step. The black paint they had adorned me with was smudged all over, and a few telltale bruises from a worthy night kissed my skin. I looked every bit the Valkyrie I once was. The braids and bits of jewelry tied in my hair, the paint, the feel of Magik under my skin. The only thing missing were my wings.

Davlin was right once again. I may have changed, but the woman staring back at me now had not been lost. "Gone for a time, but not forgotten."

I turned away from the mirror in search of the shower. Something I'd missed deeply while in Midgard. My body ached from dancing all night, among other activities. And the Magik moving through me left me feeling spent in a way I had to get used to again.

I stepped into an open air bathing room. Vines hung from the ceiling between the stone pillars, giving me a peek of the outside world, while still granting me privacy. Birds chirped a merry tune in the distance as I turned on the water, and a cascade of droplets fell from the ceiling like summer rain. I exhaled as warm water slid down my skin and soothed my sore muscles and frayed nerves.

Though I'd enjoyed yesterday's festivities, I was glad to be alone. From the moment I'd arrived in Folkvang, every second had been attended by the other Valkyrie, fallen soldiers, and my long lost friends. There'd been little time for me to process my new reality. Yesterday—or was it two days ago now?—I was in Midgard, and now I was standing here, Magik crackling under my skin. It felt both too good to be true and like a cruel joke that would be ripped from my grasp at any second.

I spent longer than I intended to in the shower, but as I

turned the water off and stepped back into the bedroom, I was ready to face the consequences of my actions and find Sigurd. Part of me hoped we could put the past behind us. But I couldn't, wouldn't, blame him if he wanted nothing to do with me. At the very least, I needed to apologize and hear him out.

As I dried off, I noticed a piece of paper on the table opposite the bed. Running the towel over my hair, I crossed the room and picked up the note.

I'll be thinking about all the ways I want to satiate that appetite of yours. See you tonight. -Ez

Warmth spread through me at his words. At least I'd have something to look forward to, even if the rest of the day went to shit.

I started down the winding pathways and bridges that led to the city below. I wanted to explore, re-familiarize myself with Folkvang, and see if some of my favorite haunts were still around. Some things had changed over the years, becoming more modern, but mostly, it still held the same charm I'd missed so much.

"Well look who it is," Talon's voice carried over the waterfall behind me. "I was wondering if we'd be seeing you today." She closed the distance between us. "I take it you had a good night then?" She wiggled her eyebrows suggestively.

I laughed and nudged her with my shoulder. "It was good."

"Only good?" She pulled a face. "Oof. Poor guy."

I laughed. "Ezra was fun." I bit the inside of my lip as the memory of his breath on my skin, his fingers digging into my waist, and the solid feel of him inside me flashed through my mind. "Maybe a little more than fun." My lips curled into a secret smile. "He was a pleasant way to be welcomed home."

We followed the curved pathway, which spilled out into a circular garden with forks leading off in several directions.

"But?" She drew out the word in a sing-song voice.

"But what?"

"You've got that look about you."

"I don't have a look."

"You do." She leveled her eyes at me. "Don't make me drag it out of you."

"If I'd known you were going to interrogate me, I would have stayed in bed."

"Touchy." She furrowed her brow. "I don't remember you being so guarded."

I shrugged. "When you have your whole life ripped from you, it's hard not to build up walls."

"Build all the walls you want." She looped her arm through mine. "I just got my friend back and I plan to interrogate every last detail out of you." She laughed.

She led us through a manicured garden filled with flowers from every realm; neon purple petals from Alfheim, tall pointed auburn leaves from Muspelheim, black and maroon sunbursts from Hel. They were all here, thriving outside of their natural environment, because of Freya's Magik.

"So, out with it." Talon took the path on our right, which was lined with lavender from Midgard.

"As great as it is to be back, it's been a turbulent transition," I admitted with a sigh.

"In what way?"

Someone I didn't recognize waved as we passed.

"Well, that for one." I waved back and gave them a tight-lipped smile. "I'm not used to being the center of attention."

"You could have fooled me." She bumped my shoulder with hers.

"Ha. Ha."

"You're just the latest gossip. They'll be onto the next thing in no time." She waved a hand dismissively. "What else?" She asked, as if we were checking my insecurities and anxieties off a list.

"Well…" I wasn't sure how to explain what happened when my banishment ended. "When my punishment was lifted, I was ripped out of Midgard like a page out of a book. It was violent and felt… wrong."

She looked as if she was weighing my words carefully. "I mean, it has been a while since you've traveled from one realm to another. And you did it without wings."

"Right. But how is that even possible?" A heaviness settled in my bones. Only a handful of Gods could travel from realm to realm on a whim. "Very few can walk between realms without the help of Magik."

She pursed her lips. "Maybe it was Freya's Magik calling you home. She spent a long time looking for you."

My eyelids fluttered, and I stared at her. "She did?" *I didn't realize anyone, least of all Freya cared that I'd dropped out of existence.*

Talon nodded. "It took her a while to accept that you were gone." Her tone was dismissive, like it was old news, and to her, I guess it was.

"I didn't realize she cared so much."

"When one of her own goes missing, she doesn't take too kindly to it."

"She didn't seem to mind barring me from the nine realms," I said under my breath.

"You killed him. There was a price to be paid." She leveled her eyes at me. "But she never would have done what Odin did to you."

Heat bloomed in my chest, up my neck and into my cheeks. I hated that she knew, that anyone knew what Odin did to me. I shared that story with Freya and the others; sparing the more gruesome details, because it was demanded of me, not because I wanted to. And hearing her speak of it so casually turned my stomach.

"Still." I took a breath. "I don't know how I got here and that just feels wrong." I redirected the conversation back to my return in the hopes she wouldn't notice my unease.

"Does it matter how you came back to us?" Her brow furrowed. "You're home, free."

"Free," I scoffed. "Free to explore Folkvang again, but I'm still bound to the dirt beneath my feet without my wings."

"You need to learn to celebrate the small things. Besides, it's only a matter of time before you're off on your next adventure."

Maybe she was right. I needed to appreciate what I had in the present. I could feel the realms again. I was free of Midgard, and Freya already agreed to give me my wings once more. "I guess it's just tough adjusting to being back."

"It's not everything you remember?" She motioned to the stone buildings covered in ivy.

It was beautiful, better than any memory I'd held onto, but like myself, Folkvang had changed in my absence. And though the shoe fit, it needed to be worn in again.

"Not exactly. My life in Midgard was... well, it was a life. I knew where I fit in. It wasn't the most thrilling existence, but I found purpose." I bit the inside of my cheek. "I'm not sure how I fit into the nine realms anymore."

"Let me get this straight." Talon stopped mid-step. "You've waited decades to have your life back and now you miss your prison?"

"You're being dramatic." I nudged her down the cobblestone path. "Of course, I'm thrilled to have my freedom, but it's more of an adjustment than I realized it'd be. It's like waking up from a dream and not knowing if you're still dreaming."

We crossed another bridge, the stream under us bubbling as it weaved its way through the terrain.

"Does that even make sense?" Talon cocked an eyebrow at me.

"Exactly, it's disorienting." I shook my head. "Though I have to say, the feel of Magik after being without for so long is delicious."

"You know what else is delicious?" She leaned in as if she was sharing a secret. "The way you and Si were sizing each other up last night."

A nervous laugh escaped my throat. "You mean the pure shock and horror?"

"That's not what it looked like from where I was standing."

Talon turned off the main street, pulling me along as we continued toward a quieter part of the city. I didn't know where she was taking me, but I was content to go along for the ride.

"After what happened, what I did..." My stomach rolled, and I felt like I might vomit my lunch.

"What happened wasn't your fault. You weren't in control."

Talon had a front row seat when I killed Sigurd and when I came to, she helped me wash the blood from my hands and defended me when everyone else turned their backs on me.

The memory of Sigurd covered in blood flashed through my mind, and I flinched. "I think he might see things differently." The way he looked at me last night, I was sure he wanted to pay me back for killing him. "I'm fairly certain he doesn't want to hear my side of things."

"Oh, I think he might, with some time." The corner of her mouth pulled into a conspiratorial smile.

"Maybe, or maybe I'll just leave Folkvang once I'm whole again." Just the thought of being able to travel through the realms once more sent a thrill through me.

"You just got here and already you want to leave us?"

"I've been stuck in one place for far too long. A little travel might do me some good." There was so much I missed about the nine realms during my imprisonment. The little diamonds of ice that fell like rain in Niflheim, the smell of steel, fire, and sweat in Nidavellir, the tingle of Magic crawling under my skin every time I arrived in Asgard.

Her head fell to one side as she looked at me. "Leaving won't make any of it easier. You'll have to face him, eventually."

"I'm not trying to avoid him. I was actually going to find him before you took me hostage," I said, as we turned down a quiet residential street.

"Si can wait until tomorrow."

"I thought you wanted me to talk to him?"

We walked through an archway and into a quaint courtyard with a beautiful willow tree in the middle of the square.

"I do, but maybe you're right, and you both need a day or two to adjust to your new reality."

"Did you just say I'm right?" I narrowed my eyes at her. "What do you want?"

"So, I know I said you'd be tomorrow's gossip." Her nose scrunched up as I looked at her. "But there are a few people who want to meet you."

I groaned.

"It's just a drink with a few friends." She held onto my arm tighter, as if I might make a run for it. I had half a mind to. I hated being ambushed, and there were plenty of other things I wanted to do today. But the way she looked at me pulled on my heartstrings.

"Lead the way."

CHAPTER NINE

SIGURD

I PUSHED the door open to the bar and stepped inside. The sound of people talking over one another, singing, and laughing hit me like a wall. I could just make out the tempo of music thrumming underneath the crowd as the door closed behind me. It was still early, but everyone in the tavern was already well on their way to a spinning head and questionable decisions.

I scanned the room, looking for a place to sit, when a flash of auburn in the back left corner caught my eye. Kara. Her table overflowed with people, empty cups, and Daiman. Traitor.

She threw her head back and laughed. Everyone in earshot looked captivated by whatever story she was telling as they laughed right along with her. A pang of jealousy shot across my chest. I was once among those who hung on her every word. Did I want to be them or did I just miss a simpler time?

As I watched her be welcomed back into the fold, I noticed an easiness to her, as if being here was a part of her routine. And maybe it was once upon a time when Folkvang was her home and not mine.

"You know, some might say staring is rude." Magnus stepped into my line of sight, cutting off my view of Kara. I blinked and my body relaxed, as if I was free of her gravitational pull.

"I just walked in the door." I took his drink and motioned for him to lead the way. *How long was I staring at her?*

We pushed through the crowd to a table in the back. A table that I couldn't help but notice was just opposite Kara's. Ragnar and Bryn were already seated and talking among themselves, and they both looked up as we approached.

"About time you showed up." Ragnar leveled his gaze on me. The snarky look on his face had gotten me into more trouble than I cared to admit.

"Whatever you've got in store for us tonight, I want no part of it." I grabbed one of the empty chairs and positioned it so my back would be to Kara. I wasn't ready for her to be a part of the background of my life. Not when I still wasn't sure how I wanted to move forward. Talk to her? Avoid her at all costs?

"Don't be such a stick in the mud." He took a sip of his drink and leaned back.

Magnus rolled his eyes. Picking up the other chair, he sat it down next to Bryn and winked at her. "Pay up." He held his hand out to her.

She scrunched up her nose and dropped a trinket into his palm. "Don't get too comfortable with it." She leaned closer to him, their faces an inch apart. "I suspect I'll be winning it back any day now." Magnus leaned in for a kiss, but she pulled away at the last moment.

"Brat," Magnus said under his breath, and Bryn winked at him.

Their banter grated on my nerves and something in my chest twisted like an animal caught in a trap.

"Do I even want to know?" I leveled my eyes at the two of them huddled together like children with a diabolical plan.

"Probably not." Bryn smirked at me over her mug.

"We wouldn't want to influence an outcome," Magnus supplied as his eyes drifted over my shoulder and landed on what I could only assume was Kara.

"Cheater." Bryn shoved him, and he caught himself before falling off the chair.

"I said nothing," he chuckled, and held his hands up in surrender.

"So nice of you to be betting on my misfortune." I turned to Ragnar. "How much do I owe you again for this?" I motioned between Magnus and Bryn.

Ragnar smirked. "My patrols for a month."

"Oof." Magnus cringed. "You should know better than to bet against us." He wrapped an arm around Bryn's shoulders.

"After last time." I cocked an eyebrow at them and they both had the good sense to look embarrassed. "I thought it a safe bet we wouldn't see the two of you within a hundred yards of one another for at least a decade."

Bryn shrugged one shoulder and smirked. "What can I say? I got bored."

"Hey, I thought you liked me." Magnus frowned.

A roar of laughter boomed through the bar and Ragnar's gaze shot behind me. "It's obnoxious how they fawn over her."

"You're just jealous." Daiman appeared by my side, drink in hand.

"I'm surprised you could tear yourself away." I cocked an eyebrow at him.

"Pfft, hardly." Ragnar pulled his gaze back to our table. "I just don't get what the fuss is about. She's just another Valkyrie."

"Weren't you the one making a big fuss over her return?" Daiman noted.

"That was before I learned she doesn't live up to the legend." Ragnar motioned for another round of drinks.

"Legend?" The rumor mill must be at work. I glanced over my shoulder and she was huddled close to Talon, chatting away without a care in the world. Must be nice.

"You know, because everyone thought she was dead the last hundred years, including Freya," Ragnar said as if it was common knowledge, but this was the first I was hearing about it. Is that what Talon meant when she said I wasn't the only one to lose something?

"Come on, you don't think Freya was in the dark, do you?" Daiman chimed in. "Who would even have the power to hide Kara from the nine realms, and why?"

"Exactly." Ragnar's eyes lit up once more. Always the gossip. "That's what made her so interesting."

"But I thought you lost interest in her?" I cocked my head in his direction.

Ragnar threw his hands up. "I did, I mean, look at her." He gestured behind me, and I couldn't help but look over my shoulder again. At this rate, I may as well join their table. I cursed myself and took a deep gulp of my drink. "She's just another sad story about love and death. I'd bet her guilt got to her for what she did to Si." He clamped a hand on my shoulder. "And so she disappeared and waited long enough for everyone to forget she got stab happy. Then she makes her return and everyone feels sorry for her and her little story."

"For someone who says he doesn't get what all the fuss is about, you sure seem invested," Bryn said under her breath.

"I have to agree. If anyone *should* be bothered, it's me." I leaned forward, resting my arms on the table, feigning nonchalance.

"Oh, because you're so unbothered?" Magnus shot me a look, daring me to contradict him.

"Her return feels like a distraction and I don't like it," Ragnar said point-blank.

"A distraction? From what?" Daiman scoffed. "The only thing that's changed around here is the topic of conversation."

"I appreciate the solidarity, Ragnar. But I couldn't care less why she's back, and I'd rather talk about anything else." I placed my empty cup on the table.

Ragnar smirked and raised his eyebrow. "Well, you're in luck. I have something in store for tonight." He leaned in and smirked. "I received a new recipe today." He motioned to the fresh round of drinks being placed on our table.

"The last time you tested a new recipe on us, I spent half a week in the forest, afraid of my shadow." I reached for a mug and tilted the cup from side to side tentatively. At least, it was a golden color this time, though darker than our typical mead.

"And the taste." Magnus looked at his cup like it was hurling insults at him.

"Like cow piss." I shook my head at the memory.

"And just how would you know what cow's piss tastes like?" Bryn grimaced.

I cocked an eyebrow. "I lost a bet to a *friend*." I shot a glance toward Magnus.

"What is wrong with you guys?" She shook her head.

"If you don't appreciate free ale, I'll take my business elsewhere." Ragnar reached for my mug, but I pulled away from him. We were never in danger of losing Ragnar's mead, but sometimes he got sensitive about it if we poked him too much. I swore he treated his operation like it was his first born child.

"Alright, alright, we're sorry." I kicked Magnus under the table.

"Hmph, well, it can't be any worse, can it?" he muttered.

"Tell us about this new concoction." I motioned for Ragnar to go ahead.

Ragnar's smile lit up his face, and he motioned for us to lean closer. "The water that was used to create the ale in front of you was harvested from the great spring, Hvergelmir." He kept his voice as low as possible, though I didn't see the point. It was so loud in here, and no one was paying any attention to us, with Kara in the other corner. I doubted anyone would even turn to look at us if we stripped naked and shouted at the moon.

"Hvergelmir? That seems a far way to go for some water?" Magnus looked at his drink with renewed interest.

"Ahh, but it's not just any water, is it?" Ragnar lifted his chin with the air of a king who knew he had the upper hand.

"Here we go with the sales pitch," Magnus mumbled, and Ragnar shot him a glance before continuing.

"Its waters have flowed since the beginning of time and helped give life to the nine realms. It's said the water contains special properties."

"What properties?" I sniffed the contents.

"The kind that breaths new life into your senses, and awareness of everything around you."

Kara's laugh reached my ears once more, and it grated my already frayed nerves. "Sounds like a recipe for disaster."

"So, right up your alley then?" Ragnar leveled his eyes at me as if to say, he'd strike me down if I tried to back out.

"I'm not sure this is the way to enlightenment." Magnus tipped his cup back and forth, studying the contents.

Ragnar placed his hand on his chest. "You have your methods. I have mine." He picked up a mug and raised it. "Skal." He brought the mug to his lips and drained the contents in one go.

I wasn't one to shy away from the unknown, even if I was feeling uneasy. "Skal." I raised my mug and took a drink. The sharp tang of citrus bubbled over my tongue, followed by a sweet floral taste.

"Flavor's not bad," I commented and took another sip.

Magnus raised his cup. "Here goes nothing." Bryn joined him and the two of them took a drink.

"That's surprisingly pretty good." Daiman held his mug up and eyed it.

"How long until we're supposed to feel something?" I took another sip, enjoying the taste more than I expected to.

"Depends. Are you going to nurse your drink all night?" Ragnar cocked an eyebrow.

I met his stare and drained the rest of the ale. "Happy?" I slammed my mug down on the table.

Ragnar smirked. "It only takes a sip, but the more you consume, the stronger the effect is.

"Of course."

"Please, like you don't need to unwind a bit." Ragnar rolled his eyes.

The roar of the bar fizzled out and there was only the lyrical lilt of her voice.

"Don't act like you don't know what you're doing." Her words dug into my skin, sending goosebumps down my arms and making my heart race.

"Flattery will get you everywhere." I could hear the humor in her voice, as if I was sitting right next to her.

I couldn't help but look over my shoulder again.

Ezra was sitting with her now, his arm draped over her shoulders. She laughed and my teeth ground together as she placed a hand on his chest.

I touched my chest, right over the spot where she'd plunged that dagger into my heart. The ghost of her hands on my body as a lover and killer taunted me. Longing mingled with betrayal inside me as I turned away from them and tried to focus my attention somewhere, anywhere else.

Ragnar raised his hand to order another round of drinks as Bryn leaned closer to Magnus and whispered something in his ear.

It was going to be a long night.

CHAPTER TEN

KARA

I BENT at my waist and kicked my leg straight up, aiming for Bryn's face. She took a step back, and I moved into a defensive position, daggers held up in front of me, ready for her to strike.

She swung her sword, and I blocked with the bracer on my forearm. The impact rattled through my tired muscles, and I stabbed upward with the other hand. She dodged my blow, and we split apart. "Has Freya set your wing ceremony yet?" She rolled her wrist, and her sword flourished next to her as she rushed toward me.

I dropped to the ground, and spinning on my heel, swept my leg out. She jumped, twisting in the air so that when she landed, she was still facing me. "Next week, with the dark moon."

"Excited?" She raised her eyebrows as we matched each other step for step.

I nodded. "And nervous." I lunged toward her and swung my left blade. She caught the strike with her sword and grabbed my wrist, pulling me off balance.

Twisting my arm, I thrust downward to free myself from her grip and backed away from her to reset. I wiped the sweat from my brow and moved into a defensive position. She was too quick for me to attack outright. As much as I tried to stay competitive in Midgard, it was nothing compared to sparing with another Valkyrie again. She was kicking my ass.

"Nervous, why?" She lunged forward, her blade sweeping toward me from the left, then the right. I blocked each swing with ease as she pushed me around the room. She was fast, not a single movement wasted, but she was repetitive too, which gave me what I needed to beat her.

"The ceremony isn't a pleasant experience, if you recall." I took a step to the left, counting each strike, waiting for the upswing I knew was coming. It wasn't a lie, being afraid of the pain, but it also wasn't the reason I felt like my entire body was a beehive. What if the Magik didn't take? What if I couldn't be a Valkyrie anymore? What if what Odin did was permanent?

"It's not for the faint of heart." She tipped her blade and before she could continue the arch, I launched forward, kicking at the hilt in her hand. The weapon clattered to the floor, and I had my dagger against her neck in the space between heartbeats.

"Nice to see Midgard didn't make you soft." She said through heavy breaths.

"I may have been lacking in worthy opponents,"—I released my blade from her neck and took a step back—"but it didn't stop me from practicing."

She picked up her sword and sheathed it. I followed suit, fastening my daggers to my belt and catching my breath.

"Can I ask you something?" Bryn started across the room toward the refreshments.

"Sure." I stepped into line with her and fiddled with the strap on my bracer.

"Are you sure you want to go through with it? I mean, I still have nightmares about my ceremony."

"Same." Though it wasn't just nightmares of the wing ceremony that woke me in the dead of night. The ghost of my wings fluttered across my back as the memory of Odin burning them off of me surfaced. "And yeah, I'm sure. Even if I am dreading going through another ceremony."

"Can't say I blame you for wanting your life back." She handed me a glass of water. "But going through it again, choosing this life now that we've lived it. It's impressive how sure you are." She raised her cup in salute and took a sip.

I thought back on my conversation with Davlin. "To be honest, I wasn't confident I wanted this life again before the curse lifted."

"What made you change your mind?" Her head fell to one side as she looked at me.

"The rush of Magik over my bones, the smell of Folkvang, the taste of the nine realms." I shrugged. "I forgot what it was like."

"The grass isn't always greener, is it?" Disappointment laced her words. Like she hoped I'd say the price of being a Valkyrie wasn't worth it.

My brow furrowed. "Would you choose not to if you were in my shoes? Could you give up this life?" I downed my water in a few gulps and refilled my cup.

She rolled her shoulders and looked thoughtful for a moment. "I was so young when I went through the trials. Sometimes I wonder if it was the right choice, you know?" She glanced at me and shrugged. "Taking on the role of a Valkyrie is so much more than any of us realize at that age."

"I think it's normal to wonder about a life without the responsibility." I'd be lying if I said I didn't have the same thoughts over the last hundred years.

A dry, humorless laugh escaped her throat. "That's the understatement of the century."

"How old were you when you started the trials?"

"Nine." A small smile touched the corner of her mouth.

Nine. Gods, that was young. I was thirteen and the youngest in my class, but nine? I did my best to school the surprise on my face.

"I know." She bristled. "I was such a spitfire. I begged my

parents for a year before they gave in. That little girl was so sure of herself, this path."

"And now?" I kept my eyes on my cup.

She let out a heavy sigh and leaned against the wall. "I haven't been sure of anything for longer than I care to admit."

"Join the club." I raised my cup and leaned against the wall next to her. "I've spent the last century wondering if losing my wings was a blessing or curse." I shook my head as I thought of Davlin. He'd been my rock through more than one of my spirals of doubt. "But knowing what it's like without them, I'd never be satisfied with a normal life."

"A life without the call of the nine realms singing in your blood?" She smirked. "How dull."

"You have no idea," I chuckled.

"What was it like?" She cocked her head. "If you don't mind talking about it," she amended.

Stalling, I took another sip of water. It was hard to share my experience with others. I found that most didn't understand what it was like to lose a piece of your soul. All too often, we're expected to pick up the pieces, put on a brave face, and move forward. Not crumble under the weight of our torment. And so, I stopped sharing. But now, being back in Folkvang with my people, there was a small part of me that wanted to start opening up again.

"After I got over the initial loss,"—I kept my eyes on the cup in my hand, rolling a bead of water along the rim—"I enjoyed the peace for a time. No souls calling to you, no longer duty bound to the fallen; the call of the nine realms only a memory." I pursed my lips, knowing the peace didn't last long, and knowing what came next. "But after a few years, the quiet itched like a festering wound. I tried to ignore it, but the silence... it drove me mad. I couldn't bear the heaviness of the loss, so I found ways to cancel it out."

The memories of those days flooded through me as I took

another sip of water. I wasn't proud of how I handled myself, nor did I feel like sharing those intimate details with anyone. "Eventually, I found a balance that worked, but the ache of being untethered never went away."

"And now?" Her voice was soft, as if she was afraid I'd shut down at any moment.

"Being back in Folkvang helps." I closed my eyes and took a deep breath. "But without my wings, the emptiness still pulls on me." I let out a heavy sigh.

"I don't know how you manage. Even the slightest inconvenience will ruin my day," she chuckled, and I appreciated her trying to lighten the mood.

"I learned to cope in order to survive." The tension eased in my chest as a smile pulled at my lips.

She pushed off the wall and let out a huff. "Okay, never give up my wings. Check."

"Zero out of ten. Would not recommend."

"If I ever complain again, I give you permission to rake me over the coals."

I laughed. Little did she know, that's exactly what it felt like when Odin held me down and burned pieces of my soul away.

"I'm ready for a drink, you?" she asked.

"I need to do some strength training first. You've got a mean swing, and I barely held you back."

"Please, you just handed my ass to me."

"True." I smirked. "But I'm still not where I want to be. Training with mortals only gets you so far."

"You sure? I'm getting together with a few people who'd love to meet you."

I tried not to bristle. It was great being the center of attention for a day, two at most. But the constant barrage of people was too much after a century of alone time. I needed to recharge and settle into my life once again.

"I'm sure. Ezra's expecting me in a bit anyway," I added, hoping it would get her to drop the invite.

I actually didn't know if I was seeing him tonight. We hadn't made any plans, and I hadn't seen him since he left my bed this morning. But she didn't know that, and I wasn't in the mood to be around people tonight. It's been such a whirlwind since I arrived, and the thought of spending the night alone sounded divine.

"You two looked cozy last night." The corner of her mouth turned up.

"At the tavern? I didn't see you."

"I was with Magnus and his friends, but from my vantage point, it looked like you were enjoying the company."

"Don't I deserve a little fun?" I raised an eyebrow.

"Hey, no judgment here." She looped her bag over her shoulder. "He's a good guy."

"He hasn't given me anything to complain about so far."

"I bet he hasn't." A devilish grin pulled at her lips. "Have fun tonight." She winked and started toward the exit. "And don't work too hard. You'll make the rest of us look bad."

"I'll do my best to remain mediocre," I called after her.

As the door shut behind her, I plopped onto the floor. There was no way I was doing any more training tonight. My limbs felt like jello, and I already ached in places I forgot could be sore. Stretching my arms over my head, my shoulder popped, and I let out a sigh.

I stared up at the beams criss-crossing the ceiling and let my mind wander. I'd only been back a few days and already my life felt fuller. The thought that I ever entertained living the rest of my days in Midgard was laughable.

If only the joy of my return wasn't overshadowed by the reason I was banished. Sigurd's death. Tomorrow I promised myself. I'd find him and start my life over with a clear conscience.

CHAPTER ELEVEN

SIGURD

LEAVING THE TRAINING FIELD, I made my way to the weapons room to return the blade I'd been practicing with. Normally I preferred my sword. But I'd learned in battle you could never guarantee you'd keep the weapon you favored. So I varied my training to be sure I was prepared for any scenario.

As I reached for the door to the weapons room, it opened and Kara almost walked right through me.

Well, I was ready for almost any scenario.

Her hand pressed to my chest to catch herself, and she took a step back. Even through my shirt, her hand felt like a cool rain against my overheated skin. "Sorry." She looked up and her eyes widened. She pulled back as if the contact had burned her and looked away. "Oh, Sigurd."

"I thought I was the only one burning the midnight oil." She stepped to the side so I could get by her.

"I'm a night owl." She shrugged.

"I remember." I looked back as I hung up the sword with the others. She leaned against the doorframe, chewing her bottom lip. Was she nervous?

"Shouldn't you be enjoying the night with everyone else?"

I cocked an eyebrow. "I could say the same about you."

She shrugged and looked at the floor. "I needed a break from all the fussing. What's your excuse?"

Surprised flicked through me. I hadn't expected such an honest answer from her. "Understandable. I needed to clear my head," I admitted. We'd always been honest with one another until—well, until I ended up here.

Her eyes met mine, and her brow wrinkled as if a war was waging on the inside. "I've been meaning to find you. It's just been a hectic couple of days."

With the sword secure and the rest of my gear put away, I turned to face her. Magnus said clearing the air might help, so here goes nothing.

"I bet. You've definitely caused quite the stir since your arrival." My eyes skated over her body of their own accord. Her leather trousers did little to hide the curve of her hips and her skin tight top exposed her cleavage and shoulders, making my mind wander to places it shouldn't. "Although you always did." My voice came out huskier than I intended, and I cleared my throat. *Not the point I was trying to make.*

She bit her bottom lip and shrugged one shoulder. "Some were born to make an entrance."

The corner of my mouth twitched. There was that confidence I remembered. "I can't argue with you there." The image of her in that gold dress from the other night seared through me and my skin flushed. *Get a grip, Si. She killed you, betrayed you.* My brain screamed at my body.

"Shall we?" I motioned to the door. I needed some fresh air, and there was so much I wanted to say, to ask, now that we were alone. But starting this conversation was proving to be more difficult than I'd imagined.

She nodded and as I followed her outside, she let out a huff. Maybe she was at a loss about how to have this conversation as well.

"You look like you enjoy being back." Talking to her in the past had always been easy. But this felt like going into battle with both arms tied behind my back.

"Do I?" She glanced at me as we walked along the fence, outlining the training field. "Honestly, it's been a long time since I've felt like myself."

"And Folkvang has made you whole again, has it?" I watched her out of the corner of my eye.

"Far from it." She paused and leaned her forearms against the fence. "If anything, Folkvang just reminds me of all the things I lost for so long." She trailed off as a cool breeze brushed her hair off her shoulder.

The smell of vanilla and rain assaulted my senses and brought a thousand memories burning to the surface. I pushed them aside, trying to hold on to the only one that mattered, her hand around the hilt of the dagger in my chest.

While maintaining a mask of indifference, I tried to filter through my thoughts. I wouldn't give her the satisfaction of knowing how truly tied up in knots I was.

"I forgot how beautiful it is here." She broke the silence.

I glanced at her, and she was looking up at the sky. Millions upon millions of stars twinkled above us like diamonds. Even after years, it still took my breath away.

"I don't recall you ever seeing beauty in the mundane."

Her face was softer than I remembered. She'd lost some of her harder edges, and I couldn't help but wonder what the last hundred years had been like for her.

"Yes, well, I wouldn't say there's anything mundane about Folkvang." A small, secret smile pulled at her lips.

"True." I looked away and studied the gold light of the land-vættir sprites dancing in the dark like fireflies. She was too close, and all the rage, all the heartbreak, and loss settled in my chest like an anchor pulling me down into the deepest ocean. "It was an adjustment at first. But Freya's been more than kind." I did my best to keep things light.

"Do you ever miss it?" She asked. "Midgard."

"Not Midgard itself, no."

She shifted, angling her body toward me. "Then what?"

"The little things." I glanced at her and no matter what I felt toward her, I had to admit, my memories didn't do her justice. My heart kicked up a notch and the urge to reach out and feel the silky smooth warmth of her skin almost overwhelmed me.

"Isn't that always the case?" She sighed and looked back up at the cosmos.

"I know that look." I chuckled at how easily some of her quirks came back to me. "What realm is it that calls to you?"

"All of them." She tore her gaze from the stars and met mine. This time, I didn't look away. I could see the pain etched in every feature of her face. My stomach dropped, my heart skipped a beat, and a thousand memories burned through me as I watched a dozen emotions flicker across her face.

"Why did you choose Folkvang upon your return to the nine realms?" The question bubbled out of me without even thinking. I was dancing around the topic, stalling before forcing myself to pick at my wound.

She paused, as if thinking about how to answer. "I was pulled here. My Magik took hold and..." she trailed off.

"So it wasn't by choice that you arrived in Folkvang?" I could hear the bitterness in my voice. She wasn't here because she wanted to make things right, but because she was forced to face me through some cruel twist of Magik.

"No." She spoke so softly, I barely heard her. "I wanted to, but no, I did not choose to come here."

Hurt flickered across her eyes and I took a step away from her. It was hard to reconcile the memory of the woman who killed me with the woman standing in front of me. Everything I remember about that day, the coldness in her eyes, the hatred in her voice, the absence of the woman I loved, was nowhere in sight now. Warmth radiated off of her as my gaze coasted over the softness of her features, the earnest look in her eyes. The woman standing with me now called to happier memories. Memories I preferred not to think about at this moment.

I let out a heavy breath as my head fell forward. "I have to ask." Bile rose to the back of my throat and my stomach threatened to empty its contents onto the ground. Conflicting emotions warred for control in my chest. I looked to the stars to give me courage. It was now or never. "Why? Why did you do it?"

She sucked in a breath and turned away from me. "I didn't know what I'd done until you were already gone. I had no control over my actions." She sighed and kicked at the grass. "The last thing I remember before..." She hesitated, and I couldn't help but look at her. "Before the incident. Was falling asleep in your arms the night before." She glanced in my direction and her eyes were glassy.

Each word hit me like a stone and my heart shattered like porcelain. She didn't know? Didn't have an answer, after all this time? Ripples of pain echoed through my chest, and I squeezed my eyes shut. The memory of her hovering over me as I died flashed through my mind and I shivered.

"I don't understand."

"I don't either." She kept her eyes straight ahead. "One minute I was me, and the next I wasn't. I spent years, decades, trying to discover what happened." She let out a huff of air and shook her head.

"Did you find anything?" I forced the words from my throat.

She shook her head. "After a while, it felt pointless. You were... gone. And no amount of me understanding what happened would change that."

"So that's it, you gave up." Frustration bubbled inside me and I stood up straight.

"It's not like I could do much in Midgard," she fired back. "Whatever caused me to..."

She went silent, so I finished the sentence for her. "Caused you to kill me." I stared at her, willed her to look at me, but she wouldn't meet my gaze.

"The answers aren't in Midgard." Her voice was soft, defeated, which only threw another log onto the fire searing through me.

"Then where?"

"I don't know." She exhaled and her shoulders slumped forward like she was caving in on herself. I was the one who'd ended up in the afterlife, and yet she looked as if she was the one whose life was ripped from her.

"So it could happen again? You losing control?" As much as I wanted to put all this behind me, could I really if she might hurt someone again?

She winced. I'd struck a nerve. "It hasn't happened since that day."

"That doesn't answer my question."

"Yes." She snapped. "I guess it could. Is that what you want to hear?" She turned to face me fully. "That I could lose myself again, cause someone else harm."

I held her eyes, refusing to look away. Her fire had never scared me before and I sure as Hel wasn't going to let it now.

"You think it doesn't scare the shit out of me, that I could hurt the people I love and have no memory of it?"

"Then maybe you shouldn't have given up so easily." I took a step toward her, closing the gap between us. "Maybe you should have fought harder to find answers to protect those that you *love*." The last word came out like a curse, and she recoiled.

She closed her eyes and stepped away. Taking a breath, she opened her eyes, all the fire gone. "You have no idea, how sorry—"

"An apology may make you feel better, but it doesn't change anything for me." Tears stung my eyes, and I swallowed the heartache and betrayal as it tried to claw its way out of me.

"Si…" Her hand reached toward me but dropped back to her side.

I wanted to grab her hand, pull her toward me. I wanted to run from her and never look back. My heart screamed in my chest as warning bells went off in my head. How many nights after my death had I dreamed of her being within reach, to gaze upon her again and to get the chance to ask why? Only for her to be here now with nothing but a bullshit excuse that she didn't know why she'd ended my life.

"No amount of apologizing will ever remove the stain on my soul for the part I played in your death." Her voice cracked, and a door slammed closed inside me.

She didn't get to feel bad about killing me. She didn't get to sit here and act like all this happened to her, too.

"The part you played." A short, dry laugh escaped my throat. "Interesting choice of words."

"It's complicated," she sighed.

"Oh, I'm sure." My anger lashed out, begging for release. "Lying to me, gaining my trust, my love." I spat the last word. To think she ever loved me was a joke. "Must have been incredibly complicated when you finally took my life."

"Have you been listening to a word I've said?" She threw her head back, and a short, humorless laugh escaped her throat. "You think given the choice, I ever would have killed you? I loved you."

The last words she ever spoke to me in my mortal life echoed through me. *"Why, because I love you?"*

"Don't." I closed the gap between us again, my anger propelling me forward. "Never say those words to me again." I didn't care if it was Magik or Odin himself that forced her hand. She gave up trying to find answers, and you don't give up on the people you truly loved.

She nodded and looked up at me, eyes filled with tears. "I may be a lot of things, and to you, I know I'm the villain." She swallowed and her bottom lip quivered. "But I never lied to you—"

"It doesn't matter." She deserved to hurt, to feel guilty for what she did, but it wouldn't change the past, and it sure as Hel wouldn't make me feel better. "It was a long time ago." I looked down at her, and her own pain and confusion stared back at me. This was not how I wanted this conversation to go. This was not the closure I'd hoped for. It would have been so much easier if she meant to kill me. If our life together was a lie. "Our past should stay where it died on the battlefield."

She nodded and took a step back. "I can't say that I expected anything else."

A small twinge of guilt zipped through me, but I didn't care to examine that right now. Not when she was standing there looking like I'd stolen her last shred of peace.

"This is your home now, your friends, family." She motioned around us. "I won't take that comfort from you." The corner of her lips twitched into a resolved smile. "For what it's worth"—a single tear fell down her cheek— "it was nice seeing you again." She turned away and started back toward town.

"Kara, wait." I took a step after her, but she didn't stop or even look back. "Streð mik," I cursed.

I ran my hand through my hair as I watched her disappear into the night. I knew it wasn't a good idea to pick at this wound. I should've stayed clear of her. Let the past stay in the past. So much for closure. All my wounds, heartache, and frustration tore through me as if they were fresh once more.

CHAPTER TWELVE

KARA

A KNOCK at the door pulled me out of my head. Thank the Gods, someone to distract me.

I'd spent most of the night tossing and turning, trying to erase the image of Sigurd's hatred from my mind, but it was no use. Even in my dreams, he shouted the same words repeatedly. *Never say those words to me again. Lying to me, gaining my trust, my love. Must have been incredibly complicated when you finally took my life.*

Rubbing a hand over my face, I opened the door and one of Freya's guards stood on my front step. She looked me up and down. "She's ready for you now."

I wasn't expecting my request to talk to Freya to be answered so quickly, since I'd only asked to see her at dawn this morning.

"Here goes nothing." I closed the door behind me and followed the guard.

A lot was said last night between Sigurd and me, but there was one thing in particular that gnawed at my conscience like a dog with a bone.

So it could happen again? You losing control? I flinched as the words echoed through me for the millionth time.

I didn't know why I'd killed him or if it could happen again. And while I tried to find answers during my exile, I'd given up when every question led to a dead end. I stopped caring about why and how. I let myself believe it was a fluke. That some kind of Magik took hold and forced me to do someone else's bidding, for reasons I might never learn the truth of.

I convinced myself it would never happen again. And when decade after decade passed, and I remained in control of my mind, I let my guard down and allowed myself to box up the past as some one-off, horrible incident.

But seeing Sigurd again. The anger and pain in his eyes when I couldn't answer his questions was like a knife to my heart.

Guilt took up residence in my chest and anxiety consumed my every thought once more. Could it happen again? Could I lose control? Could I hurt someone else I cared about? I couldn't spend the rest of eternity waiting for the other shoe to drop. I had to do something now that I had more resources at my disposal.

And so I'd requested an audience with Freya. If anyone might have some answers or an idea of where to start, it would be her.

Or at least I hoped so.

Sigurd and I may never be friends or even get along, but at the very least, I wanted to give us both peace of mind so we could move on from the past.

Freya's guard paused at a large wood door with panes of glass in the shape of flower petals. She motioned me forward, and I looked between her and the door.

I raised my eyebrows. "Freya's here?" I took a step forward and looked through the glass. Sunlight reflected on the other side, throwing rainbows in every direction into a dimly lit tunnel.

The guard nodded once, as if that explained everything. She sure was talkative.

When I pulled the door open, it was much heavier than I

expected. I made my way inside and the door swung closed with a *whoosh*. Cool air brushed over my exposed skin and sent a shiver down my spine as I started into the mountain. Folkvang was pretty temperate most of the time, so I hadn't dressed for the cool, damp air.

The smell of moist dirt, rose, and spice filled my nose as I made my way toward the soft, natural light just a few yards ahead.

The tunnel opened up into a large, domed room. And the rough, dirt walls rose at least twenty feet into the air, where they met a ceiling of glass. Vines crawled across it, creating some much needed shade and dimming the sunlight. It was as if someone had scooped out part of the mountain to create a greenhouse.

"Beautiful, isn't it?" I could hear the smile in Freya's voice as she approached me.

I pulled my gaze from the ceiling. "It's so peaceful."

"Are you not at peace being back?" She cocked an eyebrow. "Is that the reason you asked for an audience?" She motioned for me to walk with her.

"I am mostly. It's like a dream being home again." I followed her down the path on the outer edge of the greenhouse. "But I was hoping you could assist me." I bit the inside of my cheek. I barely wanted to have this conversation with myself, let alone with Freya.

"Well, well, aren't we high maintenance?" She waved her hand over an empty planter bed. Tiny spots of green pushed through the dirt and leaves unfurled. "Only back a few days and already seeking my help." She turned to face me and her eyes pinned me to the spot. "Can I assume this has something to do with Sigurd?"

"I, umm…" I balked at how straightforward she was. I'd gotten used to mortals talking around what they really wanted to say. "Is it that obvious?"

"You have the look of a woman tied in knots." The corner of her lips pulled into a smile. "In my experience, love or death is usually the cause." Her smile faded, and she cocked her head to the side. "In your case, I believe both apply."

I looked away from her to the vines clinging to the walls. "In a way, yes."

It was true. I'd once loved Sigurd, and his death had altered my entire existence. But I didn't still love him, and I'd handled my feelings about ending his mortal life eons ago.

Then why is his voice still in your head? Some part of my brain whispered. I swallowed the lump in my throat. Now was not the time to examine that train of thought.

Her fingers trailed over a leaf with brown edges. "Go on." A soft glow touched the tips of her fingers, and the dying parts of the leaf gave way to a deep, rich green.

"I want to find out what happened that day. Why I..." Sigurd's words jabbed in my head like a fire poker, forcing the next words out of my mouth. "Why I killed him."

"I see." She picked a stem with a delicate, soft blue flower. "And you think I might have some answers for you?" She twirled the flower between her fingers as she looked me over. Her gaze landed on my face as if she was searching for something.

I nodded. "I looked for answers in Midgard but came up empty handed." I let out a heavy sigh. "Midgard isn't known for Magik, so I hoped that now I've returned, there might be something for me to research or look into?"

She tucked the flower into the braid laying over my shoulder and her brow furrowed. "You think Magik forced your hand?" She adjusted my hair so the flower was front and center.

My mouth went dry. "What else could it be?" It had to be Magik, because if it wasn't—

Ice filled my veins and my heart rose into my throat as panic welled inside me. It was an impossible notion that I'd hurt

Sigurd on purpose. I refused to believe it. There had to be something else at play.

Freya's eyes turned soft, and she placed a hand on my shoulder. "My dear Kara." She clicked her tongue. "You've been looking in the wrong places."

My heart raced with the way she was looking at me.

"Then tell me where to look." The words came out more like a plea than a request. I hadn't realized just how much this issue still plagued me. Seeing Sigurd again had stirred up feelings and memories I thought were long dead. So much for time healing all wounds.

"The answers you seek can only be found within your heart." She placed a hand on my chest and gave me a tight lipped smile. "You saw an opportunity, and you took it."

I pulled away from her touch as if she'd burned me. "You think I killed him on purpose?" Adrenaline burned through me, forcing me to take a step back. My ears started to ring as the pit in my stomach doubled in size.

How could she? She thought... did everyone think I was a monster capable of killing for no reason?

Her eyes skated over my face and she pursed her lips. "Interesting."

"What is?" The words came out with a sharp edge to them.

"Even after all this time, you still believe in your innocence."

Blood rushed to my face as if I'd been slapped. "I came here for answers—"

"And that's what I'm giving you." The warmth in her voice was gone. "Don't blame me, if it's not the truth you wanted." Magik sparked behind her eyes and I had to remind myself that I was talking to the Goddess, Freya.

"It doesn't make sense." Doubt crept into my heart, replacing the fury pumping through me. "I'd never... I had no reason to hurt him. I loved him." My voice broke on the last word. *Was I really capable of murder for the sake of it?*

Freya let out a sigh. "It's happened before. It's why I imbue your wings with my Magik. It's meant to tame the less unsavory attributes of a Valkyrie's nature."

"What do you mean, it's happened before? Other Valkyrie have killed their charges without any reason?"

The corner of her eyes crinkled so slightly I might have missed it if I blinked. "Is power not enough of a reason?" Her brows furrowed as she studied me.

"Power?"

She turned away and continued along the path. "Don't you remember what it felt like? To want to take his soul for yourself? The heady, intoxicating taste of power within your grasp?" Her voice was thick, almost lustful.

I'd tried a million times over the last hundred years to pull up the memory she conjured—killing him, the call of his soul— but there was nothing. It was as if someone had edited my mind and left the entire event blank. "I have no memory of the act."

She paused mid step and looked over her shoulder. "What do you mean?" Her brow knit together and her eyes searched mine.

I shrugged. Was I going to have to explain this to everyone until the end of time? "I wasn't conscious of any of it. Not the battle, not Sigurd—nothing."

"That can't be right." She shook her head.

"Why not?"

"From all other accounts, it was clear they were in control, that they were of sound mind when they killed their charges. Enjoyed it, even." Her nose crinkled in distaste before quickly recovering herself.

"All other accounts? How many times has something like this happened?" Ice filled my veins. *Why had I never heard of this before?*

"It's neither here nor there." She waved her hand. Easy for her to say when it didn't affect her. "If what you say is true, then there may be something to your accusation that Magik has something to do with it."

"If what I say is true?" So no one believed me then. "What would I have to gain from lying?"

"Would gaining Sigurd's favor not be enough of a reason to lie?" She looked me up and down, as if taking me in for the first time.

I swallowed the lump in my throat. "I let go of him a long time ago," I said through gritted teeth.

"And yet, here you stand," her eyes skated over me with disinterest, "still trying to mend broken bridges."

I took a beat to rein in the anger simmering just below the surface. It wouldn't do me any good to lash out at her.

"I just want to understand what happened so I can put this all behind me."

"Whatever you need to tell yourself." Her lips cracked into a smile that made me clench my jaw. "But I wouldn't get my hopes up if I were you. It's possible your memory loss is just a trauma response. You did love him after all. I don't remember that being the case with the others."

I only nodded, not trusting myself to say anything more. I didn't care what she said. I knew in my soul that there was no way I killed Sigurd for power or any other reason. I'd prove her and everyone else wrong if it was the last thing I did.

"Perhaps the Norns will have something to say about your situation." She tossed their name out flippantly, and my heart faltered.

My mouth went dry at the mention of the Norns. They'd always given me the creeps with the easy way they seemed to peel back your skin and look directly into your soul.

"But Kara," she turned toward me, deadly serious. "It does not do to dwell on the past. You've paid your price; it's time to start living again."

"I'll do my best." I forced a smile, but my heart wasn't in it.

"Thank you for taking the time to speak with me." I inclined my head out of respect, even if I disagreed with most of what she'd said.

She placed a hand on my shoulder as I lifted my head. Her eyes met mine and a warm smile spread across her face.

I nodded once and took my leave. Freya may be wrong about me, about what happened with Sigurd. But her heart was in the right place, unlike many of the Gods. The least I could do to repay her kindness was to keep an open mind about what the truth might be, even if it was a truth I didn't want to hear.

I guess that meant I had to make a request of the Norns.

CHAPTER THIRTEEN

SIGURD

To think I honestly believed Kara and I could have a civil conversation about why she killed me. I'd been such a fool. A fool to think I was over it. A fool to think we could put all this behind us and get closure.

I scoffed internally. Magnus was normally right about these things, but he couldn't have been more wrong about Kara. And Talon. I shook my head. She'd always had my best interest at heart. But this time she was fighting for Kara, trying to give her peace at my expense. I wish I could say I was furious with her, but I understood it. Kara was her friend, her sister as a Valkyrie long before we kindled a friendship. And truth be told, I didn't have any space left in my heart to be put out with Talon, not when Kara's words were still bouncing around in my head.

I don't know what turned my stomach more, that I thought I'd moved on from her and what she did, or that after all this time she didn't have a single satisfying answer. What in the name of Yemir had she been doing all these years, if not looking for answers?

I took a deep breath; the smell of wet grass and soft florals settled in my chest and helped clear my mind. The air was still crisp and damp from the rain this morning as we made our way under the canopy of trees.

"Where's Magnus today?" Daiman asked as we moved toward Folkvang's barrier. "Don't you two patrol together?"

I'd asked Daiman to join me because Magnus always saw too much, and I was not in the mood to deal with his meddling. But I couldn't say that.

"Bryn has him preoccupied at the moment." It wasn't a lie. In the last couple of days, those two had abandoned all pretenses and were firmly back in their rose-colored bubble. I was happy for them both, but it was only a matter of time before they became oil and water again.

"I thought they were on the outs?" He said as we started into the dense forest at the eastern border.

I shrugged one shoulder. "Yeah, well, I guess they're working on closure." There was a bitter edge to my voice that I hoped Daiman wouldn't pick up on.

"Is that what they're calling it?" He let out an amused huff. "Those two are worse than a pair of lovesick teenagers."

A chuckle rumbled through my chest and some of the tension eased from my shoulders. I knew spending the day patrolling with Daiman was the right call. He was always easy to be around, never pried, and could be counted on to help pass the time without a fight or some deeply healing lesson.

"Either way, I'm glad you asked me to join you today. I don't have the energy to deal with Ragnar." He stepped over a moss-covered tree trunk. With the tip of his sword, he reached out and touched the invisible magical barrier that kept Folkvang a sanctuary. A kaleidoscope of colors rippled across the surface and disappeared ahead of us.

I chuckled. "Not all you thought it would be?"

He scoffed. "You know what he's like on the best of days. But when it comes to smuggling in that ale," he shook his head. "He's insufferable. He acts as if the rest of us are clueless about the risks."

"You don't have to tell me." I stepped ahead of him and tested the barrier with my blade. Nothing but a shimmer of colors. "There's a reason you'll never see me down there. I helped him once, and let's just say I rather take my chances with Fenrir than deal with Ragnar and his operation ever again."

Daiman chuckled and shook his head. "Sometimes I wonder if Ragnar's half beast himself."

"Honestly, it wouldn't surprise me." I plucked a few cloudberries off a bush as we passed and popped them in my mouth. The tart burst of flavor coated my tongue, and I grabbed another handful.

"Does anything ever surprise you?" He cocked an eyebrow at me.

The image of Kara last night, standing under the moonlight, filled my mind. At every turn, she'd proven to be a surprise. From the day we met, battle worn but still smiling, to the day she ended my mortal life. I never knew what to expect next with her. But I wasn't out here to talk about Kara, so instead, I shrugged. "Expect the unexpected and you'll never be surprised again." I offered him some berries, and he tossed them into his mouth.

"Something tells me it's not that easy." He hopped over a fallen tree and his boots squelched into the soft earth. "So how'd Ragnar even get involved with Jotunheim, anyway? It's not like we have access to the other realms." He ducked under a low hanging branch as we continued through the forest.

Sometimes I forget Daiman arrived years after Ragnar and myself. He had fit into our circle of misfits so effortlessly, I swore we were brothers in another life.

"There was a celebration of sorts. Some alliance or marriage between Freya's people and the giants."

"How did that happen?" Daiman's face scrunched up. "I thought the Gods and Giants hated each other?"

"Often, love and hate are close cousins." A ping shot across my chest and the hairs on the back of my neck prickled. I rolled my shoulders and ignored the voice in my head. While my words were true, it didn't mean they were true for me.

"You sound more and more like Magnus every day."

"Don't tell him that—I'll never hear the end of it." We both laughed as we continued our patrol.

"Must have been some alliance if Freya was willing to host the Giants." He tested the barrier once more and again, everything was as it should be.

"I remember little, honestly. The celebration went on for days, and the mead from Jotunheim flowed freely. And well, you know how good it is. Ragnar wasn't about to let it slip through his fingers."

Daiman laughed. "I hate to say it, but I'm glad Ragnar is obsessive to the point of annoying anyone in ear shot when he wants something."

"You and me both." I stepped over a thin stream slithering its way through the forest. "He can talk the wool right off a sheep. Which is how he struck a deal with one of the giants. I don't know all the details or what he promised them in return. All I know is, since that celebration, we've never been short of a supply of Jotunheim ale."

"Thank the Gods for that."

"The Gods had nothing to do with it." I raised an eyebrow at him. "It was all Ragnar."

"No need to inflate his ego further."

"It's not like he can hear us."

"It's the principle of the thing." He swung his sword lazily toward the barrier and it cut through the leaves on the other side.

We both froze, and he turned to look at me.

"Don't move." I stepped toward him, my sword raised as I reached for the barrier. I tested where the shield should be a few inches to the right of Daiman. Nothing.

My blade cut through the air, slow and steady, and I waited

for my sword to connect with the barrier. I took a step away from him and then another, searching for the Magik that kept Folkvang protected. Nothing. My heart raced. This was more than a weakness, this was a gaping hole in our defenses.

I took another step. *Come on, come on.* The tip of my blade sliced through the air, unhindered, and my stomach dropped. Another step and the tip of my blade hit the invisible barrier, sending a wave of colors shimmering to my right.

I looked over my shoulder, and Daiman was at least two sword lengths away from me.

"For the love of Yggdrasil."

"Have you ever seen a weakness this bad before?" Daiman shoved his sword into the dirt to mark his edge, and I did the same on my end.

"No. There've been cracks, a few minor tears. But they were so small you couldn't even slip a sword through. This..." I motioned between our two markers and shook my head. "This is a hole big enough for an army. It's unlike anything I've ever seen."

Daiman dropped to a knee, inspecting where the barrier ended. "What in the name of Freya?"

"What is it?" I rushed to his side as he pushed back to his feet.

"Just there." He pointed to a flattened group of bushes.

To the untrained eye, you could barely tell that the vegetation had been disturbed. But the way the branches were bent back at odd angles, with mud flung over the leaves and tree trunk nearby, told a different story. Someone or something had been here. And they were loose in Folkvang. I looked around the forest, searching for a pair of eyes or a telltale sign of what had come through the rift. But there was nothing. Not even the whisper of a shadow that didn't belong.

Daiman followed the trail while I inspected the area. "It's definitely more than one person."

116

"You're sure it's people and not beasts?"

Of all of us, he was the best tracker and could identify a trail in the thickest forest.

"I'm sure. The impressions in the mud point to heavy boots, not paws or claws." He cocked his head to the side as he inspected the surrounding dirt. Crunched over, he followed a path only his eyes could discern. "Though they seem to have wandered off in different directions, here." He paused and looked from left to right. "They came together, but went separate ways." His voice was thoughtful as he tried to make sense of the scene laid out in the earth.

Knowing he was seeing things beyond my eyes, I doubled back and searched the path for any obvious signs of the intruders.

About halfway back to the barriers, my eye caught on a black, pebble size droplet. It looked almost like a piece of midnight sky had fallen like rain onto the bright green leaves.

"What the Hel is this?" I leaned over to get a better look and several more droplets glistened up at me as a beam of sunlight broke through the canopy above.

"What is it?" He carefully made his way back to me. "What'd you find?"

I rose and, taking a step back, I motioned to the black ooze.

Daiman knelt in front of me to get a better look. He sniffed the leaves and recoiled. "Smells like death."

"What could have left this behind?" I knelt next to him and plucked a leaf with one of the obsidian droplets. I twirled the stem between my fingers, inspecting the viscous bead.

He stood, scanning the area. "Whatever it is, it doesn't belong here." Daiman's jaw flexed as his eyes stared off into the distance. "We need to report this to Freya."

"Agreed." I got to my feet. "I'll mark the rift. You take care of the trail."

He nodded, pulling his pack off his back and setting it on the ground.

I made my way back to the barrier, careful not to disturb the path Daiman pointed out, and quickly got to work.

I had to admit, I was surprised we came across anything today. Patrols were normally mind-numbingly boring. Maybe Ragnar was right, maybe Kara's return was a distraction, but why and from what?

CHAPTER FOURTEEN

KARA

I PULLED Freya's flower from my braid and tossed it to the ground as the door to the greenhouse closed behind me. The pungent, sweet perfume was making me sick, or maybe it was just the thought of the Norns that made me want to hurl.

Summoning the courage necessary, I started the trek up to the stacks to make my request. Freya's words ate at me and as much as I wanted to deny her claims, there was something to her accusation that rang true.

I barely registered anyone or anything as I made my way through Folkvang and up the winding path that led high above the city.

As the path leveled off and the stacks came into view, I stopped to catch my breath. The walk was longer than I remembered, although the last time I visited, my wings carried me to this very spot in a matter of minutes.

Only a few more days, I told myself. And then I'd fly to the house next door, just because I could.

I walked to the edge of the plateau and took in the view. Folkvang was beautiful from every angle, but from up here it sparkled in the sunlight like a prized jewel from Asgard. From the vibrant forest flanking the training arena, to the diamond-shaped homes covered in moss, to the streams of waterfalls sliding down the mountains like a lover's fingers. Every inch of Folkvang was a treasure worthy of admiration.

Turning away from the view, I wiped the sweat off my brow and made my way up to the large wooden doors. Runes were carved into the dark surface. One for insight or true vision, representing the knowledge one could glean from this place, and the other for protection. For truth and knowledge could only be gained if your heart and mind were free of the demons that sought to prey on the weak.

I pushed the door open and cool air brushed my face. Walking inside, I let the door swing closed with a heavy *thud*. It took a moment for my eyes to adjust to the dim lighting in the entry. As I looked around, warmth flooded through me and I couldn't help but smile. While many things in Folkvang have changed, this place was just as I remembered it.

Large beams crisscrossed the A-frame ceiling, and lanterns hung throughout, bathing the room in warm, golden light. Leather sofas and chairs, sat in front of the floor to ceiling windows that looked out over the valley below. And several of Folkvang's residents lounged throughout the library, reading or discussing some significant find.

I closed my eyes and inhaled the woodsy sweet musk of a thousand books and leather, and my mind was flooded with a rush of memories. Reading by the windows and watching the snowfall over a quiet Folkvang. Talon poring over ancient texts to find answers to questions she didn't share with anyone. Working in the stacks until moonlight spilled through the windows.

There were so many memories I thought were lost to me through time, but each day, small slices of who I once was made themselves known to me once more.

I took another deep breath and opened my eyes as I ran my fingers along the wood panels lining the entry and moved deeper into the library.

Making my way past the main sitting room and down a hallway, I found my way to the altar room. A chill ran across the back of my neck and over my arms as I stood at the threshold. I'd only ever been here once before to ask for the Norns' favor before my first wing ceremony, and I'd hoped to never come here again.

Stepping into the room, the door slid closed behind me, taking with it any sounds from the outside world. Candles flickered high above, casting the room in a soft glow that was contrary to the bone deep chill that emanated from the Runestone in the middle of the room. It towered over me with its sharp edges and deeply carved runes. I fought the urge to return to the stacks where life and warmth were abundant.

Taking another step inside, I grabbed one of the gold bowls nestled in an alcove to my right. The metal was cool against my clammy palms, and I took a breath to steady my nerves.

As I knelt before the stone, I placed the bowl down in front of me. Pulling a dagger from the strap on my thigh, I held my hand over the basin. Gripping the sharp edge of the blade with my free hand, I pulled it across my palm. Blood dripped in a slow, steady stream. I squeezed my fist tighter, digging my fingers into the wound until the bottom of the bowl was covered.

Magik fizzled under my skin, warming my hand and stitching the gash back together. Odin may have taken my defining feature, but Freya's Magik coursed through me once more, healing the superficial wound.

With my hand healed, I dipped my fingers into my blood, coating them with the warm, thick liquid. Looking up at the Runestone, I took a deep breath and recited the incantation that would awake the Magik within the stone.

As I spoke each word, I traced the runes carved into the stone with my blood. A heaviness fell over me. The hair on my arms stood straight up as the Magik in the stone responded to my call.

I finished tracing the last rune and pressed my palm to the center of the stone.

A warm golden light appeared in the outline of each rune. The chamber lit up with the stone's Magik and the last shred of warmth vanished from the room, leaving me as cold as the dead.

My heart hammered in my chest. Now was the time to speak my desire, but Freya's words sat heavily on my soul. What if they gifted me with a truth I couldn't handle?

C'mon Kara, Davlin's voice pierced through my doubt. *You don't back down from the truth, even when it's ugly.* His words from another time and place called to me. He was right, of course. He was always right. No matter what truth lay in front of me, I'd deal with it.

"I wish to learn the truth of why I killed Sigurd." My voice carried around the room, strong and sure.

No going back now.

A breeze ruffled my hair and the light from the stone flickered under my fingers like the flames on a dying wick. My blood seeped into the stone as if something on the inside hungered for a taste of the living. I repressed a shudder as glowing runes crawled down the stone, onto my hand, and up my arm.

The mark of the Norns.

Their Magik prickled over my skin like ice, and I shivered as the runes settled on my forearm.

As the Runestone consumed the last drop of my blood, I removed my hand from the rough surface and inspected my arm. The runes glowed, pulsed, and then sank into my flesh. If the Norns should heed my request, they would appear once more and I'd have my truth.

Bending to pick up the bowl, I deposited it into the waste area and turned to leave. As I reached the door, I looked back at the stone once more and said a silent prayer. *Please don't let me regret this.*

As I made my way back to the stacks, I ran my fingers over my arm. The sharp bite of the Norns' Magik only lasted a few seconds, but the chill of it had taken up residence in my bones.

"Kara." Talon's voice pulled me out of my head, and I looked up to find her waving me over with a broad smile. She sat at one of the reading tables, a giant book sitting open in front of her.

"We missed you at training this morning." Her gaze roamed over me, and I rubbed my arm where the runes had vanished.

"I had a meeting with Freya."

"Wing Ceremony?" Her shoulders bounced up and down with excitement.

I shook my head, debating if I wanted to tell her about my conversation with Freya, but there was no use in hiding it from her. She'd force it out of me one way or another. "Actually, you might know something." I pulled out the chair next to her. "When Sigurd died, you were there." I lowered my voice.

The smile faded from her face, and she turned to look at me.

"Do you remember anything? Anything that seemed out of place?"

"In what way?" Her brow furrowed.

I let out a huff and sat back in the chair. "I'm trying to figure out what happened that day. I believe Magik was at play."

"Is that what Freya told you?" She studied me.

I shook my head. "She doesn't think it's likely, but I know I didn't kill him in cold blood. That's why I'm here,"—I nodded toward the altar room—"I put an inquiry in with the Norns."

Talon shivered. "I don't envy you if they decide to grant your request."

A clipped laugh escaped my throat. "Believe me, as much as I want answers, I'm not looking forward to it. Which is why I'm asking you if you remember anything."

"There was one thing." She shook her head, and her brow furrowed. "It's haunted me throughout the years."

I leaned toward her, and my heart rate doubled. "What is it?"

"When I pulled you off of him..." Her gaze fell to the book in front of her. "I could tell you weren't you." She paused, and her fingers traced the edge of the book. "Your eyes, they were vacant. Like you weren't seeing anything in front of you. And there was this silver ring around the rim of your iris." She shivered. "You looked right through me and it chilled me to the bone. Freaked me the Hel out. I had nightmares for weeks."

"I know no one believes me, but I wasn't there. Physically, yes. But mind and spirit." I shook my head. "It's like I was asleep." I fiddled with my fingers and couldn't meet her eye. "Not until you snapped me out of it."

"One look at you and I knew my sister wasn't looking back at me."

"Why can't Sigurd understand like you do?" I sighed.

She placed her hand on top of mine to stop my fidgeting. "Because love clouds our perception." Her voice was soft and nurturing. "I saw the two of you together." Her lips cracked into a sad smile. "You loved one another more than I've ever seen two people love each other. I can imagine the shock of the moment made it impossible for him to see you objectively."

Lightning shot through my chest at her words. She was right. I had loved him beyond reason. "There's definitely no love left between us now."

"I don't know about that." She smirked. "But I know you wouldn't have killed him to save the nine realms. I know that and you know that." She squeezed my hand. "We'll figure this out and put things right."

Though her words were true, they did little to ease the ache in my chest.

"You know, I never got the chance to thank you for your help that day."

She waved her hand dismissively. "You would have done the same for me."

"True, but you stood by me when everyone else looked at me like I was one of Loki's monsters."

Her eyes met mine, and she squeezed my hand. "I've seen plenty of monsters in my day. You have never been one of them."

"What would I do without you?" I forced the words past the lump in my throat.

She shrugged and turned back to her book. "Probably stir in your own misery until you did something incredibly stupid."

I laughed. She wasn't wrong. "I just wish I could remember something, anything, that would help me figure this out," I huffed.

"Why the sudden interest?" Her eyebrows knit together as she studied the page in front of her.

"I talked to Sigurd last night," I said without preamble, but she didn't seem surprised.

"Oh?" She stopped mid-page flip and looked at me. "And how'd that go?"

"Well, I'm sitting here, trying to relive one of the worst days of life while hoping for an audience with the only beings in the nine realms that make me crave the comfort of my mother. How do you think it went?"

She grimaced. "It can't be that bad."

I folded my arms over my chest and leaned back in my chair. "You should have seen the way he looked at me. He despises me and he has every right to." I let out a huff. "If he doesn't want to accept my apology, I get it. I can't force him to forgive me."

"Okay." She flipped another page. "But that still doesn't explain why you're digging up the past."

"Something happened that day, Talon. I can live with the consequences. I have for a hundred years, but I can't live anymore without knowing why."

She looked up and her lips curled into a smile. "Then let's find you some answers."

CHAPTER FIFTEEN

SIGURD

I ARRIVED at Freya's chamber and let her guard know I had sensitive information for her. After a few minutes, the Valkyrie returned and motioned me inside.

As I passed, she grabbed my arm. "Make it quick. She doesn't have all day for dalliances."

I pulled my arm free. "Last I checked, Freya made her own choices about her time."

The Valkyrie scoffed but said nothing more as I walked inside and let the door close behind me.

"My dear Sigurd," Freya cooed, motioning for the others in the room to leave as I walked into the antechamber. "To what do I owe the pleasure?" She sauntered toward me wearing a sheer dress that left little to the imagination, and for the first time, the sight of her didn't stir my passions.

"I've come to report my concerns about the eastern barrier." I tried to correct her interpretation of why I was here.

Her eyes roamed over me like a starved cat. "Must you always put business first?" She wrapped her arms around my neck and her fingers tangled in my hair.

I placed my hands on her hips, holding her in place. Now was not the time to indulge in pleasures. "This cannot wait."

Her smile slipped and her arms fell from my neck. "I see."

She returned to her throne and motioned for me to come to her with one finger. "Tell me what you've found, then."

I closed the distance between us, stopping a few feet away and dropping to my knee. When I looked up at her again, that catlike smile returned to her lips. Though she was placating me, her wishes were written all over her face.

"There's a tear in the barrier," I blurted. Now was not the time for a long winded account of meaningless details.

"That's hardly a reason to interrupt my day." She poured herself a glass of wine. "Why not report the tear to command?" She folded one leg over the other, and the thin fabric fell to the side, exposing her supple skin from ankle to hip.

I met her gaze, unwilling to play this game of cat and mouse, while there was a genuine threat to Folkvang. "If this was anything like we've seen in the past, I wouldn't be here."

"Very well. Explain." She took a sip of wine, but did not let me rise. Punishment for my rejection.

"It's large enough to march an army through." I rested my forearm on my bent knee.

Her eyes flicked to mine, and her head cocked to the side. "An army? You have quite the imagination."

I shook my head, still in disbelief. "I've seen nothing like it. Cracks and gaps are to be expected. But it looks as if someone's cleaved a hole into our realm on purpose."

"Exaggeration is not a quality I thought you possessed." Her words were casual enough, but her body coiled tight with tension. She was taking this seriously, but trying to hide it. Why?

"You know better than most. I don't overstate the truth."

"No, you don't, do you?" She eyed me over the rim of her glass. "How big is this rift?"

"It's over two sword lengths wide and reaches from dirt to sky." I met her eyes, willing her to understand this wasn't some ploy to get her attention.

She leaned forward, holding my gaze. "If what you're saying is true, that would be a catastrophic breach." All the playfulness left her face, replaced by cold, hard fury.

"I assure you, it is." I refused to back down. She may be all powerful and she could make my life here a living Hel, but I wouldn't ignore the truth just because it was hard to believe.

"Very well." She leaned back and looked away. "Were you alone when you came upon this rift?"

I shook my head. "Daiman was with me. I left him to mark the trail so I could inform you of the damage."

"Trail?" She furrowed her brow and her eyes shot back to me. "You mean to tell me we have an intruder in Folkvang that didn't set off any alarms?"

I steeled my nerves. Even from a few feet away, I could feel the electric fury of her Magik rolling off of her and reminded myself to never get on her bad side.

"I believe so. Something came through the barrier, and from the size of the hole, something large."

"Something, not someone?" She narrowed her eyes at me as if I was keeping something from her.

"Daiman believes it to be a group of men, but I found evidence of tar-like ooze. It isn't anything I've ever seen before. I assume it's from some kind of beast."

"It's possible. There are countless beings in the nine realms you'd be hard pressed to identify." Her shoulders relaxed, and she took another sip of her drink.

"Whatever it is, it's not of this realm, and that's enough to cause concern."

"On that, we can agree." She motioned for me to stand. "Thank you for your report."

"That's it?" I rose, confused at her dismissal. "No orders?" I stared at her, refusing to leave. There had to be something more I could do. I'd spent the last hundred years training for a fight, to protect what we'd built here. I wasn't about to let her dismiss me.

"So eager to serve. It's why I've always been fond of you." A hit of a smile touched her lips. "But there is nothing more you can do. Unless you've somehow come into Magik strong enough to mend the barrier yourself?" She cocked an eyebrow.

"Magik isn't the only way to protect Folkvang," I said through gritted teeth.

She closed the distance between us and placed a hand on my cheek. "I'm well aware of all the ways in which Folkvang remains protected." Her eyes met mine as her fingers slipped down to trace my jaw. "But there are some things not even your strength can combat." Her words were a whispered breath against my lips.

I captured her wrist. "Won't you let me try to help?" I didn't mean to sound so desperate, but the ache to do something, to be useful burned inside me.

She let out a sigh and pity filled her eyes. "You're hurting." I let go of her and took a step back. "But this will not heal your heart."

"This isn't about my heart," I spat. "This is about protecting Folkvang." It took all of my control not to raise my voice.

"Are they not one and the same?" She stepped toward me and placed a hand on my chest, and her palm settled over the scar that was my undoing. "I admire your will to protect your fellow warriors. But your pain and frustration are what propel you into action now. I understand that more than you know." Her eyes met mine, and I placed my hand over hers. "But if you let it control you, it will only lead to destruction, not salvation."

"You speak from experience." I meant to ask it as a question, but it was plain on her face she was not speaking from a place of ignorance.

"My history is long and filled with many lessons." The corner of her lips pulled into a half-hearted smile. "Learning to let go of the pain that drives you, hardens you against the world, is the hardest lesson to learn."

"My pain is my strength. It's what's made me into the warrior I am, and you want me to let go of that?" My forehead knit together as I tried to make sense of what she was saying.

"I'm not asking you to do anything. I'm only suggesting that the emotional armor you wear may hold you back more than you know." She looked at me with pity in her eyes and I took a step back. She saw me as weak, broken.

I shook my head as the will to fight bloomed in my chest. "This is why you won't let me help with the rift?"

"I'm not asking for your help because Folkvang is not your realm to protect. It's mine." Her voice held an edge of finality. There was no arguing further, or I'd risk the wrath of a goddess. She took a step back, and a smile spread across her face when I said nothing more.

"You've already done your part. I will handle the rest." She turned away from me. "Can I trust you will keep the weakness in the barrier to yourself? I don't want to cause unnecessary panic."

"Of course." I wasn't one to gossip as it was, but the fact she asked me to keep it to myself meant she was more concerned than she was letting on.

She looked over her shoulder. "If there's nothing else," her gaze traveled the length of me. Both a question and a proposition. But I had no desire to be intimate with someone who pitied me. I took a step back and she let out a sigh. "Then you may take your leave." I was dismissed in more ways than one.

I inclined my head. "Should you change your mind and require my assistance with the rift, you only have to call for me." I turned and left without another glance in her direction.

The fact that she was hiding her concern and keeping me away from the barrier worried me. She knew more than she was letting on, and whatever had caused the breach in our realm must be far worse than I'd imagined.

She may wish to keep me away, but she had to know her warning fell on deaf ears. I would need to tread lightly, so as not to anger her beyond repair. But the Gods did not choose me because I followed the rules, and backed down when things grew beyond my understanding. I was a man of action, and despite my loyalty, I would find out what had caused that much damage to our defenses and make it right.

CHAPTER SIXTEEN

KARA

TODAY WAS the day I'd be made whole again. Waiting for the dark moon over the last week had taken more patience than I thought possible. But finally, the day was here. The misery of my first wing ceremony echoed across my skin from the moment I woke up today. I tried to remain positive and get some food into my stomach, but my nerves made me both nauseous and shaky all day. The only thing I could hold down was some stale bread and half a cup of water. It was for the best, since I was meant to have an empty stomach for the ceremony.

My mind raced and every little sound made me jump. Talon had offered to stay with me today and escort me to the ceremony site, but I wanted to spend the day reflecting on everything that brought me to this moment.

The decision to be a Valkyrie in the first place, falling in love with Sigurd, killing him, Odin's wrath. All of it, all the pain and heartache, led to today, to another choice. To be a Valkyrie once more.

I grabbed the black silk dress I'd procured for the ceremony and slipped it over my head. The fabric glided over my chest, my hips, my thighs and calves, soft as a feather. Tying at the neck, it left my shoulders and back exposed down to my tailbone. A flutter moved across my stomach as I smoothed the fabric on my sides.

You can do this. I told myself for the millionth time.

I now knew I couldn't live without my wings. I spent the last century living a half-life, and more than once, I wished the Norns would cut my string and put me out of my misery. But knowing I could choose nothing but the life of a Valkyrie didn't stop the overwhelming anxiety from compounding by the hour. Unlike the first time, I was aware of the toll the ceremony would take, both physically and mentally. And I was scared. Anyone who pretended otherwise was a fool or lying.

I stepped into the bathroom and threw some cool water on my face and neck to calm my nerves, and take one last look at myself in the mirror. My hair was slicked back and there was a flush to my skin that had everything to do with nerves. I kept my face bare, wanting to walk into my ceremony without a mask of paints and swirls. Some used the makeup to illustrate their transition from ordinary to extraordinary. But right now, in this moment, I just wanted to be me. To take back the power that was stolen from me.

I met my stare and nodded once. Within an hour, I'd be Kara the Wild Storm once more.

As the sun dipped below the horizon, filling the sky with varying shades of blue and purple, I made my way up the hill. The site was carefully chosen so that the dark moon would fall directly over us and amplify Freya's Magik.

Memories of my first ceremony played in my mind with each step. Little Kara was so excited, unaware of the pain I'd experience to gain a new life as a Valkyrie. I was full of hope for the future, unaware of the heartache that lay ahead. I was ready for the freedom of the nine realms, even though I'd never been more than a few miles from home. And I was ready to take on the responsibility of ferrying the souls of the fallen, something I didn't understand fully at the time.

With my stomach tied in knots, I climbed the hill. Cool dusk air brushed over my exposed skin and I shivered. What if I made the same mistakes, hurt people, and lost my way all over again? My hope for the future soured knowing that I might never make peace with the past. And my hunger for freedom tasted bittersweet now I understood what it was like to live with and without freedom.

The nine realms, the Gods, Sigurd, they'd all taken pieces of me, changed me, and shaped me into the woman I was now. For that, I had no regrets, but I couldn't help but wonder if the little girl who was so excited for a life bigger than any of her dreams was still inside me. I let out a shaky breath and hoped that the girl I once was, full of bravery, love, and life, was with me today as I took back a piece of our soul.

As I reached the top of the hill, I took a moment to take everything in. Starlight filled the sky and was mirrored in the river below. Lights blinked to life in the city, making Folkvang look like someone had sprinkled it in a dusting of silver and gold. I turned toward the crowd, a circle of torches lighting their silhouettes as they waited for the guest of honor. Me.

I paused and sucked in a breath. There were more than the four people I expected. It only took three Valkyrie and Freya to perform the ceremony, and yet more than a couple of dozen people had shown up for me tonight.

It was customary for others to take part in the celebration, but I didn't have many people in my corner these days. Though to be fair, just because they were here, didn't mean they were rooting for me. It was more likely they were here to see if Freya's Magik would restore me or tear me apart.

I couldn't blame them. If the shoe was on the other foot, I'd have been a front row spectator.

Talon approached as I drew closer to the circle of torches. "How you feeling?" She looped her arm through mine.

I gave her a meaningful look. "Ready."

She smiled and patted my arm as she guided me toward Freya, who stood apart from the crowd. Her white dress hung loosely to her form and her hair cascaded down her back in braids and curls. Antlers sat atop her head with runes etched into the bone. Black paint decorated her face in swirls and was smudged under her eyes, dripping down her cheeks. And a gold crescent moon medallion decorated her forehead. The flames dancing across the metal moon gave it a sentient quality. There was no question that she was the Goddess of love, fertility, battle, and death.

I bowed as my heart slammed against my ribcage and thrummed in my ears. I was acutely aware of every flicker of the flames as their heat brushed my skin. Every whisper sent a chill across my neck and down my shoulders, as if they breathed their words against my ear.

Freya touched my shoulder, and I rose to meet her eyes. She took my hand, her face remaining emotionless as she guided me forward.

"This won't be like the last time," she said as we reached the middle of the circle. "You were young then, your skin untouched, your soul without scars."

I nodded. "I understand."

"There's no shame in forgoing the ceremony and living differently from the path you planned." She was giving me an out even now, and though I knew she meant it, there wasn't a single bone in my body that wanted to live without my wings.

"I want this," I said with finality.

"As you should." The corner of her lips twitched. "But I would be remiss if I didn't remind you of the risks," she said under her breath as we came to a stop in front of a wooden chair situated directly under the dark moon's shadow.

"If I could handle the pain as a child, I can handle it now. I'm ready."

She placed her hand on my shoulders, and her eyes met mine. "I know you can handle the pain. It's whether or not your soul is still open enough to accept the call of the Valkyrie."

She pressed on my shoulders, forcing me to take a seat by straddling the chair. "The time you spent in Midgard changed you. There's no denying that." She moved around me in a slow circle.

"It's made me appreciate what it is to be a Valkyrie all the more." I felt like I was on trial, defending my decision to go through this once more.

And in truth, I was.

She was giving me every opportunity to clear my mind of any doubt. For when you sit for your wings, you must be certain of your decision.

"The ceremony will ferret out the true nature of your soul, and like before, either your wings take to you or the process will leave you less than you are now." She ran a sharp fingernail across the top of my shoulders and brushed my hair off my back.

"The risk is worth the reward." Thankfully, my voice was steadier than I felt.

"Then let us get started." Freya handed me a bowl of bluish-silver liquid that would be the only help given to me on this journey.

I tipped the bowl into my mouth, swallowing the bittersweet concoction in two big gulps. It took only seconds for the warmth to spread from my chest to my fingertips and toes. My vision blurred, and the world tilted on its axis, becoming dull and unfocused. The surrounding torches grew brighter until the crowd vanished into the shadows.

From memory, I knew the potion would only take the edge off the pain so I wouldn't pass out. Nevertheless, I was grateful for this small mercy.

"Asheria," Freya called. "Will you start us off?"

I searched the faces of the spectators in the shadows as Asheria began to sing. Her high, lyrical voice settled into my bones as she belted the hymn of the Valkyrie. I closed my eyes, letting the words take me as my skin tingled.

Someone pressed their forehead to mine. "You know the pain well." Talon's voice sounded muffled and far away. "Harness it and bend it to your will." She circled behind me as a rustled the grass at my ankles.

"I do not envy your position, but your courage is something we should all aspire to," Bryn said, pressing her forehead to mine.

"Thank you, sister," I said under my breath as she moved past me.

Asheria finished her song and turned to me. Her eyes were wide and her forehead crinkled with worry. "May all your heart's desires be answered on this, your wing day." Her voice was barely a whisper as she kissed my forehead and joined the others behind me.

"It is the will of your soul that will determine your fate." Freya's voice carried over the crowd. "The strength in your heart that shall grant your transformation. And it is with the payment of your blood times nine that will test your resolve to become one with the realms."

Silence fell over the bluff, leaving only the sound of flickering flames and the steady tempo of my heart. I scanned the crowd. Eyes glistened in the flames as they all stared at me, waiting.

Without warning, the whip came down hard on my back. It was as if a wild cat dug its claws into my flesh, exposing blood and bone to the world. The air ripped from my lungs and the world came into sharp focus. I bit down on my lip as my back throbbed with the tempo of my racing heart. A warm trickle oozed down my spine and into the grass at my bare feet.

I braced for the second lash just as it audibly cracked between my shoulder blades. My body arched as my head fell back. The potion Freya had given me felt pointless as mind shattering agony took hold of me. I gripped the back of the chair, my nails digging into the wood as I tried to take a full breath.

The breeze prickled my sensitive skin like a thousand tiny needles, and a small part of my brain wondered what was worse. This or the pain Odin inflicted on me when he stole my wings.

"This is madness," someone in the crowd whispered.

I looked up at where the voice had come from and stared into dark brown eyes. Sigurd.

What was he doing here?

The whip came down for the third time. His mouth fell open and his eyes widened as I gasped and a strangled cry escaped my throat.

CHAPTER SEVENTEEN

SIGURD

KARA'S EYES WERE GLASSY, and sweat covered her forehead. I'd never seen her look so defeated and weak. Her body slumped forward as Asheria handed the whip to Bryn. Kara had chosen this, knowing what it would take to get her life as a Valkyrie back. Guilt simmered deep in the pit of my stomach. Not only had she done this before, but she'd lost her wings as a result of my death. It all clicked as I watched in horror. This is what Talon meant, why she wanted me to give her a chance.

I was ashamed to admit that I'd never given much thought to what she lost, the pain she endured after she ended my life. Seeing her now, I wondered if my brief few minutes of pain were any comparison.

Bryn raised her hand and cracked the whip against Kara's back. Blood dripped off the cord of leather as she reached back for another blow.

"You look"—Magnus looked me up and down as if searching for the right word—"unwell."

"I don't know what I was expecting, but it wasn't this," I said under my breath as the snap of the whip echoed.

"Bryn gave me a heads up, but I honestly didn't believe her until now."

"It's hard to fathom they've all gone through this." I nodded toward Kara as the cord stretched across the space and tore through her like a knife. Her eyes slammed shut, and she screamed this time, no longer able to hold in her agony.

My stomach lurched. I may be furious with Kara, and I sure as Hel didn't trust her, but I wouldn't wish this kind of torment on anyone.

Bryn handed off the whip to Talon. How was she supposed to endure three more lashings? Blood dripped down her ribs, staining her dress.

My heart raced like I was the one sitting in that chair as Talon reached back for another strike.

Kara's body stiffened and her eyes glowed as if the stars were shining from inside her.

Crack. The whip came down on her pale sickly skin again, but she didn't flinch, didn't make a sound. I wasn't sure what was worse, hearing her scream or the silence.

Talon's eyes hardened as she drew back the whip. I didn't know how she could do this to someone she considered a friend. Valkyrie were a different breed.

Maybe that's how Kara was able to kill me, and look past the feelings she claimed to have. They were trained to put their emotions aside when it came to pain and death. Is it any surprise that she could have done the same with me?

Like a snake, the whip shot across the space and sank its teeth into the middle of Kara's back. *Crack.*

I looked away from the carnage and back to Kara's face. Anyone who would choose this as a child and then again as an adult was built differently. I had a lot of respect for Valkyrie before, but learning they'd all endured unimaginable pain to become the warriors they are left me speechless.

Talon raised her arm for the ninth and final blow and I kept my eyes on Kara. The cord cut across her back and she looked up at the sky in silence. Her head tilted all the way back and the shadow of the dark moon fell on her face.

Talon took a step back, and we all shifted behind Kara to

watch Freya's Magik in action. Kara's head fell forward as Freya spoke in the Vanir tongue.

She stepped up to Kara, holding a bowl filled to the brim with what looked like liquid gold. Raising the bowl over her head, she said what I could only assume was a prayer, then poured the contents onto Kara's bruised and bloody skin. The liquid shimmered on her back and dripped onto the grass as Kara shivered. Her knuckles were white as she held onto the back of the chair and her breathing was shallow and fast. The light around them shifted and the flames surrounding us doubled in size.

Freya dropped to her knees behind Kara. I had to blink twice as shock rocked through me. I don't think I've ever seen Freya bow to anyone. The Gods never put others above themselves.

Freya placed her hands on Kara's shoulders, and I wasn't sure she was still conscious at this point. Kara's body had all but folded in on itself, and her breathing was slow and shallow, as if every breath took an enormous amount of effort. Freya's hands touched her damaged skin, and she didn't flinch or make a sound.

That wasn't a good sign. I knew from experience that having someone touch an exposed wound was agonizing. My stomach churned at the thought, and I hoped for her sake she couldn't feel anything.

Freya spoke in the Vanir tongue once more as her hands moved down Kara's shoulders and over her arms. The welts across her shoulders and down her spine moved at Freya's touch, shaping into swirls, similar to the markings I once idly traced on her back.

I sucked in a breath and the air stilled as my vision tunneled in on Kara. The markings shifted in color and moved to her right shoulder. The swirls glowed, shining as bright as the sun. Pulsing once, the markings formed over her shoulder blades, connecting at the top of her spine. They were similar to those she'd carried before, but not the same. Each swirl, every twist and turn were more intricate, more defined than I remembered.

Kara sucked in a breath as Freya placed her palms over the marks. I could smell the sharp tang of Magik in the air as Kara's head fell back and Freya's eyes went white.

The Valkyrie circled around Kara, chanting in the same cadence as Freya. A bone-biting chill swept through me as the Valkyrie's words grew louder.

The chanting took on a life of its own as they repeated themselves, and Asheria let out a whoop of excitement. Her wings burst from her back in a sharp, swift movement. The sheer force rippled through my chest.

Talon was next, her wings springing from her back with such vigor it was a miracle they didn't knock her over. Throwing her head back, she hollered at the dark moon as she continued her dance around Kara. Bryn was next, her wings completing the barrier, making it so we could no longer see Freya and Kara in the center.

Their chanting reached a fever pitch as they danced and gave themselves over to the Magik that was thick and heady, even to me. I could only imagine what they must feel with Freya's unfiltered power coursing through their own blood.

I watched in awe as they spoke in a cadence I'd never heard before and danced in a way that called to the most primal parts of my humanity. They were magnificent, and it was no wonder people worshipped the Valkyrie just as much as the Gods. And Kara was one of them, no matter my feelings toward her. She was touched by Freya and belonged to a larger world that I'd never fully understand as a mere mortal.

They reached the end of the chant once more and, on cue, Bryn, Talon, and Asheria pushed off the ground. Their wings beat slowly as they continued circling Kara. Another beat of their wings and my heart picked up its pace. *Whoosh.* The sound of their wings vibrated through me, and I could see Kara and Freya again.

Freya's hand was pressed to Kara's back, and both their heads were slumped forward. Bright gold ribbons of Magik streamed down Freya's arm and over Kara's exposed skin.

The Valkyrie flapped their wings again, sending a gust of air over us all. Freya rose to her feet, maintaining contact with Kara the entire time as the words of her people burst from her throat like a war cry.

Kara's body rose from the chair, her head still slumped forward as blood dripped down her limp form. "Rise once more, Wild Storm." Freya's hand slid down Kara's spine as she floated into the air inside the circle of her sisters.

Another flap of their wings and Kara rose above the other Valkyrie. I could no longer make out her face, or the defining lines of her wing tattoo as she floated higher. With the shadow of the dark moon over her, I watched, heart pounding, palms sweating as her body slowly rotated above us.

Whoosh. Their wings forced the torches around us to fall into the grass. Fire sprung up in a circle in front of us, the heat of the flames brushing over my face as Kara floated higher still.

A pang of fear shot through me. Freya said it was possible her wings wouldn't take and if they didn't, it was a long way down from where she was floating. I wondered if the other Valkyrie would save her, or if they were even allowed to.

With a guttural war cry, Talon, Bryn, and Asheria tucked their wings and dropped to the ground, landing outside the ring of fire.

Kara's head fell back, and her arms splayed wide. She tipped backward and her body plummeted toward us. I looked to the other Valkyrie, but they stood as still as stone. My heart beat against my ribcage as I watched her tumble toward the flames, now reaching up to meet her.

They wouldn't let her die, would they?

I glanced to my right at Magnus, who was just as wide-eyed as myself, before looking back up at Kara's limp body as it turned end over end. My hands balled into fists. This was wrong. She was going to die. It didn't matter what I felt toward her, I couldn't stand by and do nothing as she fell to her death.

I pushed forward, but it was too late. I was too late. She was going to fall and if the impact didn't kill her, the flames would. Still, my feet moved of their own accord and I pushed my way to the front of the crowd. I wasn't the only one. Whether out of morbid curiosity or concern, everyone converged around the spot she'd disappeared into the fire.

I squeezed between Talon and Bryn as a figure rose from the flames. A dark shadow on either side of her grew larger. Blood and the gold liquid Freya poured over her dripped off her limbs, and her eyes sparked with Magik. She rose to her full height, her wings spreading out on either side of her.

Talon was the first to whistle, followed by Bryn, who threw her head back and shouted.

Kara's hand balled into fists, and her chest heaved with every breath as the fire burned around her.

She walked out of the flames, deep emerald green wings tipped with gold framed her. The woman I spoke with under the stars was gone, replaced by a warrior made by the Gods.

CHAPTER EIGHTEEN

KARA

I LAUNCHED INTO THE SKY. The breeze was cool against my feverish skin, but the warmth of the day lingered, brushing over my face and through my wings. Each feather across my back took delight in the wind's current combing through them like fingers through water.

Folkvang was laid out below me, the stone buildings basking in the starlight. The river sparkled as if filled with diamonds. People walked along the river bank, and their laughter reached my ears and filled my heart. This was my home. And seeing it from above once more helped to shed some of the weight I've been carrying.

I closed my eyes, letting my instincts take over. Instincts I thought were long dead. My chest swelled and my mouth pulled into a smile that made my cheeks hurt. I pulled my wings in tight and spun into a free fall. My stomach dipped as the roar of the wind passed over me. Falling closer to the city, I could make out the glow of lanterns lining the streets and people going about their second lives.

My wings snapped open, and I soared over the rooftops and back into the sky. By the runes, I'd missed this. I was free. Well, and truly free.

I made my way back to the bluff and landed to cheers and

whoops. For the first time in a long while, I felt like the universe wasn't against me.

Asheria reached me first, grabbing my hands and smiling from ear to ear. "Welcome back to the fold." She kissed both of my cheeks.

"Thank you for being a part of the ceremony." I squeezed her hands back as she stepped aside and Bryn stepped forward, her arm linked with a tall blue eye brunette, who I could only assume was Magnus.

"So, was it worth it?" Bryn asked as she kissed my cheek.

I rolled my shoulders, and my wings bristling. "A thousand times, yes." I might be sore for a few days as the pain and Magik settled, but I wouldn't trade it for the world.

"Congratulations," Bryn's friend said, giving me a quick peck.

"Thank you. It's Magnus right?"

"You've been talking about me?" He turned to Bryn and winked.

"Don't flatter yourself. I was only moaning about what a pain in the ass you are." She pulled him away.

"Liar." He draped his arm over her shoulder as they made their way over to the bonfire, laughing and jabbing at each other.

"Not going to lie," Talon said, pulling my attention back to my well wishers. "For a flash of a second, I didn't think you were going to make it." She grabbed my arms and pulled me into a hug, careful to avoid the sensitive skin on my back.

"You and me both."

"Welcome back." She smiled and kissed my forehead.

"Thank you for everything." I squeezed her hands before she moved on.

Ezra stepped forward, and I couldn't help the smile that pulled at my lips. "You came."

"Only Ragnarok could have kept me away." He wrapped his

arms around my waist. "That was incredible." He kissed my forehead. "Insane, but incredible." He kissed my lips. "You'll take me for a ride later, I hope?"

"If you're lucky." I raised my eyebrows at him.

"Come find me when you're done." He winked as he made his way over to Asheria and the others.

A handful of others paid tribute, with a kiss here, a hug there, and plenty of happy returns. I was about ready to join the celebration when the last of the people who watched my ceremony parted, revealing Sigurd a few feet away.

He stepped forward, his face expressionless as he closed the distance between us. His dark hair was loose around his shoulders and the collar of his shirt exposed the hollow of his throat. My heart beat in my chest like I was falling out of the sky all over again. He leaned in and the fresh scent of rain, cedar, and leather filled my nose. My head spun with a thousand memories of his body intertwined with mine and I let out a shaky breath.

His lips brushed my cheek, the feather-light touch sending heat across my face. "Congratulations," he whispered against my ear before taking a step back and putting some distance between us.

It took a considerable amount of effort to maintain a mask of polite indifference. "Thank you."

Never in a million years did I think he would be here tonight, and I hated that my heart swelled at the sight of him. Maybe he could forgive me and we could be friends. Our last conversation hadn't left me with much hope. But maybe him being here was a sign that we could move on from the past.

"That was something else." He let out a breath as he looked up at the sky and back at me.

"Not what you were expecting?" I aimed for a casual tone. The ceremony always shocked and awed those outside our sisterhood. "It's brutal, but necessary. Only the strongest can carry Freya's mark."

"I don't know what I expected, but this,"—he motioned around the bluff—"it's miles away from anything I've ever imagined."

"It's not for the faint of heart." I shrugged.

He ran a hand through his hair. "No, it's not." His shoulders were tight, and he did a fairly good job of looking at everything but me.

Was he nervous? Or just looking for a way out of this conversation?

A beat of awkward silence stretched between us. "I'm surprised to see you here," I blurted when he said nothing or made a move to leave. "I assumed you'd be keeping your distance after our conversation." I folded my arms, needing to put a barrier between whatever he was about to say and my heart.

"I may not have handled that the best." His eyes met mine and his lips thinned.

"That almost sounded like an apology." I opted for a playful tone, even though my whole body was as tense as a bowstring.

He sighed and pushed his sleeves up to his forearms. "I asked for answers and you gave them to me. It wasn't what I wanted to hear, but it was your truth." He looked toward the others, his eyes scanning the bluff as if he was hoping someone would rescue him.

My truth? So he didn't believe me. Of course he didn't. A flicker of anger simmered in my chest. "The truth often isn't as satisfying as we'd like."

"No, it's not."

"So, is that why you came tonight? To apologize?"

"I didn't know this was the plan for tonight. Magnus asked me to join him since Bryn was otherwise engaged."

I glanced toward Magnus, who was not so subtly watching us. "I'm going to go out on a limb and say your friend likes to get involved in other people's lives, doesn't he?"

He dipped his head and stifled a laugh. "That's one way of putting it. He means well, but he has no boundaries or sense of self-preservation." He said the last part under his breath as he glanced at Magnus.

I got the distinct impression they would have words tonight.

My heart gave a gentle tug for Magnus. It was rare to find a friend who cared enough to push you when most would leave things alone. "In my experience, when people are overly involved, it's done out of love." My eye met his, and I wished I could stuff the last word back into my mouth. Though I wasn't talking about love in the context of us, it still brought up the sting of his words from the other night.

Never say those words to me again.

He sighed and tucked a strand of hair behind his ear. "I didn't come here to apologize, but you deserve one."

I took a step back. "While I appreciate it, it's not necessary." I shook my head. Tonight was supposed to be about me regaining a part of my life. I didn't want to think about what happened between us or what truth still lay ahead. "We both said what we needed to say. We don't need to drag this out and make it a thing. You have your life, I have mine. And I just think—"

"Kara." He gripped my upper arm gently, and I stopped mid-sentence. "Just let me apologize."

When I didn't continue rambling, he nodded once and let go of my arm. "I was angry. I'm still angry, to be fair."

"And you have every right to be." The words tumbled out of my mouth. "I don't expect you to forgive me." And I didn't. I just wanted my life back whether or not he was in it.

"Will you let me finish?" He raised his brow and held my gaze. The words died on my tongue and I shut my mouth. The sooner he said what he needed to, the sooner I could get back to the celebration.

"I'm still angry, but until tonight, I've never thought about what you lost that day." He paused and looked back toward the fire.

"I see. And does that change things for you?" I studied his face, looking for anything that might tell me where this conversation was heading.

"No... maybe... I don't know." He rolled his eyes and looked at the stars as if they could save him. "Maybe things aren't so black and white."

"So all this change of heart because of the wing ceremony?" Heat flushed under my breast bone like wild fire. "Were the lashings enough justice for you?" I gave him the truth, and it wasn't enough, but a little pain and now he was ready to forgive me?

"Justice?" His brow furrowed and his nostrils flared. "You think I took pleasure in watching them rip the flesh from your bones?" He said through gritted teeth.

I shrugged. "Punishment fits the crime, does it not?"

He took a step back, shaking his head. "Regardless of what's happened between us, I've never wished to exact revenge upon you."

I doubted that. "Then what's caused you to have a sudden change of heart?"

"Talon told me you lost something, too. But your wings? I had no idea."

A flash of anger toward Talon burned through me. That wasn't for her to share with him.

"I didn't lose them." My temper flared as I recalled the day Odin made me less. "They were taken from me," I spat. "Burned from my body and ripped to shreds as I stood over you, mourning you." Angry tears stung the back of my eyes. "And that was just the start of what I lost." I stepped toward him. "You lost your life in Midgard, but I lost everything that day. My whole world. The nine realms. You." I said the last word through gritted teeth, trying to hold on to any composure. "And yet tonight is the first time you've ever considered that I might have been hurting, too." A dry, humorless laugh escaped my throat.

He closed the distance between us, anger and hurt etched across his face. "You act as if my life wasn't everything to me." He grabbed my hand and pressed it to his chest. "That losing what I thought we had didn't hurt more than the dagger you shoved into my heart." His chest heaved with each breath. "You took everything from me, any chance I had to become something. So forgive me if I didn't think about your heartache sooner. But I'm trying to understand, trying to see it from your side. The least you could do is take responsibility for what you did."

"I've spent the last hundred years taking responsibility for my actions. I just had my body flayed open as payment for what I did. All for something I have no memory of." I pulled my hand free, but I didn't step away. "Forgive me, don't forgive me. I don't really care. This is my chance to start over,"—I motioned to the fire, the bluff, to Folkvang—"to live again. And it doesn't require your forgiveness or understanding."

I turned and walked away, vowing to myself that I'd stay far, far away from him from here on out. Our past may be shared, but that didn't mean our future had to be too.

Davlin's words echoed in my mind. *Some people come into our lives for a season, others for a lifetime.* There was a time I thought Sigurd was for a lifetime, but turns out he was just a beautiful autumn; vibrant and full of life until winter took hold and wilted every last bloom.

CHAPTER NINETEEN

SIGURD

My head ached from the lack of sleep, but my mind wouldn't let me drift off into dreams. Kara's words cut right through me. The thought that I'd ever take pleasure in someone else's pain—I ran a hand over my face and got out of bed. If I couldn't count on the oblivion of sleep to ease my guilt and frustration, I could at least make myself useful by looking for an assignment.

Making my way to the outpost, I couldn't stop Kara's words from picking at my bones like a hungry crow. How had I become the bad guy in all this? How could she think seeing her tortured was something I'd enjoy? Deep down I knew I wasn't handling her return with the most grace, but I wasn't a monster for being angry with the woman who betrayed my love and my life.

Though I was starting to think she might be telling the truth about having no control or memory of the event. The Kara I knew would never have jeopardized her status as a Valkyrie.

Unless she didn't know she'd be punished for killing you? Another part of my brain offered.

My hands balled into fists as I followed the wooden path through the grass. I may never know the truth about that day, which weighed on me more than the event itself. How do I move forward and let go of the past without understanding how it all happened?

153

"Morning, Si. You up early or still up from last night?" Valttrie asked as I reached the patrol board.

"Little of both." I shrugged. "Wanted to see what the assignments looked like today."

"Trying to find the easy post before everyone else crawls out of bed?" He smirked.

"Something like that." I was in no mood for small talk.

"Well, you're in luck. There's nothing today. Freya wiped the board clean."

I looked at him, puzzled. "Why would she do that?"

He shrugged. "I don't get paid to ask questions."

"Alright, well thanks." I nodded and headed toward the training fields. I could at least get a workout in and hopefully ease some of the tension that had taken up residence in my back and shoulders. It wouldn't take my mind off things, but it might help tire me out enough to get some sleep.

As I approached the training field, Daiman and a few others came running out of the weapons room, armed to the teeth.

"Daiman?" I called after him. "Where are you off to? I was told there weren't any assignments today?"

"Oh, umm, we're just running drills." He looked toward the others, heading into the tree line, and then back at me.

"Drills, huh?" I closed the gap between us, but he wouldn't meet my eye. "You're hiding something."

He turned to leave, but I grabbed his arm.

"What would I have to hide?" He ripped free.

Aggressive and defensive. He was definitely lying. "What's with all the armor?" I motioned to the two swords strapped to his back, the chest plate, shield, and various daggers strapped to his body.

He rolled his eyes. "Look, we were ordered to keep this quiet."

"Ordered by who?"

"Freya, who else?" He looked toward the others, who had already disappeared into the forest.

"Does this have anything to do with the rift we found last week?" I watched his face carefully.

"I wish I could tell you more, but no friendship is worth betraying Freya's confidence." He clapped a hand on my shoulder. "You understand, right?"

I shrugged off his hand. "If there's something going on with that rift, I have a right to know."

Daiman scoffed and shook his head. "If she wanted you on this, she would have asked. There must be a reason—"

"You're right," I turned away from him. "And I'm going to find out what that reason is."

"For sorðinn's sake, Si. Keep my name out of it, will you?" he called after me.

It was still early enough that I knew she'd be in her quarters, so I made a beeline across the river and up the hill.

When I arrived at her door, two guards stood sentry, Hildr, and another I wasn't familiar with. "I wish to speak with her," I barked out the words harsher than I should've. It wasn't their fault Freya was keeping me from doing my job. And it wasn't their fault Kara had my emotions tied in knots.

"She's not accepting visitors today," the Valkyrie on my right snapped.

"She'll see me." I folded my arms and squared my shoulders. The two guards shared a glance, then one disappeared inside.

Hildr looked me up and down and scoffed. "Desperation isn't a good look on you."

"Who says I'm desperate?" I snapped. Every nerve in my body chafed as if my clothes were too tight and I ached to burst out of my skin.

She raised her brows as she appraised me. "Well, there's the fact that you smell like last night's bonfire still, which tells me you haven't seen a bed and you've got the bloodshot eyes to prove it. Not to mention the fact that you've shown up to a goddess's residence demanding to see her. Not exactly the picture of someone who has it all together." Her face scrunched up as she looked at me.

I opened my mouth to tell her off, but I probably deserved the dressing down. The door opened, and I started forward, only to be met with a hand on my chest, pushing me backward.

"Freya is not available for visitors this morning." The guard who'd made my request said. "Maybe try again tomorrow."

"Or better yet," Hildr said, "wait until she calls upon you."

I took a step back and looked between the two of them. Never, not once in all my time here, had Freya refused to see me.

"Fine. Tell her it's about my patrol last week, and I'll wait to hear from her."

"We'll pass the message along." The Valkyrie nodded once. I was dismissed.

Freya was keeping me away on purpose, and it didn't sit right with me. I wasn't sure if she was doing it to protect me from something or if she truly didn't trust me anymore.

As I walked away, I caught my reflection, and I had to agree with Hildr's assessment. I needed a shower, a change of clothes, and some sleep.

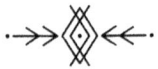

I went to check the patrol boards again the next morning, and sure enough, my name was nowhere in sight. There was still no word from Freya, either. Which sent a pang of worry through me. It wasn't like her to keep me at a distance. But I promised myself I'd be patient.

Instead, I ran drills with Magnus and declined every invitation for drinks or dinner, on the off chance Kara might be there. I wasn't ready to see her again after our conversation the other night. At the very least, I needed to sort out some of my feelings before we talked again. If we talked again.

I tried not to think about the reasons why Freya was brushing me off or why I was being kept from patrols. But ever since Kara showed up, my whole world had been turned upside down. Not that I could blame her for Freya's dismissal or the fact I was being treated with kid gloves. But with her arrival, nothing made sense anymore.

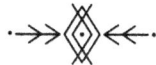

Four days after the wing ceremony, I made my way to the patrol boards. My name was nowhere in sight once again. Fury I hadn't known in decades burned through me. I wasn't made to sit around and do nothing. I wasn't chosen by the gods to do the same mundane things day in and day out until Ragnarok. My soul craved action, my blood burned with the need to be useful.

I don't know who I was fooling about being patient. It had never been my way, and I was done waiting for permission. I made my way to the weapons room, grabbed my favorite sword, and headed for the forest. Something was happening with that rift and I'd waited long enough to do something about it.

Jumping over a fallen tree, my boots made a loud, squishing sound as I landed. The weather was less than ideal today, which was perfect for doing some reconnaissance. Even with the extra patrols, I knew they'd cut the day short to warm themselves with a drink away from the elements.

As I got closer to the rift, I slowed my pace. If someone was standing guard, it wouldn't do any good to alert them to my presence. Heading left, I circled around so I would come up to the rift head on.

When the barrier, or lack thereof, came into view, it looked bigger than I recalled. Dropping to my knee behind a tree, I pulled the hood of my cloak up to hide my face as I scanned the area.

There was no one in sight and the forest was silent aside from the light patter of rain on the canopy above me. I edged closer, judging each step carefully to make as little sound as possible. Just because I didn't see or hear anyone, didn't mean I was alone.

A few feet from the barrier, I noticed a pile of wood that had been burnt to embers and paused to inspect it. A shield laid face up on the ground, the cobalt paint chipped and faded. Remnants of a camp had been scattered and half hidden in the bushes.

Was this what Daiman had been ordered to do? Guard the rift? And if so, where was he, or the others, for that matter?

I waited a few minutes, listening for the men this camp belonged to. I placed my hand against the ground, searching for the vibrations of boots through the muddy forest floor.

Still, there was nothing. Not the skittering of a woodland creature, not the chirp of a bird.

I pulled my blade, the whisper of metal against leather the only sound that cut through the forest. I moved through the makeshift camp to the edge of the rift. The forest on the other side looked just as dreary and wet, but there was an acrid smell in the air that made me cover my nose.

Reaching out with my sword, I tested the barrier, and it rippled off to my left. Then I tested the edge of the rift with my blade. The sharp clank was like steel on rock and I knocked my blade up and down the rift.

Moving closer, I stabbed my sword into the dirt at my side, ready to strike if the need should arise. I took a deep breath and ran my hand along the jagged edge of the rift. It was hot to the touch, as if the wall itself was a raging fire. Sparks danced over my fingers as I ran them down the seam, and the Magik within the barrier sent a shock up my arm.

"Step away from the barrier, Si." Daiman's voice came from behind me.

I let out a breath and turned to face him.

"What in the Gods' names are you doing here?" He shook his head like a disapproving parent.

"I could ask you the same question."

"I'm following orders. Orders to keep everyone, which includes you, away from this rift." He grabbed my arm and attempted to pull me away, but I didn't budge.

"Why? What isn't Freya telling the rest of us?"

Daiman sighed and rolled his eyes. "Give it a rest." He tried to pull me again, and in one swift motion, I grabbed my sword and pointed the tip against his neck.

"Tell me what you know."

"Or what, you'll send me to the stars?" He looked at me like I was deranged, and maybe I was.

"I don't need to kill you to get answers." I pushed the edge of the blade a little harder against his neck and a bead of blood blossomed and dripped down the hollow of his throat.

His eyes met mine and his expression turned cold. "Do your worst."

I didn't want to hurt him, but if he wouldn't give me answers the easy way, then I'd take them the hard way. I pulled back, lifting my sword to strike, when a sharp pain shot across the back of my skull and my vision blurred.

I didn't realize I was falling until I heard the *thwack* of my body hitting the mud and everything went dark.

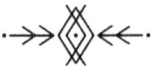

My eyes fluttered open and adjusted to the dark. Wood beams crisscrossed above me, and I sat up.

I was in bed. *My* bed. Had I dreamed of going to the rift?

I tossed the covers off and slid out of bed. Padding across the room, I pulled back the window covering. It was the dead of night, the only light from the stars peeking through the clouds. Either I'd been out for more than half the day or I'd been dreaming.

I left the window and moved through my home. My sword sat atop the table, discarded and clean. My cloak hung on the hook by the door, and when I ran my hands down the fabric, I found it perfectly dry and free of any dirt. Nothing looked out of place, nor did it look like I'd ventured outside.

Walking back toward the bed, I pulled my loose hair into a knot at the back of my head and a sting of pain shot across my skull. I moved my fingers over my head, and sure enough, there was a small, tender lump.

Not a dream.

For half a second, I thought about stomping over Daiman's place and demanding answers. But if he'd gone to such great lengths to make me believe I'd never been back to the rift, it was a long shot that he'd be honest with me. And while I'd make him pay for knocking me out and dumping me at home, I understood it. He was following orders and nothing I could say or do would change that.

Instead, I made a plan to spend the next few days watching Daiman and the others guarding the rift to see what I could glean from their operation.

Maybe Talon had some insight on what was going on. That rift was a genuine threat to Folkvang, and I wouldn't sit by and let Daiman and the others have all the glory. I deserved to be out there, protecting every soul that lives in this afterlife. My name may not be carved into stone in Midgard, but I'd be damned if I let myself fade into obscurity for a second time.

CHAPTER TWENTY

KARA

SWEATY AND GASPING FOR AIR, I crawled out of bed and slunk into the washroom. The same nightmare that had plagued me night after night pulled me from my slumber. Sigurd held me against the wall while Odin burned my wings off until the screams that lived in my memory forced me awake.

I angled my body in the mirror so I could see the tattoo on my back. Still there, I sighed in relief. Placing my hands on either side of the sink, I hung my head and took a few deep breaths to bring my heart rate back down.

After our argument, I'd spent the past week avoiding Sigurd and waiting to hear from the Norns. I wasn't sure which plagued me more, waiting for answers or dodging Sigurd and his friends.

More than anything, I wished our conversation had gone differently, but I didn't blame him for how he felt, nor did I want to change his mind. He had every right to be angry with me, but I wouldn't let him take my home.

I was careful to train during odd hours, and I selected accommodation on the other side of the river, away from the hustle and bustle of the city center, and most importantly, away from him.

Talon was insufferable the first few days, insisting that everything would blow over, that we should try to talk again when emotions weren't high. But I didn't see the point. Folk-vang was big enough for the both of us to coexist without inter-twining our lives.

I'd tried to apologize, tried to explain, but he didn't want to hear it. And sure, I could try again, but why keep beating a dead horse? Nothing I said would change what happened, and as much as I wished things could be different, it was time to move forward.

Once, it may have seemed impossible that our paths would diverge, but now it was the only option for us to live in peace. He was happy here, thriving in his second life. It was time I did the same without the heavy burden of his death riding me like a demon Hel bent on tormenting me. With any luck, the Norns would have answers for me and I could put this issue to bed.

I turned the faucet on and splashed cold water on my face to banish the sickly, sweaty feel off my skin.

"Bad dream?" Ezra's voice purred from somewhere behind me.

I patted my face dry with a towel and turned to him. "I didn't mean to wake you."

He closed the distance between us and rested a hand on my hip. "I don't mind." He pressed his forehead against mine. "Want to talk about it?" His thumb moved over my hip bone, sending a jolt through me.

I shook my head and placed a hand on his bare chest. No, I didn't want to talk. It was one thing to share my bed with him, it was wholly another thing to share the shadows of my heart.

He pulled away an inch so he could look down at me. His eyes were midnight blue pools I could happily drown in. My heart kicked up a notch for an entirely different reason as he brushed his thumb over my bottom lip and cupped my cheek. "Want me to make you forget?"

"Mmm." I lifted my chin so our lips were a breath apart. "What'd you have in mind?" I exhaled.

He cocked an eyebrow, and his lips brushed mine. I could feel him smile as his hand moved from my hip and around my backside. He gripped my ass and pulled me against him. He kissed the edge of my jaw, leaving a trio of kisses down my neck as his other hand found its way into my hair. His fingers curled around the strands and he pulled my head back to expose my neck.

"Better?" The heat of his breath warmed my skin and sent a shiver down my spine.

"A little," I gasped. I closed my eyes and let him banish my nightmare to the shadows.

He ran his tongue up the side of my neck, eliciting a shiver from me. A deep chuckle rumbled through him. "That's more like it."

He captured my mouth with his, and I melted into the warmth of his touch, the heat of his kiss. He lifted me off my feet and I wrapped my arms around his shoulders and my legs around his waist. The solid feel of him against my torso grounded me and soothed the ache in my heart.

The dreams aren't real, I told myself. But he is.

His tongue glided over mine, deepening the kiss and forcing the echo of my nightmare out of my mind. I tangled my fingers in his hair, pulling him closer, and he groaned as he carried me back to the bedroom. Laying me down on the bed, he propped himself up on his elbow above me. His hand found its way to my breast and rolled my nipple between his fingers through the thin fabric of my nightshirt. A spark of pleasure shot through me and an ache bloomed between my legs. My breath caught and my body arched up against his.

He pulled at the hem of my shirt, pushing it up to expose my breast, and I tugged it the rest of the way off. His lips met mine again, softer, deeper this time, as his fingers traced lazy circles over my bare chest. I was still getting used to the way he like to tease and take his time with my pleasure. His thumb coasted over the peak of my nipple, sending a rush of heat across my chest and into my core.

I moaned and rocked against him. His lips didn't skip a beat as they trailed down my neck and between my breasts. His tongue flicked over my nipple, the heat of his breath sending goosebumps across my skin. My hand tangled into the sheets and my hips rolled with the need to feel him. His teeth grazed my sensitive skin, sending a bolt of pleasure through me, and I groaned.

My body moved out of its own desire under him, and he pushed himself against me. The hard length of him pressed against my thigh, and my legs opened wider for him of their own accord.

A scream tore through the early dawn, and we ripped apart. He hovered above me and we both held our breath as we waited for a cue to continue or pick up our swords. As trained warriors, we were always ready for a fight, but being half naked and turned on was the worst time to be called to arms.

An animalistic roar pierced the silence, and without a word, we scrambled out of bed.

If I wasn't going to banish my nightmares with carnal pleasures, fighting was the next best thing. Either way, I needed to get rid of the anxious energy bouncing around inside me.

Grabbing a shirt, I slipped it over my head and searched for a pair of trousers. The heat of our passion was forgotten as adrenaline pumped through my chest and focused my mind on the single task of pulling my clothes on.

"What do you think it is?" Ezra slipped his shirt over his head.

I shrugged as I fastened the laces on my trousers. "Nothing good."

"Have there been any breaches? Anything that might have gotten through the wards?"

He shook his head. "Just you."

I looked over my shoulder at him. "You think I did this?" The adrenaline turned to acid in my stomach. I turned to face him, squaring my shoulders, ready to defend myself.

"What?" He shook his head and his brow furrowed as he looked at me. "No, of course not."

Guilt formed a lump in my throat, and my shoulders sagged. "Sorry, I just thought… It doesn't matter." I hated that I'd jumped to defend myself. As if Ezra would even try to blame me for whatever was happening. Not everyone thought I was a monster. I had to remember that.

Another scream sounded as I pulled my armor over my head and strapped the chest plate to my body. I slipped on the harness that held my blades as Ezra reached for the door, his sword in one hand and his shield strapped to his back.

"Ready?" He looked me up and down and his lips pulled up at the corner. "Gods, you're beautiful."

I finished fastening my bracers and grabbed my weapons. "There'll be plenty of time for that later."

I nodded for him to lead the way. "Yes, ma'am." He pushed the door open, and we paused on the threshold.

Across the river, soldiers I didn't recognize charged into the homes lining the bank. One stomped out, dragging a woman behind him. Her blond hair caught the torch light from one of his companions and I recognized her from the tavern on my first full day back. He grabbed a handful of her hair, yanked her head back, and pulled his sword across her throat.

"By the runes," Ezra's words propelled me forward, but I couldn't take my eyes off the scene in front of me as more soldiers dragged innocent people into the streets and burned their homes.

My heart lurched for each of the fallen. There was no life after this one, only the never ending expanse of the universe.

My gaze scanned up the buildings lining the hillside. I

spotted pockets of invaders running uninhibited, over the bridges and toward the Great Hall.

Whoever they were, they clearly had a mission.

"Go warn the others. We're going to need every able body," I ordered, without looking at Ezra.

"Save some of the fun for the rest of us." He called over his shoulder as he ran down the river bank to sound the alarm.

My wings erupted from my back and I thrust into the air. I pulled both of my swords from their sheaths as I landed on the other side of the river in the middle of a group of men—no, not men, monsters. Their blue eyes were as cold and unyielding as the ice of Niflheim, and their bodies were almost skeletal, as if they'd risen from a grave.

I crossed my arms over my chest and sliced through the neck of the ones nearest me. The flesh tore easily and black ooze splattered across my chest. *What, in the name of Yggdrasil, were these things?* The soft thump of three heads hitting the ground was the only thing that reached my ears, and the rest of the group turned and looked at me.

"So nice to have your attention." I smirked.

They charged forward, swords raised and screaming. I met the blade of the first one and kicked at his chest. He stumbled backward and snarled. Blocking another one, I dropped to my knees and shoved a sword through the nearest leg. A bone shattering scream tore through the air. I pulled my blade free as he fell, and used my other sword to cut his head clean off his shoulders.

Pushing to my feet, I caught another blow meant for my head. My arm shook at the awkward angle and he snarled at me. I had to fight the urge to recoil from the putrid smell of death that rolled off of him. I shoved him away, and he swung again. My blade caught his, the metallic sting of our swords clashing pierced the air.

A flash of steel to my left caught my eye, and I disarmed the monster in front of me, splitting his neck wide as my left hand moved on instinct alone. My sword connected with bone and a hand, still clinging to the hilt of a sword, fell at my feet.

Another scream punctured the air, making me wince. I turned my blade, grabbed the screaming thing by the shoulder, and shoved my sword through its neck and out the top of his head. The scream turned to a gurgle, and his body slumped against me. I stumbled backward, the dead weight knocking me off balance, as the smell of a thousand rotting corpses assaulted my nose.

A low, deep horn sounded somewhere in the distance. The call to arms. I pushed the last enemy soldier near me to the ground and pulled my blade free.

Good. This would be over soon enough.

Cleaning my blades off on my trousers, I scanned the area, looking for where I could be the most helpful.

About halfway up the hillside, on one of the smaller bridges, Bryn was surrounded. Six of the monsters crowded at her back and she held off the ten in front of her. She was doing a good job of not letting them get the upper hand, but it wouldn't last— her focus was too split.

I pushed off the ground, my wings taking over as I flew to her aid. I carefully scanned the scene in front of me, assessing where I'd be the most helpful. A hole opened up in the six behind her and I pulled my wings in, shooting like an arrow through the sky. Just as I was about to land, my wings extended, slowing me enough to drop onto the bridge.

I plunged my sword into the chest of the first one, using my other blade to slice through the muscles and tendons of his neck. The second attacked, and I caught his blow, disarmed him, and kicked his feet out from under him. He hit the ground with a crunch. I rolled the hilt in my hand so I was fisting it and pushed the tip of the blade through his eye until it hit the stone bridge. His body twitched as black ooze pooled under his head, and I pulled my sword free.

Turning on my heel, I met the next two. They snarled at me, and my lips curled into a smile. I crouched and leapt into the air, my wings helping me stay airborne as I spun over their heads, landing behind them. I shoved each sword through the back of their skulls, and their bodies twitched. Pulling my blades free, they toppled to the ground in front of me as my back hit someone else.

I turned, ready to strike. Bryn's eyes met mine, a splatter of black ooze across her face.

"I bet you didn't see monsters like this in Midgard." She cocked her head to the side as she caught another blow.

"Monsters come in many forms." I turned to face the last two and thought about all the war, all the devastation I'd seen in my years in Midgard.

No, these weren't the worst I'd ever faced.

CHAPTER TWENTY-ONE

SIGURD

THE DEEP, ancient horns of Folkvang vibrated through me, forcing me out of bed. My stomach churned and the hairs on the back of my neck prickled as I reached for my dagger.

The front door swung open, and the blade left my hand, slicing through the air.

Magnus dodged my assault and smirked. "Good, you're up."

"Never went to sleep." I ran my fingers through my hair.

"Is that right?" He scanned the room as if looking for someone.

The horns sounded again, deep and guttural. "Sounds like another pissing match with the Gods?" I tied my hair into a knot at the back of my neck.

"That or another training exercise." Magnus frowned and looked over his shoulder. "Why is it always at dawn?"

I buckled myself into my armor and grabbed my sword and shield from the table.

"Some of us don't mind first light." I pushed past him into the cool pre-sunrise air and we followed the others, rushing to find out what all the commotion was about.

A flaming arrow landed a few yards ahead, and we stopped in our tracks. Raising our shields, we drew our swords on instinct.

This was decidedly not a training exercise. Freya would never allow our quarters to be threatened.

Two more arrows, three, and then a dozen more zipped over our heads. Without a word, we sprinted forward, dodging through the flames that had found purchase and started to rise.

I turned down a narrow passageway between two long-houses that led to the main square. The only sign that Magnus had followed was the sound of his boots on the stone path behind me.

Several whistles sounded overhead, quickly followed by the whoosh of a fire catching. Glancing up, the roofs on either side of us were now engulfed. Raising my shield over my head, I ran forward as embers the size of my fist rained down around us.

The heavy thud of steel against a shield reached my ears as we spilled out into the square. For every one of ours, there were at least four of them. Bodies hit the ground and flames crackled around us as someone screamed.

It was so similar to the morning I died, I had to close my eyes. A surprise attack. Friends fighting for their lives. An enemy we didn't see coming. Kara, somewhere nearby. I opened my eyes, and I was still in Folkvang. This was happening here and now.

Ragnar burst from the fray, beheading one person and cutting through the middle of another. "Look who finally showed up."

"Couldn't leave all the fun to you, now could we?" Magnus smiled like a kid during Yuletide next to me.

A man leapt from the shadows—at least he used to be a man. In one bony hand, he held a sword, and his bright sapphire eyes bore into me as his blade cut through the air.

Blocking his attack, I sidestepped and plunged my steel into his chest. His sunken face was barely more than a skeleton, his paper thin skin stretching unnaturally as he screamed like a wild animal caught in a trap.

He dropped his sword at our feet and attacked with his skeleton fingers. Pain flashed across my chest as the sharp tips of his fingers dug into my skin and ripped. I grit my teeth, ignoring the trickle of warm blood trailing down my chest as I struggled to keep out of his reach. He was stronger than I expected for a half dead skeleton and it took all my strength to push him off me.

I took a few steps back to reposition myself, and a look of shock passed over my enemy's face for a fraction of a second. His head rolled off his shoulders and into the dirt at my feet, and his body collapsed in a heap.

"Go for the head." Daiman wiped his blade clean on his pants and stepped over the body. "It's the only thing that stops them."

I grabbed him by the arm and under my breath, I said, "The rift?" His eyes met mine and with a nod, he confirmed my suspicion.

"What do they want?" I let go of him and looked at the severed head covered in dirt and black ooze. The same viscous blood I'd seen at the rift.

"That's what we've been tasked with finding out."

"Whatever they are, they're skilled fighters," Ragnar huffed as he took down another one.

"And they have numbers." I nodded toward the path that led to the Great Hall. The entire hillside was crawling with the creatures as one Valkyrie after another landed among them and began to cut them down.

"First one to ten gets a keg of mead from Jotunheim," Ragnar announced.

"You could at least make it difficult." I ran past the others and flipped my sword in my hand. "Make it twenty-five." There was almost nothing I loved more than a challenge.

"Twenty-five it is," Ragnar shouted.

As I reached the bridge leading out of the living quarters, I swung my blade to the left and then right in one smooth move-ment. "That's two," I called over my shoulder.

"Like Hel, I'm going to let you win again." Daiman shoved me off the bridge and into the shallow water. The chill bit into my skin, but did nothing to dampen my spirits. Finally, a proper fight. "What's the matter? Can't win without cheating?" I sloshed through the water and pulled myself back up onto the bridge.

Breaking into a run, I caught up to the others in a few strides. Before Daiman could finish his swing, I jumped in front of him and shoved my blade through the neck of the monster he'd been aiming for.

"Three."

Daiman spun around me, his blade cutting through the air and sending a head rolling down the hill. "Seven."

I bit back the curse on the tip of my tongue and set my sights on the Great Hall. Attaching my shield to my back, I ran up the steepest part of the hill and through the trees. Whatever these things were, whatever they wanted, it had them all headed toward the Great Hall. If I could get ahead of them, I could take them out one by one without any interference from the others and win that cask.

As I broke through the trees, a thrill ran through me. The bridge leading to the Great Hall was crawling with half-dead men and only Talon and Asheria were holding them back.

Instinct took over as I ran into the fray. My sword cut through the air, claiming two more heads in one blow. Ducking under an assault, I grabbed my dagger with my free hand, spun around, and shoved the blade into another's throat. The howl that escaped him caught the attention of the others around me as I pulled my blade through his delicate skin and tissue. His head flopped to one side and his body crumpled at my feet.

Five more rushed me. I met the first head on. Our blades crashed as I kicked another one in the chest, pushing them back and sending them tumbling over the bridge. Swinging around and ducking another assault from my right, I used my momentum to cut the head off of the half-dead monster in front of me. I leaned backward to avoid the brush of another sword and ducked under an ax, cutting through the air as I drove my blade up through another's skull. That was a little too close for comfort. These things knew how to fight, despite being sloppy and bullish.

One came at me from each side, and I ducked as they both raised their swords to attack. I stabbed one in the thigh, and he roared like a wounded bear and fell to his knees. Jumping to my feet, I held my sword with both hands and cut through the other's neck, sending his head rolling along the stone bridge.

I turned to finish off the wounded one as another one jumped on my back. His bony arm dug into my neck, pulling me backward. I gasped as we both tumbled over the heap of bodies and I barely caught myself. I grabbed at his arm to break free, but he was unnaturally strong and I only moved him enough to take a deep breath. Another swung a flail toward me and I raised my sword to defend the next blow. The chain wrapped itself around my arm and I yanked the monster forward, shoving my head into his and knocking him backward. Pain splintered across my face, but I ignored it.

With both hands, I ripped the boney arm free from my neck and spun on my attacker. I drove my dagger through his glowing eye. Black goo oozed down his face and his scream rattled my bones. I dragged my sword across his neck, splitting his head from his shoulders, and the howling stopped as his skull cracked against the ground.

I stared down at the beaten and bloody monster and I took a few deep breaths as I pulled my dagger from the lifeless head. What were these monsters? What was their purpose here? Something about all this didn't sit right with me. The rift,

Freya's dismissal, this attack. Too many things weren't adding up.

The back of my neck prickled, and I turned to the Great Hall as forest green wings touched down in front of me. She effortlessly blocked the ax headed my way with her blade, and claimed two heads in the blink of an eye.

Our eyes caught for a moment, and memories of battles gone by with her by my side flashed before my eyes. I nodded. "Kara."

"Sigurd." She nodded back as dozens of the monsters descended on us.

We placed our backs to one another just as one jumped over a pile of bodies, driving his sword in my direction. As quickly as I took him down, another took his place. My blade clashed with another and another until the ground was littered with bodies.

"Do you know what these things are?" I called over my shoulder as I swept my foot out, sending another one to the ground.

Kara turned, dropping to her knee, and beheaded the half-dead warrior I knocked off his feet. "Disgusting." Her eyes met mine and the corner of her mouth pulled into a smile.

My feelings toward her were conflicted, but I couldn't deny that she was an exceptional fighter.

She rolled her sword in her hand and turned back to the fight, cutting a path toward the Great Hall.

The two of us fought our way through the army of half-dead men crawling all over the bridge. With each step, she was by my side, setting me up for the kill and taking her turn in beheading the monsters. We may be horrible with our words now, but fighting side by side felt like it always did. Effortless.

She turned around me, going after a handful of the undead who circled behind us as I pushed forward. Bodies fell all around us, their blood turning the weathered grey stone into a black river of death. The last few dozen monsters trying to break down the doors abandoned their mission and turned toward us as one.

They ran forward and as I pushed one back, another was on me, and then another and another. I swung out with my sword, connecting with flesh that resulted in an ear splitting scream, but the assault continued. Another jumped on top of me, forcing me to the ground, and my head hit the bridge hard enough to rattle my teeth. There were too many of them, and they were starting to coordinate their attacks.

Using my legs, I tossed the snarling thing over my head and flipped backward onto my feet. Kara landed next to me, her wings outstretched, a blade in each hand dripping with black ooze.

"You okay?"

I nodded. Her concern surprised me. After our last failed attempt at peace, I didn't think she cared if I lived or joined the stars.

Without another word, we ran forward, our weapons moving through the air like a perfectly choreographed dance. Body after body fell around us as we moved around each other and inched closer and closer to the doors.

As the last body fell and Kara's blade severed its head, a slow clap reached my ears.

"The two of you are quite impressive." Ragnar motioned between us with the tip of his blade.

"That ale is still mine." Daiman sheathed his sword as he made his way across the bridge and through the bodies.

"At the very least, it's a draw," I argued.

"Ale?" Kara raised her brow as she looked between me and Daiman. "Still making bets during battle." She smirked.

"Keeps things interesting." I shrugged.

"No way it's a draw," Daiman grabbed Ragnar by the shoulder. "He had the help of a Valkyrie."

"Sounds like someone's jealous." Ragnar shoved Daiman off of him.

"I think you all deserve a cask." Freya marched toward us through the bodies Kara and I had piled up on the bridge. Blood and black ichor smeared across her armor. "But there is still much to do before we can celebrate." She stopped a few feet short of us and turned to face the others now gathering on the bridge.

"Beheading is not enough to keep these creatures dead," Freya announced. "Their bodies must be burned before the day is out or they will reanimate."

"What are they?" I asked.

"I'll explain, all in due time," she said without looking at me. "But first we must finish this battle. Gather the fallen, including our brothers and sisters. We need to burn them all."

CHAPTER TWENTY-TWO

SIGURD

"FREYA, A WORD?" I said as she stomped past me over the heaps of bodies.

"Not now, Sigurd," she barked.

I wasn't taking no for an answer this time. She may not want to talk to me, but I followed anyway. Every fiber of my being had known the rift would bring something like this down on our heads. And I was through being kept in the dark.

"You know more than you're letting on," I said under my breath.

She looked over her shoulder and her eyes met mine for a fraction of a second before she pushed through the double doors of the Great Hall.

"Those things came from the rift, didn't they?" I motioned to the piles of bodies outside. I already knew the answer; Daiman had confirmed it. But I wanted to hear her say it.

She stopped in her tracks and turned on me. "Do not speak about things you know nothing of."

"What are you hiding from me?" I did my best to temper the anger in my voice. "Why don't you trust me anymore?" I wanted to scream at her. I could have done something. I could have helped.

Her eyes met mine and the corner of her mouth lifted as she took a step toward me. "I'm very fond of you, you know that.

But you're stepping out of place." She circled behind me. "I do not have to share the goings on of my domain with you. I've given you my favor, yes. But I can remedy that, given you've already ventured into the forest against my orders." Each word pierced my gut and turned my blood to ice. Of course she knew. Who was I to think anything happened in Folkvang without her knowledge?

"My apologies." I lowered my head. "I only wish to help, to protect my home and the ones I care about."

"You're a kind soul, Sigurd." She touched my cheek. "But there are things in the nine realms that you are not prepared for."

"The only reason I'm unprepared is because you've kept me in the dark, and I deserve to know why." I was walking a thin line. Either she'd see my passion and answer me, or she'd throw me out on my ass for being insubordinate.

"I'm trying to protect you," she snapped.

"From those monsters?"

"They are not monsters." She moved to the table between us and placed her sword down.

"Please, tell me what you know."

"The more you know, the harder it will be to distance yourself from what's to come."

"Is that why you've kept me away? Because you don't want me involved?" She didn't know me at all if she thought she could keep me from my calling.

"It is."

"Why?" I tried to keep the emotion from my voice, but my frustration was boiling just beneath the surface.

"This isn't a fight that mortals can win. A war is coming. I've felt it for some time now. The rift, the Dragur." She waved her hand. "They are warning signs of something bigger."

"If there's a war coming, I want to fight, not be kept on the sidelines."

"If you fight, you will die. And there is no life after this one." Her words were not a threat, but a promise. She didn't think I could survive what was to come, because she no longer saw me as the warrior I was. I'd become nothing more than a plaything.

"It's my life." I placed a hand on my chest. "My choice."

"Are you so miserable here that you would give it all up?"

"I have loved Folkvang, but I am a born fighter, trained to go into battle, knowing it might be my last. I'd rather die on the battlefield than safe and warm in your bed."

Her gaze dropped from mine and she shook her head. "Very well. You are here, after all, because of your skill and bravery. It was a fool's errand trying to keep you in the dark."

"So you'll tell me then? What those things are?" Relief and hope washed through me and for the first time in over a week, I no longer felt like I was on the back foot.

She nodded and took a seat. "The first Valkyrie went by another name. They were called the Disir." She poured herself a drink. "We've done well to erase their true nature from the consciousness of the nine realms." Her eyes met mine, and the embers of her Magik brushed over my skin and burned into my bones.

"They were created by Bor with crude Magik that he never understood," she sneered. "Much like the Valkyrie now, they were supposed to ferry worthy souls to us, but their hunger for power outgrew any loyalty they had to Bor."

I hung on her every word like they were morsels of food, and I was a starved man.

"It wasn't long before the Disir realized that by killing a warrior meant for the Gods and consuming their soul, they could grow more powerful than anyone living, including us."

My mouth fell open, and I blinked. More powerful than the Gods? It was unimaginable.

"How did they go from ferrying souls to consuming them?" I tried to understand what might possess someone to destroy another's soul. Kara's face popped into my mind. Could this be connected to her, to why she killed me?

"One thing the Valkyrie and the Disir have in common is that they both can sense the strength of a worthy soul," Freya explained. "It's how they're able to find the warriors meant for an afterlife with the Gods."

I nodded along, but so far none of this explained the army we'd just faced.

"The call of their charge is overwhelming, intoxicating, and impossible to resist. But for the Disir, it was something more. Their strength and abilities grew tenfold." She took a sip of her drink. "They became impossible to kill. And then, one day, the first Disir refused Bor's claim on them and called her sisters to arms along with the Dragur they'd created."

"They were—" I couldn't bring myself to say the words.

"Fallen souls, just like you. Until the Disir made them into the creatures, you fought today."

A chill ran down my arms and my mouth went dry. "Those monsters were once like me? Like Magnus and the others?" Their animalistic screams echoed in my ears. Their twisted, snarling faces flashed before my eyes. They were once us. My heart ached for the men they once were. Men who deserved to be in Folkvang or Valhalla.

"Yes, and after the Disir fell, their army, the ones you fought today, were banished to the deepest part of Hel to slumber for all eternity."

"Why not kill them? Give them peace?"

"They already had one life stolen from them. We didn't think it right to take what was left. We always hoped to find a way to free them. And in the meantime, they've been kept in a dream state."

"So how did they come to be here if they're meant to be slumbering in Hel?"

Her eyes dropped from mine. "That's a question we've been trying to answer."

A sharp pang of fear shot across my chest. She didn't know.

"And the rift. It's how they gained access to Folkvang?" Irritation prickled over my skin. There should have been more of us protecting the barrier. Lives could've been saved today. But instead, she kept it quiet. Asked me to keep it quiet. All because she didn't have answers.

She nodded.

"And do you know who broke through our defenses?" My tone was accusatory. There were very few in the nine realms who could match Freya's Magik.

"I have my suspicions," she said flatly.

"The Disir? Could they have something to do with it?"

"No, they're safely locked away with blood Magik. It would take an act against nature to free them." Freya refilled her cup.

"And you're sure they haven't found freedom like their Dragur?" I dared to ask.

Her eyes cut to me and my shoulders caved. I was dangerously close to the edge of her patience. "You've grown bold in the last few weeks."

"I only wish to be certain."

"Then rest assured. The Disir are of no concern." She took a deep sip of her drink.

I let out a sigh of relief. Thankful they weren't something to worry about, but also grateful she didn't smite me where I stood.

"Who would want to attack us? Folkvang isn't a threat."

She raised an eyebrow. "There are those who'd disagree with you."

My brow furrowed as I studied her.

"Folkvang is a sanctuary for some of the most fierce warriors in the nine realms. Would you not classify that as a threat?" Her head fell to one side as if she was measuring my intelligence.

"I see your point, but we've provoked no one."

"You're mere existence is provocation enough."

"Then where do we start?"

"I suggest you help with the fallen." She nodded beyond the Great Hall. "I will reveal all in due time." Her voice left no room for further discussion.

I had more questions than answers, but I knew when to back off. I bowed and turned on my heel.

"And Si?"

I looked over my shoulder.

Freya's stare could have pinned me to the wall. "Keep what I've told you to yourself. This information in the wrong hands could spell disaster for Folkvang."

More secrets. I didn't like it, but I nodded once and made my way out of the hall. I let out a heavy breath as I reached the bridge and looked up at the sky, now blooming with the colors of sunrise.

She was right about one thing. There was plenty in the nine realms I didn't understand and that needed to change. It was time to pay a visit to the stacks once we laid our fallen to rest.

CHAPTER TWENTY-THREE

SIGURD

I PULLED on a fresh pair of trousers after scrubbing all the blood, sweat, and black ooze off my skin from collecting the dead all day. Thankfully, most of the bodies were our enemies, but we lost a handful of our own. To die twice in a lifetime was a curse I hoped to never experience. I could only hope their souls were at peace among the stars.

Grabbing a clean shirt, I threw it over my head and made my way out the door. It was almost sundown and the boats would burn before Sol's chariot dipped below the horizon. It wasn't required that we attend, but I learned long ago that a warrior should never avoid the consequences of war. Once you turn your heart away from death, it's only a matter of time until your humanity follows.

Magnus stepped out of his dwelling a few feet ahead of me. "You heading to the rites?" I called to him.

He nodded and waited for me to catch up.

"So who do you think sent the bastards?" Magnus asked as we started down the dirt path.

"Good question." I'd been pondering the same thing since the moment I left Freya. "Who in the nine realms would risk pissing off, Freya?" I pulled my damp hair back and tied it at the nape of my neck.

"Odin," we said in unison. While Odin was the most likely

candidate based on their history, it just didn't sit right with me. It was too easy.

"But it doesn't seem like his style." Magnus tilted his head from side to side until his neck cracked.

Exactly. Odin was always meticulous, striking hard and true.

"The attack was unfocused, chaotic even," I agreed as flashes of the fight played in my head. "Though there's no doubt they were skilled fighters."

We rounded the corner, and a dozen people were headed in the same direction.

"True, but even the most skilled fighter is worthless, without direction and purpose." Magnus pulled a flask from somewhere on his person and took a sip.

"One of Loki's pranks, maybe?" I suggested, as the path declined and the lake came into view. The sun glistened off the water, and the boats sat on the shoreline, filled with the dead.

"Loki's boredom has led to more chaos than any of the other gods." Magnus offered me his flask, but I waved him off. "I wouldn't put it past him."

"It's possible our defenses were being tested to see how battle ready Folkvang is?" I relished in the notion of fighting to defend my home once more.

"If that's the case, I'd say we passed the test with flying colors." He raised his flask to the sky, then took another swig.

He was right. We handled the attack exceptionally well. Freya's warning that some might see Folkvang as a threat may have some truth to it.

As we reached the shore, I took in the couple dozen boats filled with the dead. Our own men and women were given their own boats and proper rites, but we stacked the enemy to the brim like fish in a barrel.

It looked as if all of Folkvang gathered for the burial rites and to hear Freya speak about the Dragur.

But I didn't care about everyone else.

After the fight, Kara had made herself scarce, and I hadn't the chance to thank her for fighting by my side today. I scanned the crowd. Once, twice, three times I searched the throng of faces, my heart sinking with each pass.

I shouldn't care if she's here or not.

"You coming?" Magnus turned to me when I didn't follow him.

I nodded, and we made our way through the crowd to a spot on the beach near one of the fire pits. Scanning the bystanders again, there she was, standing at the front to my right, about twenty paces away.

Magnus followed my gaze, then turned back to me. "Are we going to talk about you and your Valkyrie?" He wiggled his eyebrows, and I wanted to punch the smirk clear off his face.

"She's not my Valkyrie."

"Yeah, well, I've never seen two people fight like you two before." He took another sip from his flask.

"We trained and fought side by side for many years in Midgard." I folded my arms and tried to think of anything other than her ability to move with me and take a life like she was an extension of me.

"That was more than a lifetime ago." Magnus clapped a hand on my shoulder. "And yet, it looked as if a day hadn't passed since you last fought together."

"Some things you don't forget." I shrugged him off as if his words didn't weigh on me. But since the moment I laid eyes on Kara in the Great Hall, I'd felt heavier, conflicted, and I didn't know how to feel about the effect her presence was having on me.

"I'm sure there's a lot you haven't forgotten." He looked Kara up and down, and the corner of his mouth pulled into a grin that annoyed me.

"Sometimes, you're no better than Ragnar."

Magnus placed a hand on his chest. "You wound me."

186

"You'll survive." I stifled a laugh and shook my head.

"At the risk of courting physical harm, I have to ask. Are you going to talk to her again?"

I fought the churning frustration inside me. "I have nothing else to say to her."

I knew telling them my history with Kara was going to bite me in the ass. Magnus was like a dog with a bone. I just wanted to have one conversation that didn't revolve around her.

"Sounds like bullshit to me."

"Look," I snapped, "we tried talking, and it didn't give me any closure or make things easier." My fists tightened. "Some things are better left alone."

"Maybe." He raised an eyebrow and rested his arm on the hilt of his sword as he looked her over once more.

My eyes found their way back to her as Ezra's arm found its way around her waist. She pressed a hand to his chest as she smiled at something he said. A mix of adrenaline, anger and something that tasted like heartbreak swirled inside me. The last time I felt like this, I was dying in her arms.

Magnus bumped his shoulder against mine and handed me the flask without a word. As Freya placed a trinket in the last of our boats, I took a sip.

"I want to thank each of you for your bravery in battle today," Freya began, and turned toward the crowd. I couldn't help but wonder how much she planned to share with everyone.

A hush fell over us all. The crackling of the fire pits nearby was the only sound until she continued. "Though we have won this fight, I fear the war is far from over."

Whispers moved through the men and women around me.

"The monsters you fought today are called Dragur. They were once much like yourselves." Freya touched the shoulder of the shield maidens closest to her.

"They were soldiers, warriors meant for a life with the

Gods." She moved along the shore like a lion, graceful, full of power, ready to strike.

"It explains their fighting skills," Magnus said under his breath. "But not how they became unhinged."

Guilt at what I knew swirled in my chest as the sound of their animal screams echoed in my head.

"They are not born into the madness you saw today, but created when their soul is consumed." Freya reached Kara, and the two exchanged a glance.

"Their one purpose is to destroy." Freya moved on and I wondered if I was the only one who noticed the silent exchange between her and Kara.

"Their presence in this realm is an omen of what's to come." The flames glistened off Freya's armor as she moved through the crowd toward Magnus and me. "And today's fight won't be your last."

A few men and women whooped, and Freya smiled as the crowd parted around her like a river around a boulder.

"But you were born for this fight, hand picked by me to be here." There were more shouts of excitement, and I could feel my heart racing as her eyes met mine.

She stopped in front of me and placed her hand on my chest. "For when the Old Ones stir," she started, "a heart of flame and soul of steel"—her fingers moved down my arm— "shall stand on the final battlefield."

Her eyes held mine, and she nodded once before moving on.

"Teacher's pet," Magnus grumbled under his breath and I elbowed him in the ribs.

"The Hrafn will oversee our borders from this night forward." She raised her hands to the sky just as the Hrafn flew over us. Midnight black wings with a glint of blue extended well beyond the field we stood in and blocked out the sky above. It was as if night had descended on us in the blink of an eye. Freya's pet circled, and some primal part of me longed for cover where I couldn't be plucked from the beach. As I watched the Hrafn make another circle, it looked down on all of us with an awareness that made me shutter. Flames danced in its inky black eyes, reflecting the fire pits burning on the beach.

Freya made a motion with her hand and the Raven-like creature flapped its wings, kicking up dirt and rocking the boats where they sat in the water.

She turned toward the lake as the sun began its descent behind the mountains. "Now we honor our dead and put the Dragur to rest once and for all." With a wave of her hands, the boats were pushed into the black water.

Looking at each boat now drifting away from us, I took stock of what was lost on this day. Dozens of homes along the river burned to the ground. Blood would stain the streets for weeks to come. But it was the loss of life that would change Folkvang forever. I may not have been close to those that fell, but Folkvang wasn't large enough that you could remain anonymous. Especially when everyone here craves glory. My heart ached for every life lost to the stars. It had been eons since I'd experienced loss on this scale. It was harder than I remembered and I was sure a piece of this day would live inside me until Ragnarok took us all.

Freya raised her arms above her head, and sparks from the fires on the shore rose into the air. The twilight sky filled with tiny embers that glowed against the last sliver of light as they reached the boats and burst into flames.

"I suggest you all get some rest while you can," Freya commanded. She turned without another word and started up the hill. The Hrafn passed over us once more, the wind from its wings rustling the hair on my neck as it disappeared into the night to begin its watch.

Once the last boat drifted to the middle of the lake, the crowd dispersed. There was an electric energy in the air that always followed a battle. For when you are reminded of the end, you appreciate life all the more. It had been a long time since any of us had seen a real fight. And there was nothing more intoxicating than spending the day, heart pumping, muscles burning in a precarious dance with death.

Well, almost nothing.

My eyes skated over Kara's profile just ahead of me. A small, secret smile touched the corner of her mouth. A smile I'd been on the other side of countless times. A flash of her fighting by my side pulsed through me, quickly followed by a flirtatious grin that seduced me into accepting my death. Everything about her was wrapped up in life and death. I couldn't see one without the other.

A sharp pain cascaded down my chest to the scar that had been her doing, and I reached for the wound instinctively.

"Looks like we're finally going to have some fun around here." Ragnar draped his arms over mine and Magnus's shoulders. The shadows in my heart crept back to their hiding place, and I looked away from her.

"Speaking of fun, you owe me a cask," Daiman called back.

"You mean he owes me?" I rolled my shoulder free of Ragnar.

"Si took out half the bridge," Talon chimed in.

"We established he had help." Daiman tossed his head toward Kara. "Which is cheating."

"You would know," I fired back.

"With no clear winner, I'll just have to enjoy the ale myself," Ragnar announced.

"The only thing you'll be enjoying is the end of my blade if you rat out on your end of the deal." Daiman started to pull his sword.

"I think we all deserve a drink after today." Talon's voice caught all our attention, and Daiman sheathed his blade.

"Can't argue with that." Magnus jumped at the idea. "That is, of course, if you're both man enough to admit it was a tie."

I stifled a laugh as the muscle in Daiman's jaw flexed. Reaching out to him, I said, "Draw."

Reluctantly, he placed his hand in mine. "When the Dragur show themselves again, we'll have a rematch."

"I would expect nothing less." I smirked and shook his hand.

"Are we drinking or are guys going to kiss and make up first?" Talon motioned between Damien and me.

"Now that I would give up a cask to see." Ragnar laughed as he motioned for everyone to follow him.

"Only in your dreams." I shook my head.

"Ezra, why don't you join us?" Magnus called after him and Kara.

Traitor.

Kara stiffened, and she squeezed Ezra's hand subtly so only someone watching closely would notice. Gods, that was me, wasn't it?

"I'm going to call it a night," Ezra said. "I've got patrols first light."

"What about you, Kara?" Magnus asked.

She glanced in my direction and pursed her lips. "I have some business I need to take care of."

"You're sure?"

She nodded and waved him off. "Go celebrate your victory, and have a drink for me," she said as I walked past her.

Her eyes met mine for a fraction of a second, and a small stab of guilt pierced through me. She'd fought well today and deserved to celebrate as much as the rest of us.

I opened my mouth to say something, but she averted her eyes and kept moving. She'd been avoiding me since her wing ceremony, and though we fought well together today, it didn't change anything between us. I huffed out a sigh and kept walking. It was for the best that we kept our distance.

CHAPTER TWENTY-FOUR

KARA

EZRA AND I PARTED WAYS, and I walked back to the shore. The rest of the group's laughter and jokes faded as they made their way to toast each other on a successful fight. My heart was an anchor in my chest from all the souls lost today. To die twice in a lifetime is a fate I wouldn't wish on my worst enemies.

As I reached the edge of the lake, a breeze rolled off the water, bringing with it the smell of ash and memories buried deep in my soul. I wrapped my arms around myself as I watched the boats burn. The memory of Sigurd's last rite forced its way to the surface and my heart ached with the memory. I could still feel the chill in the air, still smell the acrid smoke. No amount of time had dulled that memory or the guilt I felt every time he looked at me.

It didn't matter that he was a few feet away now, thriving and happy. Or that we'd fought together again, side by side, like we were one mind in two bodies. The pain of his mortal death, everything I took from him, was a living, breathing thing inside me, an ache like a missing limb I'd learned to live without. But now, with him so close, it was getting harder to ignore the box I'd shoved him into so I could survive.

I let out a shaky breath and rolled my neck from side to side. I felt like I had one foot in the past and one in the present with no idea of how to move forward. How to let go of this ache that had become as familiar to me as the breath in my lungs, the beat of my heart.

One thing I did know, I wouldn't solve anything standing here in the cold. My body throbbed from a long day of fighting and cleaning up the dead. I needed a hot bath, a stiff drink, and a friendly shoulder.

I pulled on the gentle hum of Magik inside me and my wings unfurled from my back effortlessly. Life may be complicated, but at least I had my freedom back. Giving over to the Magik inside me, the nine realms opened up like a favorite book.

"Kara?" A deep, soft voice stopped me just before I stepped into the nowhere and off into the nine realms.

I turned to see who called my name, letting my wings vanish back into my tattoo.

"Magnus?" I looked over his shoulder, but he was alone.

"Going somewhere?" He motioned to where my wings had been a moment earlier.

"I was planning on it. Did you need something?"

"This may be forward." He came to a stop a few feet away. "But I wanted to see if you were okay?"

"I'm fine," I said a little too quickly.

"Fine, isn't good." He raised his eyebrows. There was such a casual easiness about him that I found myself relaxing in his presence.

I let out a heavy sigh. "The burial rite stirred up a lot of things for me."

"Ahh, the life of a warrior." He closed the gap between us and stood next to me, looking out over the water. "The dead often take a toll much larger on the living than they'll ever know."

I hummed under my breath. "It's rare you meet a poet in a fighter."

He placed a hand on his chest. "That's quite the compliment."

"I'm assuming you didn't track me down just to watch the last embers dance on the wind."

"No, though it's not a bad way to end the night." He glanced at me and smiled. I could see why Bryn was so taken with him. He was handsome in a charming way, with his hair pulled back and bright blue eyes. "I know you don't know me, and I should probably leave well enough alone."

"Probably." I folded my arms, but something told me not to push him away. Maybe it was because I wanted a friendly shoulder and instead of Davlin, the Norns placed Magnus in my path.

"But you'll learn soon enough. I don't have a filter and I can't let things go."

"I'm beginning to see that." I tried not to smile. I didn't want to encourage him too much. It was one thing to accept a gesture of friendship, but another thing to let someone open the door to the darkness in my soul.

"You fought well today, but it takes its toll. You should be with people."

I opened my mouth to argue, but he raised his hand to stop me.

"There is time to be alone and time for friends. You have the look of someone who needs to be reminded that their deaths,"—he pointed to the boats— "do not belong to you. You lived today, and that is worth celebrating."

I raised my brow and stared at him. "I get what Sigurd means now."

"Don't believe anything he says. I can almost certainly tell you it's a lie."

I laughed, and he nudged my shoulder with his. "Come join us." His smile reached his eyes and I could already feel myself wanting to give in. *He was good.*

"I promise, we don't bite. Well, except for Ragnar. He's prickly on the best of days." He folded his arms over his chest.

"What about Sigurd? I doubt he wants me to crash his party." I wanted to take him up on his offer, but I also knew Sigurd would be there and I was too exhausted, emotionally and physically, to fight with him again.

"Well then, it's a good thing it's not his party." He offered his elbow. "I didn't take you for the type to hold back out of fear of what someone else might think."

I narrowed my eyes. "Oh, you play dirty." I shook my head and fought the smile threatening to spread across my face as I took his arm.

As much as I wanted to avoid Sigurd, I wouldn't stand here and be labeled a coward.

"Whatever gets the job done." He patted my hand as a smug smile pulled at his lips.

He reminded me so much of Davlin. Saying and doing what was necessary to push me. I could already tell it would be easy to fall into a fast friendship with Magnus. Maybe I wouldn't be so alone here after all.

A couple of hours later and several drinks down, I was feeling more relaxed. Sigurd and I had yet to speak other than a few pleasantries when I first arrived. He'd been surprisingly nice when I showed up on Magnus's arm, almost like he was happy to see me. Maybe not happy, but cordial at the very least.

"So what about you, Ragnar? What's your story?" I asked as Talon refilled my drink.

"I was raised to be a warrior," Ragnar said. "Fought alongside my father and brothers until I made a name for myself."

"Any relation to Ragnar Lothbrok?" I asked.

"Could you imagine?" Daimen scoffed as he sat down next to me. "He'd be insufferable."

"As if he isn't already." Talon rolled her eyes and handed me my stein.

"Though I do not share a bloodline with the man, I share his talent for being in the right place at the right time."

"Tell us again, how did you die, Ragnar?" Sigurd cocked his head to the side, a smug smile pulling at his lips.

I'd be lying if I said his smirk didn't pull on desires I thought long dead. I forced myself to look away from him and took a sip of my drink.

"Aren't we bored with this story?" Ragnar rolled his eyes.

"How'd he die?" I looked around the room and everyone seemed to be in on the joke.

"Come now, Ragnar"—Magnus chuckled as he sat down at the head of the table— "if you don't tell her, one of us will."

"Fine." He emptied his stein and slammed it on the counter behind him. "I was enjoying the love of a good woman." He smirked. "A very good woman."

Talon rolled her eyes, and Daiman chuckled beside me.

"When the village was attacked, I didn't have time for modesty." He looked around the room, as if daring someone to interject with a snide comment.

"I defended her honor and saved as many lives as I could."

"Naked," Magnus interjected.

"Damn right. I left the world the same way I came into it: bare assed and screaming."

I almost spit my drink everywhere as the rest of the group erupted with laughter.

"That must have been quite the sight," I said once I'd regained my composure.

"Would you like a reenactment?" Ragnar wiggled his eyebrows playfully.

"I don't think that will be necessary."

"Your loss, love." He winked.

I looked him up and down. "I highly doubt that."

"She's got you there." Daiman slapped the table and laughed.

"Alright then, Daiman. What's your story?" I turned toward him.

"My story isn't half as amusing as Ragnar's," he started. "I was born in a small village in the Cathay region." He furrowed his brow and shook his head. "You know, I don't remember the name of the village anymore."

"To be fair, you were only six when you were sold into slavery," Sigurd supplied.

My heart sank as I glanced between Sigurd and Daiman.

"When my mother died, there was no one left to care for me," he shrugged.

"I'm so sorry." I placed a hand on his arm. To lose your parents at such a young age was cruel, but to be sold into a life of servitude is a fate no one should suffer.

"It was another life." He waved me off. "I ended up in the Mediterranean around the time Bjorn Ironside started raiding the area. I was fifteen when they made it to my village. I'd learned how to fight in the nine years since I was taken from my homeland. And realized I had a taste for battle." He shrugged. "It came to me easily."

"A born warrior." Talon raised a cup in salute.

"Don't encourage him." Ragnar rolled his eyes. "We wouldn't want to inflate his ego unnecessarily."

"You should talk." Bryn leveled her eyes on Ragnar, and he squirmed under her scrutiny.

"You were saying?" I motioned for Daiman to continue.

"When Bjorn and his men took my village, I fought with them for my freedom, and when it was time for them to head north once more, I went with them. I learned their language, fought alongside them, and grew into the Viking way of life. I reinvented myself as Daiman, far from my home, and survived against all odds."

"That is, of course, until you died," Ragnar pointed out.

He shrugged. "It was on a raid. They ambushed us and the rest is history."

"You chose a Viking death?" I stared at him with a mix of awe and wonder.

"I lived longer as a Norsemen, than anything else. I wanted to be with the people I fought beside, the people who freed me from my chains and gave me the chance to live my life as I saw fit."

"It would seem your loyalty has been paid in kind. Folkvang is only for the most pure of heart."

I glanced up at Sigurd, and our eyes met. His mouth opened slightly, like he might say something, and my heart fluttered. He clamped his mouth shut, his jaw flexing as he looked away, and the spell holding me captive broke.

I cleared my throat. "What about you, Magnus?"

"That's a story you'll have to earn." He winked.

"That's hardly fair, considering you're in everyone else's business." I raised a brow.

Bryn snorted into her drink, and Sigurd chuckled.

"I thought we were friends?" Magnus looked at me with puppy dog eyes and a mischievous grin.

"That's enough history for one night." Ragnar tossed a pouch on the table and rune stones spilled over the wood surface.

"You think your ego can handle losing another game?" Talon shot Ragnar a look as she took a seat across from me.

"I didn't lose the last one. We were interrupted."

"Whatever helps you sleep at night." Talon smirked.

"What's the game?" I looked around for an explanation. It's been ages since I've played a drinking game and even longer since I'd played with my kin.

"We'll each pick a rune without looking." Daiman started flipping over the stones in the middle of the table.

"Without looking at the stone, we'll all drain our cups." Magnus topped off my mug.

"The first one to finish their drink calls out the name of a rune," Sigurd said, as he took a seat next to Talon.

"The person in possession of said rune has to come up with a riddle, recite a ballad, or insult another player, to the delight of the group." Talon bumped her shoulder against Sigurd as she finished explaining the game.

"What happens if the group isn't delighted?" I asked.

"You drink another cup."

"And how exactly does one win this game?"

"Last man standing, of course," Ragnar chuckled.

"Or woman," Bryn corrected.

"Sounds easy enough." I'd spent more hours than I cared to admit firing insults at Davlin over the last few years. This should be a piece of cake.

"You say that now,"—Magnus leaned closer— "but this lot are brutal."

Ragnar pushed the stones around in circles until they were thoroughly mixed, then instructed each of us to take one.

"Skal." Ragnar raised his cup and everyone drank. I almost felt guilty for drinking such sweet ale without tasting it.

"Isa," Talon blurted as she slammed her cup down.

Flipping our stones over, Magnus chuckled.

"There once was a lass, now don't be crass. She fell for a man, and his bare ass." He shook Ragnar by the shoulder.

"To her dismay, he couldn't pay, and alas, she dumped him in the bay. Shrunken and shriveled, he mounted a horse, what was his name, well Ragnar, of course." Magnus tipped his empty cup toward Ragnar as he finished.

Everyone laughed and seemed delighted enough that Magnus didn't have to down another drink.

"Your obsession with my backside is truly frightening." Ragnar threw his stone back into the middle of the table and we all did the same.

Bryn flipped the tiles over and mixed them in lazy circles. She picked the first stone, followed by the rest of us.

"Skal." Bryn raised her cup, and I rushed to finish my drink.

"Wunjo," Sigurd yelled, and wiped droplets from his beard.

Flipping our stones over, Talon smirked and rubbed her hands together.

"The only thing more toxic than a troll's feet is Magnus and Bryn's relationship."

Ragnar threw his head back and laughed. Sigurd snickered, and Daiman choked on his drink. Bryn pulled a face at Talon, but it was clear she wasn't all that offended.

"Yeah, yeah, like any of you are the picture of a happy and healthy relationship." Magnus threw his stone into the middle of the table and pulled Bryn against his side. "At least we won't be going home alone tonight."

"I've got a round of drinks that says you don't make it another hour without irritating each other." Ragnar threw his tile into the middle of the table.

"You're on." Bryn grabbed Magnus by the shirt and pulled him in for a kiss.

Daiman whistled and Ragnar rolled his eyes as Talon shuffled the tiles.

The game continued and with each round, the insults grew more personal and the riddles turned into inside jokes. They knew how to get under each other's skin, much like siblings. Each time I thought someone had gone too far, they all erupted with laughter, refilled our cups, and continued playing.

After more ale than I cared to think about, my head was spinning, and I was pretty sure if I had a drop more, I wouldn't be able to walk home. "I think it's time to call it a night."

"Don't go." Talon reached across the table. "They should start dropping like flies any minute."

"Like Hel am I letting you win again." Ragnar leveled his eyes at Talon, but the glassy look on his face said otherwise.

I pushed to my feet. "I need to get some sleep if I'm going to have any chance of beating you in drills tomorrow."

"There isn't enough sleep in the nine realms that'll give you a chance of outdoing me." Talon smirked.

"We'll see about that."

I wished everyone a good night and made my way to leave. Stepping out into the night, I closed the door behind me and took a deep breath of fresh air. Somehow, Sigurd and I had made it through the night without arguing or talking about the past. Though we said little, it was still progress.

The tension melted out of my shoulders as I pushed away from the door. If we couldn't be friends, at least we could be cordial. I'd have to thank Magnus for convincing me to join them, even if it meant admitting his meddling was worth it.

Leaving the bustling city center behind, I walked along the north side of the river in the general direction of my place. The stars reflected in the dark water, making it look like a piece of the sky had fallen at my feet. There was something magical about seeing the stars flicker and wobble in the water like they were alive.

I looked away from the river and plopped onto the grass with a huff. Leaning back, I stared up at the stationary stars and thought of everyone who joined them tonight.

Settling into the grass, I listened to the white noise of the water rushing over rocks. It was nights like these that I'd missed most. Good friends, a beautiful night, and the sounds of Folkvang. Tiny pieces of my soul felt alive, and I was starting to realize I just might be able to live again. I closed my eyes and listened to the music that carried from somewhere in the city. Just a few minutes, I told myself, and then I'd head home.

201

CHAPTER TWENTY-FIVE

SIGURD

SHORTLY AFTER KARA LEFT, I took my leave as well. The others would most likely continue their celebration well into the early hours of the morning, but I wanted to hit the stacks first thing and see what else I could learn about the Disir and the Dragur creatures.

I followed the path along the river, needing the longer walk to work out some of the tension that had built over the last few hours. Spending an evening with Kara and my friends, the way she fit in so well with everyone, reminded me of why I fell in love with her.

And after what I witnessed her go through during the wing ceremony, it was hard to hold on to the anger that had festered and grown into a life of its own over the years. But letting go of the past and forgiving her was proving to be far more difficult than I imagined.

Is that what I wanted? To forgive her?

I didn't have a straightforward answer, but for the first time when I thought about her, the memory of her killing me wasn't the first thing that came to mind. Instead, it was how she laughed with Magnus, the brutality of the wing ceremony, the way she fought alongside me.

As I came up to the bridge that led to the other side of the river, I noticed someone lying in the grass, and I stepped closer.

It wasn't uncommon for someone to find their bed too far of a trek, especially after a night when all of Folkvang was celebrating.

Deep red hair cascaded around her head like a halo and with her hands resting on her chest, she looked far more like the people in the boats than a warrior resting and my heart lurched.

"Kara?" I called to her before my brain even had a chance to think about what I was doing. *What was I doing?*

I should leave well enough alone. We'd made it through the night unscathed.

She sat up on her elbows and looked at me with a lazy smile. She was intoxicated and her usual sharp edges were softer. From the drink or the moonlight, I couldn't be sure.

"Too much to drink?" I sidled closer and took a seat on the grass next to her.

"Never." She closed her eyes and let her head fall back, a serene smile touching her full lips. "I'm just taking a break." She took a deep breath, her breasts rising and falling and despite myself, my eyes caught on the motion.

"A break from ...?" I rested my arms on my knees and forced my eyes to behave by looking out over the water.

"Life," she sighed.

"That bad, huh?" I glanced at her.

"It's exhausting." She settled into the grass once more.

"Is it hard being back after all this time?" I lay back and turned to look at her.

She rolled her head to the side and as her eyes met mine, realization flitted across her face. Her lax features sharpened every so slightly, as if it just hit her she was sharing with me.

Guilt pierced through my chest as if the Gods had fired an arrow right through me. Again, I hadn't considered what it must be like for her. To have her life shift and change completely from one day to the next. My adjustment to Folkvang wasn't as smooth as others, and for the first time, I wondered what it must have been like for her. Did she suffer? Did she step into her new life with ease? Did she fall apart like I did?

"It's different." She fiddled with the chain around her neck. "I —well, I'm still adjusting," her gaze fell from mine.

"Is it so different from what you remember?" Free from her gaze, my eyes skated over her as a breeze tossed a few strands of hair around her face.

"Memory's a tricky thing." A short, dry chuckle escaped her throat. "So much of what I remember of the nine realms is colored by the person I used to be, and now... well, I'm not sure my memories hold the same value they once did." She looked back up at me with wide, honest eyes.

It had always been that way between us. Truth at all costs, no judgment.

Until that day.

"I don't buy that." I wasn't sure if it was the drink, fighting beside her in battle, or the starlight above us, but something in me softened as I watched her. "You may have changed, but your memories don't lose value because you're seeing them through fresh eyes." Her eyes dipped to my lips, to my neck, before she looked up at me again.

I swallowed and glanced away. Her gaze was far too intimate, and she was far too drunk even if... No. There was no point in going down that road. Even if I could forgive her, even if my body reacted to her, it didn't change one simple thing. I didn't trust her.

"Two truths?" The words barely escaped her lips.

"Okay."

My heart raced. We used to play this game when we needed to get something off our chest and didn't know how to say it.

"You first," we said in unison, and a small chuckle escaped my throat.

"Fine, I'll go first," she said, looking up at the stars and closing her eyes. "I miss Davlin." Her lips pulled into a tight smile.

"Who's Davlin?"

"A friend, in Midgard. He always had a way of saying what I needed to hear without me having to ask." She shook her head and sighed.

"Sounds like he knew you well." I folded an arm behind my head as a pang of jealousy I had no right to fluttered over my heart.

"He did—does," she frowned.

"Can you not visit him? Now that you have your wings once more?"

She nodded. "I was going to before Magnus stopped me and strong-armed me into celebrating with you all tonight."

A chuckle rumbled through my chest. "I warned you. He's a menace."

"I like him. He cares. Even about me when he doesn't know me."

"He doesn't have to know you. It's just his nature. He leaves no one behind, even when they want to be left."

She laughed under her breath and the sound warmed my heart.

"Davlin's like that. Doesn't take no for an answer. Shoves his nose where it doesn't belong. But in the end, somehow it ends up being the right thing."

"Whatever you do, don't tell Magnus that. You give him any encouragement and he will try to run your life."

"Someone else making all the decisions sounds pretty great right about now." She stared up at the stars with a wistful look.

"Trust me, it's not."

"Your turn." She knocked her knee against mine.

I let out a heavy sigh. "I fear Freya is holding back about the Dragur." My eye met hers and she frowned.

"Why do you think that?"

"Just a gut feeling." After what she shared with me and everyone else at the rites, I was sure she was leaving something essential out.

"From what I remember." She propped herself up on her elbow and leaned toward me. "Your instincts were never wrong."

"Almost never." My gaze dipped to her lips, needing a reprieve from her looking down at me. It would be too easy to close the distance between us. Too easy to fall into a rhythm our bodies had once been accustomed to.

"So you still think you were wrong about me?" She frowned and leaned away.

I reached for her arm, stopping her retreat. "I don't know." When she didn't pull out of my grasp, I continued, "It's what I was trying to tell you the other night." I reached up and tucked a loose strand of hair behind her ear, letting my hand linger longer than I should before dropping it to my chest. "Fighting by your side today, seeing you with my friends, my family, it's reminded me of a different side of you."

She sucked in a breath and her body inched closer. Whether it was on purpose or just the nature of our conversation that drew her in, I had no idea. And I realized I didn't care. Because either way, she was here, talking to me like we used to before everything went to Hel.

CHAPTER TWENTY-SIX

KARA

My heart raced as he stared at me. Every cell in my brain screamed at me to put some distance between us. But the way his eyes held mine, the truths we were sharing called to a different, more primal part of me. It had always been that way with him. This undeniable pull that was an answer to some ancient question only my soul was aware of.

"Your turn." His voice was like a caress.

"I'm…" I hesitated, not wanting to say the words aloud. We were in this delicate little bubble of peace, and I didn't want to pop it by bringing up the past. But two truths wasn't about what was convenient or easy, so I closed my eyes and sighed. "I'm afraid of what the Norns might say."

"The Norns? You made a request?" His eyes widened as he studied my face.

I nodded. "After we talked—the first time—you said something that stuck with me."

"I didn't realize my words would have such an effect on you." He pursed his lips.

"I may not have wanted to hear it, but you were right about me giving up on finding the truth, and that's not the person I am. I want to know what happened that day. Why I…" I couldn't say the words, so instead I placed my hand on his chest. He stiffened at my touch, but didn't pull away.

A few seconds passed, and when he said nothing, my stomach hollowed.

"You don't know what happened, do you?" His voice was soft, as if for the first time he might actually believe me.

With my heart in my throat, I shook my head. Being this close to him, the warmth of him under my fingers, it was making my head spin.

"You said you're afraid. What is it that scares you?" He looked up at me and his brow furrowed.

I pulled my hand back, needing the space between us, and rolled onto my back. "Freya seems to think I did it because I wanted power." I shook my head. "But I've never craved power, especially not at the expense of anyone."

"But you're worried she might be right?"

The story Freya told me about the first Valkyrie flittered to the surface of my mind. Could it be that simple? Magik gone wrong?

I shrugged. "I have no idea. It could be that, or it could be something far worse. I think not knowing has given me a sense of security for a long time. I got used to not having the answer, and it was easier than facing the truth, whatever it might be."

"That's no way to live." His voice was almost sympathetic, and it tugged at the feeling creeping out of my heart.

"Which is why I made the request to the Norns at Freya's suggestion, since she doesn't have a clue either."

Si made a noise under his breath, forcing me to look at him again.

"What?"

"It's interesting that you say Freya is clueless about the truth."

"Why?" I turned toward him. Whether it was because I was curious what he had to say or just because I missed this kind of intimacy with someone, I couldn't be sure.

"She summoned me after your return. She told me I should hear you out and implied that not everything is what it seems." He turned to me. "I got the feeling she knew why it happened and believed you were worth forgiving." His eyes searched mine, and it took every shred of sanity I had left not to close the distance between us.

Instead, I asked, "She asked you to forgive me?"

"Not in so many words, but yes." His eyes met mine, and if I hadn't known better, I'd have said he was struggling to come up with a reason not to take her advice. Or maybe I was just projecting my own feelings onto him.

"If she believed I was some power hungry monster, why tell you something else?"

He shrugged. "Either it's what we each needed to hear to push us into action. Or she knows more than she's letting on." His eyes narrowed, and he ran a hand through his hair.

"You seem very aware of her motivations." I cocked an eyebrow at him.

"She's a general. I understand the way her mind works better than most."

"I bet you do," I teased. The way he spoke of Freya, it was clear there was some sort of intimacy between them.

He propped himself up on his arm and looked down at me.

"That sounds an awful lot like jealousy." His eyes crinkled and his lips twitched into a crooked grin.

"That would imply that I care." I fought to keep the smile from my lips as my heart raced. *Did I care?*

"Don't you, though? Why else would you resort to making a request of the Norns?"

With his body so close, I could feel the heat of him through our clothes, and my fingers itched to touch him.

I shouldn't have indulged so much tonight. The ale was making me reckless and giving my body way too much control.

"Just because I care about the truth, doesn't mean I care who you sleep with." I forced the words from my mouth.

"Who said anything about sex?" His eyes dipped to my lips and lingered long enough that my next breath was a shaky one.

I groaned internally. How did we get here? I'd accepted that avoiding him at all costs was the best option, and now I couldn't remember why.

I sat up and he followed my movement so we were only inches apart. His chest rose and fell just as quickly as mine, and the warmth of his breath on my face made almost every thought fall out of my head.

I forced myself to focus on anything but sex and pushed the frustrated energy building inside me into the deepest pit of my soul. "No one. Forget I said anything."

His lips curved at the corner of his mouth, and the embers inside me sparked once more. "Alright." He sat back, creating more space between us, and I breathed a sigh of relief. "What are you going to do if the Norns don't accept your request?"

"Talon and I are looking into it." I sighed, grateful for the change in the subject.

"And what's your working theory?"

"I believe Magik was involved. Though I don't know why someone would want to kill you." I kept my eyes on the river in front of us. No longer trusting my body.

"Maybe it wasn't about me."

"What do you mean?" His words caught me off guard. How could his death not be about him?

"It's possible, if your theory proves to be true and Magik is to blame, I could have been collateral damage and you were the target."

"To what end?" I turned to face him.

"Your guess is as good as mine." He shrugged. "Hopefully, the Norns can shed some light."

"If they agree to see me," I said under my breath. "My request may not be worth their time." I settled into the grass once more with a huff, and we both fell silent.

He lay next to me, staring up at the stars in peaceful silence. Whether he knew I needed it or he needed it for himself, I didn't care. I was just grateful that he wasn't pushing me or asking questions I didn't have a satisfying answer to.

After a few minutes, he sat up. "As nice as it is out here, I promise you'll regret it in the morning if you stay here all night." He stood and offered his hand.

I sat up and smiled at him. "Have much experience sleeping outside, do you?"

"Let's just say I've lost more than my fair share of bets, and the bugs can be ruthless."

I placed my hand in his. The warmth of his touch sent a spark down my torso. He pulled me to my feet. The only thing between us was our clasped hands. I looked up at him, his dark brown eyes pulling me in like a siren song. My lips parted and he let go of my hand, but we stayed rooted to the spot as if stuck in a trance.

"You haven't told me your second truth." My words were barely a whisper between us.

He brushed my hair over my shoulder and cupped my face. "My second truth..." his eyes searched mine as if he was fighting a war inside himself. "I don't hate you." His hand slipped down my shoulder and over my arm, sending a shiver down my spine and shattering the last shred of control I was holding on to.

"What changed?" I leaned into his touch, and he stiffened, taking a step back.

"I can be angry with you, and still hurting, but that doesn't mean I hate you." He took another step back and a small smile pulled at his lips. "I'm glad you came tonight." He turned and walked away without another word.

"Me too," I sighed as I watched him leave.

As I started toward my place, the wind picked up and a bird

squawked overhead. I gripped my shoulder where he'd touched me and let out a shaky breath. One of the many cracks in my heart fused back together and, for the first time in a long while, I let myself hope the past wouldn't have its talons wrapped around me for all eternity.

CHAPTER TWENTY-SEVEN

KARA

I WOKE UP, and immediately my stomach lurched. I rushed to the bathroom and emptied the contents of my stomach. I couldn't even remember the last time I threw up from drinking. What in the name of the Runes was in that stuff Ragnar served?

Holding the side of my head, trying to ease the heartbeat in my temples, I made my way to the sink. As I reached for the tap, my eyes caught on the dirt caked to my cuticles. No, not dirt, blood. I checked my body for any signs of a fresh injury, but there was nothing except a bruise across my ribs from a well-placed kick during battle yesterday.

I didn't know where the blood had come from. I'd scrubbed my skin raw after we'd cleared all the bodies. It wasn't possible for my nails to still have blood under them, was it? My skin crawled, and without another thought, I jumped into the shower.

I scrubbed my nails clean first, then moved on to the rest of my body. A sinking feeling settled in the pit of my stomach. What if I hurt someone again and don't remember? No. I wouldn't jump to conclusions. I stepped under the water, and let it refresh my clammy skin. *It's not happening again.* I reassured myself and let the anxiety drip off my skin and down the drain. I was in a rush to get to the burial rites. It was more than likely I didn't get every drop of blood. It felt like a lie, but still eased some of my guilt. At first light, I'd inquire if anyone was missing or hurt after the rite last night. And if everyone was accounted for, then I'd known for sure I was being paranoid.

I closed my eyes and the heat of the water warmed the chill in my soul. I tried to think about every minute of last night, if there was any time missing or anything that felt out of place. But there were no gaps in my memory. That was one small victory, at least.

The image of Si, laying next to me by the river, surfaced in my mind and my stomach dipped. Now that I didn't have a copious amount of liquid courage surging through me, I felt like an idiot for the way my body had reacted. I'd practically thrown myself at him and chased him off. What the Hel was I thinking? We'd barely had a civil conversation before last night, and even if he was trying to see things differently. That didn't mean he'd want to jump into bed with me.

I don't hate you. Those husky words echoed in my head, and my heart squeezed.

Maybe he was starting to feel differently about me. Is that what I wanted? For him to look at me the way he used to? No. Not when I was still uncertain of what was happening to me. If I killed again, I didn't want him or anyone else near me.

I shut off the water and wrapped a towel around myself. I made my way to the sink to brush my teeth when my eyes snagged on the Runes glowing on my arm. A sharp sting of fear pierced through my chest and my stomach rolled as if I was going to throw up again.

The Norns had accepted my request.

I rushed into the bedroom and threw a loose shirt over my head and shoved my legs into a pair of trousers. The last thing I needed was to astral project to them naked. My heart raced as I looked down at my arm and grazed my fingers over the mark. The four Runes were inky black, similar to a tattoo, but the Magik that created them gave them a soft glow.

Placing my hand over the Runes, I closed my eyes and felt myself leave my body.

I opened my eyes and took in my surroundings. I was in my home back in Midgard. A table sat in the middle of the room and the small trinkets I'd once collected filled the shelves across from me. A fire was lit in the corner, but the flames didn't make a sound, nor did they provide any warmth.

I knew this was only happening in my mind, but something about being back here made me want to run out the door. The walls held too many memories of the hundred years I suffered without the nine realms. It was my home, yes, but also my prison, and now that I was free, it was hard to look at the life I suffered through.

"Well, well, well." Three distinct voices said in unison behind me, and I stiffened.

"If it isn't Kara the Lost." One of them stepped around me.

"Come to find answers you're not even sure you want." The second one trailed a finger along my shoulders, sending goosebumps down my arms as they stepped in front of me.

The third joined the other two. "You've had an extraordinary journey that's led you to us."

Their waist length onyx hair sat unnaturally still. Intricate gold masks adorned each of their faces with their corresponding Rune. Dread trickled down my spine as three pairs of black eyes bore into me. My bones went cold. Tiny points of light blinked to life in their eyes like stars on a midnight canvas, and I shivered.

My last encounter with them had left me with a healthy dose of fear that I didn't need or want to ever experience again. But here I was.

"It's an honor to meet you again." I inclined my head, needing a reprieve from their predatory gaze.

"I believe the honor is all ours." Skuld stepped forward, their eyes sparkling to life with all the possibilities of the future as they approached me.

"For when the Disir stir," Skuld circled around me. "A heart of flame," they twirled a braid in my hair around their finger and tugged ever so slightly. "And soul of steel," their finger slithered down my arm as they stopped in front of me, their face was inches from mine. "Shall stand on the final battlefield." Their breath bit into my skin like a winter breeze.

It was the same thing Freya had said during the burial rites.

I did my best not to bristle as they gripped my arm and twisted so the runes on my skin faced up. With a grin that promised pain, they ran a long, razor sharp nail down the tattoo still glowing on my skin. Each rune came to life, sliding down my arm, following the trail of their nail until the runes met at my wrist and formed a new symbol altogether.

"The Sigil of Enlightenment," they purred.

"How very intriguing." Urd stepped forward. Their knowledge of the past was unparalleled. "You seek more than answers: you want truth." Their head cocked from one side to the other like a bird as they stared at me.

"Are answers not the same as the truth?" I asked hesitantly.

Urd blinked several times as if deciding I wasn't worth killing. "You can answer a question to satisfaction while still concealing the truth. But that is not what your soul has called us here to do. There is much of which you are unaware." A smile brushed over their lips for a split second. "Much has been hidden from you in plain sight." The stars shifted in their eyes, and my stomach squirmed.

"Will you tell me?" I kept my voice void of emotion. If they knew how much this mattered to me, they'd toy with me and prolong this visit.

Verdandi, the keeper of the present, looked in my direction, their eyes snapping toward me like a predator catching the scent of fresh blood. "The truth you so desperately seek"—

something like disgust simmered under the current of their voice— "is bound with another's fate."

"Sigurd?" I choked out.

Verdandi nodded, and stars swirled in their eyes. "And you think it's fair for us to tell you what we know without the other present?" They held my gaze like a challenge.

I swallowed past the lump in my throat. "I understand it's his past too, but the truth I seek is my own." My heartbeat echoed in my ears.

Skuld laughed, deep and haunting, making the hair on the back of my neck rise. "Poor child, there is no truth you can glean here that belongs solely to you."

If they weren't going to answer my questions, why accept my request?

"We do not need to justify why we called you here. Whether or not you get the truth you seek," Skuld said, answering my thoughts.

"My apologies." I lowered my head. "I didn't mean—"

"We wouldn't waste our time if we didn't deem this visit worthy," Verdandi sneered and their Magik crackled around me, setting my teeth on edge. I reminded myself they could end me with a snap of their fingers.

"Tell me what happened that day?" I hated how meek my voice sounded. "Why did I kill him?"

Skuld stepped forward and grabbed my face, forcing me to look up at them. "You will share with Sigurd what we deliver unto you, no matter your feelings on the matter?" They sneered on the word "feelings" as if the idea of emotions was disgusting.

My stomach churned and chills ran down my arms and legs as I nodded. Their eyes went milky white and their grip on my face tightened. Their nails bit into my cheeks and tears sprung to my eyes. I stiffened and swallowed down the whimper building in my chest.

Skuld's long nail dug deeper and a trickle of blood dripped

down my cheek. Images flashed in their pearl-like eyes as I stared up at them, unable to look away.

A scream echoed in my head. Steel clashed. The coppery tang of blood filled my nose, and bile rose to the back of my throat. My body went rigid and my heart raced until it fluttered in my chest like the wings of a bee.

Just as I thought I couldn't take anymore, Skuld's eyes cleared, and they released my face. "The course is set." They turned back to the others. "We may proceed."

The shadows in the room moved away from the walls, curling around us like smoke.

"What's happening?" I gripped my chair, afraid to move, afraid to sit still.

"Let the Magik take you, girl," Urd commanded.

I sucked in a breath as the darkness closed in around me and the room vanished in wisps of smoke. Every breath was an effort to take as the darkness gave way to a battlefield.

Si turned toward me as the shadows cleared around him. He reached for me and a glint of silver caught my eye. A dagger. I watched as I stepped into the circle of his arms.

Oh, Gods. My blood turned to ice.

Si pulled me in for a kiss, and I plunged the dagger into his chest.

A tear trailed down my cheek as they made me watch what happened that day.

He looked at me, pained, confused, and that's when I saw my face, hollow and devoid of all emotion. A thin line of silver colored the outside of my iris, just like Talon described.

Si dropped to his knees, and I followed him to the ground. There was a glow behind my eyes that was familiar when a worthy soul called to me, but it looked different this time. Like something or someone else was propelling me forward.

"Freya said I wanted to kill Si for power," I spoke into the shadows.

"A lie wrapped in a version of the truth."

Pain shot through my heart, and I was grateful I'd already emptied my stomach before arriving here.

The darkness returned once more, curling around me, and the scene vanished. I couldn't move, couldn't think as three sets of galaxy eyes settled on me.

"When you ended his life, it was a sacrifice against what is written," Skuld said

"You were never meant to kill Sigurd," Urd finished.

"So it was Magik, then?" I couldn't help the hope that coated my words.

"Yes," they said in unison.

"Why? Why would someone want me to kill him?" It didn't make sense. Nothing was gained from his death, only loss and heartbreak.

"That's the wrong question."

"They didn't want to kill him." I measured out each word to make sure I understood what they were saying. "They wanted me?"

"His death was a necessary byproduct of the spell you were under," Verdandi said. "They needed you to kill a warrior meant for the Gods with love in your heart."

"So Si was right?" Anger filled my throat. "He was just a pawn?" I slammed my hand against the table.

All three of them nodded.

"Why, for what purpose?" I demanded.

"To bring back the Old ones." Skuld's voice was soft and solemn.

"The first Valkyrie." Urd placed a hand on Skuld's shoulders.

"The Disir as they've come to be known," Verdandi finished.

I shook my head. "The first Valkyrie perished in battle long before I was born."

"Gone yes, but never dead." Skuld leveled their eyes at me. "The Gods hid the truth with a careful lie to protect the nine realms. But the time of deception is over."

ALLISON SIPE

I was afraid to ask, but I was here for answers. "And what is the truth about them?"

"They were monsters that craved power above all else." Urd stepped forward.

"They grew strong," Skuld said, "too strong. Destroying everything in their path. Creating an army unlike anything the nine realms have seen before or since."

"They almost killed the Gods, until Freya stopped them, turned them to stone," Verdandi finished.

The way they each finished each other's thoughts made my head spin.

"So the Disir..." I couldn't bring myself to give them the same name I carried. "They live again because I killed Sigurd?"

"No, it takes much more than one life."

"How many lives?" Fear poured into me. I didn't want to know.

"One with love in your heart."

"One out of hatred."

"One to right a wrong."

"One for justice."

They took turns naming them off. Each one sent my head reeling.

"One that ends suffering."

"One who is innocent."

"One who requests it."

"And one who was never meant to be."

"Eight?" My heart broke. "Eight lives must be sacrificed for this ritual?" I exhaled a shaky breath.

"One life for each of theirs," Skuld clarified.

I blew out a breath. "Okay, how do we stop them from using others to kill?"

All three of them shook their heads.

"It's not others that they are using." Urd's lips formed a hard line.

"One must complete eight." Skuld's gaze pierced through me. I wanted to scream. "You're talking about me?"

Skuld nodded.

"Okay, simple enough. I won't kill anyone and the Disir can stay dead or frozen in stone wherever they are."

"My dear lost one. Just like with Sigurd, you have no control or memory of the deaths."

"Deaths?" The word rang through me.

"Six have already been sacrificed by your hand."

My body jolted as if someone had kicked me in the chest.

"Six?" The word barely left my mouth as the room started to spin. "I've killed six in the name of waking the Disir?"

The three of them nodded.

"I don't understand." The realization hit me like a tidal wave. "I've still been under their control? Doing their bidding. This whole time."

"Not the whole time. After you killed Si and Odin punished you, the path to their awakening halted until you returned to the nine realms."

"Why?"

"We assume the individual pulling the strings thought you dead as the rest of the universe did." Verdandi picked up a shell from my shelf of keepsakes. "Without trying, Odin put a stop to their plan by hiding you from everyone."

"It's something they didn't expect, which means they are not infallible. And they can be stopped." Skuld smiled, but it looked like it pained them.

"Why me?"

They looked at each other, and an uncomfortable silence bloomed between them. "We can't answer that." Urd spoke for the three of them.

"Can't or won't?"

"You wanted to know why you killed Sigurd and we've told you."

"Killing Si is only half the story." My blood boiled, and I gripped the arms of the chair. "But you knew that." I looked between the three of them and they said nothing. I should have been more careful about how I phrased my request. But how was I supposed to know this was something bigger than just me and Si?

"I have to tell Freya." I got to my feet. "Maybe she can find a way to stop them. Stop me." I was the problem.

"Absolutely not." A star burst in Skuld's eyes and energy crackled over my skin. "To tell the Gods is to bring Ragnarok upon us."

"Be selective with who you trust outside of Sigurd," Urd warned.

Something clicked in my brain. "Because he has a part to play in all this still?"

They nodded.

"But you won't tell me what?"

They shook their heads and started their retreat. "It's for him to come to on his own. We cannot interfere." I could see the window through Urd and realized they were vanishing. "You have a long journey ahead of you. Stay true to who you are, for there will be many temptations that could spell the end for all of us."

I nodded as they faded into nothing, and I was released. I collapsed onto my knees in my living room in Folkvang. I slammed my fist against the floor. How could they accept my request, knowing they'd only tell me half the story? I may have gotten the truth about Si, but I had more questions than ever.

A chill ran down my spine and I could have sworn the shadows moved. I jumped to my feet and rushed out the door. I didn't want to be alone in case I was summoned to kill. And I needed to find Si, tell him the truth, and pray to Yemir that he believed me.

CHAPTER TWENTY-EIGHT

SIGURD

I CLOSED the book in my lap and sat back in the leather chair. I'd read the same page five times and not a single word stuck. I couldn't stop thinking about Kara lying by the river with her heart on her sleeve. My chest tightened, and I wondered if she regretted our conversation last night, how close we were. The image of her face inches from mine, those green eyes like a meadow I wanted to lie down in.

I wiped a hand over my face as my heart picked up in tempo. My body was the ultimate betrayer. Even if I understood that she'd suffered the last century, it didn't change that I couldn't trust her. I'd always be looking over my shoulder, always wondering if she'd lose herself again. It didn't matter that my body reacted to her. It could never be the way it once was, even if I wanted it to be.

Did I want it to be like it was?

I looked up and found Talon waving someone over. When I turned to see who it was, my heart leapt. It was as if my thoughts had conjured her. Kara looked like she had gotten little sleep. Considering the way I found her last night, I was surprised to see her up and out of bed during the first half of the day.

"You look like you woke up on the wrong side of the bed."

Talon's gaze shot to me and back to Kara. Without a word, I knew she was accusing me of Kara's sleepless night.

"It's been a long night or morning." Kara shook her head and wiped a hand over her face.

"Oh, do tell." Talon sat forward, resting her chin in her hands.

"Can I talk to you, actually?" She turned to me, ignoring Talon.

"Uh, sure." I stood a little too quickly, and Talon looked between the two of us.

"Did something happen between you two?" Talon moved to the edge of her seat.

"Leave it Talon." I shot her a glance as I motioned for Kara to lead the way.

Without so much as a glance backward, Kara made her way toward the racks at the far end of the library. I followed, wondering if this had to do with last night. We'd both had too much to drink and neither of us was thinking clearly, but considering nothing happened, I didn't think she'd be this upset. Unless she was upset that something didn't happen?

She looked down the aisle we passed. Right, then left. Then the next aisle—right, then left.

Skitr, I cursed internally. This couldn't be good if she was making sure we were alone.

Right, then left. All the way to the last stack when she turned right and disappeared down the aisle. I followed her, and she was already pacing back and forth in the small space.

"Was it necessary to drag me all the way down here just to tell me off?"

She paused and looked up at me. "Tell you off?" Her eyebrows knit together and she cocked her head to the side.

I ran a hand through my hair and shifted on my feet. "For last night?"

"Last night?" She drew out each word as if trying to remember what I was talking about.

Ouch. Maybe it was all in my head. "Things got a little familiar and if we crossed a line—"

"Considering I've had your mouth all over my body in the past, I hardly think a few stolen glances could be considered crossing a line." She shook her head. "Besides, this has nothing to do with that."

Heat coursed through me as a memory of her laid out before me, my lips on her bare skin, jumped to the forefront of my mind. "Then what is it?" My voice came out huskier than I meant it to, and her eyes caught mine for a fraction of a second.

"I saw the Norns this morning," she said deadpan.

"Oh." Her words doused the lustful memory and sharpened my focus. "That's why you look—"

"Like shit?" A dry laugh escaped her throat. "Yeah."

"And you're here to tell me what they said?" I tried not to sound hopeful. When she told me she'd made a request of the Norns, I didn't allow myself to hope that she would share what they said.

She nodded. "It's your past too." Emotions flashed across her face that I couldn't place and her lips tightened into a frown that was almost a smile.

"What did they say?" I swallowed. Why was I nervous? The damage had already been done. Knowing the why wasn't going to change anything.

She leaned against the rack to my right and pinched the bridge of her nose.

"It's much more complicated than I ever imagined." She shook her head. "I'd always thought someone was being vindictive or cunning in taking you out and using me to do it." Her eyes danced back and forth as I closed the distance between us and leaned against the opposite stack, facing her. "But this is far, far worse."

I met her eyes and a mixture of fear and heartbreak stared back at me.

"Magik played a part," she said after breaking our gaze. "It's why I have no memory of the act." She laced her fingers together.

"I sense a but." I folded my arms, needing some small barrier over my chest as my heart lurched.

She looked up, her eyes glassy and bloodshot. "But you were right. It wasn't entirely about killing you."

"They wanted you?" The realization hit me like a tidal wave. "For what?" My ears started to ring. Someone had used Kara and killed me for some sick game.

"Not for what, but for *who*." Her head fell back against the stack, and she let out a breath.

Her words barely registered as the pain, frustration, and anger building inside me all these years surfaced. "So I was just collateral? A pawn in someone's game?" I ground my teeth.

She shook her head. "Not exactly." She swallowed. "It had to be you." She looked up at me through her lashes, and tears sparkled in her eyes.

I had to fight every nerve in my body to stay quiet and let her take her time telling me. She took another breath and looked up at the ceiling as if she was trying to force the tears back into her eyes. "It had to be you because the Magik demanded a soul meant for the Gods."

"I wasn't the only one meant for the Gods." I tried to keep the bite out of my voice. I wanted to hear everything she had to say and showing my anger would only lead to her shutting down.

"No, you weren't." She bit her bottom lip and looked at me. "But you were the only one I loved."

I squeezed my eyes shut as a sharp pain shot across my chest. I was killed because she loved me? What kind of sick joke was this?

"The Magik required I kill with love in my heart." A tear fell down her cheek, and I had to fight every instinct not to go to her.

I wanted to believe everything she was saying, but this could all be an act. Another trick to get me to let my guard down and let her in again.

"How do I know you're telling the truth?" It pained me to say the words when she looked to be hurting as much as I was.

A sound came from the back of her throat as she shook her head and wiped the tears from her eyes. "I should've known you wouldn't believe me."

"I want to believe you." I pushed off the stack and shifted my weight. "I do."

"Don't you think if I was making it up, I'd find a better way of letting myself off the hook?" Her voice broke, forcing me to look at her.

Dark half moons hung below her eyes from being out late. Red veins spider-webbed across the whites of her eyes from little to no sleep. The frown she wore looked as if it was permanent, and her shoulders caved in defeat. She was broken and hurting.

And I was partly to blame for her pain.

As much as I wanted to keep her at a distance, and hold on to my reservations about her motives, some part of me knew I was fighting a losing battle.

"For argument's sake, let's say I believe you." I held up my hands in a truce. "You said they wanted you for a *who*, not a *what*?"

She let out a heavy sigh and folded her arms. "The first Valkyrie."

"The Disir?" A warning bell went off in my head.

"They were—wait, you know about them? How?" Her brow furrowed, and she blinked in rapid succession.

"Freya mentioned them to me."

"Why?" Her eyes narrowed.

"I've had my suspicions that something's been going on for a while now and I confronted her after the battle."

"You confronted Freya?" She scoffed and shook her head. "You two must have quite the arrangement. I've seen very few go toe to toe with her and walk away from it."

"We have an understanding."

"So are you saying the Disir have something to do with what's happened here, with those monsters?" She asked.

I shifted, wondering if I should tell her. Freya warned me not to say anything but seeing how the first valkyrie were linked to Kara and myself, somehow it felt wrong to keep this from her.

"She told you not to tell anyone, didn't she?"

"How'd—?"

"You're not the only one who understands Freya. She enjoys playing her games and keeping things close to the chest."

"This isn't a game."

"To you and me, no. But to the Gods?" She shrugged. "Keep her secrets. It's only a matter of time before the cat's out of the bag."

"What's that supposed to mean?" I don't know why I was being so protective of Freya. Maybe it was my connection to her or the fact that she'd always been kind to me, but Kara was right. The Gods did like to play games.

"Someone's trying to bring them back. It's why I killed you. The Magik was a part of some ritual to restore them."

"Someone? The Norns didn't tell you who?"

"They're blind to the movements and motivations of the one pulling the strings."

"Freya said it's not possible to bring them back."

She rolled her eyes. "Of course, you'd believe her."

"Why would she lie?"

"The Gods are arrogant, blinded by their own power. It was

Freya's Magik that turned them to stone. And what can be done with Magik can also be undone. I'm living proof of that." She patted her chest and pain flashed across her eyes like it was a strike from the whip that had made her whole once more.

"If that's true, then we need to warn Freya." I turned, but she grabbed my arm.

"No, we can't go to Freya." Her grip tightened on me as if she was ready to fight if I tried to argue with her.

"Why not?" I eyed her.

"The Norns were very clear. I was to share what I learned with you and a trusted few. The Gods can't know what's happening."

"If someone is waking a God-killing weapon, don't you think she deserves to know?"

"This isn't about what I think. It's about making sure we don't mess up the future any more than it already is."

My hands balled into fists. "You're being about as cryptic as the damn Norns."

"This path we're on wasn't written, it was created. You were never meant to die by my hand. Everything that's happening started with us, and according to the Norns, it's supposed to end with us. If we involve the Gods, it could bring about Ragnarok."

A nervous laugh bubbled from my throat. "You're joking." She held my gaze, her face deadly serious. "You're not joking." She shook her head. "I wish I was."

I ran a hand through my hair and turned toward the window. I had no words. After all this time, I had the truth, or at least a version of it. But it didn't make me feel any better. Someone was out there, playing with our lives from the shadows. The Gods had always been fickle. Starting wars and ending civilizations for their petty squabbles. But Ragnarok? Who would want to bring that upon the nine realms?

"So let me get this straight. Someone used Magik to force

you to kill me and now the Disir are running around with their Dragur army again?"

"They aren't back. It takes eight deaths, one for each of them."

"Well, that's one bit of good news."

"About that." Her eyes were on the floor like a scolded child. "You were also right about something else." She bit her lip and I could have sworn she shivered. "Whoever forced me to kill you is still controlling me." She winced.

"What are you saying?"

A tear fell from her eye and hit the wood floor. "You aren't the only one I've killed."

Dread curdled in my stomach.

"Six lives have already been taken by my hand. And I have no memory of it. Just like with you."

"Oh, Kara." I closed the distance between us and wiped the tears from her cheek. Cupping her face, I forced her to look up at me and when her eyes met mine, my heart broke for the both of us.

For so long, I'd held onto the belief that she never loved me. That she had killed me because she saw me as less than her and her kind. It was easy to believe—she was a Valkyrie, and I was mortal. But the more I've learned, the more I was starting to believe I was wrong. She didn't do this to us and she didn't deserve the anger I directed at her. Whoever was behind all of this would pay for what they'd put us both through.

"I'm sorry." She grabbed my wrists. "I'd hoped the Norns would give us both some peace so we could move on with our lives and let go of the past. Never in my wildest dreams did I think..." She pulled my hands from her face. "I understand if you want nothing to do with this. I'll do everything in my power to fix it without you—"

"And let you have all the fun?" I took her hand in mine. "I've spent countless years wasting away here. Doing the same thing, day in and day out. I was born for more than this." I motioned, indicating Folkvang. "I've always known that. So, if you'll have me, I will help you put things right. And if not, I'll do it myself. Because whoever is pulling our strings deserves to pay for what they've done to us."

"You're not afraid of me? Of what I might do?"

"I didn't say that." A nervous laugh escaped my throat. "Anyone who doesn't have a healthy fear of you is asking for trouble."

She laughed, but it didn't reach her eyes.

"We can't do this alone." I chose my words carefully. I wasn't sure if she wanted to tell others, but we needed to if we had any chance of getting ahead of this. "Only a fool goes into battle on their own."

"I know," she sighed. "The Norns warned me to be careful with who we trust."

I nodded. "We need to be strategic in who we tell. Talon is safe, and Ragnar, he's good at keeping secrets."

"Magnus & Bryn?"

I nodded. "But not Daiman. He's been working with Freya, keeping things from me. I don't trust him right now."

"Okay. And anyone else, we run it by each other first?"

"What about Ezra?" I asked, and I couldn't help the sting of jealousy.

"Ezra?" She looked at me like she was confused.

"I'm not blind. I know the two of you have something going on."

"I didn't realize you were paying attention." She cocked an eyebrow.

"It's not like you've been discreet."

She shrugged. "I don't know him well enough to trust him with this."

"If you're sharing a bed with him, he at least deserves to

know that you could wander off in the middle of the night to go on a killing spree."

She flinched, and I immediately felt guilty.

"Sorry, but he should know something. I was in his shoes once, and I would have wanted to know what was going on with you."

"I'll handle it." She nodded. "And if we're going to do this together, we can't keep secrets from each other. I need to know what Freya told you."

A small part of me wanted to remain true to my word and not tell her. But with all of Kara's honesty and heartbreak lying between us, I didn't have it in me to keep her at arm's length.

CHAPTER TWENTY-NINE

KARA

ONCE SI FINISHED TELLING me everything he'd learned about the Disir from Freya, we made our way back through the stacks and toward the main lounge area. Even with everything on our shoulders, somehow the tension between us felt lighter. I knew deep down he would never forgive me, not entirely. But finding out the truth about that day seemed to have released something in both of us.

And for the first time, when I looked at him, it wasn't with loss and heartache. But hope. Because if we could get past this, then maybe I could get past what was happening to me now.

As the corridor opened up into the lounge, soft, warm sunlight from the windows on my left truly made me feel like I was stepping out of the shadows for the first time since I'd arrived in Folkvang.

"Okay, what in the name of Odin is going on between you two?" Talon accosted us before we could take another step.

"Nothing," Si and I said at the same time. We sounded like kids caught playing with weapons we had no right to be touching.

"Last night you barely said two words to each other and now you're running off into the stacks, thick as thieves?" Talon looked between us like a disapproving parent. "Is there some emergency the rest of us should be aware of?"

Si looked at me and shrugged. "Why do you automatically assume something is wrong?"

"Maybe because you both swore to stay away from the other." I flinched. It was one thing to know we were avoiding each other, but hearing it out loud sent a ping of guilt through me. "So either you've suddenly pulled your head out of your ass or Ragnarok is upon us. Which is it?" She leveled her eyes at Si, then me.

"You're not entirely wrong," I said under my breath.

Si leaned in, his cheek brushing mine. "I'll let you handle this," he whispered, and Talon tracked the movement. "I'll see what else I can find in the archives." His eyes met mine as he pulled away. The spark from last night danced in his gaze just beyond his careful control. If I didn't know what I was looking for, I would have missed it.

I wasn't sure what to think about it or if I even wanted to pull on that thread. But at least he wasn't looking at me like he wanted to kill me, so I'd take the win.

"The archives?" Talon's voice pierced the quiet library. "What are you looking for in those old tomes?" She looked between Si's retreating form and me.

Si gave me an apologetic smile as he walked away.

"Look, I know I'm not half as interesting as him, but are you just going to stare at him all day, or are you going to tell me what's going on?"

I shot her a look. "If you must know, I spoke with the Norns this morning."

Her mouth fell open, and she looked at me like I'd grown horns. "They actually granted your request?"

"You seem surprised."

"Aren't you? As far as I know, they haven't answered anyone in decades."

"Count me lucky, I guess."

"So they told you what happened? Why you..." She mimed a stabbing motion and nodded in Si's general direction.

"Come on, there's a lot to catch you up on." I looped my arm through hers and started toward the couches facing the windows.

·→→⟨◊⟩←←·

"Okay, well, why do we care if some old Valkyrie are brought back to life?" Talon asked after I finished explaining everything the Norns shared with me.

"Because they aren't just Valkyrie anymore. Their power grew stronger than the Gods. They tried to kill them all. Whoever is trying to bring them back, it's not for a good reason."

"And you have no idea who it could be or why?"

I shook my head and picked up the cup of tea in front of me. "I mean, it has to be someone with Magik, or at least have access to it, right?"

"Not necessarily." Talon sat forward, her eyes bright. "You said the Norns can't see the one pulling the strings. Maybe it's because they don't have Magik, and that's how they're able to stay hidden."

"If they don't have Magik, what other means would allow them to control me and use me as their weapon?"

I looked to the window, but instead of seeing the mountains surrounding Folkvang and the city below, I saw the threads that tethered this world to the other realms. All it would take was one tiny pull on the Magik inside me, and I'd be somewhere else entirely. I was the perfect weapon from that standpoint.

"Speaking of which, did the Norns mention why you were chosen to carry out these sacrifices?"

"They wouldn't say." I shook my head and took a sip of tea to settle the frustration simmering in my chest like a shark in chummed waters.

"Why not?"

My lips formed a hardline. "Because that was not the question I requested them to answer."

"But it's all connected," Talon yelled and several people looked our way. "If we knew why they chose you, then maybe we could stop it."

I shrugged. "Apparently, they see it differently."

"That is beyond infuriating," Talon said through gritted teeth.

"Believe me, I know." I took another sip of my tea and barely tasted it. "And whoever's hiding in the shadows knows how to operate in the Norns' blind spot. So we basically have nothing to go on."

"How do you blind those who can see the past, present, and future?" Talon shook her head and took a sip of her tea with a bewildered look on her face.

Inspiration zapped through me. "You're a genius."

"This is hardly the time for stating the obvious," Talon said deadpan.

I dismissed her with a wave of my hand. "I'm being serious. Whoever is trying to bring the Disir back has to be operating outside of their vision, outside of time." My eyes widened.

"You don't mean—"

"Just like us, when we jump from one realm to the next."

"Yes, but we pass through time with our destination as our anchor. We can't tread water in the nowhere. Or at least, I can't?" She eyed me as if I'd been keeping some secret from her.

"I can't either, but it doesn't mean it's impossible." She visibly relaxed, and a pang of sadness shot through my chest like an arrow.

I made her nervous. And rightfully so. Until this morning, even I didn't know what I was capable of. I couldn't fault her, but it didn't stop the sting of disappointment from ringing through me.

"Who would have that kind of knowledge?"

"Those who created the realms," I said under my breath for fear of being struck down on the spot.

"That's a dangerous accusation." Talon stilled and I could swear she inched away from me as if she too thought I'd be punished for my words.

"I don't say it lightly. I know the wrath of the Gods better than most. But *He* can harness Magik, and it was his father who created them." I didn't dare say the Alfather's name out loud for fear he might appear out of thin air and do worse than take my wings this time.

"But why? What could he gain from releasing them on the world again if they are as terrible as we're to believe?"

"Why do the Gods do anything?" I shrugged and laid my head back against the couch.

"Power." She leaned back.

"Vengeance," I said, staring at the ceiling.

"Spite," Talon sighed.

"Amusement."

"Who in the nine realms would find this entertaining?" She snorted.

I rubbed a hand over my face. "I can think of a few Gods who take pleasure in others' misfortunes."

"Only a few?" A short, clipped laugh came from her throat.

"Fair point. And it might not even be one of the Gods. There are plenty of others who might be motivated to have a God killing weapon on their side."

"Motivated, yes, but stupid enough to try? I don't know." She shook her head.

"If I've learned anything from Midgard, it's that it doesn't take stupidity to charge down a path that can only lead to destruction. Quite the opposite, actually. All that's required is blind faith that they're in the right. Some of the greatest villains I've witnessed only needed a silver tongue and absolute belief in their convictions to cause the most harm."

Talon sighed. "So we're either dealing with an all powerful God or an unhinged mastermind. Great."

"Or both." I rubbed my temple. My heartbeat had slowly taken up residence in my head over the last couple of hours. It was either from a lack of sleep, drinking too much last night, or coming down from the anxiety of meeting with the Norns. Whatever the cause, I was ready to crawl into my bed and sleep for a week straight.

"You okay?" She turned toward me, resting her arm on the back of the couch.

"Just tired. I didn't get to sleep until almost dawn."

"Odd, I remember you leaving in the dead of night. Someone keep you up all night?" A playful grin spread across her face.

I rolled my head to the side to look at her and she smirked. "The fate of the nine realms hangs in the balance and you want to know who kept me up all night?"

"The world isn't ending at this very moment. And did you say, *who* kept you up?" She leaned forward. "Based on the way you two were looking at each other, can I assume it was Si?" She nodded toward him on the other side of the room.

"He found me after I left you all, and we talked. That's it." I sat up straighter and looked at him over her shoulder.

His hair was pulled back, but several strands had come free, framing his face as he talked to one of the librarians. It was getting harder and harder to ignore that I still have feelings for him. Especially after last night. The way he looked at me. The heat of his body so close to mine. Sure, I could blame it on the ale, but deep down, I knew it was more than that.

Talon leaned forward, impeding my view of Si. "You have your fuck me eyes on."

"Do not." My cheeks and neck flushed red hot.

"You know, there's nothing wrong with having feelings for him."

"There's everything wrong with it." I picked up my tea only to find my cup empty.

"Why?" She stared me down.

"You're joking?" I rolled my eyes, but she waited for me to continue. "I ended his mortal life, Talon. Everything he ever wanted to accomplish, to experience, was stolen from him because of me." I tried to keep my voice down as I poured another cup.

"And we've learned that wasn't your fault."

Her casual attitude on the subject made me want to hurl my cup across the room. Being used to kill didn't absolve me of my guilt. How could she not understand that?

"I don't think it matters."

"I do." She shifted closer to me.

"Well, if I ever kill you because some asshole is using me like a puppet assassin, I'll be sure to remind you that you should forgive me because it wasn't my fault."

"What to know what I think?"

"Not really." I brought my cup to my lips.

"I think you're afraid."

I froze and looked at her over the rim. "Of what?"

"To forgive yourself, to let yourself be happy, to love again."

I took a sip of my tea, letting the heat burn my retort back down my throat. "Can we not make this some deeply emotional life lesson right now?" I said instead.

"I'm serious."

"Maybe when this thing is over, I can try to forgive myself. But people are still dying because of me."

"Not because of you."

"It's by my hand," I argued.

"You're the weapon someone else is wielding. The blame lies with them, and them alone." She met my eye, daring me to argue with her.

"Still, until I'm free of whatever hold they have on me, I can't —I won't be able to move forward." I searched out Si across the room as the librarian handed him another stack of books.

"There will never be an ideal moment to start living your life again."

"Who says I'm not living my life?" My gaze slid to hers.

She smirked. "Merely breathing and going about your day is not living."

"Tell me then, since you're such an expert. What is living?"

She looked over her shoulder toward Si and back at me. "Doing the things that make your soul sing."

"There are some songs that should be lost to history."

Talon sighed and leaned back against the couch. "If that's truly what you want, I'll support you. But I wouldn't be a good friend if I didn't tell you, I think it's a mistake to shut yourself off."

"I haven't shut myself off. My friendship with you is proof of that. Ezra is proof of that."

She rolled her eyes. "Ezra is a passing fancy."

I opened my mouth to defend him and she held up her hand.

"Don't get me wrong, he's a worthy distraction, but you deserve more."

"What I deserve is to be free of the strings that have been tied to me. I deserve to be in control of my mind, body, and soul. You want me to live? Then help me be free."

Si sat down in the chair opposite us and placed a stack of

books on the table between us. "This is everything they have on the first Valkyrie."

"Can we not call them that?" I grimaced. "I hate sharing a title with the creatures who treat life so carelessly."

He nodded once and handed me the book on top. "Not much has been written on the Disir."

"I find that hard to believe. The Gods fought a war against them and won. Wouldn't they want their heroics on display?" Talon grabbed a book from the pile.

"Unless they were hiding something," I supplied.

"It wouldn't be unlike the Gods to hold back the truth," Si added.

"And the Norns were adamant about the Gods not finding out about the Disir's potential return." I shrugged. "Maybe there's more to their warning. Maybe they don't want them to know because of what really happened."

"If that's the case, then these," Si motioned to the pile of books in front of him. "Are most likely useless."

"Not necessarily." Talon flipped open the book in her hands. "Often, the truth is hidden among lies. We just have to find the right lie and untangle it."

"And how are we supposed to unravel and decipher the stories written by the Gods?" Si asked.

"One page at a time," Talon flipped a book open with a smile.

CHAPTER THIRTY

SIGURD

AFTER SEVERAL HOURS of flipping through dusty tomes and being no closer to any answers, I slumped in my chair and rubbed the sting from my eyes.

"Rome wasn't built in a day," Kara sighed.

"Rome?"

She waved her hand dismissively. "I know it seems like this is a waste of time, but there's bound to be something that gives us a clue. It's just going to take time."

"Time, I fear we are running short on."

She sat back and scanned the room for the tenth time. She'd grown more on edge with each passing hour. It was as if she was watching and waiting for the darkness to creep across the room and drag her away.

"Everything okay? You look like you're afraid of the shadows."

"To be honest, I kinda am." She didn't meet my eye. "I don't know when they'll come for me again. When they'll use me to do their bidding."

"I know you don't want to hear this." I sat forward, resting my arms on my knees. "Especially from me. But you shouldn't be alone, in case—"

"In case I turn into a walking liability and start killing people? Yeah, I'm aware." Her words were clipped.

"I don't mean to be—"

"Don't apologize." She shook her head. "You're not wrong for saying what we're both thinking."

"Maybe Ezra can—"

"No. We hardly know each other. I'd rather not involve him in all this."

Was she protecting him, or did she not want to share the truth with him? I honestly wasn't sure which option I was hoping for.

"Talon then?"

She nodded. "She's probably the best option. If we can find where she ran off to." She glanced at me and the instinct to offer to keep watch nearly overtook me.

Even if we were on better terms, there was nothing I could do if she lost herself and vanished to another realm. I had no way of following her, no way of stopping her. The strategic part of my brain agreed that Talon was the best option. But another part of me, a part I was trying to ignore, screamed at me to stay with her. Like some lost instinct knew we were better together than apart.

"We can send word to her." I motioned for one of the librarians to come over. "And I'll stay with you until she arrives."

"You don't have to stay with me." She grabbed a sheet of blank paper and scribbled a note.

I placed my hand on her arm, and she paused mid-sentence. "Yes, I do. Until we figure out how to free you," I paused, the rest of my sentence getting stuck in my throat. "I can't trust you to be alone."

She closed her eyes and grimaced. "I understand." Her voice was soft, defeated as she finished the note, folded it, and handed it to the librarian at her side. "See this gets to Talon?"

The librarian nodded once and took the folded piece of paper.

"I'm sorry," I said once we were alone again. Guilt had settled like a boulder in my chest. She'd been open and honest with me today and here I was still telling her she couldn't be trusted. It felt like a step backward, and the look on her face said just as much.

"Don't be." She stood, grabbing a stack of books. "It's not your fault I can't be trusted. And whether I like it or not, I'm dangerous."

I couldn't deny her words and my chest ached with the knowledge. I picked up the remaining books and followed her to the return counter. Her shoulders hunched forward and her pace was sluggish. It took all of my carefully crafted strength to keep my distance, but I couldn't ignore the voice growing louder in my head, pushing me closer to her. It was as if I was caught in her gravity and no amount of fighting would change my orbit.

We returned the mountain of books and made our way outside. She shifted from one foot to the other and glanced at me.

"What is it?" I watched her carefully, not liking the way she was looking at the steep drop off to the city below.

"I'm beyond exhausted." She glanced toward the path that cut down the side of the mountain and led back to civilization. "There's no way I'm walking down." The swirls of her tattoo glowed and her wings slowly unfurled. She held out her hand to me. "Shall we?"

"Must we?" I stared at her with wide eyes.

"You can take the long way down, but that will leave me without a chaperone. And we wouldn't want that now, would we?" She cocked an eyebrow.

I wasn't overly fond of being ripped from the ground, and she knew it. "You're enjoying this, aren't you?"

She shrugged, but did nothing to hide the smirk on her face.

I folded my arms. "What will it take to get you to walk down?"

"Nothing you can give me." She looked me up and down and there was a playfulness to her gaze that sent a shock through me.

I stepped in front of her and had to fight the urge to throw her over my shoulder and carry her down the mountain. "If memory serves, you were always happy to take what I could give you."

Surprise flickered across her eyes as she looked up at me and her lips parted ever so slightly, pulling my attention.

"I was much easier to please then." She kept her expression neutral, but the hitch of her breath made it clear my words had landed as I intended.

"Many things have changed over the years…" I leaned in, pressing my cheek to hers. "But I doubt pleasing you is one of them," I whispered against her ear, and the warmth of her heavy breath on my neck sent a shiver down my spine.

"I doubt someone who's intimidated by a short flight has the adventurous spirit to satisfy anyone." She closed the gap between us, her chest pressing against mine, and my whole body stiffened. The warmth of her was intoxicating and the soft smell of her–vanilla and lavender–wiped every thought from my mind.

"The way you fly has nothing to do with adventure." I looked down at her, the control I'd been holding onto all afternoon slipping through my fingers.

"Like I said." She smiled up at me as if she'd won, but there was something she was forgetting.

I never backed down from a challenge, even when I knew better.

I wrapped an arm around her waist and pulled her against me. Her breath hitched as her eyes met mine. "Do your worst."

She smiled and this time it reached her eyes as she wrapped one arm around my shoulder and the other across my back. Her wings beat around us and she launched us into the air. My grip tightened around her waist and I crushed her to me. My stomach plummeted as she dropped over the edge of the cliff.

The brisk twilight air whipped around us and was a welcome reprieve from the heat of her body. Her right wing tipped upward, and we banked to the left. My stomach landed somewhere in my throat as the sound of music and laughter reached my ears. Her fingertips pressed into my back as if she was playing the music herself, and a hum from her chest resonated through my body.

I let myself look at her and found her eyes closed. A soft smile touched the corner of her mouth as her hair swirled around her like wild flames. The furrow in her brow had relaxed, and she looked as if she'd left the weight of the world back on the ground.

Slowly her eyes opened to meet mine, and for the life of me, I couldn't look away. It was the first time since she arrived in Folkvang that she looked at me with an open and unguarded gaze. Her truth lay bare between us, and I was quickly losing the battle within myself to remain neutral in regard to her.

"The skies suit you."

Her lips curled as she dropped her gaze from mine. "Even if I am a little too adventurous?"

"Don't—"

She tucked her wings, and we plummeted toward the ground. My stomach left my body altogether, and I tightened my grip on her, pressing the length of her body against mine. I wasn't sure if it was the fear of falling to my death or the feel of her against every inch of me that made my heart threaten to beat out of my chest. Gods, I needed to get some space between us.

Her wings snapped open as the temperature dropped and we glided over the river that split Folkvang in two. A mist off the water coated my exposed skin, dousing some of the fire that had been building all day between us.

Her wings flapped behind her, slowing us down until we were hovering just a few inches off the ground. My boots touched the grass first, followed by hers. Her grip on me eased, but she didn't let go as her wings shimmered into a green and gold mist, vanishing on her command.

Fire sparked in her eyes and her chest heaved with each breath. My grip on her eased, and she took a step back. This was a delicate game we were playing, one I don't think either of us was in control of.

"Now that wasn't so bad, was it?" She sketched a casual smile, but her eyes were anything but.

"I've done worse." Clearing my throat, I dropped my hands and took a step away from her. "I'm surprised you chose a place on this side of the river." Fresh air filled my lungs, giving me back a kernel of sanity. Though it would take an act of the Gods themselves to help me forget the feel of her curves under my hands and the press of her body against mine.

"Why is that?"

Focus, Sigurd. "It's umm, quiet over here, out of the way," I managed.

"And what's wrong with quiet?" She shrugged and started down the path.

"Nothing. I just thought you would've wanted to be closer to the city center. Closer to everyone." I stepped in line with her.

"I did. But I thought it best to give us both some space."

Understanding bloomed in my chest, followed quickly by guilt. Yet another thing I hadn't realized she had sacrificed in my name. "You didn't have to."

"I know. I wanted to. After everything…" She looked at me and sighed. "I wanted you to have peace."

"What about your peace?"

"Being back in Folkvang has been enough." The tone of her voice didn't match her words, and I wondered if it really was enough. I could press her to share, but we'd gotten along today

247

and I didn't want to ruin it by forcing her to talk when she wasn't ready to.

"It would seem your plan to keep your distance isn't going all that well." Our eyes caught and a desire I thought long dead burned to the surface. I'd be lying if I said it didn't scare me. How easy it was to fall back into a rhythm with her.

She stopped in front of one of the diamond shaped houses, all covered in moss, and turned toward me. "I know. As much as I've tried to give you space, to let you live without the shadow of our past, I think fate has other plans for us." An air of melancholy surrounded her. Did she regret she couldn't escape me, couldn't escape our past?

"I don't know if I believe in fate anymore."

"Anymore? What changed?"

"When I lost my mortal life, and everything I believed I was destined for... it made me realize that fate is just another fallacy we tell ourselves to feel good about the path we're on."

"That's very glass half-empty of you."

"It's realistic."

"It's jaded." She folded her arms over her chest.

"Maybe," I shrugged.

A half snort, half laugh came out of her throat. "So you believe the Norns have this grand design for everyone, but you don't believe in fate?"

"You said yourself, the Norns did not write what's happened to us. Which means free will has to have some measure of strength over fate." I edged closer to her, unable to keep the distance I knew I should. "What happened to the woman who believed in creating her own destiny?" I held her gaze. Her eyes were a deep greenish-grey today, making her features softer and less intimidating.

"She died a slow and painful death over the last hundred years." The fury that always simmered just beneath the surface flashed in her eyes and in the set of her mouth.

"Now, who's the jaded one?" I raised an eyebrow.

She rolled her eyes and her lips twitched into a smile. "I've spent a hundred years paying for your death, and setting this whole mess into motion."

"But that's just it. You and I are proof that fate or destiny isn't set in stone. You were never meant to end my mortal life and yet, here we are."

"You don't get it, do you?" She frowned and took a step back. "I have to believe in fate, that I was meant to be here in this moment for some bigger reason. Otherwise, I'm just a pawn in someone else's game."

"I hate to be the bearer of bad news, but we're all pawns in someone's game. It's not about who's moving the pieces around the board, but what you do right here and right now that makes a difference." I felt like I was giving her a speech before war, and maybe I was. There was an uphill battle in front of us, and if we're to have any chance of a victory, we both needed to believe that our choices matter.

She shook her head and her gaze fell to the ground. "I don't know if it really matters."

I placed my fingers under her chin and made her look at me. "Why not?"

Her eyes searched mine as if she was wrestling with every word on her tongue. "Because if freewill was at play, I never would have killed you." She stepped closer. "Not now." Her hand pressed against my chest and my heart caught. "Not then." She tilted her head up. "Not ever." She leaned into me, leaving just a breath between us.

Someone cleared their throat, and I took a step away from her. "Am I interrupting something?"

I glanced over my shoulder. It was Ezra, of course.

CHAPTER THIRTY-ONE

KARA

SORÐINN. "Ezra, hey. What are you doing here?" With everything going on, I'd forgotten he was meeting me tonight. I stepped around Si. A part of me was relieved at the interruption. We were heading down a path I wasn't sure we should be.

"I can go if the two of you are working something out." He pointed the way he'd come.

"No, stay. Si was just leaving." I glanced back at him and I did not miss the heat in his eyes. We were so close to crossing a line that we absolutely shouldn't.

"I'll wait for Talon." He nodded, turned, and walked toward the river.

With each step he took, a small shred of my sanity came back to me. What the Hel was I thinking? We couldn't go down that road again. If we were going to stop the Disir from becoming a reality once more, we couldn't lose ourselves to one another. There was too much at stake and our alliance was still too fragile.

"Come inside?" I started toward my front door, shoving aside anything I felt for Si.

Ezra followed and closed the door behind him. "If the two of you are rekindling things, I don't want to get in the way."

"We're not."

"That's not what it looked like." He closed the gap between

us and cupped my cheek. "You are an incredible woman. And I'd be happy to enjoy your company for as long as you'd like. But I'm not blind, nor am I confused about what it is you and I are doing."

"And what is it we're doing?" I met his eyes.

"Having fun. Passing the time." He shrugged with a soft smile. "But you and Si—"

"Sigurd and I have a complicated history, some of which is bleeding into our present. That is all. But we are not rekindling things."

A smile touched his lips, and his arm wrapped around my waist.

I pressed a hand to his chest. "But there is something you should know." He took a step back, but kept his hands on my hips. "I'm not safe."

"There's a threat on your head?"

"Nothing like that."

His brow furrowed and his eyes searched my face. "Does this have to do with your time in Midgard?"

I nodded and closed my eyes. I didn't want to drag him into this, but Si was right. He deserved to know at least some form of the truth.

"Do you know mine and Sigurd's history? How he ended up here?" I stepped out of the circle of his arms, needing some space between us to think.

He nodded and a small part of me cringed. The rumor mill really did work overtime around here.

"Then you know I killed Sigurd, but what most don't know is that I was being controlled through Magik. I was forced to do someone else's bidding." I started to pace, trying to dispel the nervous energy building inside me.

"Okay, but what does that have to do with you not being safe?"

I swallowed and took a deep breath. "It appears they still have influence over me."

Ezra crossed the space between us and took my hand. "Did something happen again, like with Si?" He guided me to the couch and we sat down.

"According to the Norns, yes. But, just like with Si, I have no recollection of it."

He brushed the back of my hand with his thumb in a soothing rhythm. "So it's not that you, yourself are unsafe, but you're worried you're not safe for others?"

I nodded. "I know I'm not."

"That's hardly a fair assessment. I saw you fight the other day to save lives." His wide, hopeful eyes pulled on my heart strings. "We would have been worse off without you."

"It doesn't change the fact that I'm being used to kill, whether I'm aware of it or not."

"No, it doesn't." He turned to me. "But you're forgetting something."

"And what's that?" I looked up at him.

Brushing my hair behind my ear, he held my eyes. "You are not the thing they force you to be. You are a Valkyrie. Touched by Freya. You are Kara, beautiful and kind."

My heart swelled and then cracked. I didn't deserve his kindness. Not after everything I've done. My title as Valkyrie may as well be forfeit, now that I know the Magik inside me is nothing more than a weapon.

I shifted, putting some distance between us. "None of that changes the truth of my situation. The man I once shared a bed with was stripped of his mortal life because of me, and I'll be damned if I'm going to repeat history."

"I see." He nodded. "So, are you pushing everyone away, or just me?" His tone was reminiscent of Talon's earlier today and it grated on my nerves.

I was done having the same conversation with everyone. If I wanted to put distance between myself and anyone else, that was my business. "Do you want to wait around and see what happens?"

"I'd rather you didn't make decisions for me."

"I—"

He raised his hand. "If you don't want me around, you just have to say so. I'll go. But don't pretend you're doing me a favor and protecting me. In case you've forgotten, I earned my place here."

"You're right. You earned your place here with your mortal life. I won't be the reason your story ends and you rejoin the stars."

"Very well." He stood and held out his hand. I let him pull me to my feet and into his arms. "If you ever need a friend"—he pressed his forehead to mine—"or someone to warm your bed. You only have to ask." His lips brushed mine and I let myself enjoy his embrace one last time. "Take care of yourself." He pulled away and started toward the door.

"Ezra?"

He paused on the threshold.

"Thank you for everything," I said, and I truly meant it. He was a welcome place to land upon my return to Folkvang, and I wouldn't forget it.

"It's been my pleasure." He smiled, and then he was gone.

I stared at the door for several heartbeats, and then I made my way toward my bed. I couldn't say I was happy to see him go, but we'd both known from the start that this was nothing more than a fling. Better to walk away now than end up causing more damage down the line.

I plopped down on the bed, not bothering to change out of my clothes. The last couple of days had taken more from me than I cared to examine at the moment. I closed my eyes and let my mind wander. Dark eyes stared back at me from the shadows. The press of Magik laid over me like a blanket. A familiar voice pulled me in as the beat of wings *whooshed* around me, and I gave over to the heaviness in my soul.

CHAPTER THIRTY-TWO

SIGURD

I STOOD on the edge of the river, telling myself I didn't care that Ezra was the one who followed her inside. She was free to do as she pleased, even if it felt like we were having a moment. I had no right to her or my jealousy. But knowing that and separating the ache that was festering in my gut were two different things.

I took a deep breath and tried to push the memory of her pressed against me out of my head. The silky feel of her skin under my fingers. The smile that touched her lips as she soared through the sky.

I wiped a hand over my face. Gods. I was in trouble.

The sound of a door opening caught my ear, and I turned to her cottage as Ezra appeared at the threshold. He looked over his shoulder and nodded once before heading down the path.

The pressure in my chest eased as I watched him go, and I shook my head. I shouldn't feel relieved. Who Kara spent her time with was none of my business.

I started down the path, needing to move so I wouldn't find myself at her door. But I made sure to keep her cottage in my sights. I felt like a prison guard, moving up and down the river's edge, watching and waiting for—well, I had no idea what I was waiting for. Where the Hel was Talon already?

I ran a hand through my hair and looked up at the sky. A hawk circled above, gliding over the breeze. It dipped its wing, banking off to the right, and disappeared beyond the treeline. How did I end up here, watching over Kara, when I told myself I'd stay away from her? Could she be right about fate? That no matter what decisions we make, some things are ordained to be?

I started back the way I'd come when I spotted a figure in the shadows dart away from Kara's cottage. If it was her, she was either sneaking away because she didn't want to be babysat or… I didn't want to finish that sentence. With my heart in my throat, I picked up my pace.

A flash of Auburn hair caught my eye and my stomach bottomed out.

"Kara?" I called out to her as she walked across the grass and headed east. "Kara," I called her name louder and moved toward her, but she didn't answer, nor did she look my way.

By the Runes, where was Talon? I jogged to catch up with her.

Either she didn't care that I was following her, or she wasn't paying attention, because it only took me a few seconds to close the gap between us.

"Kara?" I grabbed her arm, and she swiveled toward me.

My heart plummeted into my stomach and my mouth went dry. Her eyes were vacant and a silver ring glowed around her iris.

Her above me. Silver rings in her eyes as I bled to death. The memory hit me like a tidal wave.

This wasn't the woman I'd spent the day with.

She tried to pull free of my grasp, but I held onto her. Grabbing her other arm, I pulled her toward me. I was careful not to use my full strength as I held her in place. I looked over my shoulder the way Ezra left and suspicion prickled the back of my neck.

"Did he do this to you?"

She tried to rip free from my grasp and I dug my fingers

tighter. "Look at me. Did Ezra do something to you? Is he the one pulling the strings?"

"You'd like that, wouldn't you?" she sneered. "It would give you a reason to kill him." Her voice was bitter, harsh, and so unlike her own.

Whether it was Ezra or someone else, I wouldn't hesitate to kill whoever did this to her. They deserve all the wrath and fury coming their way for the part they played in my death, as well as five others.

"Kara, this isn't you." My gaze bounced between her eyes, but they were empty pits of green and silver and my stomach hollowed.

Her lips curled back like a wolf, and she pressed herself against me. "You have no idea who I am," she snarled.

It was like reliving the past. My heart raced, my ears rang, and I lost my grip on her. She swiveled away as the memory of her shoving the dagger into my chest assaulted me.

Her wings unfurled, snapping me back to the present, and I lunged for her. Wrapping my arms around her waist, I tackled her to the ground. This wasn't the past. This didn't have to end the same way. We rolled down the incline toward the river and I was able to get on top of her. I pinned her arms to the grass and sat on her pelvis.

"Wake up, Kara." My fingers dug into her forearms as she thrashed against me. "Please." History was repeating itself and there was nothing I could do to stop it.

She screamed like an animal as she tried to buck me off of her. "Let go of me." Her voice was a savage scream that echoed in my bones. *For Sorðinn sake! Where the Hel was Talon.*

"I won't let you hurt someone else," I swore. There was no other option. She couldn't be allowed to kill the seventh person in this sick ritual.

She lifted her head as far as she could, bringing her face a few inches from mine. "You can't stop what's coming." Her breath was warm on my face, but it turned my stomach. It was hard to look at her now, after the tender moment we shared.

"I can try." I struggled to keep her pinned without using more force, but she was strong and murderous, which was a dangerous combination.

Her body went still under me and she looked into my eyes. "You'll have to kill me if you want to stop me." Her lips curled into a smile and a chill went down my spine.

There was nothing left of the woman I knew, the woman who'd apologized to me, the woman who took nine lashings to have her wings back. The Kara, staring back at me now, was a bloodthirsty monster, Hel bent on tearing the realms apart. How could I have not seen the difference before? How could I have been so blind?

She bucked her hips, tossing me off balance. Her legs tangled with mine and she flipped me off of her. "And you're not man enough to do it." She got to her feet and adrenaline rang in my ears.

"If it means saving another's life, I'll do what I have to." I rose and squared my shoulders.

She laughed, but it wasn't the musical sound that pulled on my heartstrings. It was the laugh of a madwoman. I hated seeing the undiluted fury in her eyes, the snarl on her face that contorted her features into something wild and menacing. How had everything gone sideways so quickly?

She pulled her sword from her back and stepped toward me. "You and what weapon?" She pointed the tip of her blade at my chest.

"It is a fool who thinks steel is the only weapon one possesses." It wasn't ideal, but I'd trained for any scenario, and I would get that sword out of her hands and stop her from killing anyone else. I pushed down my feelings for her, along with the guilt and worry for her well-being. There was no more room for being gentle. Not when lives were at stake.

Her smile faltered, and she lunged toward me.

I ducked and spun out of her path, grabbing her free arm in the process and pulling it behind her back. I shoved my knee into the back of her leg and she tumbled to the ground on all fours.

She scowled up at me, pounded the dirt, and got back to her feet. I just needed to keep her distracted long enough for Talon to get here, and then we'd be able to stop her together.

She lunged, and I dodged to the side as she swung again and again. Her form was wild, messy, and propelled by anger. She looked nothing like the woman who fought beside me during the attack; full of grace and precision.

"Kara. Remember what the Norns told you?" I tried to distract her, keep her off balance and talking.

"The Norns hold no influence over me." She jumped over me, her wings suspending her in the air.

I turned just in time to catch her arm over my head, her sword inches from my skull. I twisted to the side, and she swung at me with her free hand.

I caught her fist, blocking the punch, and pulled her against me. The tight quarters made it impossible for her to reposition and swing her blade again.

She threw her head forward, crashing her forehead into my nose. I heard the crunch of bone before the sharp spiderweb of pain fired across my face.

A trickle of blood made its way down my throat as I twisted her sword arm to the side. She gritted her teeth but refused to drop the blade. If I pushed any further, I'd break her arm and as much as I wanted to stop her, I didn't relish the idea of causing her pain. She was right; I wasn't man enough to kill her. But I couldn't let her hurt someone else.

As if she knew what I was thinking, the corner of her mouth pulled into a grin. She dropped the sword and fisted my shirt in both hands. Before I could even register what she was doing, she pushed off the ground and shot into the sky.

"You may be able to fight, but only one of us can fly." The air whipped around us and I wrapped my arms around her. She moved higher and higher until the river below became nothing more than a thin line cutting through the valley.

A pang of fear shot through me and blood rushed to my ears, drowning out everything but my racing heart. If she dropped me from this height, I'd die and it would be for good this time.

"Kara, please wake up," I said, voice stuffy from my swollen nose, but she ignored me, flying higher still.

I tightened my grip on her with one arm, and with the other, I cupped her face. "You don't want to do this." I couldn't fight her with my body, not here in the sky. But I could try to fight her with my words and hope that some part of her was still in there.

We stopped rising, her wings keeping us in place far higher than I ever wished to travel off the ground. Her eyes met mine and nothing more than a predatory look gazed back at me. "And how would you know what I want?"

"Because I know the truth of your soul." I stared into her foreign eyes, forcing myself to look beyond the Magik that was controlling her.

"No one can truly know the depth of another."

I shook my head. "When you love someone, you can. You taught me that."

She grimaced. "Don't pretend you have any love left for me in your heart." She pulled my hand from her face. "You're just trying to fulfill your hero complex by saving some poor innocent life and making a name for yourself."

"Of course I want to save innocent lives, but that doesn't change the truth." My heart slammed against my ribcage.

"The truth," she scoffed. "The truth is, you'll never forgive me and I don't want you to." She twisted out of my grasp and shoved away from me.

My stomach lurched and my heart skipped a beat as the air whipped past me.

She let go.

I kept my eyes on her as I plummeted toward the ground. She hovered for a moment, watching me fall, her wings beating with the breath in my lungs, and then she vanished. Off to Gods knew where to kill some unsuspecting soul.

I'd failed her. Failed myself. And now I was going to crash into the world below and return to the universe. After everything, she was still my undoing. No matter how hard I tried to stay away, to leave the past where it belonged, her hand would always be the one to steal my last breath, the last beat of my heart.

Resigned to my fate, I closed my eyes and waited for the impact.

A part of me wished I could summon the anger I once felt for her, but seeing the vacant expression in her eyes. There wasn't a doubt in my mind that Kara, the woman I knew, the woman I cared for, was not in control today, nor was she in control the day I lost my mortal life.

Wind roared in my ears, and without looking, I knew the ground was getting close. I took solace knowing that in the end; I knew the truth, I'd seen it with my own eyes.

I braced for the impact.

At least it would be over quickly.

My body smacked into a hard surface, knocking the air from my lungs, but there was no pain.

"You just had to be a hero, didn't you?" A voice said above me.

CHAPTER THIRTY-THREE

KARA

THE DISTANT SOUND of Talon and Si talking under their breath pulled me out of my slumber. My body ached like I'd tumbled down a mountain and my head throbbed with every heartbeat.

I opened my eyes and glancing at my surroundings. I wasn't in my home or even in my bed, which I distinctly remember climbing into. The pointed ceiling was like mine and so were the dark wood panels. But this place was much bigger, more open.

To my left, a large bed with different color furs laid across it, calling to my tired soul. In front of me, behind Talon and Si, a large wood burning fireplace crackled with a few dying embers.

I tried shifting my weight in the chair and found my wrists and ankles were bound.

My stomach rolled and my head spun. *Shit. This can't be good.*

Si and Talon looked my way. Neither of them wore a friendly expression. Si's nose was swollen and Talon's eyes were bloodshot. Neither of them looked as if they'd slept.

Talon stomped up to me, her lips tight and eyes narrowed. She grabbed my chin and forced me to look up at her. Her eyes scanned mine, and she let out a sigh of relief.

"It's her." She dropped my chin and Si stepped forward with a grave expression.

"It happened again, didn't it?" I said, past the lump in my throat.

He nodded and knelt to undo the restraints around my ankles.

"Were you able to stop me?" I looked down at him and back up at Talon.

"No." Talon leaned against a support post. "I was too busy saving him"—she nodded toward Si— "to do anything about you." She folded her arms over her chest.

I looked down at Si as he freed my legs, but he didn't look back. A sinking feeling flashed down my torso. *It had to be bad if he wouldn't even meet my eye.*

"Did I. . hurt you?" I choked the words out, eyeing his swollen nose. The fact that he couldn't look at me was proof enough I'd crossed a line yet again with him.

"Hurt him?" Talon scoffed. "You almost killed him. Again." She emphasized the last word.

My heart throbbed in agony. The thought that I'd gone after him again without my knowledge broke something essential in me, and the world tilted.

It didn't matter that I wasn't in control. It didn't matter that we seemed to be finding our way toward a tentative friendship.

Because in the end, I was nothing more than a liability, capable of killing anyone in my path.

Sigurd rose to his feet and looked down at me. None of the warmth from yesterday remained in his eyes. His stare was cold and just as unforgiving as it was the day I returned to Folkvang.

"How? What happened?" I choked out.

Sigurd moved behind me and worked the knot around my wrists.

"You dropped him from about a thousand feet up." Talon shook her head and stared daggers at Sigurd.

I waited for her to say she was joking, but when her eyes met mine, the cold steel of her gaze cut through me, and bile rose to the back of my throat.

The rope keeping me bound went slack, and I pulled my arms around the front of me. As I rubbed the tender skin around my wrist, I noticed bruises on my forearm. Were the black and purple fingerprints on my skin from the person I killed?

I closed my eyes and folded my arms, trying to hide the evidence of what I'd done.

"Sorry about that." Sigurd's voice was devoid of emotion. "I did my best not to hurt you, but you put up a good fight."

"You have nothing to be sorry for." I couldn't meet his eyes. Shame and guilt ate away at me like locusts from the inside out. "I'm the one who should be apologizing. If Talon hadn't…" The thought that he might not exist in the nine realms was too much to bear.

"Maybe that'll teach him not to fight out of his league." She cocked an eyebrow at him.

"Talon." I snapped toward her. How could she be angry at him when I was the monster?

She shrugged. "He's a skilled fighter, but we have the Magik of a God running through us. There's no competition, and he knows it. Maybe if he was thinking with—"

"You've more than made your point, Talon," Sigurd said through gritted teeth.

"I hope so, because next time you might not find yourself so lucky." She pushed off the post.

"Why are you pissed at him, when it's me you should direct your anger toward?"

"Because you had no control over your actions. He did." She looked him up and down. "Though an argument could be made that he didn't either." She closed the distance between them as if she was challenging him.

He turned on her. "That's enough. You may have saved my

life, but it doesn't give you the right to question my motivations. I would have done the same for any of you."

She raised her hands in surrender and he sat on the couch across from me in a huff.

"So, what do we do now?" I asked when it was clear neither of them was going to elaborate further.

"That depends. Do you remember anything?" Talon asked.

I shook my head. "The last thing I remember was saying goodbye to Ezra and then I crawled into bed."

Sigurd scoffed.

"Something to say?" Talon's head swiveled in his direction.

"You already know my thoughts on the topic." He folded his arms over his chest and leaned back.

"What thoughts?" I looked at Sigurd, but he kept his gaze on his lap. Whatever wall had fallen between us was firmly back in place. As much as it stung to see him so closed off, I couldn't blame him. The fact that he was even here spoke volumes.

"He thinks Ezra has something to do with you turning murderous." Talon rolled her eyes. Clearly, she didn't feel the same way.

"Ez, has nothing to do with it."

"You wouldn't know, though, would you? You have no memory of how you lose control." Sigurd looked at me, but he wore a calm mask of indifference.

"I remember him leaving. I remember getting into bed. And when I fell asleep, I was alone."

"Doesn't mean—"

"Would you give it a rest? It can't be Ezra," Talon snapped at Sigurd. "He's mortal, and there isn't even a whiff of Magik about him, which he would need to control her."

Sigurd sighed and Talon stared at him while the silence grew.

"Moving on then." She turned back to me and Sigurd stared out the window to his right.

"Does this only happen when you fall asleep?"

I blinked, confused. "I have no idea."

She leaned over and grabbed my shoulders. "Think."

"What does it matter?" Sigurd commented.

Talon stood, gritting her teeth and rolling her eyes. What had transpired between them while I was out?

"Because if she only loses control when she's asleep, then it might mean they can only gain access to her when she's unconscious." She spoke to Sigurd like he was a toddler incapable of understanding the grownups.

"Honestly, Talon. I wish I could tell you." I jumped in before they could start arguing again. "But I only know what happened with Sigurd, because you woke me up from it and told me."

"You pulled her out of it?" Sigurd looked at Talon. "How?"

"I don't know." Talon's face scrunched up as she tried to remember. "I pulled her off of you and..."

"You hit me repeatedly and were screaming my name." I recalled the sting across my face.

"I tried to reach you." Sigurd's gaze met mine for a fraction of a second before settling on the floor.

"I don't remember," I said under my breath.

"It was like you were a different person. Harsh, cold." He didn't look up at me, and guilt rushed through my chest and into my stomach. "You said a lot of things." A dry laugh escaped his throat. "But it didn't matter what I said. I couldn't reach you." He looked at me and pain flash across his eyes.

"I don't think there's anything you could have said. If I had to guess, it's the kill that sets her free, not anything we did or didn't do." Talon gripped his shoulder in a comforting gesture.

"If that's true, how did I end up here tied to a chair?"

"You materialized shortly after you disappeared," Sigurd explained. "Your hands were covered in blood and your eyes were still lined with silver. Whoever you killed, it was quick." He ran a hand through his hair.

"I was the one who knocked you unconscious," Talon said, and they shared a look that clearly said more had happened in that moment than they were going to tell me. "After some debate, we brought you back here."

"And where is here, exactly?" I looked around at the unfamiliar surroundings.

"My place," Si said, picking a piece of lint off his pants.

I waited for him to explain why, and when he didn't, I looked at Talon.

"Why?"

"It's the most convenient for the time being."

"What about your place?" I asked her.

"I've been appointed as one of Freya's guards, so I'm up on the hill now," she said nonchalantly. "You're better off here. Magnus is just a couple of doors down, and Bryn is with him all the time now. And Ragnar is just around the corner, as well as Asheria."

"I don't understand. Sigurd almost died trying to stop me. But you want me to stay here with him now? How does that work?" This was the worst idea any of us has ever had. "You should lock me up so I can't hurt anyone else. I shouldn't be sharing a dwelling with the man I killed once and attempted to kill on another occasion." I looked between the two of them, searching for a shred of common sense.

"There is strength in numbers," Sigurd said definitively. "You won't be able to take us all on."

"And what happens when it's the middle of the night and I'm summoned to kill? What makes you think I won't try to kill you again?" I tried to reason with him, and get him to see me for the threat that I was, but he wouldn't look at me.

"What would you have us do?" Sigurd's eyes finally met mine, and they were full of anger. "Kill you? End this insanity once and for all?"

"Maybe you should." I held his stare, refusing to back down from the threat.

"No one is killing anyone." Talon rolled her eyes and stepped between us. "I swear you two are worse than children."

"Look, I get you're both just trying to help, but maybe—"

"If you say maybe you need to do this alone, I swear I will smack you clear to Yggdrasil."

"That's not what I was going to say." It was, but I didn't want to argue anymore. My head was killing me and I wanted a shower to scrub the stench of death off my body.

"Mmhmm." She eyed me skeptically. "Then what were you going to say?"

"Maybe, if we clip my wings—"

"You'd give up your wings?" Si looked up from his lap and some of the anger had melted to confusion. "After what you went through to get them back?" He was looking at me like I'd sprouted horns.

"I don't mean give them up. But maybe there is something that dampens the Magik, makes it so I can't travel the realms."

"That will help protect everyone else, but Folkvang will become your hunting ground." Talon met my eye. "If we're to believe the Norns, you only have one more sacrifice to make. Are you really willing to kill someone here?"

"I'm not willing to kill anyone."

"You know what I mean. You'd be making a choice to put the people here in danger. Can you live with that? Can you live with sending someone to the stars?" Talon folded her arms over her chest and stared at me. She wasn't asking because she was judging me, but allowing me a moment to fully understand what I'd be agreeing to.

"The people of Folkvang have a better chance at surviving than others," Sigurd said. "We're born fighters. It won't be easy pickings like the other realms."

"You may have a death wish, but you don't speak for everyone in Folkvang," Talon snapped at him.

"Neither do you." Tension rolled off of Sigurd as he and Talon stared each other down.

"Before the two of you kill each other, why don't we find out if it's even possible to subdue the Magik in me? And until then, I'll stay here and hope I'm not called into action again." I rubbed my temples, desperate for the bickering to stop so I could close my eyes and find oblivion.

"I can ask around," Talon said. "But I wouldn't get my hopes up. Freya's Magik isn't easily tampered with."

"No, it's not. But it's worth a shot if we can control even the smallest part of all this." I pushed to my feet.

"You monitor her." Talon pointed a finger at Sigurd. "And don't press your luck again."

Sigurd looked up at her, cold steel in his eyes, as he nodded once and looked away.

"Good. Try not to kill each other while I'm gone." She sighed as she made to leave.

The door shut behind her, and a heavy silence fell between Sigurd and me.

"You might've been right," he said without looking up at me.

"About?"

"Maybe fate is conspiring to force us together, even if we'd choose otherwise."

I didn't miss his choice of words, nor did I miss the sting that radiated through my core. "Say the word and I'll leave."

He looked up at me, a flicker of surprise crossing his features.

"I mean it. You don't have to do this." I met his eyes, forcing him to tell me what he wanted.

"I won't risk anyone else getting hurt by you." His words cut through me like a hot knife.

269

"Then I guess it's your own choices that will seal your fate, not the other way around."

He looked out the window and sighed. "I assume you want to get cleaned up. Talon brought you some clean clothes and you can wash up through there." He nodded to the right.

"That isn't what I asked you."

"What do you want me to say, Kara?" He shot to his feet. "That it'd be easier if you weren't here. That you're dangerous and this is a horrible idea."

I lifted my chin. "If that's how you really feel."

He closed the distance between us, a flash of fire in his eyes. "It would be easier if that's all I felt."

I opened my mouth to tell him I'd leave, to tell him I'd be happy to make his life easier, but he raised his hand and closed his eyes.

"For once, please don't make this more difficult that it has to be." He walked away from me and with one arm, leaned against the mantle of the fireplace. "I don't have the energy to fight with you, not right now."

"Then let me leave. You don't owe me anything. I can figure this out-"

"On your own?" He looked over his shoulder and the worry etched into his forehead, the sleepless night in his eyes, hit me like a brick wall. "How's that been going for you?"

His words felt like a slap to the face and I took a step back.

"Either you accept the arrangement or you don't." His head fell forward. "But you're not leaving here."

"So I'm your prisoner then." The idea was almost laughable. My former lover, the man I killed, was now my jailer. The Norns really had a sense of humor.

"I don't like this anymore than you do."

"I doubt that."

He turned toward me. "I'm asking you, please." His gaze met mine, and the venom died on my tongue. A silent plea stared back at me. He was hurting, and it was my fault yet again. As I stared into the endless depth of his mahogany eyes, the fire inside me died.

Would it really kill me to stay? No. No, it wouldn't.

"Fine, but only for tonight." His gaze fell from mine and he let out a sigh. "Tomorrow we find a more permanent solution." I started toward the bathroom.

"If that's what you want."

I opened the bathroom door and stepped over the threshold. "I think it's for the best." I closed the door behind me before he could say anything else and sunk to the floor. How had things gone so wrong so quickly?

CHAPTER THIRTY-FOUR

SIGURD

I ROLLED over onto my side, and my eyes automatically searched her out on the sofa. She stared up at the ceiling, one arm behind her head, her other hand resting on her chest with her fingers drumming softly. I'd offered her the bed, but she'd refused. Stubborn as always.

Though she looked relaxed at first glance, the longer I watched her, the more I realized she was anything but. Her lips pursed into a hard line, her breathing was much too rapid for someone at peace, and her gaze darted around the ceiling as if she was trying to solve a problem written in the grain of the wood.

She turned to me. "I feel entirely myself at the moment if you're concerned." Her voice broke through the silence.

"I wasn't…" I abandoned my justification. She knew I'd been watching her. No use in denying it. "Can't sleep?" I sat up, swinging my feet out of bed and resting my hands on either side of me.

She shook her head and looked back at the ceiling. "Kinda hard when at any moment they might summon me to destroy another life. What's your excuse?"

"Would you believe me if I said I'm worried about you?"

Her brow furrowed, and she looked back at me. "You have every right to worry about what I might do to you."

Of course, she'd take it like that. I'd been cold toward her since the moment she came back to us. But it was only because Talon was right. I did let my feelings, however complicated they may be, cloud my judgment of her. I couldn't do what was necessary to stop her, and I almost lost the last life I'll ever have in the nine realms.

"That's not what I meant."

Her fingers stopped tapping on her chest as she took a breath. "Then what worries you?"

I let out a heavy sigh. "You only have one sacrifice left, and then what? What happens to you when this is all done?"

"Does it matter?" She sat up. Moonlight illuminated the right side of her face, while the other remained in the shadows.

"Doesn't it?" My brow furrowed. How could she be so callous about her life?

"To me, yes, but why does the thought plague you?" Her face was devoid of emotion.

My heart beat in my chest like a wild drum. "Should I not care what happens to you in all this?" I met her eyes. "Would you prefer my indifference?" I forced the question back onto her.

If she didn't want me to care, if she preferred we kept up the walls between us, I would give her what she wanted. But I was growing tired of the war inside me.

"Would it not be safer?" She cocked an eyebrow.

"That's not what I asked you."

"No, but I think I've more than proven you're better off when I'm not a part of your life." Her eyes fell to her lap.

"By the runes, Kara." I pushed to my feet and crossed the room. "Just answer the question." I sat down next to her as she pulled a feather from one of the cushions.

She took a deep breath. "It's not a simple yes or no." I waited for her to continue, allowing the silence to stretch between us.

"I've never wanted your indifference, but I understand and respect it."

It wasn't an outright declaration of what she wanted, but it was enough to keep me from closing the door in my heart. I lifted her chin and her meadow green eyes met mine with a thousand questions.

My heart sped up, and I shifted my hand to cup her cheek. It was now or never. "I'm tired of pretending you don't matter to me."

Her lips parted, and she shifted toward me. Every nerve in my body strained toward the movement, but I had to fight the urge to close the distance between us. Just because she wanted friendship didn't mean she wanted anything else from me.

"When did that change?" Her hand found its way up my forearm, her fingers leaving a trail of heat along my skin.

I itched to grab her, crush her against me, and savor the feel of her hands on the rest of my body.

The corner of my lips pulled into a smile. "About a thousand feet above Folkvang."

She frowned and pulled my hand from her face. But instead of letting go, she laced her fingers through mine.

"If I'd known threatening your life was the way to get you to stop hating me, I'd have done it the moment I arrived." A sad smile touched her lips.

"I don't think I've ever hated you." A low chuckle rumbled through my chest. It was why I'd been so conflicted, so unable to keep away. No matter how angry I was with her, how hurt or confused, I still never hated her.

She cocked her head to the side and pinned me with a knowing look.

"Okay, maybe for a few minutes. But I was hurting. I..." I couldn't bring myself to say the words. I cleared my throat and tried again. "I couldn't understand how I could be so wrong about someone. About you." My heart thrummed in my chest.

Looking at her now, it was hard to believe I ever harbored any ill will toward her. I'd let my pain and anger fester into its own version of the truth, a truth that wasn't a fair representation of the woman in front of me.

"Maybe you weren't wrong?" She turned, so she was facing away from me and rested her head on my shoulder. "Maybe they picked me for this, because of who I am at my core." She sounded defeated, like some essential part of her believed she really was a monster capable of unspeakable things.

"You may be a lot of things, but I struggle to believe they chose you because of some darkness in you."

"Just because you don't believe it doesn't mean it isn't true."

I shifted so I could see her face. "We all have darkness in us, some more than others. But your shadows don't define you unless you let them."

"That may be true for most, but there are some stains on a soul you can't cast aside, can't escape from, no matter how much light you shine upon them."

"Life's not meant to be lived without shadows. It is the nature of the universe. Where there is darkness, there is light."

She sighed. "I don't remember you being an optimist."

"I blame Magnus." I rolled my eyes.

A soft laugh rumbled through her. "He's made quite the impression on you. I approve."

"Oh? I didn't realize you were taking stock."

She sat up, placing a hand on my chest. Her eyes pinned me to the spot. "There isn't a woman in the nine realms who wouldn't measure the kind of man you are."

Her honesty sent a wave of heat through my chest, down my torso, and below the belt as her gaze held mine. Our alliance may be fragile and tentative, but the things I wanted to do to her were anything but.

"And what kind of man am I?" I managed to hold on to the last shred of my control and not close the gap between us. Until she was clear, she wanted more from me, I wouldn't touch her the way I wanted to, the way I needed to.

A smile pulled at her lips. "Honorable." Her hand trailed down my chest and my hand balled into a fist. "Confident." She bit her bottom lip as her hand moved back up my chest. "Honest."

I grabbed her wrist as her fingers skated over my heart. Her lips parted and sparks danced in her eyes. "If you don't stop touching me like that, you're going to get a much less honorable version of me."

"Maybe that's what I want."

"Don't start something you're not willing to finish."

She leaned closer and whispered, "Who said I wasn't willing?" The warmth of her breath skated over my face, and I grit my teeth.

I brushed her hair over her shoulder and cupped the back of her neck. "Then say it." I pulled her against me. "Tell me what you want."

"I want you to make me forget the shadows exist."

That was all the permission I needed. I pulled her toward me, crushing her lips against mine. Damn the past, damn the future, and damn the consequences.

Her lips parted, and she opened up to me, sending a pulse of heat down my neck and chest. Her fingers tangled in my hair and I pulled her closer, eliciting a small sound of contentment from her that shot through me like an arrow.

She threw one leg over me and straddled my lap. More years than I could count had passed between our last meeting, and still, her lips moved against mine with a practiced rhythm that even the closest of lovers couldn't rival.

Breaking the kiss, my mouth fell to the hollow of her neck. Her skin felt like silk against my burning lips, and it took all of me to hold on to the sliver of control still in my possession. Brushing her hair back, I exposed her collarbone and kissed the star shaped scar along one edge, as I unfastened the belt around her vest and tossed it aside. Sliding the vest off of her shoulders, she rolled her hips on mine, stealing the last shred of hesitation left in either of us.

She reached for the hem of my shirt and lifted the fabric over my head, tossing the garment behind her. Her breath caught at the sight of my bare skin and she ran her hands down my torso. I watched her take me in, the hunger in her eyes, the sorrow in the set of her jaw, and the desire of her swollen lips.

Her fingers traced the scar on my left side, just under my rib cage. It was the blow that had taken me and my heart ached with the memory. I caught her hand, and she looked at me before sliding off of my lap. Kneeling in front of me, she kissed the scar that was my undoing, sending a shiver down my spine.

I sucked in a breath as her lips moved up my torso and my hand found its way into her lush, fiery hair.

"Kara," I breathed, and her grip on my arm tightened as she reacted to the husky sound of her name on my lips.

Standing, she lifted her shirt over her head and tossed it to the floor. I caught her bare waist and pulled myself to the end of the sofa. I kissed the smooth skin across her stomach, and she shivered at the touch as her eyes met mine. Gods, my memory didn't do her justice.

CHAPTER THIRTY-FIVE

KARA

HIS CALLOUSED HANDS moved up my back, his fingers digging into my skin as his lips danced up the side of my rib cage and a moan escaped my lips.

In the space of two heartbeats, he wrapped an arm around my waist and stood. He pulled me against him and I wrapped my legs around his middle. His skin smelled like cedar and leather, sending a wave of pleasure through my core. He was strong, purely male, and every part of me wanted him.

A voice in the back of my mind screamed to stop, to put some distance between us. Because surely this couldn't lead to anything good. I'd only hurt him again.

My back hit something soft as he laid me down. His lips crashed against mine. His body pressed into me as if he was trying to make us one. My head spun, and I moaned as his fingers gripped my thigh and dug into my flesh.

You're only going to hurt him again.

He bit down on my bottom lip and my nails dug into his back. He groaned into my mouth, and I swallowed the sound like a woman starved. Gods, I'd missed the feel of him, the taste of him. My memory didn't do him justice.

I trailed my hand down his chest and touched the scar over his heart. Another memory assaulted me, the one the Norns had shown me. Dagger in his chest, blood on my hands.

My body went still, and I broke our kiss. He looked down at me, his eyes glazed over with lust. Neither of us were thinking clearly right now. He leaned in to kiss me again, but the voice that had been yelling at me was too loud to ignore.

"Wait," I exhaled, and he froze above me. "We can't do this."

He pushed himself up on his arms. "Did I—?"

Of course, he'd blame himself. I shook my head. "No. I just can't." A mixture of guilt and disappointment punched through my stomach.

He pushed off the bed and took a step back, his chest rising heavily with every breath, his erection straining against his pants. For a fraction of a second, I wanted to say screw it, and lose myself to this beautiful man in front of me.

"I tried to kill you yesterday." I forced myself to say the words that would be the bucket of ice water we both needed. "It's too dangerous to let our guard down." I pushed off the bed and started toward my shirt on the floor, but he grabbed my arm, stopping me in my tracks.

"If you don't want this, that's more than fine. But don't do it because you're protecting me. I can make my own choices." His eyes burned into mine.

Ezra had said something similar, but didn't they understand I was trying to protect them, to keep them from meeting the stars?

"I don't want to hurt you again. I can't. I won't survive it this time," I said with a little more bite than I meant to.

His grip on my arm loosened, but instead of letting me go, he pulled me against his chest, wrapping his arms around me. "We'll find a way to free you, I promise."

A relieved chuckle escaped my throat. "Oh, so now that sex is involved, you're motivated to help me?"

He pulled back and grabbed my chin between his thumb and forefinger. "It has nothing to do with sex. Though it's not a bad motivator." He smiled, and all the guilt and unease I felt melted away.

"No, it's not." I reached up on my tiptoes and pressed my lips to his.

"Come on." He nodded toward the bed. "That sofa isn't fit for sleeping."

I couldn't argue with that. It was too small to really stretch out and relax. He picked both of our shirts off the ground and walked back to the bed.

"Get comfortable." He tossed me his shirt. His dark hazelnut eyes seared into me. "I promise I'll be nothing but honorable." A crooked grin touched his lips and warmth pooled between my legs.

He turned and started across the room.

"Where are you going?" I asked, feeling guilty that I'd taken his bed.

He looked over his shoulder, his eyes roaming over my skin in such a way that I could feel the heat of his gaze. "To be a little less honorable." He turned away, leaving me flushed from head to toe.

He stepped into the bathroom and closed the door behind him. The shower turned on a moment later.

Gods. Not taking him to bed was going to be an exercise in strength. I slipped out of my trousers and pulled his shirt over my head. The smell of him engulfed me and made my head spin.

I lay back, pulled a blanket over me, and stared at the bathroom door. My heart pounded in my chest and I couldn't help imagining him. The water cascading down his chest and back while he pleasured himself.

My hand found its way between my legs and I ran my finger up my slippery seam before sliding it inside me.

To be less than honorable. His words rang through me and the image of him fisting himself propelled my fingers to glide in and out.

I could still feel the heat of his mouth on my skin, the length of his hardness pressed against me. I let out a moan and my hand tangled in the sheets.

I slid another finger inside and writhed at the sensation. The memory of his tongue gliding across mine sent a shiver through me as I imagined his tongue lapping me up, his fingers working me into a frenzy.

I let out a ragged breath as I curled my fingers and coaxed my orgasm to the surface. But it was the memory of Si's calloused fingers against my skin that spurred me on.

I withdrew my fingers, sliding them up my middle before plunging them back inside me. Only this time, it was Si's hand that I rode into oblivion. My back arched off the bed, and it was Si that I saw in my mind, his lust-filled eyes like liquid pools of fire that shattered my self control as I came undone in his bed, surrounded by the scent of rain, leather and wood.

I laid there panting. An ache I knew I wouldn't be able to satisfy alone built inside me when I heard the shower shut off.

I looked at the closed door, and my heart gave a gentle squeeze. If I didn't think about it, I could almost pretend that nothing horrible had ever happened to us.

Almost.

The door clicked open, and Si walked into the room. His hair was slicked back, and he had a towel wrapped around his waist. He didn't look my way as he padded across the room and pulled a pair of cotton trousers from his wardrobe.

He turned his back to me and tossed his towel to the side. Muscles stretched and pulled across his back as he dressed. Even in the shadows, there was no doubt that this man was sculpted for war. Every line of his body honed to fight to the death. I'd always known that to be true. But seeing him dressed down, all the sensitive parts of him on display, reminded me that someone could be crafted for battle and still be vulnerable to the whims of death.

He scrubbed his towel over his head, sending strands of dark hair flying in all directions. He threw the towel onto the table and ran his hands through his hair to gather it at the back of his neck. With his arms raised, I got a full view of what I was missing, and my body pulsed in frustration.

His eyes met mine as he stalked across the room, tying his hair back. He smirked at whatever he saw on my face, and I rolled onto my back and stared up at the ceiling, trying to think about anything other than the feel of him pressed against me.

The bed dipped next to me and every nerve in my body sparked to life at his closeness. I scooted as far away from him as I could without falling out of bed and tucked the blankets around me. As if the thin layer of fabric would do anything to shield me from the heat of his body, the smell of his skin.

We both lay there in the dark, staring at the ceiling without saying a word. It was as though we were both afraid if we spoke, the fragile truce we'd agreed upon would shred to pieces like a sail in a storm.

I didn't know what was worse, thinking he hated me and wanted nothing to do with me, or lying next to him when I could still feel his hands and lips on my skin and knowing I couldn't, wouldn't touch him.

CHAPTER THIRTY-SIX

SIGURD

"You two look chummy." Magnus looked between Kara and me. "I assume last night went well?"

"Excuse me?" Kara's eyes widened, and I felt her stiffen next to me.

"It was fine," I said quickly. "Nothing to report."

"Oh, you mean, did I try to run off and kill someone?" A nervous laugh escaped her throat, and I glanced at her. She'd been jumpy all morning and disappeared into the bathroom the moment the sun crept through the window.

"Of course. What else would I mean?" Magnus smiled, but a knowing look crossed his face as he glanced between me and Kara.

I grabbed another piece of toast and slathered it with butter. "We haven't even finished breakfast yet. Can we not?" I said under my breath.

Magnus raised his hands in surrender. "I said nothing."

"You didn't have to." I met his eyes and took an angry bite of toast.

"Would the two of you stop bickering like an old married couple?" Bryn sat down next to Magnus and poured herself a glass of elderberry juice.

Kara snorted next to me. "You stole the words right out of my mouth."

"You're supposed to be on my side here." Magnus shot Bryn a wide eyed look.

"Oh no, I told you I didn't want any part of your meddling."

"Meddling?" Kara glanced between the two of them.

I leaned into her. "You don't want to open up that can of worms," I said under my breath.

Her bright green eyes widen in understanding and she mouthed the word *oh*. My gaze drifted to her lips for a fraction of a second. The heat of last night's kiss seared my lips and liquid warmth burned at my resolve to keep my hands to myself.

Bryn whispered something to Magnus, and Kara looked away. Gods. I shouldn't have kissed her. Our situation was already precarious as it was, but now it felt like we were teetering on the edge of a cliff.

I glanced up as Bryn handed Magnus that damn token from their bet. "You two are incorrigible," I said under my breath.

"We have to get our kicks somewhere." Bryn chuckled.

"It's a shame Magnus can't keep you entertained enough to give up your little game." I leaned back and place my arm on the back of Kara's chair.

"Why do I feel like I'm missing something?" Kara glanced between the three of us.

Bryn waved her off. "You're not missing anything worthwhile. Just another pissing match."

"Don't–"

A deep boom rattled the fixtures above our heads. We all froze.

"What in the name of Odin was that?" Bryn looked to the window as she set the carafe of juice on the table.

"Nothing good," I sighed. Can a man not have one moment of peace?

I pushed away from the table, pulling a dagger from its

sheath. I moved to the door and pulled it open ever so slightly. Peeking through the gap, I didn't see anything or anyone.

Another boom rattled the windows, quickly followed by the horn that called us to arms.

I looked over my shoulder at the others. "Another attack."

Magnus jumped over the table and joined me by the door. "You were right. Something bigger is at play here."

"Are we just going to stand here all day, or are we going to fight?" Kara looked between Magnus and me.

"We need weapons." I turned from the door.

"Not a problem." Bryn walked behind the bar and opened a false wall. Swords, axes, arrows, and a quiver stared back at me.

"Has this always been here?" We'd been told to keep a weapon with us in our homes, but all others were to be stored in the weapons room so no one would hoard their favorites.

"First lesson of war, always be prepared." Bryn threw a sword in Kara's direction and she plucked it out of the air.

Magnus grabbed one of the other swords, leaving the double-headed ax for me and the bow and arrow for Bryn.

"I didn't realize we were at war." Magnus tested the weight of his blade.

"When you live as long as us,"- Kara flicked her sword from side to side— "you learn that even when you're not at war, you should prepare for it."

I pulled the door open, and Bryn and Magnus filed outside. Kara started after them, and I caught her arm. She looked up at me, her brow furrowed in confusion. "Stay close to me."

She started to pull away, but I held on. "I mean it."

"I'll be fine." She stared up at me, a challenge in her eyes. "I'm more than capable of taking care of myself."

"I'm well aware. But it's no coincidence that all these attacks started after you arrived."

"You think this has to do with me, with the Disir." Understanding flitted across her face.

I nodded and let go of her. "Do not leave my side."

"I guess you'll just have to keep up then." A glint of playfulness shot across her eyes, and she rushed out of the door.

I couldn't help the smile that pulled at my lips. So many things had changed between us, but this, this felt like old times as I followed her into battle.

We made our way through the alleyways, Magnus out in front, and I picked up the rear. I strained to listen for the sound of steel clashing, but there was nothing. Where the Hel was everyone?

Magnus turned left, and I checked our rear before following. A few more people were spilling into the streets, swords in hand as the horns sounded again. This time, it came from the east. Magnus changed course almost immediately. We made our way into a courtyard, dodging people as they joined the call for battle.

A horn blared again, this time right above us, and we all froze.

"Back to back," I called out, and people all around us jumped into formation. Magnus, Bryn, Kara, and I formed a circle, protecting our backs as we watched the shadows and looked to the rooftops.

"There!" someone yelled, and as if on cue, Dragur jumped from the roofs and out of doorways. They ran from the shadows and burst from crates as they charged us from all directions. The horns had been a trap, I realized, a ploy to gather us into one area.

The sound of steel clashing reached my ears as I raised my ax to strike. A skeletal Dragur ran at me, and I caught his sword with the edge of my blade and kicked backward. Another one jumped from above, blade poised to strike me dead on. I dodged out of the way, and then another was on me.

"We need cover," Kara said from somewhere behind me.

"On it." Bryn shot past me, her wings unfolding, and up into the air she went in two strides. She notched an arrow as I dodged another swing of steel. Kara spun in front of me, taking the head clear off the Dragur that had just attacked me.

"You're welcome." She smiled, her eyes bright before she shifted her weight and went on the attack.

I lunged forward, swinging my weapon and cutting down a Dragur to my right. Their body hit the stone floor with a heavy wet sound. With both hands, I lifted my ax over my head and in one swift motion, I detached his head from his shoulders.

An arrow whizzed past me, finding its mark between the eyes of a Dragur whose blade was raised above Magnus's head.

Magnus turned and winked up at Bryn before cutting down another Dragur.

One of the monsters roared like a dying animal, and the rest went into a frenzy.

"Don't let them get away," someone yelled as they moved through the courtyard, toward the east.

"Follow me," I called to Kara as I picked my way across the makeshift battlefield. For once she didn't argue, and a body dropped next to me, her sword still stuck in its throat.

"No one gets past us."

She nodded, retrieving her sword from the body, and we made our way to the other side of the courtyard where four Dragur were waiting for us. I turned my ax over in my hand, itching to feel the resistance of flesh and bone as they ran toward us, snarling and screaming.

Kara caught the first one, shoving her blade into his stomach. She grabbed his hair, forcing his head backward. Raising my ax, I came down on his neck and his head hit the ground with a thud. She pulled her blade free and the next two were upon us.

I ducked out of the way and spun around the back of one of them. With both hands on my ax, I swung, and another head rolled to the ground.

Kara was still fighting the other one, and as I turned to take on the next, I realized there were very few Dragur still standing. Steel clanked to the stone floor behind me and I turned to see Kara thrust a dagger upwards, through the Dragur's chin, and up into his skull.

"Didn't realize you had a dagger on you."

She yanked the blade free and kicked the body to the ground. "I always have a blade on me."

"Funny, I didn't come across one last night." I cocked an eyebrow at her as she wiped the black ichor off on her trousers.

"Guess you didn't look hard enough." She stashed the dagger in her boot.

She bent to pick up her sword and her body went stiff.

She rose to her full height, her face pale. "Something's wrong."

My heart fell into my stomach, and I grabbed her instinctively. "What is it?" I searched her eyes for the silver rim around her iris, but they were clear and devoid of Magik.

"No, not that." She looked around the courtyard and then, as if someone called her name, she whipped around, pushing me behind her as her wings burst from her back and she raised her sword.

I looked over her wings to see what had ignited the Magik within her, and saw a wall of Dragur. They stalked back and forth, snarling at us like we were their prey, but they didn't attack.

"Bryn," I yelled over my shoulder. "We need more of you in the sky." I pointed outside of the courtyard and her face paled. "Go," I shouted, and she shot off to get reinforcements.

"Magnus," I searched him out in the crowd.

His sword punctured through the neck of the last Dragur in the courtyard and the body slumped to the ground, revealing my friend.

"You need to see this."

He jogged over to me, jumping over the fallen bodies.

When he reached us, his eyes went wide, and he looked between the army in front of us and me. "What the Hel are they waiting for?"

"We need to get out of here," Kara barked, and stepped backward. "We can't fight them all."

"We don't back down from a fight." Magnus reached down and picked a sword off one of the dead bodies, and I did the same.

"While that's admirable, only a fool lets their arrogance stop them from doing what they should," Kara snapped at him. "Now fall back." Her voice was commanding and some invisible force tugged at me, forcing me to take a step back, and Magnus did the same. I looked around and noticed the others in the courtyard had also followed her command.

Some of the Dragur whooped and hollered, sending a shiver down my spine. Kara took another step back, her wings forcing Magnus and me to move with her.

I scanned the army in front of us, looking for a weakness, a hole in their defense, but the way they moved back and forth, shifting their lines, made it hard to pinpoint anything other than their size.

The Dragur started to part down the middle, making room for something or someone, and I froze.

My heart battered against my chest, and adrenaline pumped through my veins. The Dragur parted and a tall man dressed in black shadows stepped forward. His long jet black hair and pale skin were striking, flawless and God like. A wicked grin spread across his face and he held out his arms.

"Loki." Kara said under her breath.

Ice filled my heart and pumped through my veins. Freezing me to the spot.

"Hello, Kara," he purred.

CHAPTER THIRTY-SEVEN

KARA

"How's my favorite murderous little Valkyrie?" He sauntered toward me. His shadows moving of their own accord as they swirled around him. The caw of a hawk sounded overhead and my heart faltered.

The bird.

It was always there. In my dreams, in Midgard when I killed Si, here when I lost control. It was always watching, always waiting.

"It's been you all this time?" My ears rang as a fury I'd never felt before ripped through me.

It almost felt too obvious. The games, the secrets, using others to do his bidding. The only reason I dismissed Loki early on was because his games always skewed towards inconvenience, not domination. Waking the Disir, it wasn't his style. Or so I thought.

He made a sweeping motion with his hand and took a bow. "I'm surprised you didn't figure it out. Disappointed, really."

My fingers tightened around the hilt of my sword.

"Good, you're in the mood for blood." His black eyes sparked with amusement. He waved his hand and the sound of bodies dropping to the ground curdled my stomach. I turned to find Si, Magnus, and every other warrior and shield maiden on their knees in the courtyard.

I turned back to Loki and raised my sword. "Let them go."

"Or you'll do what?" He snarled. "You have no power here." He stalked toward me and my mouth went dry. Bryn and the others would be here soon.

I held my sword up to my neck. "Oh, no?" I didn't want to kill myself, but if it ended this insanity, I would do it.

Loki's eyes flashed as he stalked toward me, and the corner of his lips twitched. Either he was unsure if I was serious, or he was enjoying this.

"I doubt you want to start your whole ritual over when you're so close. Only one more sacrifice, right?"

He kept moving closer, and I held the blade tighter to my throat. A warm trickle of blood skated down the side of my neck.

His eyes tracked the blood dripping down my skin and then flicked back up to me. "Someone has been talking to the Norns, I see." He looked me up and down.

"I have. They seemed disappointed in how remedial your plans are." My heart slammed against my ribcage, but my hand stayed steady.

His eyes flashed with excitement, and he smiled. "Lying doesn't suit you, Kara."

"Who says I'm lying?" I swallowed past the pain in my throat.

He cocked his head to the side and frowned. "Because I know how blind they really are." He stalked closer. "And not being able to see what I'm up to is just the tip of the iceberg."

"I don't believe you." If that's true, we're in a lot more trouble than I realized.

"Believe me, don't. What do I care?" He shrugged as he casually walked through the men and woman on their knees. "The only thing that matters right now is finishing the ritual."

I didn't have time to think about the Norns, and what they did and didn't know. Every life in this courtyard was on my shoulders, and I'd do whatever I had to, to make sure they all walked out of here to see another day.

"Let them go or I will end this, right here, right now."

Loki stopped a few feet in front of me and sighed. "You're right about one thing." A devilish grin pulled at his lips.

He raised his hand, rotated his wrist, and palmed his fingers. Si lifted off the ground and flew toward Loki. "We will be ending this right here, right now." Si landed at Loki's feet, and he caught himself before he could fall flat on his face. Loki grabbed him by the hair and pulled his head back. A gold dagger appeared in his hand and he pressed it to Si's exposed throat. "Now, do you want to be the reason I kill him, or do you want to put that sword down?" Loki leveled his eyes at me as he yanked Si's head back even further. There wasn't an once of humor in his face. He'd do it, he'd kill Si like it was nothing.

"Let him kill me," Si snarled and pulled against the Magik, holding him in place.

"This doesn't involve you," Loki snapped at him and smashed the hilt of the dagger into his face. The crunch of his nose breaking made me want to vomit, and I removed the blade from my neck.

"Good girl," Loki purred, and my skin crawled. "Now, since you've been so accommodating to my plans, I'll allow you this one act of kindness. You get to choose your last kill."

I shook my head. "I won't kill any of them."

He cocked his head to the side. "You misunderstand. Someone is dying in this courtyard. Either you pick someone or he dies, and then we try again." He yanked Si's head back again, pressing the tip of the blade against the hollow of his throat.

"The Norns said each sacrifice must fit a specific type of death."

"Quite right." Loki smiled. "It just so happens that everyone here fits the criteria. How fortunate are we?"

My mouth fell open as I looked around at the men and

women around me. "You orchestrated the horns to bring them here?"

"One of my finer tricks," he said, clearly pleased with himself. "Do you want to know which sacrifice their death will count toward, or do you prefer to do your work blind?"

"My work?" I stepped forward and had to fight the urge to close the distance between us and rip his head clear off his shoulders. "None of this is my doing." White hot rage burned through my veins.

"Are your hands not covered in their blood?" He looked down and nudged his chin toward me.

Looking down at my hands, they were coated in blood, and large drops fell from my fingers. I dropped my sword, and it clanked against the stone floor. I brought my shaking hands up and turned them over as my mouth went dry and my stomach threatened to empty its contents.

My dagger, deep in Si's chest. The man from my dreams, bloody and dying in the snow. A woman, her throat cut wide open, a tear falling down the side of her face. Someone kneeling in the shadows and my sword shoved into their back, between their ribs, and into their heart. Another slice of a throat, another dagger in someone's chest, a body slumping against me as I push them to the ground.

My hands shook, and tears stung my eyes.

"That's right, you did all that," Loki cooed. "You killed each and every one of them." A grin spread across his face that made me want to scream.

"Why are you doing this to me?" My voice shook.

"You mean the Norns didn't tell you?" His brow furrowed. "Interesting." He was like a cat playing with a mouse.

"Tell me what?" My voice shook with a mix of rage and disgust. I don't know who I hated more, him for forcing me to kill all those people or myself for not being strong enough to fight against his influence.

"All in due time, my pet. First things first. It's time to pick someone, or I'll do it for you, and I doubt you'll enjoy my choice." He pulled the dagger across Si's face, opening up a gash on his cheek. Blood trickled down his face, staining his dark linen shirt, but he didn't make a sound.

"I can't." I shook my head.

Loki disappeared from Si's side, and the wind rustled my hair. "Oh, but you can," he whispered behind me, sending a shiver across my whole body. His arm wrapped around my middle in an intimate embrace, and he placed the gold dagger in my hands.

He moved my body slowly, as if he were guiding me through a dance. "It's just one more life and then you're free," he breathed against my neck, and I recoiled.

I couldn't kill one of them. They didn't deserve this fate, and I wouldn't condemn them. I gripped the dagger tighter, steeling my nerves for what I had to do.

"Just one more life and that's it, you swear it?" I asked as I scanned the courtyard and my eyes met Si's.

Loki hummed under his breath, the vibration radiating from his chest into my back. "Just one more life by your hand." He whispered against my ear. He took a step back, but his hands remained on my elbows.

I spun on him, lunging with the dagger raised, but he rolled his eyes and snapped his fingers. The dagger vanished from my hand and reappeared in his. "How predictable." He reached down and pulled the head back of the person closest to him. Without even looking, he pulled the dagger across his throat. Blood streamed down the man's chest and he slumped to the ground.

I shuddered, unable to keep my composure. I'd seen more than my fair share of death in battle. But to rob a defenseless person of their life to prove a point ignited a rage inside me that left me shaking.

"Shall we try again?" Loki's eye met mine and my body went cold.

"You're a monster."

"I've been called worse." He stepped over the person slumped at his feet and handed me the dagger again. "Last chance before I take things into my own hands." He stared me down as I wrapped my fingers around the hilt of the dagger.

I looked around the courtyard at Magnus on his knees a few feet away. At Si, bloody and bruised in front of the army of Dragur. A woman I'd seen in the bar my first night here. A man with dark curly hair I spoke to before the burial rite. My heart ached, and I knew with every bone in my body, every fiber of my being, that I'd rather die right here and now than hurt any of them.

I turned back to Si. His eyes met mine across the courtyard, and my heart broke. I wish we'd had more time together, but fate had different plans for us. I gave him a small secret smile and then turned the dagger on myself, shoving it into my stomach and twisting.

"Oh, for sorðinn's sake," Loki grumbled. "Must I do every-thing?" The dagger vanished from my stomach, and the wound stitched itself together in the space of two heartbeats.

Loki stood in front of me, smoke curling from his fingertips.

"No!" I heard Si yell from the other side of Yggdrasil, as a heavy darkness settled over my eyes and into my bones. My heart rate slowed as the world faded around me. Every thought emptied out of my head. My concern for the people in the courtyard. Sigurd, bloody at Loki's feet. Magnus helpless and on his knees a few feet away. Talon and Bryn who were probably on their way.

Everything vanished. Leaving me an empty shell until there was nothing left but the sound of Loki's voice and the cold talons of his Magik under my skin.

CHAPTER THIRTY-EIGHT

SIGURD

"So much for being the nice guy." Smoke curled out of Loki's fingers and slithered over Kara's skin. She exhaled, and the smoke entered her mouth, her eyes, and her ears until there was nothing left and her body went rigid.

"Now be done with it."

Kara pulled the dagger from her boot in a mechanical movement and stepped up to Magnus. He didn't flinch, didn't cry out or beg for his life. My heart shattered, and I tried to get free, but Loki's Magik kept me pinned to the spot.

Magnus's eyes met mine, and he nodded. "It's okay," he mouthed.

"Please," I screamed. "Don't make her do this."

He closed his eyes as Kara stood over him and placed her dagger at his neck.

"Kara!" Desperation clung to me as I tried to free myself from Loki's Magik. "Kara, please," I choked, but she couldn't hear me, couldn't see what she was about to do.

She was no longer the woman I kissed last night, no longer the woman who sat beside me at breakfast or fought with me to save these people. She was an empty shell, another monster of Loki's making, forced to do his bidding.

She pulled the blade across his throat. I stopped breathing, stop fighting against the Magik as the delicate flesh of his neck split open slow and steady. He didn't make a sound as blood trickled down his collarbone and over his chest.

Rage and agony tore through me as his body slumped to the ground. Kara stepped over Magnus and looked up at Loki without a single emotion on her face as his blood dripped from her dagger.

A scream tore from my throat and I pushed against Loki's Magic once more. My blood demanded revenge for my best friend, for my brother. My soul begged to feel the heat of Loki's lifeblood on my hands, and watch the light die out in his eyes.

I'd make him suffer for the pain he's caused not just to me, but to Kara, Magnus and all the others lives he's taken for this sick game of his.

"That's more like it," Loki cooed and held out his hand to her. Kara handed him the weapon that ended my friend's life as she stepped toward him.

"Let her go, you bastard." My words came out in a snarl.

"Watch yourself, or I'll have her kill you just for fun." He pinned me with an icy stare, and I recoiled.

"You can fight this, fight him," I pleaded with Kara.

She leaned down, so we were face to face. "I don't want to." She held my gaze and the silver rim of Magik shimmered around her deep jade eyes.

Loki chuckled as Kara stood and took his hand. The two of them walked out of the courtyard and toward the Dragur army. They split down the middle once more and she disappeared into their ranks.

The moment Loki was out of sight, his Magik lifted, and I ran to Magnus. Pulling him into my lap, his eyes met mine as blood poured out of his neck.

"It's okay." I combed his hair back. "You're going to be okay."

He reached up and touched my face as tears fell from my eyes.

"Please don't go." I rocked him in my arms and his hand slipped from my face.

His body went limp in my arms and something essential tore open inside me. It should have been me. He didn't deserve this, not after everything he's done for me, for Kara, for everyone in Folkvang. Magnus was the best of us, and now I'd never get to tell him how much I loved him. How much I owed him for meddling in my life.

A tear fell from my face and landed on his forehead as I rocked him in my lap. He was gone, well and truly gone, and there was nothing I could do about it. There was no Magik that would bring him back from the stars. No bargain I could make to trade my life for his.

"Si." Valttrie touched my shoulder. "We need to move him." I clung to Magnus, barely hearing his words. "Si, the fight isn't over."

The Dragur roared, echoing the scream building in my chest. I nodded at Valttrie.

I closed Magnus's eyes, and he helped me carry him to the back corner furthest from the army.

Grabbing the weapon closest, I turned to face the Dragur. Every single one of them would pay for Magnus's death.

The Dragur edged forward now that their master was gone. They howled and screamed like wild beasts as the men and woman still alive formed ranks on either side of me. There weren't enough of us, but every person here would fight to the death if that's what was required.

"Kill them quick, with no hesitation," I ordered.

"For Folkvang," someone yelled.

For Magnus, I thought, and my heart lurched as fury pumped through my blood. Not now, I told myself. I couldn't allow myself the luxury of mourning my friend. These people needed me, Kara needed— I faltered as the image of her slicing Magnus open played for me again.

The Dragur rushed forward, their swords raised as they funneled into the courtyard. Vengeance propelled me forward as the first reached me. I cut the head off one in a single swing. I sliced through the next one, his blood splattering across my chest, and pushed forward.

Half a dozen ran at me, and my blood cried out for war. Everything blurred around me, as steel clashed with steel. I swung with both hands, using the force of my entire body to cut them down. One by one, their bodies piled high as the image of Magnus's blood pooling under him assaulted me.

Dozens more poured into the courtyard, where one went down, two more took their place. I hadn't seen a battle like this since my mortal life in Midgard. I turned on my heel and blocked an ax from slicing through my shoulder when something sharp and blunt ripped through my side. I disarmed the ax wielding Dragur and cut his hands off at the wrists, before shoving my sword through his skull.

I looked down at my side—the hilt of a dagger stuck out. I shifted and pain shot through my back and down my leg.

Another Dragur rushed me, and I raised my sword. They swung again, and I met their blow once more. The thing snarled at me, black ooze dripping down his temple. He swung for a third time and when I reached up to block him, the dagger shifted.

White, hot pain seared through me as if someone had shoved a blade fresh from the forge into my side.

I lost my footing, and my vision blurred. It couldn't end like this. Not with Kara missing, not with Magnus dead in the shadows.

The Dragur stalked closer, his form shifting and moving out of focus.

I have more to do, more to fight for. I sucked in a breath to steady myself.

He swung, and I dodged to the right, but I wasn't quick

enough. The edge of his blade sliced across my arm. The sting of my skin being torn open brought everything back into focus and I rushed him, dagger be damned.

I kicked at his chest, forcing him backward. He stumbled, and I shot forward, shoving my sword through his chest. I twisted the hilt and gasped as he fell against me. The smell of death surrounded me as I pushed him off my blade.

Stumbling backward, I gasped for air. I needed to get this dagger out of me so I could move. Taking another step, my back hit the wall as I took in the chaos in front of me. I could barely make out the warriors on our side through the mass of Dragur that had piled into the courtyard.

I wrapped my hand around the hilt of the dagger and took a deep breath. I grit my teeth and forced myself not to hesitate.

One, two, three. I ripped it out and threw it to the floor.

A throbbing ache replaced the sharp stiffness of the blade, and I pressed my hand against the wound. My fingers were instantly slick with blood, but at the least the pain had eased some.

I stared down at the dagger, shining with my blood and a soul deep fury filled my body. For every drop spilled today, I'd make up in ten fold before this was over.

A Dragur noticed me against the wall and started toward me. I lifted my shirt over my head and whipped it into a tight band of fabric. Wrapping it around my middle, I pulled it as tight as I could bear and tied off the two ends. It would do for now.

The Dragur raised his sword to swing when an arrow struck between his eyes. I turned to see where the arrow had come from. Bryn hovered above me, her wings outstretched, and she notched another arrow. Her eyes met mine, and she nodded once before shooting again. Her arrow found its target, pinning another Dragur to the stone wall across from me.

I stepped forward, cutting through the neck of the monster

Bryn had incapacitated. His head fell off his shoulders and rolled across the bloody stone floor.

Another Valkyrie joined her in the sky and another. Arrows shot past the men and women in the courtyard, picking off the Dragur like they were nothing more than insects.

Dozens of Folkvang residents piled into the courtyard and pushed the Dragur back. Thank the Gods.

Someone grabbed my shoulder, and I turned to shove my sword into their chest.

"Friend, not foe," Talon deflected my blade, and I let out a huff. "I'm surprised Kara's not with you." She scanned the courtyard.

"Loki took her." A flash of her grabbing his hand made me flinch.

"Loki?" Her brow furrowed as she searched my face.

"All this is his doing. The Disir, controlling Kara. It's been him all along." The words were like poison in my mouth.

"Mother above," she said under her breath.

"At least it finally looks like a fair fight." I nodded toward the Valkyrie, soldiers and shield maiden now pushing back the Dragur.

"We had no idea—"

"I know. Another one of Loki's games." I shifted my weight and pain flashed through me, hot and urgent. "He used the horns to call a select few here to be the last sacrifice."

"Please tell me she didn't…" Her eyes widened, and I wished I could tell her what she wanted to hear.

I shook my head.

"Who was it?" Her voice was deadly serious.

I couldn't bring myself to say his name. Instead, I pointed to where I left him, safely out of the fray slumped against the wall.

She looked at him, and her hand went to her mouth. "Gods."

Shouts and cheers called my attention back to the fight. The Dragur were retreating, running toward the cover of the trees.

"Don't let them get away," someone yelled and dozens of warriors and Valkyrie alike chased after them.

As the courtyard emptied, a quiet I'd only ever known on a battlefield settled over us. I stepped forward and flinched as pain shot through me like lightning.

"There will be more boats to come before this is over," I said, looking over the piles of bodies.

Talon gripped my shoulder. "You're hurt."

"I'll be fine." I ignored her.

"You're no good to any of us, half dead."

"We don't have time."

"Make time," she ordered, and I felt that familiar pull all Valkyrie had that made it impossible to ignore her. "Besides, we need to regroup and plan our next step."

"How do we even begin to plan the next step? He's a God, Talon. A sorðinn God and we don't know where he's taken Kara or why. This was all supposed to be over with eight deaths. He said so himself."

"What did he say, exactly?"

"That she'd be free after the last kill," I repeated what he'd so lovingly cooed to Kara.

"Free doesn't mean finished." Talon's eyes met mine and realization bloomed in my chest.

"He's going to kill her, isn't he?" I had nothing left in me to mince my words.

She pursed her lips. "That would be my guess."

I ran a hand down my face. "Before we do anything else, we need to tell the others about Magnus." I closed my eyes, fighting back the anger and grief that threatened to spill over. Why him? Why did it have to be him?

"Go see Asheria. Let her patch you up." She clapped a hand on my shoulder. "I'll gather the others and we can tell them together."

"They can't know it was Kara." I met her eyes, willing her to understand.

She furrowed her brow.

"They won't be able to forgive her."

"They deserve to know the truth." She frowned. "I thought you, of all people, would understand that."

"The truth doesn't change that he's dead and we need their help if we're going to save her." I hated myself for even saying the words out loud. But I needed all the help I could get if we were going to stop Loki.

"I don't like it."

"I'll tell them when this is all over, I swear it." I held my hand out to her.

"Fine." She clasped my hand. "But if you don't tell them, I will."

I nodded. Still unsure if it was the right thing to do. I knew they would blame her, just as I had. It wouldn't matter that she fought it, that she'd tried to sacrifice herself, because in the end, Magnus had gone to the stars and it was her hand that had spilled his blood.

CHAPTER THIRTY-NINE

SIGURD

DAIMAN WALKED THROUGH THE DOOR, the black ooze from the Dragur covering his shirt and arms.

"Where the Hel have you been?" I shot to my feet.

"Looking for you," he said, out of breath. "They have your Valkyrie."

"She's not—"

"We know," Talon interrupted me. "We're working on a plan to get her back."

"Only problem,"—Ragnar leaned back in his chair—"we don't know where to look. They could be anywhere."

"Not anywhere." Daiman's eyes met mine.

Realization hit me like Thor's hammer. "The rift?"

"Rift, what rift?" Ragnar sat forward, resting his arms on the table in front of him.

Daiman nodded, ignoring Ragnar. "There's a temple on the other side."

"Anyone care to explain what in the nine realms these two are talking about?" Ragnar got to his feet, but I ignored him.

"Temple? For who?" I didn't know what I'd expected to be on the other side of the rift, but it wasn't a temple.

"Your guess is as good as mine. We could never get close to it. The Dragur have been guarding it day and night," Daiman finished.

"So that's what you all have been up to." I met his eyes, and he had the good sense to look ashamed.

"I'm sorry I didn't tell you."

"And what about knocking me unconscious?" I cocked an eyebrow at him. It would take more than an apology for me to forgive that transgression.

"Wait, what happened?" Talon looked between us.

"And that," Daiman said sheepishly. "She gave the order to keep it quiet, we couldn't—"

I held up my hand to stop his explanation. "Now's not the time."

"Right. Well, if we want to help Kara, we should start at the Temple."

Ragnar grabbed my shoulder. "I'm as keen as the rest of you to slaughter every one of those monsters, but first, you need to tell us what in the Gods' names is going on."

"Daiman and I found a rift in the protective barrier about two months ago, along the eastern border in the forest."

"It's how the Dragur have been gaining access to Folkvang," Daiman continued.

"Did you report it?" Bryn stepped forward, her words cold as steel.

We all turned toward her. They were the first words she had spoken since we'd told her about Magnus. She stared at me and Daiman, eyes red from the tears she'd cried over Magnus's body, but that's where her sadness ended. The rest of her was pure, hard steel, ready to be aimed at the person responsible.

"I did." A pit opened up in my stomach. "Freya said she was handling it." I should have done more. Should have tried harder to keep everyone safe. Magnus might still be here if Freya would have let me help.

"Clearly she didn't," Bryn said through gritted teeth. If Freya wasn't a goddess, I had no doubt that Bryn would've added Freya to the list of people who'd feel her wrath.

"She tried to seal the rift," Daiman jumped to Freya's defense, and I cringed internally. Now was not the time to go to bat for Freya, especially not with Bryn. "But whatever created it was immune to her Magik. So she told us to explore the other side, try to glean any information we could."

"How convenient." Bryn placed her hands on the table and stared down at Daiman like a wolf hunting its prey. I didn't envy him and I don't think a person in this room would stand in Bryn's way if she wanted to shut Daiman up.

"You think Freya did this on purpose?" Daiman squared off with Bryn. "She's done nothing but try to protect us."

"Oh really? Is that why Magnus is dead?" Her voice cracked and her words pierced through my heart. I looked to the ground, guilt, shame, and anger warring inside me. The image of Kara pulling the blade across his neck would haunt me until the end of time.

"Was she protecting us when the Dragur marched through our streets? When they killed mercilessly? Can you honestly sit there and defend her inaction?"

Daiman looked around the room, clearly just now realizing we were missing one of our own. "I... Bryn, I'm sorry. I didn't know."

"No, because your head is so far up Freya's ass you didn't even realize he wasn't here," Bryn yelled at him, her arms shaking with unbridled rage and grief.

It wasn't Daiman's fault that Magnus wasn't here. He wasn't in that courtyard. He couldn't have stopped what happened. But it didn't matter. Bryn would take her pain out on anyone and everyone around her.

I glanced at Talon and then at Bryn. Talon nodded and moved to her side.

"Come on, let's get some air." Talon had to force Bryn out the door.

I was right to sit on the truth of his death. If she had any idea that it was Kara who'd killed Magnus, the only way she'd help me get her back was if I promised to let her spill Kara's blood.

Guilt squeezed my heart and sent an ache through my chest that I knew would never ease. When the time came, I'd pay for my dishonesty with open arms. Until then, I would put everything I had left into stopping Loki and whatever he has planned for Kara and the nine realms.

"I'm sorry." Daiman clapped a hand on my shoulder. "I know the two of you were close."

I shrugged him off, unable to sit in my grief with the lie eating away at me. "We don't have time to mourn. Loki plans to wake the Disir and for whatever reason, he needs Kara to do it."

I explained everything we knew about the Disir and the sacrifices, careful to leave out the detail that each death had to be by Kara's hand.

"Sounds like we have a job to do." Ragnar stood. "Let's get her back and send Loki to the fiery pits of Muspelheim."

CHAPTER FORTY

KARA

THE SMELL OF MUSTY, wet earth filled my nose, and I opened my eyes. I tried to sit up, but only made it a few inches before I felt the chains on my arms and legs pull tight. Crude, jagged stone walls rose hundreds of feet above me, and a small patch of twilight sky was all I could see of the outside world.

Where the Hel was I? My heart raced as I looked from side to side. White stone statues surrounded me in a circle, their features worn down with time, but unmistakably female.

By the runes. They weren't just statues of women. They were the Disir.

My vision blurred and my head spun as my eyes settled on the first statue with wings frozen in an upward position, like she'd take flight any moment. The second held a sword in each hand, a frozen scream forever etched on her face. The third stood stoically, like she'd already accepted her fate.

God's, no. This couldn't be happening.

A chill ran down my chest and over my arms and legs. I strained my neck to look behind me. The fourth's arm was raised, dagger in hand, ready to find a home in someone's back. The fifth statue's wings were also out, but instead of being ready to take flight, they hung behind her like a cloak, as if she too had accepted there was no way out. The sixth wore a snarl, her sword crossed in front of her mid-swing.

My stomach heaved, and my ears rang. Every time I tried to imagine the Disir, I saw them as creatures beyond recognition. But these statues could have been Talon, Bryn, Me.

The Norns' warning about their true nature rang clear in my mind and I reminded myself that looks were deceiving. They may have once been like us, but their souls were corrupted the moment they took a life that didn't belong to them.

My eyes skated over the last two, and my chest tightened as sweat beaded on my brow. I had to get out of here. I pulled on the chains, but they didn't budge an inch.

"Finally, you're awake," a deep velvet voice purred from the shadows, sending a jolt of panic through me. "Does it always take you this long to come back to yourself?"

Loki, the courtyard, the Dragur, Si. *Oh Gods, please tell me I didn't kill him.*

"Who was it?" I strained to look at him. I needed to know that Si was still alive, that I didn't hurt him.

"Who was what?" Loki moved from the shadows and stood over me. His dark hair spilled toward me like a curtain as his jet black eyes met mine.

"Who did you make me kill?" I forced my voice to stay even. If it was the last thing I did, I wouldn't show him my fear, my anger, my pain.

"Ahh, yes." Amusement flickered across his face. "Of course, you don't remember." He snapped his fingers, and I was back in the courtyard. I watched the scene unfold as I pulled my dagger from its sheath and stood behind Magnus. Tears filled my eyes. The person who'd befriended me and treated me with kindness when I didn't deserve it.

I pulled my dagger across his neck, and his body slumped to the floor. A tear escaped my eye and rolled down my temple. I stepped over his body and, without a glance in his direction, I walked to Loki and took his hand.

Bile filled the back of my throat, and I had to fight the urge not to throw up.

"I warned you that you wouldn't like who I chose," he said in a sing-song voice.

I blinked away the tears and met his stare. Now was not the time for grieving. "I'm going to kill you."

"Don't make promises you can't keep, pet." A crooked grin pulled at his lips. "Now, shall we get started?"

"Started? I thought there were only eight sacrifices and the Disir would live again."

"You were misinformed. The Norns can be like that sometimes. Doling out information and holding it back when they feel like it." He circled, pulling vials from his coat and placing them around me. "One of their own must spill the blood of eight, and in turn, that hand shall be the ninth sacrifice to wake them."

"One of their own?" I laughed. "Sorry to disappoint you, but I am not a Disir."

Loki paused, placing the last vial next to my head. The deep maroon color staring back at me was unmistakable. Blood.

He placed a hand on my head and smoothed back my hair. "And that's where you're wrong."

He uncorked the vial and dipped his finger in the blood. He hovered over me like he was about to cut me open for the birds to feast on as he traced a design on my outstretched arm. When he stepped away, I glanced at the marking. It was a rune I didn't recognize.

"The Magik only works because of what flows through your veins." He walked over to the stone figure to my right and poured the contents of the vial over it. Blood dripped down the screaming face of the white stone figure. I watched the blood slide over the hollow eyes, down her blunt nose, and down her cheeks. I couldn't pull my eyes from the statue as blood dripped from her chin like a melting candle.

My stomach rolled, and my heart beat fast and shallow. It wasn't the sight of blood, but the spark of Magik that burned where he'd traced the rune on my arm that made me sick.

Loki grabbed another vial, dipped his finger in the blood again, and drew another rune just below the first one. "You are not who you think you are." He moved to the next statue and poured the vial over its head, just like the first.

The second rune burned on my arm like a brand, and I bit back the pain.

"You carry the blood of the old ones within you," he said, starting on the third vial. "A key left behind. A key to the lock on their cage."

I tried to jerk from his touch as he painted a rune on my other arm. "I am not a Disir," I said through gritted teeth.

"Didn't you wonder why I chose you for the ritual?"

I said nothing. There was no way I was what he claimed. The Disir were imprisoned for their crimes long before I was born. And who would dare to create more of those monsters after what they did?

"You are one of a kind, Kara. Truly unique. For only one of their own can return them to the nine realms. It was a clever little trick, impossible to break until I learned about you."

"I don't believe you."

A kernel of doubt wiggled in my brain. The Norns refused to tell me why I was chosen. Could it be because I carried the Disir blood?

No.

This was just Loki playing another game. There had to be some other explanation for all of this. Something that didn't bind me to the murderous, power hunger women standing frozen around me.

"Thankfully, your belief is not required for the ritual, only your blood." He shrugged and emptied the contents of the third vial.

My arms throbbed in time with my heartbeat as the runes roared to life. The pain grew with each mark on my skin and sweat beaded on my forehead. I took a deep breath to keep the pain at bay. Pulling on all my training, I quieted my mind and focused on the tiny window of sky above me.

He picked up the next vial, drew the fourth rune on my left arm, and poured the blood on the statue.

My vision blurred as white, hot fire licked at my arms. We were only halfway there and already I wanted to jump out of my skin. If he didn't kill me soon, the pain from all eight runes surely would.

He picked up the next vial, but his fingers froze on the cork. His gaze lifted to the hole above us and he cursed under his breath. Setting the vial down, he waved his hand and transformed into a hawk. He flew toward the hole high above me and disappeared.

I had to get out of here.

CHAPTER FORTY-ONE

SIGURD

AS WE MOVED through the forest, a pit opened up in my stomach. What if we were too late? What if Kara was already dead? Or worse, what if the Disir had already returned to the nine realms?

The deeper we moved into the woods, the quieter it got. There wasn't a single bird song, or rustling of woodland creatures in the bushes. Even the air felt stagnant and heavy, like the forest was also holding its breath.

I shuddered as if spiders crawled under my skin. Not only was it too quiet, but there was a thick haze of Magik in the air. I had to ignore every instinct screaming at me to turn around with every step.

I glanced between Daiman and Ragnar ahead of me and unease churned in my stomach. The hairs on the back of my neck prickled as if a landvættir sprite was whispering against my skin, and my heart raced as I stepped over a fallen tree. My gut screamed at me to turn around.

I stopped in my tracks and placed a hand on my sword. Every nerve in my body coiled, ready for a fight as I opened up my senses to the surrounding forest.

"What is it?" Talon said, coming to a stop next to me.

Bryn paused on my other side, deathly quiet, and I wondered if she could feel it too. I scanned the trees in front of us, searching for some unseen threat, when I noticed a Rune carved into the bark of a tree just ahead of me.

Why would there be runes carved into the trees here?

"Daiman," I called ahead, and both he and Ragnar turned. "Have you seen this before?" I pointed to the Rune. He spent more time in the forest than any of us and would know if it was out of place.

Daiman doubled back and inspected the tree in question. He ran his fingers along the bark. "It's freshly carved." He looked behind him. "We're close to the rift. It could have been done to ward people off."

"Or to warn someone of intruders?" I scanned the treeline.

"Keep your eyes and ears open. I doubt we're alone." Talon looked around as though something or someone might show themselves.

We started forward again, Ragnar and Daiman still in the lead, their hands on the hilt of their swords, ready to fight at any moment. My boots crunched through the dry leaves and brush when my ears started to ring. I stopped again and strained to hear beyond the high-pitched tone.

"Is it your wound?" Talon placed a hand on my upper back. "I thought you had Asheria take care of it."

"I did." I scanned the trees. "It's something else. Something's out there. Can't you feel it?"

She looked around but shook her head. "Are you sure?"

The distinct call of a hawk sounded overhead and my heart stopped. Tendrils of dark smoke crawled across the forest floor. Just like in the courtyard.

"Positive." I grabbed her arm and pointed as a wisp curled past us and disappeared into the bushes. "It's Loki." I pulled my sword from its sheath and yelled to Ragnar and Daiman, "Watch your boots!"

They both turned toward me, and Ragnar's eyes were

rimmed with Silver, just like Kara when she was under Loki's spell.

"Streð mik," I cursed under my breath.

"I guess there's no point in hiding anymore, is there?" Ragnar pulled his sword from his side and flipped it over effortlessly.

"Knock it off, Ragnar." Daiman gripped his shoulder, but Ragnar swung at him.

"You're joking, right?" Daiman jumped out of the way and pulled his sword to block the next blow.

I stepped forward to help Daiman when an arm wrapped around my neck and yanked me backward.

"Let him go, Bryn." Talon turned, sword in hand, eyes on Bryn behind me.

Moving as little as possible, I reached for the dagger at my side as her arm cut off my air supply.

"Or what? You'll kill me. Go ahead." Her breath was hot on my neck and it set my teeth on edge.

"It's Loki," Talon said. "He's playing with your mind."

I wrapped my fingers around the hilt of my dagger as the fight between Ragnar and Daiman heated up behind Talon.

"Last chance, put the sword down," Talon ordered as she stepped closer. Her eyes met mine and crinkled ever so slightly. I didn't relish hurting any of them, but we didn't have time for this. I plunged the dagger backward into Bryn's leg and freed myself from her grasp.

She snarled as I coughed and took a deep breath.

"Take care of them. I'll handle her." Talon nodded toward Daiman and Ragnar.

"Try not to hurt her." I turned on my heel and ran. "She's not herself."

Talon nodded once, and I ran to help Daiman.

Ragnar swung, pushing Daiman backward. He tripped over a

root hidden in the bushes and fell on his back. My heart lurched. Ragnar was brutal when he wasn't trying to kill you. With the state he was in now, there was no way he'd stop until Daiman was dead.

Ragnar stalked toward him and tightened his grip on the sword, his knuckles turning white.

My legs burned as I closed the distance. I wouldn't let another one of us fall today.

He raised his blade with both hands and my sword cut through the air, knocking him to the right and giving Daiman the chance to roll out of the way.

Ragnar turned on me, swinging like a madman, all technique and skill gone as unbridled rage propelled him forward. I blocked the blow and spun backward, putting some distance between the two of us and catching my breath.

"I don't want to fight you," I said as Ragnar's sword cut through the air and collided with mine again.

"This is insanity," Daiman yelled. "Snap out of it." He rushed Ragnar, taking his focus from me and allowing me to choose my next attack carefully.

Out of the corner of my eye, I saw Talon kick Bryn square in the chest, pushing her backward as Ragnar jumped out of the way of Daiman's sword.

The hearty snap of branches being ripped from their trees reached my ears, but I didn't have time to worry about Talon and Bryn.

I shot forward with both hands on my sword's hilt and sliced downward. My blade struck Ragnar's with enough force that his blade fell to the ground. Daiman was on him again. With the tip of his blade pressed against Ragnar's chest, he pushed him backward into a tree.

"Pathetic," Ragnar spit at Daiman. "Can't even fight your own battles. You don't deserve to be here."

I winced as Ragnar cut right to the heart of Daiman's insecurities.

Daiman pressed the sword harder and a trickle of blood stained Ragnar's green linen shirt.

"Daiman." I grabbed him by the shoulder.

"You can't deny the truth." Ragnar smirked. "No matter how hard you train, you will never be as good as us."

"Sorðinn off, Ragnar." Daiman closed the gap between them and cracked the hilt of his sword against his head. Ragnar's head fell forward, his legs gave out, and he crumpled to the ground.

Daiman cleared his throat and turned back to me.

"Was that really necessary?" I raised an eyebrow.

"You telling me you wouldn't have capitalized on the opportunity to shut him up?" Daiman snapped.

He had a point.

"Bryn's down, but I don't know for how long," Talon said, out of breath as she jogged toward us.

"So it's just the three of us, then? Against an army of Dragur and a God," Daiman huffed.

"I've had worse odds." Talon shrugged.

"There's no shame in turning back," I turned to Daiman. "This isn't your fight." Now that it was just the three of us, I felt guilty asking him to march into a battle that we had little chance of walking away from.

"Isn't my fight?" Indignation laced Daiman's voice. "They killed Magnus and countless others. They've turned our home into a battlefield. And I don't know about you, but I'm not keen to live with Loki as ruler of the nine realms. There's no way I'm turning back now."

I clapped him on the shoulder and smiled. "Then lead the way."

CHAPTER FORTY-TWO

KARA

I TUGGED on the chains holding me to the stone platform, testing their strength. They didn't budge and there was very little wiggle room, but it was worth a shot. Taking a deep breath, I pushed the searing pain in my arms to a corner of my mind. There would be time later to lick my wounds and give in to the ache settling into my bones. But right now, I had to get out of here before Loki returned.

I inhaled deeply through my nose, and I relaxed each muscle in my arms, one by one. Deep breath in, relax, deep breath out. One more time. Deep breath in, release the tension in my shoulders, deep breath out. Turning my wrists over, I gripped the chains in both hands.

Deep breath in and out. I pulled on the chains, trying to curl my arms toward my chest. My biceps shook with the effort and the runes continued to burn my flesh. But I ignored it all, pulling as hard as I could.

There was a reason becoming a Valkyrie was a brutal and trying experience. It was for moments like this. To know you were strong enough to push through the pain, to dig deeper when you thought you had nothing left.

The chains budged a fraction of an inch, and I relaxed against the stone. Heart pounding and panting, I took a few seconds to recover before adjusting my grip on the chains.

I inhaled deeply, filling my lungs until they burned. Controlling the exhale, I pulled on the chains again. My left arm jerked as they loosened another inch. "Come on," I said through gritted teeth. The chain on my right side gave a little, and then my arms were flattened against the stone by some invisible force.

"Valiant effort, I'll give you that." Loki stepped out of the shadows.

I tried to move, to thrash out of the grip of his Magik so I could tear his head off, but I was frozen to the spot.

"But unfortunately for you, there won't be any more interruptions." He stalked toward me.

"I doubt that," I snorted.

"They can try, but they're going to have to kill a few of their own if they plan to reach you." A crooked grin pulled at his lips, and his eyes gleamed as if he relished in the idea of people killing each other for sport.

At least someone was coming for me. All I needed to do was stall, keep him talking, or at the very least distracted. If I could buy some time, it might be just what I needed to survive, because there was no way I could take him on by myself.

"You underestimate them."

"I doubt it." He picked up the vial he'd uncorked before he disappeared. "I've found that killing your loved ones against your will has a tremendous effect on one's psyche." His eyes met mine and the corner of his lips curled into a grin that made my stomach churn. "Wouldn't you agree?"

He was baiting me, but I wouldn't give him what he wanted. "Or you may have just given them another reason to kill you." I smiled up at him. Two could play this game.

He lowered his head, and a chuckle rumbled through his chest. "I'd like to see them try."

I sat up as far as his Magik and the chains would allow and looked him square in the face. "So would I."

His lips parted and some emotion I couldn't place crossed his eyes.

"Even if they defy all odds and make it here. You won't be alive to watch them fail." His eyes sparkled like he'd love to see people fighting over my dead body.

I thrashed against the chains, desperate for blood. His blood.

"I've always admired your fiery spirit." He looked at me like we were kindred spirits. "It's a shame to snuff out such a bright soul." He shrugged. "But we all have our parts to play."

"What happened to you? How can you care so little about destroying people's lives?"

"A few lives are nothing compared to making the Vanir and Aesir pay for their unchecked wrath. I'd think you of all people would want me to succeed."

"Me?" I snorted. Was he so delusional that he thought I'd understand and sympathize with this insane plan?

"Does it not bother you that my father punished you for something that was not your doing?" His head cocked to the side as if he truly didn't understand how I might see things differently.

"I may hate Odin for stealing my wings, for punishing me when it was your fault Sigurd died by my hand, but I would never kill innocent people to get back at him."

He shrugged and dipped his finger in the blood. "That's the difference between you and me. I'm willing to do what's necessary to serve justice."

"You think the ends justify the means, but when all is said and done, you're no better than him."

He leaned over, his face inches from mine. "I don't make it a habit of taking the opinion of those on death's door."

"Maybe you should." I tried to shove my head into his face, but his Magik held me tight.

He traced the next Rune on my right palm. The moment his finger touched my skin, flames galloped through my veins and I had to bite back the scream that threatened to burst from my chest. I wouldn't give him the satisfaction of hearing my pain.

Just like before, he poured the blood over the head of the statue and moved on to the next vial. He painted another Rune on my left palm, one on my forehead, and one on my chest.

By the time he was done, I was sweating and panting from the pain. Every muscle in my body felt stretched to its limit, and my legs had started to cramp. My head spun from exhaustion and the agony of the Magik consuming me. It was unlike any power I'd felt before. It pulled at the fabric of my soul, and devoured the Magik inside me like it was nothing. My vision blurred as I tried to hold on to consciousness.

The only thing keeping me attached to the physical world was the pounding of my heartbeat in my ears, my arms, my teeth, my fingers. My whole body pulsed as the muscle in my chest threatened to smash through my ribcage.

A distant part of my brain hoped I'd stalled long enough, that whoever was coming would still get here in time to stop Loki.

CHAPTER FORTY-THREE

SIGURD

NIGHT HAD FALLEN AS TALON, Daiman, and I made it to the rift without further incident. It had doubled in size, maybe even tripled, since the last time I was here.

"By the runes," Talon said under her breath.

"If Freya doesn't figure out how to control it soon, it will leave all of Folkvang unprotected." I took in the sheer size.

"I thought time was of the essence?" Daiman stopped halfway through the rift.

I approached and touched the barrier to the right. It sparked at my touch and rippled in a kaleidoscope of colors. My heart raced as I looked to the other side. Millions of stars lit up a night sky so different from our own.

"Here goes nothing." I walked through the rift with Talon right behind me.

"Weapons ready," Daiman called over his shoulder as he hid behind a tree.

I pulled my sword and pressed against the tree next to him. "Where's this temple?"

Daiman pointed through the trees to a cliff face about a hundred yards away. Torchlight flickered at its base, lighting up stone pillars on either side of an arch. Shadows moved in front of the pillars and dimmed the firelight frequently enough to denote there were a handful of guards at the entrance. Dragur.

"You two take the ground, keep to the trees," Talon said, eyeing the cliff face. "I'll take to the sky." Her wings unfurled slowly, keeping tight to her body.

I grabbed her forearm, and her eyes met mine. "Be careful."

"Always am." She winked and a gust of air threw my hair back as she thrust into the sky.

"This way," Daiman whispered, and motioned for me to follow.

We skulked through the trees and bushes, making our way as fast as possible while trying not to make a sound. The closer we could get without alerting the Dragur, the faster we'd be able to dispatch them.

When we were close enough that I could make out their faces, I grabbed Daiman's arm and pulled him behind a group of trees. We watched their movements for a few minutes, taking stock of the paths they walked, which were distracted and which were closest to the treeline.

"We take those two first," I said, pointing to the guards patrolling further away from the cliff face. "Then we aim for—"

Talon landed in the middle of their encampment, and they started shouting.

"I swear Valkyrie can't help making an entrance." A smile lit up Daiman's face, and we both ran toward the fight.

Talon looked like an angel of death as firelight danced over her bronze skin and black feathers. Her shadow cast on the cliff face, flickered and shifted with her movement. It was something straight out of a nightmare. Thank the Gods she was on our side.

I closed the distance to her as her sword sliced through the air, and cut a Dragur's head in half, from eyes to throat. Black blood oozed from the monster as his knees buckled and he collapsed. By the time I reached her, she'd already decapitated four of the guards.

I jumped into the fray, my sword connecting with one of the

Dragur guarding the temple entrance. He snarled at me like a bear and lunged. His blade came down on me repeatedly, each hit rattled through my arms as he kept me on the defense. He was stronger than the others I fought, more controlled. Counting his swings, I noticed a pattern. When he came down on my left side again, I dodged to the right and moved behind him, slashing across his arm.

His roar was deafening, and it threw any chance we had of sneaking into the temple out the window. He turned toward me, and I swung again, putting him on the defense and pushing him toward the treeline, away from the others.

He stabbed forward and swung with his free hand. I pulled my head back, but I wasn't quick enough and his fist connected with my jaw. A jolt of pain shot across my face, but with the adrenaline pumping through me, I barely registered the blow before I shot forward again.

My sword connected with his forearm and I sliced through his skin. Blood poured from the wound and the putrid stench of death filled the air.

As he met my blow, our swords connected and the crash of steel rang out, echoing off the cliff. I closed the gap between us, pushed his blade aside with my own, and knocked my forehead against his face, cracking his nose. I grabbed the dagger at my side and plunged the blade into his eye. He fell to his knees, and I brought my blade down on his neck, separating his head from his shoulders.

I pulled my dagger from his eye, wiped the blood off on my trousers, and turned to pick my next victim.

CHAPTER FORTY-FOUR

KARA

THE CLASH of steel rang through my ears and the flicker of flames flashed across my eyes like a dream. Nothing felt real anymore as shadows moved around, casting images on the walls of battles gone by.

Loki's face appeared above me, frantic and panting. I saw his face in double and triple, his eyes wide with anticipation as he blurred in and out of focus.

"Your sacrifice will bring in a new age for the nine realms." His voice echoed and my stomach heaved like I was out on the sea, cresting a massive wave in a storm. He cupped my cheek, and I pulled away from his touch. "Your sacrifice will not be forgotten."

Out of the corner of my eye, there was a flash of gold. I turned toward it just as he sliced the dagger across my wrist. There was no pain as my skin split open, a small silver lining, but I could feel the warmth of my blood trickle down my wrist.

He shifted to my other side, and I rolled my head with the movement. He placed the golden dagger against the blue veins in my wrist and pulled. Blood bloomed to the surface and spilled over.

Maybe this was what I deserved for killing Magnus, for ending Si's mortal life, for killing all those other poor souls. A single tear spilled from my eye as I stared up at the tiny window of sky above me. Maybe it wouldn't be so bad to be among the stars.

I closed my eyes as another clank of steel sounded somewhere in the nine realms.

"You're too late." Loki's voice echoed around me.

The sound of my name being screamed from what seemed like the other side of Yggdrasil reached my ears. I felt like my head was in a fog and I couldn't see, hear, or feel anything clearly.

My eyes fluttered closed, too heavy to keep open any longer. Fire and shadows flickered across my eyelids, but I couldn't bring myself to watch as the Disir returned to the nine realms.

CHAPTER FORTY-FIVE

SIGURD

I FORCED the double doors open and my breath caught. Kara was chained to a white stone, runes painted on her skin. Her wrists were cut and dripping blood into a pattern on the floor. Eight white stone statues surrounded her, covered in what I could only assume was blood.

The Disir.

"Kara," I yelled, hoping she was still alive. I rushed toward her and an invisible force slammed me against the wall.

Loki stalked toward me. "She was right." He closed the distance between us. "I underestimated you." He placed a finger under my chin and looked into my eyes. "What kind of man goes on a suicide mission to save the woman who betrayed him and ended his mortal life?"

"You ended my life, not her," I practically growled at him.

I could still hear Daiman and Talon fighting the Dragur just outside, and I hoped they finished the last of the Dragur quickly. As strong as I may be, I knew my limits, and I knew I couldn't take on Loki alone.

He clicked his tongue and shrugged. "Was it really so easy for her to convince you of her innocence?"

I refused to rise to the bait. "I was in the courtyard when you forced her to kill Magnus."

"Did I, though?" He cocked his head to the side like a bird

inspecting its prey. "I only pushed the issue. It was she who chose his death."

"She wouldn't have killed him." I refused to believe anything that came out of his mouth.

"Just like she wouldn't have killed you?" A smirk played on his lips as he toyed with me. He enjoyed this. "I guess some men have to learn a lesson more than once for it to stick."

I pushed against the force holding me to the wall, but his Magik was too strong.

Daiman stumbled into the temple, a Dragur impaled on his sword.

Loki raised his hand, and Daiman's sword clattered to the floor as he flew into the wall adjacent to me. "I must say, I'm surprised the two of you made it this far, but I'm afraid it's the end of the line."

The crack and crunch of stone splitting open and hitting the floor pulled all of our attention. I looked at Kara first, but the stone she was laid out on remained intact. I scanned the circle of statues. The one with her wings ready to take flight had a crack down her face and over her chest.

I didn't know how to stop what was happening. I didn't even know if we could at this point, but I couldn't do nothing. I pulled my feet up, placing them against the wall, and pushed. Loki's Magik was like a heavy door I was trying to force open, and I could feel a weakness in the pressure over my arms. He wasn't paying enough attention to me or Daiman now that a second statue started to crack open.

I took advantage of the weakness and pulled my shoulder off the wall and then the other. My core screamed with the effort, and my thighs shook as I pushed against the wall with my feet. I dropped free and caught myself on my hands and knees.

Loki didn't turn to me, and I quickly ducked behind one of the statues. I caught Daiman's eyes, and he nodded.

"How do you know they won't kill you on the spot?" Daiman called Loki's attention to him.

Loki's head swiveled in his direction. "Because I have something they'll want more than my blood."

As quietly as possible, I moved behind the next statue, placing Kara between myself and Loki.

"Says you. Considering they've been encased in stone for Gods knows how long, it's not like you could ask them what they want. Typical God," Daiman taunted, "imprinting your desires on others."

"And what would you know of it?" Loki's voice was ice cold as I moved to Kara's side.

I turned her face toward me. She was ghostly white, and my heart sank into my stomach. I pressed my fingers to her throat, looking for a pulse. It was there, but only just.

"Get away from her," Loki growled, and I was tossed backward into one of the statues.

Loki stalked toward me, his hand raised, smoke curling around his fingers. I tried to get to my feet, but his Magik rocked through my body, keeping me pinned to the spot. There was no mercy, no weak spot this time.

The smoke curled toward me, and I was powerless to get away.

"When are you going to learn, Loki?" Talon dropped from above like a stone through water. "You never come out on the winning side of your games." She held a sword in each hand, her wings splayed wide in front of me.

The smoke crawling toward me dissipated, and Loki's Magik released me. I scrambled to my feet, moving out of the line of fire.

"My dear sweet, Talon. I think you'll find I have the upper hand this time," Loki cooed.

I searched for Daiman where I'd last seen him, but he was no longer pinned to the wall. *Please still be alive.*

Loki flicked his wrist at Talon, but she didn't move. A smile pulled at her lips, and Loki frowned.

"Your Magik can't touch me." Talon lunged forward.

Loki jumped back, and a gold sword materialized in his hand. He blocked Talon's blade in the nick of time as she struck with her other weapon.

With my back pressed against the wall, I moved around the temple, looking for Daiman. *Please still be alive.* He was in this mess because of me. I had to get him out. I couldn't lose another friend.

The ground rumbled under my feet, and I looked to the circle of Disir encased in stone. The last statue cracked down the middle, and a ripple of Magik burst through the room, hitting me square in the chest, sending shards of ice through my veins.

My head cracked against the rocky wall, and my ears rang. Everything seemed to move in slow motion. Talon swinging her sword, Loki dodging out of her way. The tiny dust motes floating in the air all slowed down. I steadied myself, shook my head and took a breath. I was no match for the Magik in this temple, and neither was Daiman.

Pushing off the wall, I ran around the outer edge of the room until I found Daiman slumped against the floor.

"Come on Daiman." I pulled him upright and tapped his cheek. "Wake up." I shook him and his eyes fluttered open. "Are you hurt?" I searched his eyes as he let out a breath.

He shook his head. "I don't think so." He winced as I pulled him to his feet, and his gaze went to the fight between Talon and Loki. "Is she really going hand to hand with a God or am I seeing things?"

"No, she really is." I let out a nervous laugh.

"Remember when we said we'd have a rematch?"

I nodded. The memory of the first Dragur attack and the competition for Ragnar's ale felt like years ago.

"I win this round."

I laughed in relief as I nodded. He could have this win; I was more than grateful he was still alive.

Kara let out a scream that made my blood still. All my attention went to her as her body lifted off the stone. The chains around her wrist and ankles were the only thing keeping her from floating away.

Blue-white light burst from the cracks in all eight statues and centered on Kara. The rumbling grew more intense and rocks fell around us. Chunks of stone crumbled away from the statues and the light grew more intense.

Kara's body arched as more light concentrated on her. The stone she was attached to exploded like wood under a blast of lightning, and the chains dangled from her floating body.

I ran toward her, Daiman by my side, and grabbed the chains. We both pulled, trying to bring her back to the ground, but she didn't budge.

"What do we do?" Daiman and I looked up at Kara as the statue closest to us erupted, leaving nothing but a woman covered in white dust and blue light.

"You've done quite enough," Loki snarled, and the chains wrapped around our necks like the chilly hand of death and I sucked in a breath.

Another statue exploded as I struggled against the chains cutting off my airway. Kara's wings erupted from her back above us, and another statue shattered into a million pieces. Stone and dust flew in every direction, and the chains squeezed tighter.

Loki let out a roar as another of the Disir was freed. The chains relaxed enough for me to free myself. I coughed, trying to pull fresh air into my lungs, but the air was full of Magik and stone, and dust.

Next to me, Daiman gasped as another statue shattered into

a million pieces. "We've got to get out of here." Daiman coughed and pulled on my arm. "We can't save her."

Boom. Another Disir freed.

"She doesn't deserve to die alone," I yelled over the rumble of the temple crumbling to pieces with each explosion.

"She's not alone," a sickly sweet voice said behind me and my heart jumped into my throat as Daiman's eyes went wide.

A blade kissed my neck, and I went still as another did the same to Daiman. The Disir dragged us away from Kara as another statue exploded, sending vibrations through the entire temple.

The last statue shattered, and the rumbling stopped. The Temple went utterly still, the only sound coming from me and Daiman gasping for breath.

Kara dropped like her strings had been cut. Her body hit the stones below her, and her limbs twisted at odd angles.

Bile rose to the back of my throat as Loki screamed again. They stretched his arms wide, one Disir on each side of him, and I immediately scanned for Talon. Like us, one of the Disir had captured her, and she was on her knees watching Loki be dragged toward one of the Disir.

"At least he'll die with us," Daiman said through gritted teeth.

If that was all we accomplished today, I could return to the fabric of the universe knowing justice was served, not only for me and Kara, but for Magnus and all those other souls Loki stole for this ritual.

CHAPTER FORTY-SIX

KARA

"Bring the girl," a woman's deep voice boomed through the temple.

"Don't—*hrumpf!*" someone shouted behind me, but their protest was cut off.

Arms grabbed at me from multiple directions, forcing me to my feet. I could barely open my eyes, and my body begged to melt into the floor. Supporting my weight on either side, they dragged me forward. I didn't bother trying to keep myself upright or hold any of my weight. If they were going to kill me, I wouldn't help them escort me to the hangman's noose. Not that I had the energy to, anyway.

The light changed behind my eyes, and I managed to look up. We stood in the moonlight from the skylight above. And so the stage was set, the spotlight shining with an audience in the shadows to see me take my final bow. The two holding me lowered me to the floor. The stone surface felt warm against my icy skin. I didn't have much longer. I'd lost too much blood.

A woman with long reddish-brown hair that curled to her waist stepped forward. Her features were soft, motherly, and it surprised me. She didn't look like the soul sucking monster the Disir were described as.

She looked down at me with a soft smile. "You have sacrificed much tonight." She placed a hand on my cheek. "And my sisters and I thank you." She cocked her head to the side to meet my gaze. Bright blue eyes like the dawn stared back at me. "You do not deserve the fate *he* has thrust upon you," she sneered as she looked at something over my shoulder.

She nodded once as my breathing became short and shallow. My eyelids drooped as the coldness disappeared. There was a struggle somewhere around me, but it might as well have been in another realm for how distant it seemed.

"Open your eyes, Kara." Her voice cooed at me as warmth spread through my body.

"You can't do this," Loki growled, the warmth of his breath touching my cheek.

I opened my eyes to find him on the ground next to me, his face pressed tightly to the stone. Our eyes met. What was he doing on the floor with me? Why were we still alive?

A glint of gold caught my eye as his eyes widened and his mouth fell open in a gasp. A dagger stuck out of the side of his neck. Blood so dark it almost looked black trailed down his skin, and I realized there was no escape for me or my friends. They were going to kill every last one of us.

"Take him," someone whispered. "The power is yours."

Chills ran down the length of my body as a spark ignited deep in my abdomen. My mouth went dry, and the air was ripped from my lungs.

"Do it, girl," the voices whispered.

Heat spread from the spark inside me, lighting my veins with fire, and a hunger unlike anything I'd ever felt before propelled me toward Loki's bloody form.

The familiar note of a death song called out to me in the darkness, and Magik bloomed in my chest. Loki shuddered as I inched my way toward him. He shook his head and his eyes went dark as another note of his song played for me, echoing in the temple like a siren's melody in a cave.

"You don't want to do this," he sputtered, but his words were lost on me as his soul cried out, pulling me in.

Reaching out, I placed a hand on his cheek. His features softened, and I drew in his breath as my own. He blinked slowly and when his eyes met mine once more, there was no pain in them. I took another deep breath, and light sparked on his lips.

The hunger inside me snarled at the sight, and strength I didn't know I had propelled me forward. My mouth hovered over his, the light brushing against my lips like the sweep of a lover's tongue, and the predator inside me purred. I brushed my mouth against his, and the spark found its way into my mouth, my blood, my soul.

The song grew louder, pulling me under its spell, and I deepened the kiss.

He didn't fight me as I pressed myself to him, and my heart beat with a renewed fever as I sank into the kiss. My body warmed as his song danced over my skin and echoed in my bones. I wanted—no, needed more. I wanted to taste every note, breathe in every beat of his heart, and luxuriate in the power of his Magik swimming in my head.

I grabbed his face, my fingers digging into his skin as the heady desire to take every last shred of his soul, every drop of his Magik, reached a fever pitch. My heart raced, my vision blurred, my head spun, and the music of his soul drowned out the nine realms. His sound poured into me, slaking my thirst and bringing me back from the brink of death.

And then it was silent. He'd vanished entirely.

It was as if he'd been plucked from under me, and the hunger inside me bucked in response.

I looked around the temple, but he was gone and so were the Disir. A hollowness settled in my chest as I met Talon's eyes, Daiman, and then Sigurd's. They stared back at me in horror, like I was a caged animal finally free of my chains.

I closed my eyes and searched the nine realms for the

familiar song of Loki's soul, but there was nothing. Not a single note reached me. He was gone, taken from me before I could take him completely. Anger flared in my chest as the primal spark inside me purred and settled.

More. A voice whispered in the back of my mind. *I want more.* It growled.

CHAPTER FORTY-SEVEN

SIGURD

"Where the Hel did they all go?" Daiman was the first to speak.

"A problem for another time," I said. "Kara?" I stepped toward her hesitantly. I wasn't sure what the Hel just happened or if she was even still herself.

"Don't." Talon stepped in front of me, reaching out to Kara. "You're safe now." Kara let Talon help her to her feet and my heart lurched.

Chains still hung from her arms and legs. The manacles around her forearm had rubbed her skin raw. The wounds on her wrist had stopped bleeding and a little color had seeped back into her face. I tore a strip of fabric from my shirt and moved to bandage her wrists, but Talon stopped me.

"It's okay." Kara's voice was hoarse and deep. "I'm okay."

Talon dropped her arm, and Kara held her wrist out to me. Blood and dirt caked her skin, and I tore off another scrap of fabric and wrapped it around her other wrist. It would have to do until we could get back to Folkvang and get her properly healed.

"Anything we can do about the chains?" She winced through each word. Whatever she'd done to Loki had brought her back from the brink of death, but it hadn't refueled her strength.

"Here." Daiman handed me a dagger.

"Let's give them a minute." Talon took Daiman by the arm and directed him back through the double doors.

"Come here." I guided her to the largest piece of rock still standing and motioned for her to rest her arm on the stone. "I'll be as gentle as I can," I said without looking her in the eye.

Digging the tip of the blade into the keyhole of the manacle, I banged on the hilt to wedge it in.

"I'm surprised to see you here." Her voice was soft, tentative, like she was afraid.

"Why wouldn't I be?" I grabbed a piece of stone and bashed it against the hilt. The tip of the blade wedged into the lock.

"Loki told me"—she touched my arm, and I looked up at her —"about Magnus." A tear fell from her eye. The frown between her eyebrows and the quivering of her lip reminded me of my own heartbreak. "I'm so sorry."

I forced myself to focus on the manacle and banged the stone against the dagger again. "It wasn't your fault."

"It doesn't change that he's—"

"Please don't." I glanced up at her. "I can't..."

She nodded, and I knocked the stone against the dagger again, and the manacle sprung open. She rubbed the raw skin of her forearm and winced. Worry flicked through me. She'd been hurt much worse in the past and didn't even bat a lash.

"How bad is it?"

Her eyes met mine, and she opened her mouth to speak.

"Don't lie to me."

She closed her mouth and let out a huff. "I should be dead."

"But you're not because of what you did to Loki?" I asked tentatively.

She nodded.

"And what exactly did you do to him?" I had an idea of what happened, based on what Freya told me about the Disir consuming souls. But Kara wasn't a Disir, was she?

Her eyes dropped from mine. "I don't know."

A lie. My stomach sank, and I motioned for her other arm. I didn't blame her for not wanting to talk about it. Whether she fully understood what had transpired between her and Loki was anyone's guess, but now was not the time to push for answers.

I repeated the same steps with the dagger and bashed the stone against the hilt.

"Do the others know about..." She paused. "The courtyard?"

I understood what she meant without her having to say the words. "Talon knows the truth of what happened. But I thought it best not to share with the others until you were safe."

"Why?"

"Because I needed their help, and we didn't have time to explain everything."

"I see. So what will you tell them?" she asked, deadly calm, as if she'd already resigned herself to another hundred years of isolation.

"The truth." I smashed the stone against the hilt and the manacle sprung free. "That Loki forced you to kill him. That you had no choice or control."

"It wasn't so long ago I told you the same thing and you didn't believe me. What makes you think they'll be any different?"

"Because you're not the only one who's had Loki meddle with their mind." I got to work on the chains around her ankles.

We fell into a tense silence. There was a lot to say, but I had no clue where to start. I honestly thought we'd all be dead right now.

She held her arms around her middle, a barrier between her and the world. I could feel the walls around her as if they were my own. So much had happened over the last twenty-four hours. I'd yet to sort out how I felt about us before our world was turned upside down yet again. I couldn't imagine what she was thinking or feeling after the ordeal she'd been through.

"Where do you think they went?" She finally broke the silence once I freed her ankles.

"I don't know." I sighed and got to my feet.

"I have to go after them." She shook her head.

"I know." I held my hand out to her. "But first let's go home." She nodded and placed her hand in mine.

"Thank you for not leaving me behind when you had every right to." She squeezed my hand like it was a lifeline.

My heart cracked, and I had to force down the lump in my throat. "I was taught to never leave someone behind, no matter the circumstance." Magnus's words rang through me and tears pricked my eyes. I'd spend the rest of my days trying to live up to the man Magnus thought I could be.

We made our way out of the temple to find Daiman and Talon waiting for us. Kara went to Talon and the two of them led the way back to Folkvang.

"Is she okay?" Daiman said under his breath.

I studied her ahead of us and a nagging feeling unfurled in the pit of my stomach. "I don't know."

Kara may not know what happened in that temple with Loki and the Disir, but I wouldn't wait around to find out. From now on, I'd be prepared for whatever was thrown at us.

END CREDIT SCENE

The blue flame leaves cast a glow over the eight Disir lying among the roots of Yggdrasil. They were alive, but nowhere near full power.

"You will need to take from the tree of life if you are to be restored to your former glory," a voice said from the shadows.

Eight pairs of eyes turned toward the voice.

"Why have you brought us back to the nine realms?" The one who helped save Kara demanded.

"Are you not thankful to be saved from your slumber?" the shadow voice asked.

"Depends." Her blue eyes searched the darkness.

"You wanted to kill the Gods, almost did before they turned you to stone. Can I assume your wish to destroy them remains intact?"

"You speak of the Gods as if you aren't one yourself." Her reddish-brown hair swirled around her like seaweed as she stepped forward and narrowed her eyes.

"The Asier have always been a blight on the universe. Taking what they want and destroying anything and anyone in their path. I too would like to see Odin's reign come to an end."

The Disir smirked. "And what's in it for you?"

"I want to rule the nine realms."

"What makes you think we'd bow down to you?"

"Ahh, that's the best part. You wouldn't bow to me or anyone ever again. You'd be free to do as you please once we secure my throne."

Her eyes narrowed. "How can we be sure you're telling the truth?"

Loki stumbled out of the shadows, tied up and gagged. Wide-eyed, he stared at the Disir and then back toward the shadows.

"I present to you a son of Odin. Let him be the first to fall in their line."

The Disir's lips curled into a smile as she reached down and placed a hand on one of the roots of Yggdrasil. Magik crackled as she pulled from the tree of life. Her eyes glowed as she let go of the root and stepped forward.

Grabbing Loki by his shirt, she leaned closer and pulled the gag out of his mouth. Before he could say a word, she pressed her lips to his. He grunted, and she exhaled.

White light glittered from his mouth into hers. His skin became more sunken with each second that passed, his bones more visible as his eyes started to glow with the sapphire blue of the monsters he'd once commanded.

She let go of his shirt, and he slumped to the floor.

"You have yourself a deal."

AUTHOR NOTE

I started writing this book in July 2019 at a writers retreat in Edinburgh. To say I was living life to the fullest is an understatement. In October of that same year I got married in England surrounded by friends and family. Life was grand and I felt like I was hitting my stride.

Then 2020 kicked us all in the teeth and I struggled. I struggled more than I have in over a decade. I stopped reading, I stopped writing. It seemed trivial and irresponsible to not be paying attention to what was happening in the outside world. Ahh, the outside world...sometimes I forget that we were allowed to frolic through this world without a care.

Like many others, I stayed glued to the news or as some like to call, the Reality TV show called America. I educated myself on topics of politics, Black history, American history, Vaccines and Viruses, and with each new thing I learned, the more enraged and frustrated I became. How did we get to this point?

My heart hurt, I felt lost in a life I never expected to be living. Eventually my characters packed their bags and stopped talking to me altogether and I didn't have the strength to chase them. The things I once loved were too much of a reminder of all the things we've lost. They were a part of a world that didn't exist anymore and I didn't know how to make those pieces fit into this new reality. I couldn't turn to the things that made me whole the last time I was lost. Travel, friends, school, Soothsayer. So now what?

Well, one of my favorite authors, and I mean favorite, I will one-click buy anything she writes, released the second book in her new fantasy series.

A Kingdom of Flesh and Fire.

With each page I read, it was as if I was uncovering the key to who I used to be. Strong, confident, creative. Jennifer's words, her characters, the world she built turned a lock inside me and rekindled the fire in my soul.

Books can be like that sometimes. They can read you, understand you, take your pain, make you laugh and hold you at 3am when it's just you and the words on the page. Books have always been a unique, personal kind of Magic to me. When I finished reading, A Kingdom of Flesh and Fire, I felt like the pieces of me, I thought I lost, were slowly making themselves known again.

My characters started talking to me once more and the confidence I once had to create my own Magic bloomed in my chest. I sat down to write Kara and Si's story with renewed excitement and finally, after a year of unprecedented change and growth, I knew I was strong enough to write their story.

2020 took a piece of all of us, but it can never steal our Magic. If you are still in the dark, struggling to find yourself again in this new world, you are not alone. Be kind to yourself and know your Magic will find you again.

Enjoy this book?
You can make a big difference

Reviews are the most powerful tool in my arsenal when it comes to getting attention for my books. It's reader like you, who share their love for a story that helps, authors like me get their stories out into the world.

Only about 1% of readers actually leave a review, good or bad. So all I ask, is that you join the 1% of readers who leave reviews and share your thoughts about, Realm of Flames & Steel!

I hope you enjoyed *Realm of Flames & Steel*. This book took me on a wild adventure from 2019 to 2022. Kara and Si have taught me so much about myself and I hope they do the same for you.

The next book is in progress already, so you won't have to wait too long to find out what they are going to do about the Disir, or whether or not Kara and Si are ever going to get over themselves.

In the meantime you can read my other series, Soothsayer. It's filled with Arthurian Magic, Destiny, Love, and lots of Adventure! You can check it out on KDP or buy a physical copy on my website, Allisonsipe.com

I would love to hear from you and what you think about Kara & Si! Please feel free to email me any questions or just drop me a line and say hello on my website.

Until next time, Embrace Your Magic!

ALSO BY THE AUTHOR

Soothsayer

Avalon: A Soothsayer Novella

Trivium

Le Fay: A Soothsayer Novella

Elysium

ABOUT THE AUTHOR

Allison Sipe lives in Southern California with her husband and two dogs. She has a degree from California State University Northridge in English Literature and is very proud to have gone to school for something she loves.

When she's not writing or spending hours obsessing over other books with friends, she loves to travel the world, go to Disneyland and look for Magic is ordinary places.

 facebook.com/allisonsipeauthor

ACKNOWLEDGMENTS

It takes a village to get a book from the idea stage to a completed novel…and about a 1,000 cups of coffee.

First, I want to thank my Beta readers: Apollo, Ev Harrell & Marielle Allen. I am so thankful you took the time to read ROFAS and give me feedback. I loved all your notes, comments and reactions to Kara and Si's story. This book is a better book because of the three of you. Wishing you all the Magic in the world!

Speaking of Magic, I have to give props to my editor, Clare. You are a word wizard and helped beat this book into shape. All your little reactions along the way, had me laughing and smiling as I worked through all your notes. Every time I write a book, I learn a little more and your edits were by far some of the best lessons. Thank you for being amazing and I can't wait to work on the next book with you.

Cal & Chey, our writing club helped me breath new life into this book. I met you both at the perfect time and I'm so thankful we spent 2021 writing, laughing and reading together. To many more years of supporting one another. Thank you both for being such bright lights in my life.

Matt, I mean how much more do you need really... you got the book dedication! But seriously, thank you for always being willing to talk story with me, look at a millions different book covers, and always give me advice. You're the best brother a sister could ever hope for.

Eric, thank you for all the cups of coffee! I'm so lucky to have a partner that wants to see all my dreams come true. Your support, encouragement and belief in me keeps me going when the writing gets hard. And thank you for always letting me talk your ear off about made up worlds, even when all you want to do is go to sleep.

And thank you to everyone at my old day job for telling me to go after my dreams and reach for the stars and dare mighty things. I'm lucky to have so many wonderful people in my corner rooting for me.